THE BOY IN THE SHADOWS

CARL-JOHAN
VALLGREN

Quercus

First published in Great Britain in 2015 by

Quercus
55 Baker Street
7th Floor, South Block
London W1U 8EW

A CIP catalogue record for this book is available
from the British Library

PB ISBN 978 1 78429 129 7
EBOOK ISBN 978 1 78429 128 0

This book is a work of fiction. Names, characters,
businesses, organizations, places and events are
either the product of the author's imagination

Prologue

He had taken bus 49 from Stadshagen with the younger boy sleeping in the pushchair. It was early June. The seventh of June, to be precise. He would remember the date for the rest of his life.

The older boy was now walking alongside him, holding on to the canopy of the pushchair. The little brown hand was sticky from all the sweets the boy had eaten at the party. A minute ago he'd said that his stomach hurt and he had to throw up, but now they were out in the fresh air and he seemed to feel better.

They had got off at the bus stop at Nordenflychtsvägen. As they waited for the bus to drive off so they could cross the street, the older boy studied the front pages of the newspapers outside the shop. On *Aftonbladet*'s was a photo from the World Cup in Mexico. The Swedish players' faces sombre after their loss to Italy at the group stage. Ove Grahn was quoted on the possibility of getting revenge when they played Israel. *Expressen* had gone for Palme's state visit to the US.

'Dad,' said the boy. 'I'm hot. Can I take off my jacket?'

'Sure. Put it in the pushchair.'

Summer had finally arrived, a bit late this year. He had

been stressed out all day. First he'd been out on Lidingö to look at the property Gustav had bought for them, where they would build a house in the autumn. Then he'd come in to Stadshagen, where Kristoffer had been invited to a friend's party, and then he'd gone off to Fridhemsplan with the little guy to have a bite to eat while Joanna visited a friend.

He'd taken the opportunity to have a few beers while Joel slept in the pushchair – three large, strong beers, to be on the safe side – and he'd lost track of time and had to run to the bus to pick Kristoffer up in time.

They walked over the pedestrian crossing. A wino was pissing in Kristinebergs Slottspark. The man hadn't even bothered to turn away; he was casually showing his cock as he stood there watering the flowers. At least he hadn't gone *that* far. He was careful; he never drank so much that he was obviously tipsy.

'Can I have an ice cream, Dad? It's hot.'

The boy's voice warmed his heart, even when he was nagging.

'Isn't your bag of sweets enough? And didn't you have ice cream at the party? Peter's mum said you did, anyway.'

'But I want more. Please, Dad . . . it feels like I'm burning up.'

'Listen, a few minutes ago you were complaining that your stomach hurt and you had to throw up. And now you want ice cream. Which is it?'

'But I feel better now. My tummy ache is almost gone.'

He loved this little boy, who had come to the world seven and a half years earlier, and who was walking at his side and whining about ice cream and refusing to hold his hand because he thought he was too old for it. That amiable, high little-boy voice. The sense of humour he'd developed, even though he was only seven. And then, the moving fact that he was black, that the blood had skipped a generation, skipped him, and instead settled in a little Swedish boy.

But no matter how much he loved him and no matter how hard it was to resist him, he had no intention of giving him any more treats.

'Sorry, no more.'

'But, please . . .'

He yanked the boy towards him as a Volvo Amazon came speeding down Hjalmar Söderbergs Väg and passed them only half a metre away. Fucking roadhog. The boy could easily have run out into the street just now, angry because he hadn't got his way.

He held tight to the boy's arm and took a deep breath to calm himself. He looked to the right, where the Traneberg Bridge rose up against the sky. A train that looked like a gigantic caterpillar on wheels rolled into the metro station. No point in getting stressed. They could take the next one. Joanna had gone straight back to the apartment after visiting her friend, and she was making dinner. They would have a cozy evening at home, enjoying Saturday night together, the whole family. And when the children had gone to bed, he and Joanna would open a bottle of wine and look at the drawings for the new house. The house with which his father was trying to buy his love.

The Volvo disappeared down towards Stadshagen and they crossed Hjalmar Söderbergs Väg. The little boy had woken and was sitting up in the pushchair. Joel. The very opposite of his big brother. Pale skin, almost snow-white, with no hint of biracial features. The man loved him just as much as he did Kristoffer, of course, but in a different way – a bit less intensely, a little less painfully. As if Joel hadn't had time to make as big an impression on him yet.

The door to the ticket hall slid open. He walked a metre to the side in order to look at the timetable. The trains were still running every five minutes; he had two Green Line trains to choose between.

The little guy had started howling – maybe he'd had a bad dream. He looked at the clock on the wall: five thirty. That couldn't be right. Had he lost track of a whole hour? He looked at his wristwatch: four thirty. But the second hand wasn't moving. The damn watch had stopped.

A woman came out of the Pressbyrån kiosk with a newspaper under her arm.

'Excuse me,' he said, 'do you happen to know the time? Is it really five thirty?'

'Sure is. Five thirty. A few minutes past, even.'

She gave him a friendly smile. She was in her fifties. Wearing a kerchief, a colourful cotton dress and rubber boots. She made him think of a farmer's wife. The way they had looked when he was little, out in the country.

'Thanks.'

'It was nothing. Have a nice weekend!'

So he had lost track of a whole hour, which meant that Joanna was waiting for them at home, with dinner ready, wondering where they were. He accidentally ran the pushchair into the metal column in front of the turnstiles.

What a fucking place to put a bearing element. The little guy was crying louder; his legs had probably been bumped, even though the collision hadn't been all that hard.

'Everyone calm down,' he said. 'We're a little late. Mum is waiting with dinner. We have to try to hurry.'

He handed the ticket to the turnstile guard in the booth and went through the pushchair gate. The little guy was screaming even louder now. He was working up to hysterical tears, and only Joanna could comfort him.

'There. Shh, please don't cry now.'

It was the beer. He shouldn't have had it, or at least not the last two. Even if he wasn't drunk, they had made his judgement waver, had made him get out of rhythm with the world, lose track of time, run into posts and barely avoid traffic accidents.

Another train was coming into the station; he could hear the thuds in the rails overhead. Several people were streaming in from the street, shoving from behind. The little guy tried to get out of the pushchair, still screaming, and he had to hold on to him with one hand while clutching Kristoffer with the other, thrusting the pushchair ahead with his stomach.

The stairs or the lift?

The stairs would be faster. But the pushchair ramp looked steep, and with Joel about to unravel it was probably a better idea to take the lift. He pressed the call button.

'Dad, can I take the stairs?'

Kristoffer looked at him with those eyes he couldn't refuse. Those Caribbean eyes. His own mother's eyes, although he could barely remember them.

'No.'

'Please? I can walk by myself if you take the lift. It'll be fun.'

'You're too little.'

The half-empty bag of sweets he held firmly in his hand. The chocolate-brown child's hand that wasn't even half as big as his own. The red goo from a lollipop that was stuck on his cheek. How could he be drunk in the company of his sons?

'Please! I'll wait for you up there.'

'I said no.'

All of a sudden a shadow fell across the boy's face as someone stopped beside them.

'You can walk with me if you like. I'll hold your hand until your dad arrives in the lift.'

It was the woman in the kerchief again. She had come through the turnstile behind them, politely making room for a dad alone with a pushchair and two whining kids. Kristoffer looked at her with wide eyes, judging whether this was someone he ought to be shy of or accept right away. Then Kristoffer looked at him, pleading.

'Please, Dad, can I go with the lady?'

'Okay. But hold her hand so you don't fall. You can see how crowded it is. Lots of people everywhere. And then sit down on the bench up there and wait until I arrive in a minute.'

'I'll sit with him until you're there,' the woman said gently. 'Come on now, young man, let's go.'

Kristoffer smiled at him, showing his missing teeth. The woman gave him a motherly look. He would never forget it. Some moments, some images, would forever drill their way into his consciousness.

He watched as they started up the stairs. Kristoffer's little hand in the woman's larger one. She said something to him and he looked up at her with his big eyes and nodded in agreement just as the lift dinged its arrival in the ticket hall.

He pushed the pushchair in and pressed the up button. His brain took small Polaroid pictures that would later etch themselves into his memory: the coffered ceiling with its three lights. The sign: 750 kilograms or ten people. The cigarette butts on the floor, the half-empty beer can in one corner.

The lift stopped at platform level, swaying slightly. He opened the door, having no idea why he had broken out in a cold sweat, and abruptly he felt sober. The little guy was totally quiet now, as if he no longer wanted to be a bother. He walked quickly along the walkway to the tracks. A wall of metal grating on one side. Plexiglas on the other – you could see across the tracks, but you couldn't see the stairs. A westbound train was in the station; the last few passengers were getting on. The driver shouted the usual 'Please take your seats, the doors are closing' as he hurried forward. He heard the sucking sound as the train doors closed and the squeal of the metal wheels as the train began moving.

The glass door to the stairs opened. Soon he would see Kristoffer sitting there on the bench, waiting for him with his bag of sweets in his hand, beside the woman.

His beloved Kristoffer.

He turned the corner with the pushchair and looked around. The stairs were empty. No one in sight. He could see the lift door he'd stepped through a minute earlier on the lower level, the white tiles on the walls of the stairwell, the two large, fluted glass lights hanging from the ceiling. The graffiti on the empty bench.

Joel had started whimpering again. He unstrapped him from the pushchair and put him down on the floor. Then he turned in the other direction, towards the platform. That was empty, too. Just the rear lights of the train as it disappeared towards Alvik. He turned towards the stairs again, and the ticket hall below. A lone senior citizen with a cane was reading something on a bulletin board.

He called the boy's name:

'Kristoffer!'

He was nearly whispering at first, as if he had lost his voice. Then, loudly, in a full panic:

'Kristoffer! KRISTOOFFEER!'

His voice echoed off the walls, and then, as far off as if it were coming from another world, another time, he heard Joel, who had started to cry again.

PART I

Stockholm, May 2012

For Katz, it all started with a melody. Six notes in each phrase, floating between major and minor:

I hurt myself today/To see if I still feel . . . Dull and distant, as if the music, or he himself, were underwater. *I focus on the pain/The only thing that's real.*

To his surprise, there was a strange woman squatting next to him, holding a spoon. She didn't seem to hear the music, or else she didn't care. *Too desperate*, Katz thought; the brain had an incredible ability to shut out anything that wasn't essential.

She handed him a ten-pack of five-millilitre syringes from a handbag. The standard orange-topped kind, which matched the veins in most people's arms. She had separate implements for herself. Tuberculin syringes with detachable needles. To draw blood from the feet or hands, where the veins were smaller. He sneaked a look at her arms. Long-sleeved blouse. The same trick he used. Always long-sleeved shirts with cuffs, to hide the scars.

The needle tears a hole/The old familiar sting/Try to kill it all away/But I remember everything . . .

He thought he saw his parents at a distance, under the bridge abutment. Anne and Benjamin, arm in arm, always so bound up in their love, always keeping everyone else out – not least him. He hated them for it, his Norrlander mother and his Jewish father. Wasn't it true, even though he never wanted to admit it? Then they disappeared, dead as they were, behind a pillar marred with graffiti.

He looked around. Was this where he lived now, was he back at square one, on the street? On a dirty mattress next to a ventilation grate under a bridge in north-western Stockholm?

Someone had used stones to mark a sort of property line around the sleeping place, or maybe it was meant to depict a symbolic bedroom wall. A pair of boots stood nearby on a piece of tarp. His own?

He looked down at the water, towards the swimming area and the marina on the other side of the sound. Traneberg Bridge, once the world's longest concrete-arched bridge, rose above him; it had been built at a time when a belief in the future ruled the country, but nowadays it was a refuge for addicts and the homeless.

'Dol Fool', 'Drag' and 'Sork', he read on the pillars. The taggers had thrown their spray cans on the ground afterwards. Farther off, there was a scattering of small cotton balls; one might mistake them for flowers in the May warmth – daisies, he thought.

Katz remembered the desperate addicts at Kottbusser Tor in Berlin fifteen years earlier, toothless Kotti junkies who crouched by the canal, setting fire to old cotton balls to squeeze out the last bit of junk, collecting enough for half a shot of brown horse to mix with citric acid. People who took water from puddles on the street, or from toilet tanks in public lavatories. He'd done it, too, he had to admit, when he was at his worst. He'd been lucky to survive.

You could have it all/My empire of dirt . . .

The melody went on, mechanically somehow, from far away. *A kingdom of shit*, he thought; he wanted to give it away – he thought he'd already got rid of it.

'The tar is plugging up the syringe, fucking crap heroin.'

The woman was desperate. And he was, too, he realized. That terrible bodily longing for the kick, to kill everything with the buzz. The longing for emptiness. Timelessness. The bodily homecoming. The woman swore . . . *goddamn fucking shit* . . . as she fumbled with the equipment. Where had he met her? He recognized her, but he didn't remember where from.

A newspaper lay open on the ground. And on it was a soup spoon with a bent handle, to lessen the risk of losing the dose. He could see the fear in her eyes now, and he suggested that she snort a little of it to calm down.

'Shut up, don't mess me up . . .'

'Fuck it, then.'

He didn't care any more. He prepared his own dose instead, taking the bottle of water out of his jacket pocket, filling the syringe and emptying it into the bottom half of a Coke can, where the heroin was already waiting. Cooking, waiting. He tore a piece of cotton from the tampon she'd taken out of her bag, he rolled it into a ball for a filter and pulled the dose into the syringe. He was surprised at how sure his hand was after all these years; it was like swimming or cycling – once you'd learned how, you could do it for the rest of your life.

He rolled up his sleeve, took the nylon stocking she'd laid out and knotted it just above his elbow. He tapped the last few air bubbles out of the syringe and pressed the plunger down until it touched the solution.

It had been ten years, and every motion was still there. And he was just as good at injecting with his left hand as with his right; he'd practised it because it had been a matter of life and death back then, because he took so much junk that he constantly had to rotate injection sites and he had to be able to shoot up into his right arm if the left one didn't respond, and to do it quickly and painlessly before withdrawal made it impossible.

Sunlight filtered in between the pillars of the bridge. A metro train rushed past thirty metres above his head, slowing down as it approached the station in Alvik. It was a sunny afternoon; the warm May weather had arrived suddenly after a period of cold and snow that had lasted late into April.

Did he live here now? Was he homeless again? No, his office was only a few hundred metres away in Traneberg – he'd just been there, bent over his computer . . . or had someone changed the timeline, placing the end at the beginning, or the other way around?

That wasn't right. He knew who he was: Danny Katz, forty-four years old, only child of two parents who died young. Former interpreter at the Ministry of Foreign Affairs. Former civilian translator and computer programmer with the armed forces. Former homeless drug addict. But he was on his feet again. Self-employed. Nothing remarkable – he ran a small translation firm and received freelance assignments from private firms and, sometimes, the military. It didn't bring in that much money, but it was enough for him to break even, to pay for the two-room apartment in the same building as his office, for his modest life with no excesses, because excesses would inevitably lead him back here, to a life on the street.

Farther down by the water, where his parents had just disappeared, there was now a man. Naked, it seemed. It was as if he had built-in binoculars and could zoom in on him. Yes, a naked man, wounds on his legs, leaking blood. He didn't understand it. The vision. A sign of some sort. But when he blinked and looked again, the man was gone.

He fixed his gaze on the inside of his forearm instead, tapping it a little with his fingertips, pulling a bit at the tie, and found the vein he needed. He aimed the needle at his arm at a twenty-degree angle, towards his heart; always in the direction of his heart. A good angle, he thought, not too steep; otherwise, he risked going through the vein.

He didn't understand. Why was he doing this? Ten years after he finally managed to get clean. Ten years of NA meetings, ten years of daily struggle. The short time on methadone, the first treatment programme down in Ytterjärna, paid for by his former military colleague Rickard Julin, who had dedicated so much power and prestige to getting him into the system again, giving him a job, managing the old network, smoothing the way for him, putting him in contact with clients. That would all be in vain now. He was throwing it all away.

This couldn't be right. What had his last assignment been? An IT firm had requested information about a Belarussian telephone company; he had translated a couple of balance sheets for them, as well as some articles from a business journal in Minsk.

He hesitated, the needle one centimetre deep in his arm, mechanically pulling back the plunger to see if he'd hit his mark. *Dark-red blood, never bright red, then you've missed the vein.* He didn't want to inject the dose into tissue by mistake, then it would just swell up and hurt terribly, and it would take forever for the kick to hit him.

Now!

He had found it; the blood was dark red, trickling into the syringe. He pulled off the tie with his teeth and injected. The rush came immediately. He collapsed around his own skeleton, let his flesh rest on the scaffolding of bones and cartilage, and his eyelids came down like blinds. The feeling was divine; he realized how much he had missed it. He pulled the needle out slowly; the blood squirted up on the front of his shirt, but he didn't care any more – he just took a handkerchief out of his jacket pocket and pressed it against the site of the injection.

There was a different man standing where the naked man had stood, and he was wearing a black suit and a wide-brimmed hat. He blinked until the man disappeared like the dream-vision he likely was. Another train rumbled above his head.

He looked at the woman again. Her dose was ready now, and she held the syringe up to the light and emptied it of bubbles. Her raven-black hair framed a symmetrical face with vaguely Asian features. Blue-green eyes, beautifully formed mouth. White skin. Like Snow White.

'I recognize you,' he said. 'Where have we met?'

'We don't know each other . . . you just think we do.'

Strange answer, he thought, as she searched for a vein, first at her hip; she pulled her pants and burgundy underwear down a bit, but then she changed her mind and her broken nails felt around up by her jugular. *Too close to the carotid artery*, he thought, *please don't inject it there!*

To his relief, she found a vein in her right upper arm instead and injected the dose with a resolute expression. Right away she started booting – pulling the plunger back and forth, drawing out blood which she then re-injected, to rinse out every microgram of the dose.

'So we just met right here?' he slurred, gesturing at the mattress.

'I just happened by. But you live here.'

'Under the bridge?'

'Yes – shit, you're badly off. And people are looking for you. Someone wants to set you up.'

He nodded as if accepting what she'd said, as if he had already submitted to his new reality.

'So who are you?'

'Me? I'm no one . . .'

Her pupils were so small he could hardly see them. She had collapsed and was half lying against him; her underpants stuck up above her waistband at the back. Lifeless. He wondered if she'd overdosed, if he should call 112 for an ambulance, ask them to bring Narcan, which they could inject straight into her chest to bring her back to life.

Then he saw the bite marks. A line of bloody wounds around her neck made by teeth, bites that had ripped through the skin. Like that time with Eva Dahlman, his first girlfriend, whom he had been accused of beating unconscious and biting like a wild animal. He had been convicted for it. Sixteen years old. He'd been sent to yet another reform school, where things had finally turned around for him: he had decided to make a break with his old life, get away from crime. But it hadn't been him! He hadn't been in a condition to do anything like that, no matter what the technical evidence had shown.

I wear this crown of shit/Upon my liar's chair/Full of broken thoughts/I cannot repair . . .

Where was the music coming from? He looked around, but he couldn't find the source.

And the woman who seemed to have fallen asleep on his lap – who was she? He stroked the black hair away from her face, laid her on the mattress and got up.

Five notes in each phrase now, the shifts between major and minor, just a melody, no words any more; he had added those in his head. He recognized it. Nine Inch Nails' 'Hurt'.

The notes . . . getting stronger and stronger, seeming to reach him from the bottom of his consciousness, erasing his surroundings, the bridge, the woman, the dirty mattress, the syringes, the junk. It was the ringtone on his mobile, he remembered triumphantly as he climbed ever faster towards the surface of consciousness, but just as a melody, without Trent Reznor's bitter voice. And the melody kept playing until he managed to grab the phone, which lay next to him on the floor of his apartment.

He sat up and answered the call. He saw the grey light

filtering in through the blinds of his bedroom window; he listened to the voice on the other end of the phone.

She sounded like the woman under the bridge, like Eva Dahlman, except at the same time she didn't. As if the timeline were out of order.

Angela Klingberg was a strikingly beautiful woman. Beautiful in a way that must cause her problems, Katz thought as he sat down across from her in one corner of Ritorno, the old café on Odengatan where they'd arranged to meet. Considering to whom she was married, it was natural that she was dressed so elegantly. He made note of the Hermès handbag at her feet, the expensive gloves on the table, her angora sweater, her discreet make-up and the almost as discreet diamond bracelet around her left wrist. She was about thirty-five, blonde, lanky, with an aura that was simultaneously sad and attentive. He felt a stab of pain at the thought that she was taken, and he was surprised by that feeling, by how low it was – but also how honest.

Until her phone call that morning, he hadn't even known she existed. Actually, despite the wedding ring on her left hand, he had a hard time picturing her married to Joel Klingberg – or maybe it was just difficult to picture Klingberg being married at all.

As he took off his jacket and hung it over the back of the chair, he wondered why he'd agreed to meet her. Curiosity had to be one reason. Twenty-five years earlier, when he'd just managed to break away from his life as a juvenile delinquent, he and Joel Klingberg had both been students at the Armed Forces Interpreter Academy. They had been in the same barracks during their basic training in Karlsborg, and after that they shared a room for two intensive semesters of Russian studies in Uppsala. What little he knew about Klingberg's life since then was only what he'd read in the papers – gossipy reports about the upper-class circles he moved in; pictures of parties where Klingberg, with his sombre looks, didn't seem to fit in; items about a real-estate firm he and a few friends from his boarding school in Sigtuna ran on the Riviera for a short time, just to get some business experience. After that, he'd studied law and done a year at the London School of Economics, before he was brought into the family business, Klingberg Aluminium AB, and disappeared into the anonymity of the business world.

'Thanks for taking the time to meet me,' said the woman in front of him, aiming an embarrassed smile across the table.

'No problem. How did you get my number?'

'It was on Joel's computer, in his contacts.'

Which was strange, too: Katz couldn't picture Klingberg having any plans to contact him.

'Would you like something, by the way? Shall I order for you?'

'No, thanks. Just tell me why we're here.'

So she told him.

Joel Klingberg had disappeared three weeks earlier, by all indications – according to the police – voluntarily. There was no reason to search for him actively, nor was there any evidence that a crime had been committed. He had left the couple's home on Östermalm on the morning of Sunday 22 April to run a few errands, and he simply hadn't returned. She had called his mobile every day since, she explained, but only got his voicemail. And there was something like a farewell letter.

She took it out of her bag: an email, printed out on A4 paper, originally sent from Klingberg's phone. Katz quickly read through it – a few lines saying that he was going away for an unspecified amount of time to be alone and think. He apologized for not having the guts to say this to her in person and wrote that she shouldn't worry about him or try to find him.

'I got it four hours after he disappeared,' she said. 'And it's not like him. Joel's not the type to run away from his problems.'

'So what do you think happened?'

'I honestly don't know.'

She folded up the paper and put it back in her bag, and somehow Katz was reminded of Klingberg's girlfriend from their time at the interpreter academy, a girl their age whose upper-class mannerisms had bothered him but whose name and appearance had been erased from his memory.

'The police think he left because of a fight we had that morning. About kids . . . or rather, a lack of kids. Joel wanted to wait. A middle-aged man, married ten years, and he still wants to wait! I'm sure you know about his baggage, what happened to his brother. I told him that his fear of responsibility is because of that – his fear that it might happen again. That's what we were fighting about.'

Oh yeah, his brother, Katz thought, as he followed her gaze, which moved nervously from object to object on the table: the coffee cup she wasn't drinking from, a forgotten newspaper that was open to the page of horse-racing results, her gloves – the same colour as the nails on her beautiful hands. The brother who had disappeared, the centre that everything circled around, the loss that Klingberg hauled around like invisible shackles.

'I know how it sounds,' she said. 'A wounded man leaves his argumentative wife to get some peace and quiet for a while. But, as I said, it's not like him. We had already made up by the time he left. He said he was going to do a few errands and would be back for lunch. We had even made a reservation at a restaurant. It seems that I'm the last person who saw him. And the only one who refuses to believe that he took off voluntarily. According to the police, he amused himself by driving around in his car for a few hours . . .'

Klingberg had taken the car after leaving the apartment. They had examined the GPS log, she explained. It seemed he had driven around at random, from their home to Skeppargatan, circling the city for a while, before he continued to Kungsholmen. He had stopped at a petrol station on Thorildsplan, driven on through Stadshagen up to the Kristineberg metro station, and then on to Alvik and Tranebergsparken, where he stopped at the public tennis courts for a few minutes.

'That's near where you live. I checked the local directory. Strange, isn't it?'

Katz felt a sudden unease at the thought that Klingberg

had stopped his car at that particular spot. If he'd looked out the window that morning, he probably would have been able to see him between the trees on the other side of the park.

'Where did he drive after that?' he asked.

'Over to the industrial area by Ulvsundasjön, then he turned around and drove back to the city and wrote his so-called farewell email.'

According to Angela, Joel Klingberg had parked the car in a car park near Central Station, and his trail ended there. It seemed that he had taken a train south. There was a ticket to Copenhagen in his name for that day; he'd bought it himself online, but the Swedish Railways system couldn't tell if it had been used.

She grew quiet and Katz noticed that his gaze was caught up in her eyes. In the anxiety she radiated, the sadness that made her who she was. His type more than Klingberg's.

'And why did you contact me?' he asked.

'I know it sounds strange. But it's what Joel would have wanted.'

'You're going to have to explain that.'

Angela Klingberg had never heard of Katz until one evening a few months earlier. Joel had mentioned him out of the blue as they ate dinner: Danny Katz, his old friend from his time in the army.

'He said that you were the only person he'd ever trusted.'

'He said that?'

'Yes: "The only person I've ever trusted in my whole life." I happened to think of it after he disappeared.'

Where had Klingberg got that idea from? It was true they had spent time together during their military service, but they came from two different worlds – Katz was from the gang world of the suburbs, and Klingberg was from a sheltered upper-class environment. At the weekends, after the weekly vocabulary exam, he was picked up by a private chauffeur and vanished back to his rich man's life with his grandfather, behind tall garden walls in Djursholm. Katz had never got to know him on a personal level.

'I defended him in a fistfight one time,' he said. 'Maybe that's what he was referring to?'

'He never mentioned that. I think he meant something else.'

She took a package from the chair next to her.

'Also, not long before he disappeared, he received this. I found it a few days later, by chance. It was at the very back of his wardrobe.'

It was a padded envelope with no return address, post-marked in Stockholm one month earlier. She opened it and placed the objects on the table in front of him.

'I don't know what these are all about. But Joel ought to have said something. It seems so . . . strange.'

A square piece of cloth, about eighty by eighty centi-metres, ochre-red and black, unfolded before Katz's eyes. Embroidered in the middle was a naïve motif depicting two crossed arrows. And, to the right of the arrows, enclosed by a sequinned frame made of rounded mirror fragments, was a genuflecting man sewn in coarse cross-stitching. Two fabric letters were glued under the motif: M.K.

'Initials?' said Katz.

'Don't ask me. And there's this . . .'

She touched the other object, a similar piece of cloth, but a bit smaller; the embroidered motif depicted a man surrounded by dogs which were licking his legs.

'I don't even know if this has anything to do with anything,' she said. 'It's just so mysterious.'

'Did you show them to the police?'

'No. Like I said, there's no indication of a crime. If you'll excuse me a moment . . .'

She stood up and vanished in the direction of the Ladies. And Katz thought about that time again, in 1987, when he'd gone to the interpreter academy. *Verba arma nostra*: 'Words are our weapon' – that had been their motto. And it was words they would be armed with – Russian ones: they were tested on a daunting amount of vocabulary each week. They completed six semesters' worth of university-level Russian in ten months. Katz remembered the endless hours in the language lab, his studies in behavioural science and psychology, topics they were expected to have some knowledge of as interpreters in a war situation. He remembered his interrogator training – PBI, people-based intelligence, as it was called in military language – and a live drill on Gotland, when they'd practised their skills on coastal commandos. He remembered that they'd watched a training film on *skendränkning*, which they would later call by its English name: waterboarding.

It was incredible, he thought now, that they hadn't reacted to what seemed to be a lesson in torture. In the film, a Swedish ensign had tied a towel over the airways of an anonymous man, who was bound to a hospital trolley with his head tilted backwards. The ensign had poured water over the towel. The reaction was immediate: convulsions, violent retching. The subject, the ensign explained, while facing the camera and continuing to pour water over the man's face, experiences drowning because he can't breathe and he inhales water: 'This method doesn't cause any physical harm, but the experience is extremely unpleasant. Waterboarding is not expressly forbidden in Sweden, though it might be comparable to unlawful coercion.'

For his part, Katz had been most astounded at finding himself where he was – the only one who didn't come from a high-class family – and he was confused by the fact that he'd been selected at all, much less hand-picked.

He looked over to the bathrooms, but Angela Klingberg still hadn't come out.

And Joel . . . he, too, had been an outsider, but for different reasons, still dazed by family tragedy. His parents, like Katz's, had died when he was young; they'd gassed themselves to death in the garage of their manor-like country home in Sörmland. After that, Joel had lived with his grandfather, Gustav Klingberg, founder of Klingberg Aluminium, who was at that time a greying patriarch who ruled the family empire with an iron fist. He had died a year or two after they'd been discharged; Katz had seen an obituary in the newspaper.

But the underlying family tragedy had happened even earlier: his brother had vanished in the early seventies, and that was the incident which had driven his parents to suicide just short of a decade later. The pain and guilt seemed to be carved into Klingberg's being; they defined who he was. He was only a bit older than Katz, but he had the posture of an old man, always running away from the pain, from the guilt of being the one who survived, the one who was left behind, escaping into theory, his studies, the Russian vocabulary.

Only once had Klingberg told him about the incident, a very brief description of how his brother had been carried off by a strange woman at a metro station in Stockholm and had never been found. There wasn't a day since that he hadn't asked himself what had really happened, who or what was behind it, whether it was the work of a lone madwoman or whether several people were involved. Had it been an extortion scheme gone awry – although as far as Klingberg knew, his family had never received a demand for money – or were there perverts involved, maybe paedophiles?

It was as if his brother had left his shadow behind, he'd said. *Imagine, Katz, his body is gone but his shadow is still here.*

When Angela Klingberg came back from the Ladies, Katz could tell she'd been crying. She sat down at the table again but avoided his eyes.

'I want you to try to find out what happened to him,' she said resolutely. 'I'll pay well. If there's anything Joel and I have a lot of, it's money.'

She was fiddling with something inside her handbag – a pen, he saw. And then he remembered the muddled letter he had sent to Klingberg fifteen years earlier, when he was at his very worst, the letter asking for money, the begging

letter which Klingberg had never answered, or which perhaps had never arrived.

'It's not easy to trace missing people,' he said. 'Especially if they don't want to be found.'

'I just want you to give it a try.'

'I don't even know where to start. It's not my area of
expertise.'

'Your background is in intelligence, isn't it?'

'Is that what Joel said?'

'He said that the army arranged embassy jobs for you
after your military service.'

'That was a long time ago. I was a military interpreter,
translator and computer programmer. Nothing special.
I'm still a translator. That's what I do – I translate documents and articles for people who are willing to pay for
them. I'm not a secret agent. Or a private investigator.'

But she already knew what he knew: that he needed the
money.

'Joel would have wanted it to be you. I need your information. Bank account. Mailing address. Home phone
number, so we can communicate as effectively as possible.'

Katz took a business card from the inner pocket of his
jacket. It contained all the information she needed. As he
handed it over, he realized he had doodled on the back.
A heart and a flower. For some reason, he found this
embarrassing.

Katz made a living from his way with languages. On translating and transcribing documents into understandable Swedish for clients who had greater purposes for that information. Military and external analysts, businesses that wanted to keep an eye on competitors or be at the cutting edge of their business. Sometimes purely technical translations that demanded perfect rendering in order to be useful to the client. It was not a glamorous job. Hour after hour in front of the computer. Hour after hour of reading, writing, note-taking, looking things up in dictionaries.

Katz's most recent position had been at Capitol Security Group in Solna. The founder of the firm, Rickard Julin, had enticed him to come to the company just as he'd started to get his head above water ten years earlier. But they had met each other long before that, in the early nineties, when Katz had been working as a military interpreter and Julin had been serving at the same consulate.

Later that decade, as the cuts in the military reached their peak, Julin had resigned and started the firm with a group of risk capitalists. At that point, Julin and Katz hadn't been in contact in several years. Katz had been destitute, living on the streets, occupying himself with a painfully protracted suicide, until, incredibly enough, Julin had chanced upon him, managed to get him into a treatment centre and then offered him employment. But Katz had never felt at home there. After a few months in an office module in Solna, where he translated articles from Russian military journals for Capitol's clients in the defence industry, still bewildered at how life had taken such a strange turn, he had resigned and started his own business. Generously enough, Julin hadn't been angry; instead, he made sure that Katz received assignments he couldn't take on himself, jobs that were outside his own field of expertise.

Capitol was one of a handful of companies in Sweden that had special authorization to work with personal security details. They also dealt with travel escorts, camera surveillance of property, the tracing of funds, background checks on people – so-called 'due diligence' – and also what Angela Klingberg was looking for: searching for missing persons. So Katz wondered if he had been right to accept the job. He ought to have sent her to Julin, who had the resources Katz lacked. On the other hand, he needed the money.

This thought was still occupying him as he returned to his office, sat down at his desk and looked out across his little world: the two computers, the visitor's chair that never received visitors, the bookshelf with its binders and technical dictionaries, the safe on the wall where he kept sensitive material. One of his assignments in the spring had been for a pharmaceutical company. The company had ordered an investigation into illegal sales of their medications on Eastern European Internet sites. Katz's task had been to find material that could potentially be used in a trial. The information he gleaned from following transactions between virtual wallets was enough for the company to start legal proceedings. But this was hardly the sort of information – about Slavic languages, Russian pirate sites and how the Internet worked on the other side of the Baltic Sea, about hidden information-gathering, advanced rootkits, cloud computing, VPN tunnels, and how to sneak past firewalls – he needed to search for a vanished businessman.

He sighed and took out the padded envelope Angela had given him, fished out the pieces of cloth and laid them in front of him on the desk.

The motifs were mysterious: a man genuflecting in front of two crossed arrows. Another man, his legs apparently being licked by dogs. A religious thing, or just decorative objects, crafts of some sort? It wasn't even certain they had anything to do with Klingberg's disappearance.

He took the first one and held it up to the desk lamp. The fabric looked old. It was worn. The stitches had started to come loose on the back. Antique? Klingberg could afford to collect precious objects if he wanted to, after all. The men on the canvases were embroidered in black thread, and something about their stylized physiognomy carried his thoughts to Africa. Slaves, Katz thought, without really understanding the association; black people, imprisoned.

He put them in the desk drawer, pushing away the memory of Angela Klingberg's endlessly sad eyes as she introduced herself to him at Ritorno. Instead, he started up his computer to do an image search on his old army comrade.

An instant later he had Klingberg before him in full-screen format. It was a photograph taken in connection with a shareholders' meeting about a year earlier. Joel was standing beside his uncle, Pontus Klingberg, the CEO of Klingberg Aluminium. Behind them was a group of suit-clad men with champagne glasses in their hands. Pontus Klingberg was holding a bound volume of papers under his arm: the company's annual accounts, according to the caption. And then Joel, in the dark uniform of the business world, with a tie, handmade shoes, his hair thinner than when Katz had met him and without the glasses he'd worn back then, but with the same aura of being lost.

Why had he started to talk about Katz a few months after the photo was taken? 'The only person he had ever trusted'?

Perhaps it did have something to do with the incident Katz had mentioned to his wife, after all: that Katz had once defended him in a fistfight.

It was during their basic training in Karlsborg. Another conscript, a paratrooper recruit, had attacked Klingberg at a fast-food stand. Compared to those types, people like Klingberg were nothing more than bookworms, know-it-alls, four-eyes and former student-council members – which, surprisingly enough, was often accurate. Katz had hesitated at first. He had decided to make a break with his old life as a fighter. But, on that night, something had made him forget it: Klingberg's defencelessness.

Klingberg had been terrified, unable even to run away. And it had woken a primitive protective instinct in Katz. He knew he had nothing to be afraid of. Not because he was faster or better trained than the large elite soldier in front of him, but because he had learned to ignore all rules. At the same instant the guy in front of him had started to shove the frightened Klingberg, Katz had taken a step up and head-butted him in the face. In the next, he had broken one of the guy's kneecaps by kicking it full force and had thrown him to the ground and smashed the Coke bottle in his hand against the back of his opponent's head. It had all been over in less than ten seconds.

Incredibly enough, he had got away with it. No charges. There wasn't even a report filed. Perhaps his victim's shame had been too great.

Afterwards, Klingberg had been fascinated. Where had his coldness and ruthlessness come from? Where had he learned to fight? And Katz had told him about his years in care, the gang crime, his school problems, about the little 'Jew boy' who hadn't allowed anyone to mess with him, about a life that had been the exact opposite of Klingberg's.

It was somewhere around this point that their friendship had begun. The incident had taken place just a few weeks after they'd joined up. Klingberg had clung to him after that.

He minimized the photo and reached for his phone. He dialled Julin's direct number. Three rings later, he had him on the line.

'It's Katz,' he said. 'I wonder if you could check out a few things with the police.'

He briefly described Joel Klingberg's disappearance and the assignment he'd received from his wife, and he heard Julin's hearty laughter when he heard that a language and computer nerd like Katz was on Julin's turf;

then he heard his characteristic hemming and hawing, the expected objections that he didn't want to use his contacts without cause but that he would see what he could do.

'I want to know what sort of investigation they started. It seems that they looked at his GPS, for example, before they decided to stop investigating. It's possible that his wife is on a wild goose chase. But I want to know if there was something else that caused them to shelve the case. And if I can't get anywhere with this in a few days, I promise to send her on to you or someone else who knows what they're doing.'

'Don't underestimate yourself, Katz. Look at it as a chance to broaden your horizons.'

'If you promise to help me.'

'I'll see what I can find out. Just have some patience.'

It's for the best, Katz thought. Julin had contacts he didn't.

It took only a few hours for Julin to obtain the police material on Klingberg's disappearance. The investigation had been dropped after twenty-four hours, and no description of Klingberg had been issued. There was nothing to suggest that a crime had been committed. There was no information stating that anyone in the Klingberg family had been contacted by a kidnapper. An investigator had dutifully called the hospitals to see if Klingberg happened to have been involved in an accident, but he didn't get any leads. It looked undeniably like a voluntary disappearance, and the police had no reason to investigate further. Joel had sent an email to Pontus Klingberg, the CEO, saying that he would be travelling for an unspecified amount of time. According to the police report, this had made company management more angry than worried. Several important contracts were about to be brought to a close, and Joel, as the chief counsel, should have attended the signings.

As for the car that had been parked in the garage, Klingberg's ticket was still valid. The vehicle had been located and searched by the police; after that, it had been picked up by Angela Klingberg. Julin had attached the GPS log in his email. It was consistent with what Angela

Klingberg had told him, except that Joel had stopped at the tennis courts in Traneberg a second time before he drove back into the city, parked the car and vanished into thin air.

As Katz glanced through the route a second time, he toyed with the thought that Klingberg had wanted to tell him something, that this was why he had been sitting in his car two hundred metres from Katz's home. But why would that be the case? Everything pointed to it just being a coincidence.

What would cause a person to disappear voluntarily? What if he assumed that Angela Klingberg was right, that it didn't have anything to do with their fight? Could there have been some sort of threat? Had Klingberg been so scared of something that he chose to disappear? Something criminal? Was he involved in something illegal? Or was he an addict, or a former addict, and had suffered a relapse?

Unless it was a case of infidelity, and he had gone somewhere with a mistress. But no normal man would leave a woman like Angela for someone else. He pictured her in front of him at the café table in Ritorno, the sadness she radiated – which, to his surprise, turned him on. Her long, elegant fingers had trembled slightly, with a tension that came from worrying about her husband, and, unable to stop himself, he started fantasizing about her. She unbuttoned his shirt, one button at a time, running her nails down his chest to his navel, cupping her hand around his sex; her hand with its wedding ring started to massage him through his pants until he grew hard, and then soft again from something that was like self-contempt but might actually have been envy.

He devoted the rest of the afternoon to Googling Klingberg but didn't find anything that might be connected to his disappearance. The family company, at least, seemed to be doing well. They had signed new contracts with manufacturing industries in Russia and China. Joel popped up in a few business articles; among other things, he had changed his position on the board of directors, from being a regular member to becoming vice-president. There was no mention outside the business world. Nothing on LinkedIn, Facebook, or any other social network.

At four thirty, he called Klingberg Aluminium to try to speak to Joel's uncle, but he didn't get beyond a secretary who explained in an authoritative voice that she would contact him once she'd checked the calendar. He hung up, but then picked up the receiver and dialled Angela Klingberg's number instead.

'Could I take a peek at Joel's car?' he asked once he had her on the line.

'You mean in case there's something there the police missed? When?'

'Now, if possible.'

He heard her long, even breaths close to his ear, as if they were lying beside each other in bed and she'd placed her mouth against his cheek and was about to fall asleep.

'Would later this evening work?'

'Of course. And I'd also like to examine his computer.'

'No problem. It's in his study, just as he left it.'
'Great, is there a particular time that works best for you?'
'How about eight thirty?'
'Sure. It won't take long.'

The Klingbergs' flat was on the top two floors of an art nouveau building on Skeppargatan, not far from the prestigious Strandvägen. Katz walked through a stairwell with plasterwork mouldings and giant marble pilasters on the walls and took the lift right up into the Klingbergs', where Angela Klingberg met him in the hall, unlocked a black security gate and let him in.

She was dressed in jeans and a pussy-bow blouse, and her hair was up in a ponytail. Katz was painfully aware of her perfume, and just as painfully aware of the strap of her cream-coloured bra, which was visible on her shoulder where the fabric of the blouse had slid down.

'Sorry I couldn't meet you earlier,' she said. 'I had a couple of things to arrange. The car's in the garage. We can look through it first, and then come back here and look at the computer.'

They took the returning lift to the basement, and then the stairs down another level until they came out into the garage. In the farthest corner was Klingberg's red Lexus. A hybrid, Katz noted, powered by both petrol and electricity.

'I'm the environmentally conscious one in this household,' Angela Klingberg said, as if she had read his mind. 'If Joel had had his way, we would have driven an SUV like all his friends. Or each had our own car. But I happen to be the chairperson of an organization that deals with environmental issues. You have to practise what you preach.'

'Is that what you do for work? Environmental issues?'

'Only as a volunteer. I used to give lectures on sustainable development at businesses where the level of environmental awareness is, to put it mildly, negligible. I started out as a marine biologist. Although a lot of people have trouble believing that.'

She gave him a defiant look. And Katz realized that this was the price she had to pay for her looks: people didn't take her seriously.

As he opened the driver's-side door and looked around the interior, he asked her how she had met Joel.

'Through mutual acquaintances. I grew up in Djursholm, just a few blocks from Joel. But, strangely enough, we had never met before that party. I was abroad for a few years; I lived in Paris until I came back to Stockholm to study. That was twelve years ago now. And, of course, it turned out that we had tons of common denominators. My grandfather was on several boards of directors with Joel's grandfather. And Joel's uncle, Pontus, moved in the same circles as my parents for a while. They even founded a golf club together in Marbella in the seventies. And we both went to boarding school. Joel was in Sigtuna and I was at Lundsberg.'

Katz let his eyes roam across the car's interior. It was very clean. Not so much as a chewing-gum wrapper in sight. He called up the GPS log from the past few days. Angela Klingberg had gone out to Djursholm at one point. Otherwise, she had taken only a few short trips in the neighbourhood, to Östermalmstorg, among other places. He scrolled the computer back to the date of Klingberg's disappearance and saw that the display matched the information he'd received from Julin.

'Has Joel ever disappeared like this before?' he asked.

'Not as long as we've been together.'

'Does he have any enemies?'

'What an odd question. No, not that I know of.'

'A mistress?'

He could tell that she was hurt by this question.

'No,' she said firmly. 'Joel is incredibly loyal. Besides, I don't think he has the nerve to lead a double life. He's not cold-blooded enough.'

Or else he was, but he was also clever enough to keep people in the dark. Katz didn't know him; he hadn't even really known him during their time in the military. He didn't know anything about his or Angela's world, the existence of truly wealthy people.

'And what about the firm, Klingberg Aluminium – Joel never said anything about a threat against the firm?'

'We never talk about Joel's job when we're home. It's a silent agreement we have. It's bad enough to have a husband who works sixty hours a week at a family business and all that involves – a sense of duty and family tradition. We try to talk about other things. Books we're reading. Movies we see. Theatre . . . on the few occasions that Joel can come along.'

A workaholic, Katz thought. Maybe that was what all of this was about. Being burnt out. A man who hit a wall and fled, wild with panic.

He climbed out of the car and bent down to peek under

the front seat. A crumpled tissue spotted with blood lay next to an old parking disc.

'He gets nosebleeds sometimes,' said Angela Klingberg, taking it from him. 'For no particular reason. It runs in the family. The Klingberg family.'

Cocaine, Katz thought as he closed the door, but that didn't square with the image he had of Joel.

He walked around the vehicle and opened the trunk. Nothing of interest. Just a warning triangle and an empty paper bag from the department store NK. He noticed that his jacket and his shirtsleeve had pulled up a bit when he'd bent to look under the seat. His scars were clearly visible in the light of the garage – the yellowish lunarscape the drug abuse left behind, sticks from thousands of needles. Angela saw them, too, and averted her eyes.

'I had a thought,' Katz said, as he continued around the vehicle. 'Did the police look at the surveillance cameras in the garage where he parked? There should have been film of the car when it was driven in and parked.'

'I didn't hear anything about that. But, as I said, they didn't take me seriously.'

'Okay,' he said. 'I understand.'

He checked the back seat without finding anything of interest; then he opened the door to the passenger seat, looked around and closed it again.

'We're finished here,' he said. 'I'd like to look at the computer, too, before it gets too late.'

Katz followed Angela Klingberg through what he imagined was a servants' passage from the olden days. Behind a half-open sliding door he caught sight of a bedroom as large as his own flat. They passed a renovated luxury kitchen and a dining room with tiled heating stoves and stained glass in the bay windows; then they walked through a gigantic living room and up a flight of stairs to the top floor, finally arriving in an office. Before a picture window that faced a roof terrace stood a desk with a computer on it.

'No one has used it since Joel disappeared,' said Angela. 'Except for me . . . I went through his email to see if there was anything there. But I didn't find anything that seemed suspicious. Joel isn't a particularly secretive person. You don't need a password. Just turn it on.'

As the hard drive began to whir, Katz took in the rest of the room. A built-in bookcase full of binders and folders ran along one of the long walls. A lone painting hung above the door; it looked like some sort of still life, depicting two crossed feathers, a champagne cork and a perfume bottle, clumsily painted by an amateur. A wedding picture stood in the window that looked on to the roof terrace. Klingberg in tails. Angela in a cream wedding dress. They looked genuinely happy.

Katz called up the web browser. The history had been deleted in the middle of April, a week or so before Klingberg had disappeared. He restored it with the help of a recovery program but didn't find any conspicuous traffic. In recent weeks, Klingberg had mostly read foreign business journals on the net: the *Wall Street Journal*, *The Economist*, *Finanzwelt*. He had searched Wikipedia for Bordeaux wines and had Googled the addresses of a few restaurants.

Katz moved on to the email program. The farewell letter to Angela had been sent from Klingberg's mobile phone, so it wasn't there. The trash contained only spam, and the saved emails seemed to be about only the family business.

'I'd like to install another program,' he said. 'Is that okay? I might find things you don't want to know about.'

'Strange tendencies?' She gave a crooked smile. 'I'm prepared to take that risk.'

Katz connected a USB drive to the computer, clicked on the icon that popped up and dragged a program to the hard drive. He had written the code himself and was quite pleased with the results. Essentially, the program would miss nothing of importance but, above all, it didn't waste time on worthless information, the binary trash heap that every computer contained.

Ten seconds later, the search was finished. Klingberg didn't seem to have anything to hide. The only hidden information on the hard drive was a zip file that had been saved as a system file, whether consciously or by mistake. Katz tried to open it, but the file appeared to be damaged. He dragged it to the USB memory to check it later. Everything else was transparent.

'And the computer has been here since Joel disappeared? No one else has been here? No one has borrowed it?'

'No . . . why?'

'It's almost too clean.'

'You didn't find anything strange?'

'Nothing.'

'You're sure?'

'Completely sure.'

Angela Klingberg shook her head and looked over at the wedding picture in the window.

'That was taken ten years ago, almost to the day,' she said. 'I was twenty-five. We left for our honeymoon the next morning. Went to the Dominican Republic. That was where Klingberg Aluminium was founded once upon a time. Joel's grandfather, Gustav, started dealing in sugar and bauxite in Santo Domingo in the forties. He was from a Swedish missionary family that was stationed on the island. Gustav's parents did poverty-relief work out in the country. There's even a road named after them in Comendador, a city on the border with Haiti. Joel told me that they saved a lot of people's lives when the Dominican army massacred Haitian refugees in the borderlands. The Parsley Massacre, I think it's called.'

'Was that why Joel wanted to go there, to travel in his family's footsteps?'

'At least partially. He had been there a lot as a child, with his grandfather, every summer. We visited the company's first bauxite quarry and the family grave in the Lutheran cemetery in Santo Domingo.'

Angela Klingberg smiled dreamily.

'It was a wonderful trip. I taught Joel to dive. He got his PADI certification in a village on the northern coast. I was already studying marine biology. The Caribbean has fantastically rich marine life. We saw barracudas and tiger sharks. I would have loved to go back this year as a sort of anniversary. We even talked about it . . .'

She grew silent and looked over at the still life on the

wall. 'Joel did the sketch for that painting while we were there. It's terrible, isn't it?'

'I didn't know he painted,' said Katz.

'He doesn't. As far as I know, that's the only painting he's ever finished. It's a sort of commemorative picture of the day his brother disappeared. Joel was only a few years old when it happened, but he claims to remember things from that day. There was a woman who promised to wait on a metro platform with Kristoffer while Joel and his father took the lift with the pushchair. When they came up to the platform, the woman and Kristoffer were gone. They were supposed to have waited by a bench, but no one was there.'

'What does that have to do with the painting?'

'Joel claimed that there were two feathers lying in a cross on the ground under the bench. And on top of the feathers was a champagne cork. Somehow he was reminded of all of this when we were in Santo Domingo.'

'That's peculiar.'

'Yes, isn't it?'

'And what about the perfume bottle?'

'I don't really remember. I think the woman who took Kristoffer from them was wearing an excessive amount of perfume. Anyway . . . whether or not the memories are correct, they were real to Joel.'

Katz stood up from the desk and turned off the computer. Angela Klingberg brushed away a strand of hair that had fallen into her face. The same way Eva Dahlman used to. They looked like each other; why hadn't he noticed it before now?

'Is that all?' she said.

'Yes.'

'Is there anything else I can help you with?'

'I need to get in touch with Joel's uncle. But that doesn't seem to be the easiest thing in the world.'

'Don't worry,' she said. 'I'll call Pontus and make an appointment for you.'

It was ten o'clock by the time Katz parked the car near Central Station and then walked the short distance to the multi-storey car park. A uniformed guard was sitting in a Plexiglas booth on the ground level, doing sudoku. The man was in his thirties, and he was bald and sallow. Katz introduced himself and was admitted through a door at the rear of the booth.

'You're the one who just called and wanted to see the surveillance films?' said the guard. 'I got them out for you. There's not much to do here, you know; any sort of interruption is nice. It was 22 April you were interested in? Around lunchtime? A red Lexus.'

Katz nodded.

'It'll cost you, of course, unless you're a cop. Let's say a thousand kronor for you to think of this place as a non-stop video booth . . . as long as my boss doesn't show up.'

Katz fished out two 500-kronor bills and placed them on the table in front of him.

'The car was parked on the second basement level,' said the guard. 'Next to a pillar, at eleven fifty-four.' He pulled up videos sorted by date on a screen and clicked on one of them. Eight frames popped up. 'We have two cameras on each level and one at the entrance, but that one's on a different system. The guy you're looking for is visible in the two frames on the bottom left, first when he drives in and parks, and then when he gets out of the car and walks to the stairwell door, but, if you ask me, there's not much to see.'

The guard clicked on the frame on the lower left and it entered full-screen mode. Klingberg's Lexus rolled down the ramp from street level; it was impossible to see what the driver looked like. But he appeared to be alone.

'Can you enlarge the image?'

'Nope. It'll just get grainier. Here, you can see him as he gets out of the car.'

The screen had shifted to the other camera. Klingberg's car turned into a parking space, but a pillar blocked the view.

'Hold on . . . you can see all of him here. You can't see what he looks like, but I bet a thousand kronor he's an immigrant. They're the only ones who can afford to drive luxury cars.'

A man stepped in shot from the blind spot; he was wearing a grey raincoat with a hood. It was a Fjällräven jacket, Katz noticed; he had bought one like it the previous autumn, but it had been stolen when his building's storage area had been broken into.

'Can't you see his face?'

'No. And it sure as hell wasn't raining that day either. I checked on the camera at the entrance. It was fucking cold. It was below freezing, even though it was April, but it wasn't raining. The sun was out full force!'

The man was aware that he was on camera. He pulled up his hood so it covered his whole face. Then he looked at the ground and started walking quickly towards the exit. He opened the door to the stairwell and disappeared.

'Not much action, huh?' said the guard, and he nodded at the screen, where the tape was still rolling but nothing else was moving. 'Not so much as a pigeon or a rat. We usually have lots of those. And gangs from the suburbs. Junkies. It's like a fucking zoo here at night. What's all of this about, anyway? Is there something important about that guy? This is the second time I've shown someone that tape.'

'Who else did you show it to?'

'The cops.'

Katz was mystified. Angela Klingberg didn't think the police had looked at the surveillance video. Julin hadn't mentioned it either.

'When?'

'Just a few days ago. A chick. She was actually pretty cute. In good shape. In her forties. Probably a dyke. She showed ID, but I don't remember her name. Actually, maybe she was a DA.'

The guard reached for a can of Coke on the shelf, took a sip and gave a nasty sneer.

'Speaking of zoos, check out this clip.'

He had clicked on another frame: a gang of teenagers walking in the stairwell. They stopped right under the camera. As if in response to an inaudible command, they took out cans of spray paint and started tagging the walls. It was over in less than a minute. Four walls, full of graffiti. One of them, a young boy with dreadlocks, turned to the camera and smiled before taking out a bottle of beer and throwing it at the lens, missing. Then they vanished down the stairs, and all that was left in the shot were the tagged walls and the shards of glass from the beer bottle on the ground.

'Fucking scum. Did you see the monkey who threw the bottle? Know what I've started to think recently? That that Norwegian guy, Breivik, is right. All this multi-culti shit is going to hell. But people don't have the guts to speak up. Even Åkesson and the Swedish Democrats have gone all PC. So what would you say if I told you that Breivik did the only right thing? We have to get to the root of the problem, dig it all up before it's too late . . .'

The guard stopped talking and scratched his scalp.

'So, there's one more camera,' Katz said calmly.

'What?'

'In the stairwell. Are you the one who rigged it up? The company doesn't have permission to use cameras outside the parking area.'

'Like I said, nothing happens here. Eight hours in a glass cage every night. You have to do something for fun. Anyway, I took it down. My boss complained.'

'Was the camera in the stairwell there on 22 April?'

'Maybe . . .'

'And you didn't say anything to the police.'

'Like I said . . . she was a dyke.'

'I want you to find the video from when the guy in the Lexus was here. He did go into the stairwell, after all. You have him on tape somewhere. A close-up.'

The guard sighed.

'I think he's here somewhere, but it'll cost you another five hundred.'

Katz placed another bill on the table, and two minutes later he was looking at another shot of the man. He was going down the same stairs the teenagers had vandalized, with his back to the camera. He still had his hood up. The man was of average height, just like Klingberg or Katz himself or another one of a million men in the country. There was nothing particularly striking about the way he walked or held his body. Then he was out of shot, without having shown his face.

'That guy isn't taking any risks. He doesn't want to be recognized. Can I turn it off now? I have a job to do.'

'Wait a minute!'

The camera was still rolling. Katz saw the light shift in the picture as a door was opened one floor down. Two shadows appeared against the wall; two people meeting, stopping and exchanging a few words, until one of them – the man in the raincoat – disappeared through the door and the other came up the stairs.

Katz recognized him when he entered the shot: a young guy, maybe seventeen years old. He stopped on the landing, directly under the camera. His clothes were dirty; he was wearing a backpack over one shoulder. *Homeless*, Katz thought, *and a junkie*. But clean for the time being. He looked scared stiff.

'A druggie,' said the guard. 'This place is crawling with them. I found a dead junkie here just last week, in a car. I thought he was sleeping at first . . . he was in the back seat of a Toyota Corolla. Look at him, he looks like he's fucking dying of AIDS.'

Katz had seen him at an NA meeting in the city the

previous winter. Katz had been the one to open the meeting, 'sharing', as it was called. He had listened to the others' stories, noticing how far behind they were in their personal development, how they were just scraping the surface of their problems, and then he had noticed the guy who was sitting by himself at the very back of the room. He looked vacant, as if he didn't really understand what was going on around him. Dirty. Flecks of blood on his jeans. With the same backpack at his feet.

'Is it possible to print out pictures?' he asked.

'Individual frames? Sure.'

'I need one of the man in the raincoat and one of this guy.'

The guard did as he asked.

'You're lucky,' he said, as he handed them over. 'The pictures are included in the final price.'

Katz stared at the photo of the junkie. *He's terrified*, he thought, *but of what? Of the man he met in the stairwell? And he's far too young to be an addict.* Just as he himself had been once upon a time.

Katz had gone to six different schools in the first ten years of his life. His parents, Benjamin and Anne, had been teachers, but Benjamin had a terrible disposition so he had never been able to keep a job for very long. At the last school Benjamin worked at he broke the collarbone of a caretaker after an argument about the ventilation in the teachers' room. He couldn't control his outbursts; they were in his blood. Katz had inherited the tendency, too; he'd spent his life trying to keep it under control, but hadn't always succeeded.

Benjamin had died of lung cancer just after Katz's fourteenth birthday. His mother had died shortly thereafter; she stopped eating and withered away at a nursing home in Sollentuna. The family had no other relatives, and Katz was placed in a youth home. Actually, it was amazing he hadn't ended up there earlier. He had begun to go astray several years before – he was caught shoplifting at the age of only eleven and had his first case come up in the social welfare office at twelve.

After his parents' death, there was not even a shred of superego left to control him. After being sent to the youth home in Hässelby, he got to know other troubled kids from western Stockholm: gangs from Blackeberg and Rissne, young thugs who couldn't see a future, no matter where they looked. Katz quickly blended in. They committed burglaries at the request of older criminals, waded through the water at the yacht clubs along Lake Mälaren with bolt-cutters in hand to cut the locks on boat engines, dabbled in stolen goods and hold-ups, assaulted people they didn't like the look of, and functioned as drug mules between dealers and distributors across half of Greater Stockholm. The heroin was everywhere. Katz saw what the drug did to people, how it broke them down, but he was a teenager and could see no reason to resist. His first love story with the drug lasted only a few months, and he never had time to develop a total addiction. Strangely enough, it was the catastrophe with Eva Dahlman that saved him. He had met Eva the summer he turned sixteen. His best friend from the youth home, Jorma Hedlund, had introduced them. Eva was tall, shy and preferred not to speak because she was ashamed of her mild stutter. At first, Katz took her silence as arrogance; later on, he thought it was inscrutability. She was two years younger than him and came from a troubled home, just like he did; she had lived on the street when things were at their worst, and sometimes she spent the night in Katz's room at the youth home if he managed to smuggle her in without the staff noticing. She was with him when he took his very first shot in the basement of a high-rise on Astrakangatan, and his hands shook so hard that she was the one who finally had to inject it for him.

They had been together all summer long, doing drugs, having sex outdoors, shoplifting from department stores together, hanging out with the same crowd. In August they had burgled a luxury yacht that was anchored outside the marina at Hässelby Strand. Katz and Jorma Hedlund had seen the crew leave the boat and vanish in a taxi, and they had waited a few hours for it to get dark before swimming out to the vessel. Eva had stood guard on the beach. Except for a thousand kronor in cash, they hadn't found anything of value. They had vandalized the boat before they left – trashing the interior, tossing food out of the refrigerator, pouring a can of paint they found on to the clothes in the wardrobe. Later that same evening, Eva and Katz had got high together in a bike-storage room not far from there. The horse was hardly diluted and Katz felt how strong it was as soon as he injected it, felt his limbs go numb in an alarming way, and then it had all gone black.

When he woke up, he was in a forest. He later learned he was on Grübbholmen, an uninhabited island across from Hässelby Strand. A torch was shining in his eyes, and he heard dogs barking and saw police everywhere. His pants had been pulled down to his knees. He was holding a pair of panties in his hand. Someone grabbed him by the hair and turned him over on his stomach. He saw Eva Dahlman, naked, blood all over her body, being carried off on a stretcher; he heard people yelling at him, felt someone yank him up into a sitting position and slap handcuffs on him.

At the youth detention centre he was sent to, he met a psychologist who tried to help him remember what had happened. According to the police report, he had beaten Eva until she was unconscious and had then bitten her neck severely. But Katz's memory was blank. Eva didn't remember anything either. She had been placed in a treatment home for young drug abusers in Norrland and refused to believe that Katz was guilty.

The incident had haunted him for several years. The uncertainty was the worst part. Was he really the sort of person who could do something like that? He had tortured himself with doubt. But, in the end, the idea that he was guilty was unbearable. He wanted to move on, make a break with his old life.

Katz's salvation turned out to be his academic abilities. At detention centre he was granted permission to study at a school in Huddinge, where he completed a course in natural sciences. He achieved top grades, not least in foreign languages and maths, and his teacher allowed him to work at his own pace, outside the curriculum. In his final year he studied computer programming and even stepped in as an instructor when the regular lecturer was ill.

At eighteen years old he underwent the examinations for his compulsory military service. The military psychologist suggested he take the extra tests that were required for special training. Katz had tested sky-high on the Stanford-Binet and other intelligence tests. One month later, he received a call from a major at the recruiting office, who asked if he would like to do his military service at the interpreter academy; they had reserved a space for him in case he was interested.

Katz became one of three military interpreters from the school to be offered employment at an embassy immediately after finishing his education. In autumn 1988 he was placed in Helsinki as a defence assistant. For two years he translated Russian documents for the military attaché: newspapers, military communications, transcripts from Finnish radio intelligence across the border. Apparently, he did a good job, because after this appointment he was sent to the Consulate General in Leningrad, or St Petersburg, as it would soon be called.

That was where he met Rickard Julin for the first time.

Officially, Julin was employed by the Swedish Ministry for Foreign Affairs as a consul in the bureau of visas, but in reality his employer was the armed forces. The old Soviet empire was about to collapse, and the consulate was still responsible for official contacts with north-western Russia: the oblasts of Arkhangelsk, Murmansk, Novgorod and Pskov, the republics of Karelia and Komi, Nenets Autonomous Okrug and the Kaliningrad region. Julin's task was to gather information about munitions that had gone astray, what was going on with the arms industry and who was taking responsibility for weapons stockpiles and missile facilities.

Katz only saw him once a week or so, since Julin spent most of his time travelling. But Katz liked him because of his calm demeanour and his natural warmth – he was light years from how one would imagine a career officer. As he understood it, Julin had once had on-the-job protection, a number and an alias in order to stave off attempts by foreign powers to recruit him, and all of this made an impression on Katz.

Julin was sixteen years older than he was, and it wasn't

until a year later, when Julin vanished to take a job as a peace observer in the Balkans, that Katz realized what Julin had meant to him, that he had looked up to him like an older brother.

Katz's tour of duty as a military interpreter ended in the spring of 1992, as suddenly as it had begun. He returned to Stockholm to apply as a jobseeker in the midst of the impending recession. When he landed at Arlanda airport, he realized that he had nowhere to go. By then he hadn't seen Julin in over a year, and it was a long shot that he would be able to reach him at an old work number. But Julin answered, and not only that – he acted as a guardian angel. In under a week he arranged a job for Katz as a civilian translator at the FRA, the National Defence Radio Establishment.

He sat alone in a room on Lovön, producing basic data for the military's external analysts. He dealt with small fragments of information that other people put together to create an intelligible whole. He saw Julin now and again. He had moved up through the defence establishment, as a travelling attaché at NATO headquarters. They got together sometimes when Julin was home – meeting at a café in the town, speaking Russian together for fun or exchanging gossip about old colleagues from the Ministry for Foreign Affairs.

Katz started using heroin again during his second year in Stockholm. He could hardly explain to himself how it happened. Maybe it was just because of loneliness. The loneliness that closed ever tighter around him, isolating him more and more, encapsulating all his other feelings:

his sorrow at the loss of his parents, his frustration over his lost teenage years and over what had happened to Eva Dahlman, his sadness at the way they had been separated and had never seen each other again, the nameless rage he had carried inside him for as long as he could remember.

He bought the drugs from a distant acquaintance from his time at Hässelby, a South American by the name of Jorge who had the porous, chalky skin of the old IV junkies. But he did his job – he never took drugs during working hours, he made sure his sleeves covered his track marks and he delivered what he was supposed to deliver on time.

In the summer of 1993, Katz was suddenly sent to the Consulate General in Berlin on behalf of the FRA. The old Berlin Agreement had expired when Germany was reunited. The Russians packed up their last weapons stores and sent the goods from the East Berlin suburb of Erkner to Moscow by train. Katz gathered information about how this was organized – how long the Russians took, how the decampment was administered, which branches of the military were involved, and how it was reported in the Russian and German media. He went to Berlin on a diplomatic passport, with ten grams of Dutch heroin in a bag in the inner pocket of his jacket. At the time, his doses were three times stronger than what he'd started with.

The consulate had arranged an apartment for him on Wiener Strasse in Kreuzberg, just a stone's throw from Kottbusser Tor. So he had no problem getting his hands on drugs. Kottbusser Tor was the headquarters for the heroin trade in south-central Berlin. Toothless junkies sold Turkish horse in three-gram envelopes for a fraction of the price in Stockholm. You could buy ten-packs of syringes outside the chemist's.

After a few months in the city, he needed the poison round the clock in order to function. He started taking risks, injecting small doses at the office, taking time off more and more often, starting to hang out with other junkies. And then came the first periods of calling in sick, weeks of being in a fog; afterwards, he could hardly remember what had happened.

He found temporary salvation when he was called back to Stockholm to go through computer training at KTH, the Royal Institute of Technology. The armed forces knew of his programming abilities and his general gift for languages and information-gathering, but a new day was about to dawn with the Internet and ever-faster personal computers. They were looking into the future and realizing that they needed people like Katz.

He managed to detox and control himself until he finished the course. But, immediately after it, he once again found himself going steeply downhill.

It happened very quickly. In less than a year, he had lost his job and become homeless.

He got money by committing burglaries and by selling drugs himself. Jorma Hedlund was the only one of his old friends he was still in contact with. Jorma was still a criminal, but he had tried to help Katz. The only problem was that Katz didn't want help.

He stayed in shelters, temporary lodgings where you

could get a bed for the night but were kicked out again as soon as the sun came up. Later, he stayed in dope dens or, as he became sicker and sicker and cared less and less about himself, outside: in doorways, in parks.

He fell and fell through that darkness, towards a bottom that didn't exist, until his salvation was finally standing before him in the form of Rickard Julin.

Katz still remembered that day as if it were yesterday. Julin had discovered him at the Gullmarsplan metro station. Katz had been on his way somewhere, but he could no longer remember where. He had been standing on the platform, barely noticing how people kept their distance as they walked past him because his clothes were dirty, his hands were covered in track marks and he was talking to himself out loud. At least, that's what Julin had said later, that he had heard him before he saw him, and recognized his voice.

That's where it had started: Julin had given him a business card and asked him to call, even if it was only to chat for a while. That's just who he was — a man who fixed things for other people. One month later, Katz found himself at an Anthroposophical Society treatment home in Ytterjärna.

Katz opened the door to his flat just after midnight. He immediately sensed that someone had been there. He felt the keyhole with his thumb. No trace of lock lubricant. If someone had picked the lock, it had been cleaned afterwards. He walked into the hall and closed the door behind him. Faint light from the streetlamps shone through the windows. He stood still and tried to listen for any sound: an intake of breath, the soft rustle of clothes against a body. But he couldn't hear anything.

He went into the bedroom. The light from the clock radio was reflecting dimly off the walls. His bed was untouched, but the door to the wardrobe was ajar. He opened it carefully. Everything seemed normal, except for the strange feeling that someone had moved his clothes around and put them back in the right place.

In the kitchen, the fan was making its usual gentle buzz. The dishes were in the rack; a dry Wettex rag was hung across the tap. The floor and the wall tiles were sparkling clean. Everything looked just as he had left it.

He moved on, into the living room. The sofa looked like a sleeping animal in its spot against the wall. The digital receiver blinked under the TV. A folded newspaper lay on the coffee table. The objects in the bookcase and on the windowsill . . . they were all in the very spots he remembered them being in.

He looked through the rooms once more, systematically, finding no traces of a break-in. He knew from experience where a person would look for valuables. He had done the same thing himself in his darker years. But nothing had been stolen. And nothing was out of place.

The feeling slowly dissipated as he made a sandwich and ate it in the kitchen.

He noticed on his mobile-phone screen that Angela Klingberg had sent a message. He looked at it: she had booked a meeting for him at Klingberg Aluminium headquarters at ten o'clock the next morning. Pontus Klingberg would be expecting him.

Katz thought of the young junkie in the multi-storey car park. He ought to try to get hold of him, ask after him at shelters, check with the NA group downtown. He had seen the person who was driving Klingberg's car; he'd exchanged a few words with him and had somehow been frightened by him.

Then there was the female police officer who'd asked to look at the surveillance tapes just a few days earlier. According to Julin's contacts, the investigation had been dropped after one day. But, apparently, someone had opened it again.

Something wasn't right, he thought: something about the whole Klingberg story was fundamentally wrong.

He walked into the living room, started up the desktop computer he used when he didn't want to go down to the office and put the USB stick into the port.

The file he'd copied from Klingberg's computer seemed to be corrupt. He downloaded a zip-fix program from the

Internet, and a few minutes later the file was restored and opened. It contained a write-protected folder named 'MK'. The same initials as on the cloth he had received from Angela Klingberg.

The folder contained a few scanned black-and-white photographs. Family portraits taken more than half a century earlier in what appeared to be a tropical country. A man and a woman posing for a photographer, along with two boys. Another few pictures of the same family in a city somewhere. Signs in Spanish in the background. The family patriarch, Gustav, with his wife and children. The youngest boy was presumably Joel's father.

There were a few notes further down in the document; key points that, according to the file date, had been written the day before Klingberg's disappearance:

Kristoffer abducted June 1970.
Mum and Dad found in September 1979.
    Why in the country?
Marie Bennoit died in 1978. How?

Klingberg seemed to believe that there was a connection between the events – between the abduction of his brother and the deaths of three people. The photographs in the file depicted his father, uncle and paternal grandparents. They had been taken decades earlier, probably in the Dominican Republic. Who was Marie Bennoit? A relative? Why else would Klingberg mention her along with his brother and parents?

At precisely ten o'clock the next morning, Katz stepped through the door of Klingberg Aluminium's main office in Vasastan. A secretary asked him to take a seat in the foyer and wait. The room was sober, almost sterile. Grey walls; black, wall-to-wall carpeting. A faint buzzing sound came from the air conditioning. A few weekly magazines lay on a coffee table. The view was magnificent: it looked over Vanadislunden and the Wenner-Gren Centre and the waters of Brunnsviken just beyond them.

Katz helped himself to coffee from a machine next to the reception desk. As he let it cool, he called Angela Klingberg. She didn't answer either her mobile or on her home number. He hung up and called Julin instead, and he gave him a summary of the information he'd learned from the guard at the multi-storey car park: that the police had looked at the security tapes although the investigation was officially suspended. Julin promised to check up on this and call back as soon as he knew more.

There was a Klingberg Aluminium brochure among the magazines. Katz paged through it listlessly until he came to a portrait of the founder, Gustav Klingberg. The company's history was given under the picture: Gustav had been born in the Dominican Republic in 1914, the eldest son of the missionary couple Einar and Astrid

Klingberg. After graduating from grammar school in Santo Domingo he received a scholarship to study mining engineering at a technical college in Havana. Three years later he returned to the island to start his own business.

In a short time he had made a fortune in the sugar industry and in bauxite mining. Along with an American mining company, he refined bauxite for the production of aluminium and the manufacturing of highly refractory clays.

In the early forties, the text went on, he had married the daughter of a Swedish missionary; her name was Lisbet and their families were acquaintances. Their sons, Pontus and Jan, had been born in 1941 and 1942.

In the early fifties, Gustav and his family returned to Sweden as the result of a strategic business decision. He founded Klingberg Aluminium and established its headquarters in Stockholm. The company imported bauxite from Africa and the West Indies for the manufacture of aluminium for car rims, ball bearings, aircraft hulls, façades and roofing. After just a few years, the Klingberg Group controlled a conglomerate of companies in the metal industry.

On the last page of the brochure was a family portrait taken in the late sixties; Katz assumed it was meant to symbolize continuity in the company. It showed Gustav Klingberg, his wife, Lisbet, and their two children and four grandchildren standing on the veranda of their family home in Djursholm. Joel was second to the left, standing, according to the caption, next to his big brother, Kristoffer.

Katz looked straight into the eyes of the boy with the sad smile. Kristoffer was black.

Joel had never mentioned anything about his brother being adopted. And yet they looked alike, as if one's environment really could influence one's looks, as if there was something chameleon-like about children.

Katz put down the brochure. A female receptionist smiled at him from the other side of the desk. Shortly afterwards, he was shown in to the CEO of the company.

Pontus Klingberg didn't seem to think it was odd to get a visit from a stranger who asked questions about his nephew's disappearance. He received Katz while sitting on a leather sofa in the boardroom. The view was just as magnificent from here.

'My dad was a great admirer of Axel Wenner-Gren,' he said, when he noticed where Katz was looking. 'That's why he absolutely wanted the company's offices to be adjacent to the old man's showpiece. Axel was a lover of the Caribbean, too, just like Dad. He had a house in Barbados; he actually lived there during the war, until '42, when the Brits blacklisted him for selling Bofors guns to the Germans. I remember him from when I was a kid. Gustav and Axel used to eat at the Stallmästaregården hotel together; they always had the *gubbröra* as an appetizer and fried herring as the main course, and they would discuss commodity prices, the future of Electrolux or the Wallenberg family's rampages through the main branches of Swedish industry.'

He reached for a bottle of mineral water that stood on a serving trolley behind him; he opened it and poured a glass, which he handed to Katz.

'What's on your mind, young man? Is it Angela – is she worried about my nephew?'

Katz took the glass and sat down in the chair across from him.

'She doesn't believe that Joel vanished willingly.'

'It's natural for people to be nervous when someone disappears without warning like that. I don't know what kind of problem Joel has with Angela, and I'm not sure I want to know. Money, maybe? That can happen when a girl marries rich . . . or richer than what she's used to. It creates a certain amount of inequality. But Joel has a great deal of loyalty to the company. He'll be home again soon.'

'Where do you think he is?'

'What do I know? In Denmark, maybe, like the police think. Or maybe he's still here in Stockholm. It shouldn't be too hard to find him. One could start by calling around the hotels. But that's not my job. You have to respect people's integrity. I'm sure my nephew has good reasons for going away for a while.'

Pontus Klingberg laced his fingers together behind his neck, leaned back on the sofa and looked up at the ceiling. Katz studied his silver hair, his double-breasted suit and the well-manicured hand that suddenly moved down and rested on his knee. He's not used to being contradicted, he thought. He's a man who is used to getting his own way.

'You didn't notice anything out of the ordinary about him before he disappeared?'

'No, everything was normal. Business as usual. We were working on a deal in England, a company we've had our eye on for a while. Aluminium structures for furniture.

The majority shareholder is prepared to sell to us for a reasonable price. I'm actually on my way to London tonight for the final arrangements. Joel was supposed to come with me; that's the only thing that bothers me.'

A woman of about twenty-five stepped into the room to say that his younger daughter had called. Pontus Klingberg nodded and gave her a fatherly smile before she disappeared again.

'Joel used to do things like this when he was younger,' he went on. 'At that time, he still lived with his grandfather. He would vanish and stay away for a few weeks. He would sit and read in a rented apartment somewhere. And then he'd suddenly show up again, as if nothing had happened. He hasn't had an easy time of it, as you may know. It's been a lot for him to process. First, his big brother's abduction. And then he was orphaned nine years later, when my brother and his wife . . .'

He stopped talking in the middle of his sentence and a streak of sadness darkened his gaze. He looked down at his lap before continuing: 'He must have left a message for Angela, right?'

'They had fought that morning.'

'About children, I'm guessing? Always their big problem; that discussion has been going on for ten years. Her financial lifeline, should their relationship go to pot. But I think Joel will end up giving in. I have two daughters myself. And four grandchildren. Children are the spice of life, or whatever the expression is.'

Pontus Klingberg looked out the window, down at Brunnsviken, where the trees were in their late-spring bloom. Faint opera music emanated from hidden speakers in the room; Klingberg swayed gently in time to it. There was something fragile about him, Katz thought, which one didn't notice at first glance. As if he didn't really fit into himself, into his own body.

'The police contacted you about Joel's disappearance.'

'Very briefly, by phone. I told them what I knew, and that was about it. Who are you, anyway? Angela said something about you and Joel doing your military service together?'

Katz told him how he had got to know Joel. A few words about the interpreter academy, his memory of Joel being picked up by a private driver on Fridays.

'Katz?' Pontus Klingberg said, when he was finished. 'Jewish background. Don't worry, I'm not prejudiced; I have several Jewish business associates. A gifted people. They know how to make money.'

Which was a typical prejudice, Katz thought, as he watched Pontus Klingberg stand up and walk over to a bookcase; his own father had been a teacher, and his grandfather, if he understood correctly, had been a shoemaker in Vienna before he moved to Sweden with his wife and fifteen-year-old son just before the war broke out, and he had vanished to Israel after the war – they were hardly rich Jews. But Katz was used to this, and he had heard worse, ranging from harmless stereotypes about the business acumen Jews were assumed to have to how they controlled world politics in secret. Maybe this was what it meant to be Jewish: that there were always comments about you being a Jew.

When he turned around, Pontus Klingberg had picked up a framed photo from the bookcase. Two smiling young girls on a yacht. There was a second portrait on the bookcase: Pontus Klingberg with the same girls – now grown up – on a smaller sailboat.

'My daughters,' he said. 'Ebba and Julia. From a cruise in the Caribbean when they were little. The other one is from Sandhamn, a few years ago. We usually compete in the Gotland Runt race every summer. Soon their children will come along, too, my grandchildren . . . I have pictures of them, too, if you're interested. The Klingbergs always do well.'

He smiled proudly, but then his face twisted into a grimace.

'I used to think, *What if Ebba or Julia had been kidnapped instead of Kristoffer?* And it hurt so much just to think it. I don't think you can imagine the pain it caused us when it happened. A seven-year-old boy disappeared, and his fate is still unknown. It completely broke his parents. Jan never recovered. I suffered so terribly alongside him. Our only comfort was that the incident brought him back to the family. He had tried to distance himself from Gustav all his life . . . and from me, too, but after that loss he came back. Not that we could do much to ease his pain. He never forgave himself. He'd had a few drinks before he and the children walked to that metro station from a children's party in Stadshagen. He never stopped torturing himself with guilt. And he kept drinking. Ironically enough, the alcohol that had once caused him to use poor judgement became the thing that consoled him. That was what killed him and Joanna, his wife. The suicide was just an extension of their drinking.'

Pontus Klingberg gazed out of the window, sighed and swallowed hard.

'None of us got over it. Gustav was a broken man. First he lost his grandson, and then his son.'

He grew quiet. There was laughter from the hallway outside.

'Wasn't there anything to suggest that the kidnapping had been planned?'

'No. It was a coincidence, the work of a lone mad-woman. That woman, whoever she was, just took Kristoffer on impulse – God only knows where. That was more than forty years ago now. Kristoffer would have turned forty-nine this year. Hardly a week goes by that I don't think of him. And when you see things in the paper . . . about what happened to that Austrian girl, Kampusch, or about devils incarnate like that Belgian, Dutroux, it makes your thoughts start whirling again, and that sick feeling comes. Or the hate comes.'

Pontus Klingberg gave him a vacant look and shook his head quietly.

'Was Kristoffer adopted?' Katz asked.

'Why do you ask?'

'Well, he was black.'

'Didn't Joel ever tell you about his brother?'

'No, not in detail.'

'His paternal grandmother was Creole. But the blood, or whatever the word is, skipped a generation. It was hardly visible at all in Jan, except for his curly hair . . . and in the summer . . . he would go browner than the rest of us. It was damned strange; Joel didn't get it either – the blood, the inheritance – but it showed up in Kristoffer. It's a long story.'

Pontus Klingberg didn't look at Katz as he told it. It was as if he were deep inside himself, as if he were just a medium for the family's story.

He told Katz about his paternal grandfather, Einar, the missionary who had saved the life of a fifteen-year-old Haitian girl during the Parsley Massacre in 1937. He had adopted her and let her grow up as his own daughter: Marie Bennoit. But Gustav had fallen in love with her. Or maybe the two step-siblings had fallen in love with each other. Despite this, Gustav had married the daughter of a missionary, Lisbet, Pontus Klingberg's mother. But soon after that he had an illegitimate child with his mistress: Jan Klingberg.

'Dad was a businessman through and through. He did business with Ramfis Trujillo. Do you know who that is? He was the son of the dictator of the Dominican Republic, Rafael Trujillo, and he was just as crazy and just as much of an erotomaniac as his father. Dad would stop at nothing to get his way; he was ruthless, but there was never any question that Jan was a full member of the family. He was taken away from his mother shortly after he was born, and he only got to see her sporadically. Lisbet, my mother, never accepted Gustav's relationship with Marie, but it was a matter of course that Jan was part of our family and would come with us to Sweden when we went back. It was a tough blow for Marie; she wanted to

75

keep him. But, naturally, Gustav got his way. Marie wasn't left empty-handed, though. Considerable sums of money were transferred over to her throughout the years. And she had more children to support. Dad wasn't her only lover. She was very beautiful. Timeless, somehow.'

Pontus Klingberg stopped talking and got up from the sofa.

'Do these have anything to do with your family history?' Katz asked. He had taken out the pieces of cloth Angela Klingberg had given him; he placed them on the coffee table.

Pontus Klingberg looked at them expressionlessly. 'What are they?'

'They were sent anonymously to Joel shortly before he disappeared. Do they mean anything to you?'

Pontus Klingberg shook his head.

'No,' he said sadly. 'Unfortunately, I can't help you.'

He walked slowly towards the door that led back to the foyer.

'If you'll excuse me,' he said. 'I promised to meet my daughter for an early lunch.'

Pontus Klingberg led Katz out to the foyer, his arm across his back. Almost tenderly, as if he were confusing Katz with his nephew.

One hour later Katz found himself in the microfilm room at the National Library in Humlegården. The room was quiet. There were only two other visitors there, plus the librarian, who was working on a computer.

He walked over to the compact shelves and moved two sections in order to get to the evening papers. He took out the boxes containing microfiche issues of *Expressen* and *Aftonbladet* from June 1970, the papers which, according to the catalogue, had published the most articles about the abduction of Kristoffer Klingberg.

He opened the first box, inserted the roll into the holder on the microfiche reader, lifted the glass plate and advanced the film to 8 June, the day after the incident.

Six different headlines, but none of them was about Kristoffer. Thirty thousand people were feared dead in an earthquake that had taken place in Peru a week earlier. Olof Palme was on an unofficial state visit to the United States and had given a speech to the National Press Club in Washington.

Katz moved on through the newspaper. Sports headlines about the World Cup in Mexico. Lee Hazlewood visiting Stockholm. Cigarette ads he hadn't seen in Swedish papers since he was a child: 'I switched to Prince, too.'

The movie listings, with *Love Story* and *A Man Called Horse*, before the weather forecast showed up on the last page.

He didn't get a hit until the 15 June issue of *Expressen*: 'Boy abducted at metro station.'

The article was short, and it was on the very bottom of the domestic news page. It was practically just a notice. It was made clear that the incident had happened a week earlier at the Kristineberg station. No names were mentioned.

It took a few more days before it became big news. But then the entire Klingberg family was splashed across the centre spread of both evening papers. The boy had been abducted by a woman who had managed to trick the heartbroken father into trusting her. There was specula-tion that it was an extortion scheme, but the police and a spokesperson for the family denied this. And, for the first time, there was a photograph of Kristoffer.

The picture was clipped from his first class picture. A toothless little boy smiled at the camera. Naturally, there was no mention of the colour of his skin, but at the same time it was puzzling when one saw the pictures of his par-ents and little brother.

The articles continued for two weeks before they faded away and were replaced by other news. Nothing new turned up. The story was stylized as a Greek tragedy, where Nem-esis afflicted the rich and powerful. A nationwide alert had gone out, and the story had been publicized in neighbour-ing countries as well. There had been some tip-offs, including anonymous ones, but none of them had led anywhere.

*

Pontus was the crown prince of the family company, Katz thought as he put the microfiche back in the right place. Jan didn't seem to have anything to do with the firm at all, except symbolically, by way of his name. According to the articles, he had studied to be a teacher and hadn't had any interest in making himself a career in the company. He was a child of his time, passionate about things other than business; he was married to a woman who was two years his elder, Joanna, a social anthropologist; he dressed in line with the post-hippie fashions of the time, travelled by public transport on principle – a very wealthy heir disguised as a bohemian. Gustav had provided financially, of course; among other things, he had bought beach-front property on Lidingö for the family, and he had also planned to pay for the construction of a luxury home there. By golly, his grandsons would live in dignity even if his son was slumming. But then catastrophe had struck.

Katz took a break to eat lunch at the restaurant in the library: potato pancakes with pork and two cups of coffee to go with them. The canteen was full of researchers and students. The people at the next table were speaking Russian; three men were gossiping about a female research colleague. Katz shut them out. He felt distant in the sudden buzz of people.

He drank up the last of his coffee and called Angela Klingberg. She wasn't answering now either. He logged into a computer on the ground floor and checked his mail. There she was. She had sent a short message an hour earlier, asking if he could come to Skeppargatan at eight o'clock that evening. She needed to see him, she wrote; could he confirm that he could come?

For a brief instant Katz pictured her walking naked and perfect through the quiet flat, her hand touching the objects she passed. He pushed away the thought and replied that it was fine; he would come at eight.

Then he took the lift back down to the microfiche room and walked over to the catalogue computer.

He entered Kristoffer and Jan Klingberg's names in the search field. There was an article in the magazine *Se* that seemed interesting. A few minutes later, the library had retrieved it for him.

It was a frank interview with Jan Klingberg on the ninth anniversary of the tragic incident. He had been photographed on the metro platform where his son had disappeared. He had consented to an interview because he wanted to help others who had experienced similar tragedies.

In the interview he said that he still dreamed about his son – sometimes several times a week – and in his dreams the boy was still seven years old. Just like the last time he had seen him, when he disappeared hand in hand with the strange woman. He had been frozen in time that afternoon, Jan explained, 'glassed into my memory'.

The years had gone by extremely slowly for Jan, the reporter wrote, but the days went by far too quickly. And they carried him farther and farther from Kristoffer. The boy was slowly fading, even though Jan did everything he could to keep him in his memory. He could no longer remember his voice, and he was angry with himself for that.

The seventh of June 1970. That was when his life had ended. And now it was that time of year again, the reporter wrote – early summer, the end of school, graduates in their white caps – the worst time of year for Jan. His son would have been sixteen.

On the metro platform where he was photographed, Jan Klingberg expressed amazement that life went on with so little concern in a place that he found so terrible. People getting on and off the trains; the bus stop where he had disembarked with Kristoffer after the party they'd been to in Stadshagen. It was inconceivable. From where he stood he could see the paddling pool in Fredhäll, the children playing down there, boys of Kristoffer's age, the age he'd been when he was taken away.

The journalist wrote that the mystery remained unsolved, that Kristoffer had disappeared without a trace. No ransom letter had ever been sent; the international searches hadn't brought any results. And the boy himself would have contacted them if he had managed to get away from his kidnapper. Jan had come to terms with the thought that Kristoffer was dead.

The journalist asked Klingberg what the woman might have done to get Kristoffer to come with her on the metro.

This was a question he had asked himself every day since the train had vanished off in the direction of Alvik, Jan explained. Because the boy would have protested. But maybe the passengers had mistaken them for a grandmother with a fussy grandchild; maybe she'd even said as much to a sceptical fellow passenger: 'Don't pay any mind to my grandson; he gets like this sometimes.' And he also asked himself where she had got off with him. At the next station? Alvik? Anyway, that was the direction he'd gone in right after it happened, he explained, in a total panic and with his younger son in the pushchair, ice-cold inside, as if he were already dead; he thought that the woman wouldn't have dared go any farther with him, but no one had been there, and the turnstile guard hadn't seen or heard anything.

He talked about the time after the kidnapping. He remembered it in a sort of haze. The newspaper articles. The police interrogations. The nationwide alert. The search. The tip-offs that had come in, which had kept his and his wife's hopes alive for a few days or weeks but which had later fizzled out. And the newspaper articles that became fewer and farther between because the fate of a single person – even if it was a child, even if it was the child of a rich family – didn't mean anything as time went on. The flickers of hope had been extinguished one by one, replaced by darkness.

The body of a boy had been found in Denmark that summer, and Jan had hoped it was Kristoffer so at least they could have some closure. But it wasn't Kristoffer; it was another child. One year later, a madman had taken responsibility for the kidnapping; he'd claimed that he'd killed the boy but couldn't give the location where he'd buried the body. Jan had hated the man for that, for giving them a bizarre hope of an answer and then taking it away.

Now that nearly a decade had passed, Jan realized that Kristoffer's body would never be found, but not a day went by that he didn't wonder what they'd done to the boy. He consciously thought 'they', because he felt there must have been more than one person. He couldn't imagine that a lone woman was behind the kidnapping.

The journalist asked once again about the ransom rumours; after all, the Klingberg family was incredibly wealthy.

But Jan Klingberg denied any such rumours. In his darkest moments he believed that sexual offenders had been involved. He had heard of people like that. Adults who assaulted children. Paedophiles.

In the concluding paragraph, the reporter wrote that Jan now lived for his younger son, for Joel's future and well-being. The tragedy had taught him to cherish the days, to see what was important in life.

Katz spooled back to the beginning of the article and looked at the picture of Jan Klingberg. It was impossible, of course, to tell if a person was suicidal just by looking at him, but it seemed inconceivable that the same man would be found dead of carbon monoxide poisoning a few months later in a garage at the family's country home in Sörmland, along with his wife, Joanna.

They were connected, Katz thought as he sat in his car later that afternoon. Joel Klingberg had received two mysterious objects shortly before his disappearance, embroidered pieces of cloth that probably had something to do with Kristoffer's abduction.

Someone must have contacted Joel Klingberg by telephone and claimed to have information about his brother. The same person who'd sent him the package? Joel seemed to have received the information while driving; otherwise, why would he have suddenly cut his errands short and driven toward Kungsholmen?

Where had he met the person? At Thorildsplan? In Stadshagen, where Kristoffer had been at a party before he was abducted?

Katz looked at the printout of the travel log. It was clear: Joel had followed the path Kristoffer had taken before being abducted. He'd gone through Stadshagen and up to the Kristineberg station, as if he'd wanted to follow in the kidnapper's footsteps. Because it had to have been planned: the person or people – the woman, with or without accomplices – must have been shadowing the family until they arrived at a golden opportunity, more or less by chance.

Joel had stopped at the site of the abduction and then

kept going, across the bridge. He had stopped again at the station where, forty-two years earlier, his panicked father had got off the train to ask the turnstile guard if he'd seen Joel's brother.

Then he had kept driving. The person who had been with Klingberg, or who had spoken to him on the phone, had told him to stop at the tennis courts. It had nothing to do with the fact that Katz lived nearby; it had to do with Kristoffer's disappearance, just like the rest of the journey that Sunday three weeks earlier.

It had been cold, Katz remembered, as he followed Klingberg's route down to the industrial area. It had been cold throughout April; they had hit record low after record low. He tried to imagine the cosy warmth in Klingberg's Lexus, the scent of the leather seats, his confused thoughts deep down in the middle-aged businessman he'd become . . . and the person he'd been talking to. Who was it?

Katz kept driving, going down Margretelundsvägen, past the newly built light-rail bridge that led to the Solna side of the water, on past the small industrial buildings along Missionsvägen, the old sheet-metal shops and boat-cover manufacturers. Run-down brick buildings from the thirties, annexes made of Eternit from the late sixties, before development in the area stagnated. He stopped where Klingberg had, at a lay-by near a community garden. He turned off the engine and removed the key from the ignition.

First a stop at the tennis courts, and then here.

Or was he wrong? *Was* it a case of extortion? Had he been there to hand money over to someone, or to pay for information?

To his left was a wooded hill; on his right was a spit of land extending into the lake. Farther off was a shipyard for small boats and a marina.

Or was this just a good thinking spot for a tortured man who had fought with his beautiful wife?

Katz put the key in the ignition, started the car and drove back in the opposite direction.

If Klingberg *had* disappeared, he thought, and he didn't show up again, there wasn't anyone left in his little branch of the family. No children of his own. His parents dead. His brother abducted as a child.

Joel had started to suspect that there was a connection between Kristoffer's abduction and the death of his parents. Had he been lured into meeting someone who claimed to have information about the incidents – a person who had sat in the car with him? The same person who had parked it in the car park near Central Station? Because Joel wasn't the one Katz had seen on the tape, he was sure of that. Something had happened to him before then.

At five thirty in the evening, just as Katz stepped out of the shower, he got a call from Rickard Julin.

'Before you ask any questions . . . I've taken the liberty of checking out your client. Out of pure curiosity. Angela Klingberg seems to be something of a marriage swindler. Or at least she used to be.'

Katz wriggled into his bathrobe and went out to the kitchen.

'Pontus Klingberg suggested as much, too,' he said. 'But he seems to have a personal grudge against her.'

'She comes from a Djursholm family that lost status. Her father ran an auditing firm that went bankrupt. It was seized, and the family had to move from a luxury home in Stocksund to a rented flat in Täby Centrum. Social climbing in reverse.'

'What are you trying to say?'

'You can come to your own conclusions. But she has a criminal record. She was fined for cheating a former boyfriend out of money.'

Katz looked at the clock. He had more than two hours before he was supposed to meet her. He took an apple from the fruit bowl, looked in vain for his kitchen knife and grabbed a table knife instead. He cut the fruit into slices as he held the phone between his shoulder and ear.

'When was that?' he said.

'She was eighteen. The guy was at Lundsberg with her, the boarding school she had to leave when her parents could no longer afford tuition. She confessed during interrogation. She said she needed the money for clothes . . . she wanted to maintain a certain way of life.'

'She was a child. And that doesn't make her a kidnapper twenty years later.'

'And then she was married once before, to another multimillionaire, a Frenchman, but just for a year. She tried to get a record-breaking amount of alimony after the divorce, but it wasn't granted. Her husband had managed to include a lot of fine print in the pre-nup.'

Katz heard a dog barking in the background, and then he heard Julin yelling something at his children.

'Sorry for the racket,' he said. 'We bought a dog and the

kids are absolutely beside themselves. It's an Ovcharka, a Russian shepherd dog. The company is thinking about starting to import them. They're not exactly child-friendly. I have to keep it in a cage in the garage to start with. But the kids want me to let it out so they can pet it. That would be a bad idea. I don't know how much longer I can talk. Whatever you do, Katz, don't have kids in your old age.'

'Did you check up on what I asked about – the police officer who looked at the surveillance tapes?'

'There's something odd about that. My contacts don't know anything about it. They seemed truly surprised.'

'Could it have been another department doing parallel work on the same case?'

'That should have come up by now. If it's not someone working half privately, something being done "outside normal working hours", so to speak. If it even was a police officer?'

'Why wouldn't it have been?'

'Don't ask me. Katz, one more thing.'

'Sure.'

'They don't have any kids, right, Klingberg and his wife?'

'That's right.'

'So she's the sole heir. And that guy is good for a couple of hundred million, maybe more.'

'Angela just isn't the type to organize someone's disappearance.'

'How do you know that?'

'If she were, why would she have hired me? Why not

just leave it alone? After all, everyone, including the police, thinks that he left of his own volition.'

'Maybe she wants to stay a step ahead. If he doesn't come back, or if he's found dead, she's above suspicion.' Julin sighed on the other end of the line. The dog barked again; it was loud and agonizing. 'I have to go now,' he said. 'Before the kids do something stupid. The dog is just here on trial. We're going to test him out later tonight. Do a few guard-dog tests with a proper dog-handler.'

'Can you do me one last favour, Rickard?'

'What?'

'An archive search with the criminal police. It's about the disappearance of Joel's brother in 1970. I want to know if there's anything about crime scene evidence in the investigation file. Things they found at the place where he disappeared. A champagne cork, among other things.'

'Sounds strange. What's it all about?'

'I don't know. Can you just check for me?'

'Okay, I'll see what I can find.'

'Great. Talk to you later.'

'*Poka*, Danya!'

'*Poka!*'

It occurred to Katz later that Julin had planted a small seed of doubt, but it never received the sustenance it needed to sprout. Because what he found in the flat on Skeppargatan changed the rules of the game.

He had called Angela again after his conversation with Julin, in order to move his thoughts in a different direction. But she hadn't answered.

He realized he was going to arrive more than an hour before they had planned to meet, and if she wasn't there he had decided he would wait for her. He needed to talk to her, to get rid of any suggestion that she was involved.

Katz had no problem remembering the entry code.

He thought of Jan Klingberg as he took the lift up to the flat. The panic that had sneaked up on him when he suddenly realized he had left his son with a total stranger, the suspicion that had started to gnaw at him, saying that something wasn't right. Katz felt vaguely nauseated as he listened to the creak of the wires in the lift shaft; he had the sense that something was wrong, but he didn't know what.

The security gate and the door to the flat were wide open.

He called her name as he walked through the servants' passage he'd followed her through just a day earlier. He was aware of the bitter taste of fear when he saw the overturned furniture in the dining room, the sheets pulled down on the floor in the bedroom he passed and the wide-open doors that seemed to be inviting him in to look at everything he didn't want to see.

Spatters of blood on the stairs up to the top floor. Bloody streaks on the wall, made by human fingers.

The silence in the flat was broken only by his breathing. A cold sweat erupted on his forehead. He heard someone moaning, a high, cat-like whine, and he realized that it had come from him.

It took an eternity to walk up the stairs. Light was streaming into Klingberg's office from the terrace windows. The computer was on; it was displaying a slideshow from the photo album. Angela and Joel were in most of the shots: holiday pictures, everyday pictures, pictures from a crayfish party accompanied by classical music that sounded like Wagner.

More blood, on the oak parquet: a broad track of blood, as if someone had dipped a rag in red paint and dragged it across the floor. A door was open beyond it, leading to another room.

Everything swam before Katz's eyes as he stepped in.

Her body was in an unnatural position, as if it had been tossed on the rug. She had her mobile in her hand, as if she had wanted to make one last call to say goodbye.

He nearly vomited. The reflex was so powerful that he had to hold his hand to his mouth when he discovered the bite marks on her neck. Like Eva Dahlman that time. A sort of bloody necklace, from her throat and around to her nape. Her skin was torn to shreds. Those bites had been wild; the force and the hate behind them had been incredibly strong.

He seemed to be able to absorb only one detail at a time. His own clothes spread through the room. Her naked lower body. He saw the curl of her greyish pubic hair. Recognized the handle of the knife that stuck out of her chest. His kitchen knife. That was how she had died. Like an animal to slaughter. The knife had gone straight into her heart.

Never checked the laundry basket in the bathroom. Never checked the kitchen drawers to see if anything was missing.

Without realizing it, he had sunk to his knees beside her body. The screen of her phone showed the list of missed calls. His own number was at the top – six missed calls from his phone, the last one from his attempt to call her just half an hour before.

He looked around the room. There were bookcases on each wall: the Klingbergs' library. He suspected that there were more objects in the flat that belonged to him, planted there by whoever had done this, more of his clothes, perhaps, in the bedroom on the lower floor.

The raincoat on the surveillance tape from the garage, he realized now, must have been his, too.

He backed out of the room, returning to Klingberg's office. He retched again and couldn't hold it back this time; he threw up on the floor next to the desk.

What did it matter? His fingerprints were already in the room, on the computer and the desk, on the door handle and the handrail of the staircase, on the security gate in the hall, in the car that was probably still in the garage.

He touched the mouse. Her hotmail account was open on another tab. The mail she had sent, asking him to come, and his reply, which could be taken to suggest that they were having an affair.

Katz heard distant sirens. He looked around again at what would soon be transformed into the cordoned-off crime scene of a murder. He ought to wait for the patrol car, explain himself, just stick to the truth – but he knew that he wouldn't. It was too perfectly executed, the whole set-up, the whole scene; it would point straight at him.

The sirens were getting closer. They were in the neighbourhood now, and it sounded as if there were several cars.

Katz left the room, almost running down the stairs and back to the hall. His hands shook as he locked the security gate. There were three locks; the key was in the top one. Had she opened the door to her own murderer?

The sirens had stopped. The first patrol officers must be in the stairwell already.

He locked all three locks. Then he closed the door to the flat, bolted it and threw the key away. How much time would this buy him – fifteen minutes before they forced the gate and the door?

He went over to the glass door that led to the roof terrace, opened it and stepped into the fresh air. There wasn't the smell of blood any more, that sickly-sweet scent of slowly congealing blood, from the clotting film like the thin skin on a sauce. No more smell of mortal fear.

The terrace was sunken for better shelter, but he could

get up on the roof over by the railing. He caught hold of the snow guard and pulled himself up. Roof tiles covered in years' worth of shit from the gulls of Nybroviken. He was six floors up, and the pitch of the roof was steeper than he could have imagined. Katz was afraid of heights; he always had been, and the feeling of dizziness had only got worse as the years went by.

He closed his eyes and realized that he wasn't going to make any progress, that he was paralysed with fear.

He forced himself to look again.

Five metres to his right was a ladder that led up to one of the chimneys. Katz braced his foot against the top part of one roof tile. It ought to be able to take more weight at the lath.

He stretched as far as he could, fumbling until he could grab a couple of tiles, then lifted his right foot and shoved his body sideways.

He slowly got closer. Three metres away. Two metres. He couldn't go back now. With his stomach pressed against the roof, he pulled himself the last little bit until he reached the ladder.

Then he climbed up.

He reached the ridge and peered down. He saw police cars on the other side of the street – a van and a regular patrol car. Onlookers had started to gather on the pavement. Straddling the ridge, he slid towards the next building.

Fifteen metres on, he found what he was looking for: an attic window. He managed to get it open and he slipped through the gap feet first.

Five minutes later, he walked out through the front door of the neighbouring building. He didn't look at the police vehicles or the people assembling nearby; he just walked purposefully up the street to his parked car.

How much time did he have? One hour at the most, before suspicions would alight on him. *This isn't happening,* he thought, and yet happen it had.

The headache was like a sort of shimmering fairy-tale colour in the back of his head, yellowish-red with hints of baby blue. He felt strange stabbing pains in his chest. His throat was as dry as a bone. As he drove past Gallerian towards Jakobsgatan he searched the glove compartment for a bottle of water. He pinched his arm to feel something other than his internal pain. The evening had a denseness he'd never noticed before. The rain was falling strangely. There was a parking ticket on his windshield; he discovered it when he turned on the wipers, but the wind took it and it fluttered away in the sparse evening traffic.

A sudden burst of tears came over him, first as stomach cramps, then as a bestial sob as the tears forced their way into his eyes.

He turned right on Vasagatan. He felt as if he were seeing the world in telegram form. Happy-hour pubs. Illegal cab drivers. Russian and African prostitutes. A junkie was standing outside 7-Eleven, crouching with his back against the window as if he were about to fall asleep on his feet, but Katz knew it was the other way around: the heroin made him feel very much present, but it carried him miles into his own body. He felt a sudden thirst for the drug. He felt his body screaming for heroin, and the thought made him break out in a cold sweat because it had been several years since he'd felt that way.

A red light just before Norra Bantorget. He breathed slowly so as not to hyperventilate. In the rear-view mirror he saw a man stagger across the street with his belongings in a shopping trolley, waving his free arm at honking cars like a bullfighter. The heroin addict slowly slid down the window of the 7-Eleven as if he were melting.

He couldn't shake the image of her body. She had been put to death, he thought. Put to death and thrown away.

He didn't understand it.

Every detail. Even the bites around her neck. It would all point to him.

He drove on, towards the Barnhus Bridge, drove across to the Kungsholmen side, and took Fleminggatan towards Fridhemsplan.

If he stuck to the truth, told them exactly where he had been and what he had done, why would anyone doubt him?

And yet he knew they would. He felt it instinctively – he would be nailed for this.

Katz was out on Drottningsholmsvägen. His brain had started working again; his thoughts had started to organize themselves according to a functional grammar. He knew what he ought to do, or at least where he would start.

He stopped the car two hundred metres from the flat and approached on foot. The lights were off in the stairwell.

There were no police cars outside the door. To be safe, he went around the back. No strange movements. The first-floor neighbour was standing at the kitchen window, looking through an advertising flyer.

Katz went in via the basement and walked quickly up the stairs to the second floor. His legs were still shaking; his heartbeat felt irregular. His nausea had come back.

It took him only a few minutes to gather up what he needed: a bag with a change of clothes, a torch, an old mobile phone and its charger.

He locked the door behind him and went down to the office. He dug a hammer, pliers and a screwdriver out of his toolbox. The street outside was still empty. No vehicles, no people. Without warning, he started to sweat and felt it dripping along his armpits and his back.

He opened the safe and took out one of the small hard drives, a laptop and his passport and put them in the bag. He had five thousand kronor in cash in an envelope. He stuffed it into the inner pocket of his jacket. He looked around in the dark. He didn't need anything else.

Then he went outside again, crossed the street and walked to a nearby car park.

His fingers trembled as he pressed the screwdriver against the rubber along the side window of a silver Ford Sierra. He pulled on the shaft until the window came down five centimetres. Just like before, he thought, with Jorma Hedlund. With both hands in the opening, he pulled down with all his strength until he could fit his arm in to open the lock from the inside.

A man walked by on the other side of the pavement

with a dog on a lead. Katz stood stock-still until the man had disappeared from sight. Then he got into the driver's seat, placed the tip of the screwdriver in the ignition and struck it with the hammer.

No stop-lock on this model; easy to hotwire. Only the Saab 900 is easier to steal. Worthless locks; if they get worn out you could start them with the stick of an ice lolly.

Jorma's voice in his head, from twenty-five years before, when this was an average day for them.

Katz grabbed the wheel and pulled it towards him as hard as he could until he heard it come unlocked.

Then he turned the screwdriver, using the pliers, and heard the engine start.

He came across the first police car two hundred metres from his place. He saw it slowing down, saw the cop in the passenger seat looking at his licence plates before they turned on to his street, with lights but no sirens. He kept driving calmly, stayed below the speed limit, and met two more police cars going in the same direction. The Sierra purred like a cat.

Julin's house was in Smedslätten in Bromma – not more than a few kilometres from where Katz lived and yet in a completely different world. Things had gone well for Capitol Security in the past few years, so well that Julin had been able to leave his old military rental in Solna and purchase a luxury home: three hundred square metres, daylight basement, a view of Lake Mälaren. It was obvious that this man was in the security branch. A three-metre-tall garden wall surrounded the property. A modern security gate led into the grounds.

Katz parked the car on the darker side of the street, walked up to the gate and rang the bell. He heard a dog barking from a distant building. It took a minute or two before Julin answered the gate intercom.

'It's Katz,' he said. 'I need help.'

It took him an hour to explain what had happened. He noticed his hands starting to shake as he came to the scene that had greeted him in the flat on Skeppargatan. He stopped talking and looked out of the window.

'What are you going to do now?' Julin asked cautiously.

'I don't know.'

'I think you should call the police and say that you're here at my house. They'll come and pick you up, take you into the city and question you, and all you have to do is stick to the truth. I'll come with you if you want. Shall I call the company's lawyer?'

'Maybe later. There're a few things I have to check up on first.'

'Like what?'

'There's a witness . . . from the multi-storey car park. A young guy who saw who parked Klingberg's car. I need to get hold of him.'

Julin sighed.

'This is crazy. Call the police now.'

'But what if this is what I think it is?'

'A conspiracy? Forget it, you're imagining things. It's the shock. I remember it from the Balkans, when you see people dead . . . it does something to you, shakes up your thoughts.'

'There were a lot of my things there.'

'All kitchen knives look the same.'

'Believe me, it was done perfectly. Strands of hair. DNA. My clothes. The murder weapon.'

'Listen to me. They're going to determine the exact time of death, and you'll tell them you weren't at the flat then.'

'Wasn't I? How do you know? My fingerprints are everywhere – on Klingberg's computer, on the security gate, the stair rail . . . in their car.'

Julin sighed and got up from his chair. Katz suddenly noticed the silence in the house.

'Should I leave?' he said. 'Am I going to wake the kids?'

'They're not here. They left for Skåne with my wife a few hours ago, shortly after we talked on the phone.

They'll be there for a week. We have an old half-timbered house down there. You should visit sometime.'

'How did things go with the dog?'

'The Ovcharka? Didn't you hear it? It's in the garage. Totally impossible to deal with. We're going to send it back to Moscow.'

Julin opened a glass cabinet, poured cognac into two snifters and handed one to Katz. He shook his head dismissively.

'I don't get it . . . whatever it is that's behind all this. Why go to all the trouble? Why not just arrange a car accident to bump her off? Call the police, Katz, that's my advice.'

'Did you find anything out, by the way? About what I asked you to check . . . the circumstances surrounding his brother's disappearance?'

'Sorry, haven't had time. Do you think it has something to do with this?'

'Klingberg was on the trail of something. He had started to put things together . . . his brother's disappearance and the death of his parents nine years later. Officially, it was suicide, but he seemed to have reason to doubt that. He had contacted someone who had information about the kidnapping and maybe about his parents' death. But then something went wrong, or maybe he was lured into a trap.'

'Good God, Katz . . . that's all speculation.'

'I know when I'm right.'

He stood up and looked through the window at the dark lake and the distant lights in Mälarhöjden, on the other side of the sound. He felt the panic sneaking up on him again.

'Can you do me one last favour, Julin? Print out a picture of Klingberg from the Internet?'

Julin nodded and disappeared into an adjacent room. Katz heard the buzzing sound of a printer. Then Julin was back again with a picture, the same one Katz had seen online, from the company's annual meeting.

'So, your old army friend . . . it's unbelievable.'

Katz nodded and tried to capture a brewing thought, but he missed it.

'I'm going to disappear for a while,' he said. 'Don't tell anyone that I was here.'

'What if I need to get hold of you?'

'You can't. Not if I don't want you to.'

PART 2

Scheduling the handover for Monday evenings had not been well thought out. The kids were out of sorts, tired from the first school day of the week and emotionally unstable after a weekend in the company of Ola and Erika. Their baby took attention away from its older half-siblings, and she didn't like the way this kept them outside the new family constellation. She had said as much to Ola, but his only reply was that she shouldn't interfere in his life.

She didn't understand how things had gone so wrong. Most divorced parents did the handover on Fridays. It had to do with her old work schedule, she realized; as the prosecutor on call, she had been relieved of duty early Monday morning, and then the routine had just stuck – even though now, several years later, she kept normal working hours at the Swedish Economic Crime Authority, or EBM. She had tried to change the schedule, but Ola thought things were fine the way they were.

She could hear the children through the door of the flat. Arvid, bawling something about a missing Bakugan toy, those odd little figures that could be folded into a ball and fulfilled some mysterious but crucial function in the life of a five-year-old boy. Lisa, who had a children's song on repeat in her head and couldn't stop singing.

Ola yelled at them from the hall. He was presumably trying to get their things on so they would be ready the instant she showed up. So he wouldn't have to see her, just hand them over as quickly as possible and close the door behind her with an aggressive bang.

Fucking asshole, she thought. But the children loved him, and they needed their father; she couldn't take that away from them.

The smell of fried food filled the stairwell. The building had been jerry-built in the early eighties, slapped together among the turn-of-the-century buildings on Ringvägen. Naturally, when Ola moved in with Erika two months after the divorce, he had chosen to live on the other side of the city, as far from their old home on Sankt Eriksplan as possible. He was a master of messing with her. He even messed with her in her sleep, in her dreams.

She stared at the name on the mail slot: Westin. The last name she still went by, because her maiden name bothered her even more, if that was possible. It was amazing that they had tolerated each other for so long. Because she had hidden who she really was, because she had so wanted to be part of his bourgeois life. Until it all fell apart, until he had started to glimpse the darkness behind the façade, the weaknesses he couldn't deal with.

She hesitated, her hand at the doorbell. Erika's voice inside, shrilly yelling something at Lisa – that she had to stop singing because the baby needed to sleep. Why didn't *she* shut up, that fucking slut? A lawyer, just like Ola. They had met at work, likely on the sly, for quite a while before things ended between Ola and her.

She tilted her head to the left and looked at herself in the stairwell mirror. She was more underdressed than casual. Trainers, jeans, a grey hoodie. She was forty-two, but sometimes she still turned the heads of young men out on the town. She didn't know why. She had never considered herself pretty, and it wasn't a manifestation of feminine self-contempt; it just didn't fit into her idea of the world.

The light fixture on the ceiling flickered, and she ran her hand under her scarf. Leftovers of an old indulgence of vanity, from back when the scars were still visible on her neck, before the plastic surgery had erased them. Like a reminder of her youth, the time and place she had come from. She had never told anyone what had happened to her, not even Ola.

She took a deep breath and rang the bell. She heard the children shouting for her before the door opened and they tumbled out like two happy calves. Lisa first, dressed in the red leather jacket she had got for Christmas the year before, which she refused to give up even though it was too small. And then Arvid, the little actor who pretended to be grumpy even though she knew how happy he was to see her.

'Hi, sweethearts.'

'Mum, you're super late, it's past eight o'clock!'

'I know, I'm sorry, there was a lot going on at work.'

'You could have called earlier, damn it.'

Ola's aggressive voice cut through all that love, cut in among the children's arms around her neck, their wet kisses, the warmth of their small bodies. But she wouldn't let him provoke her.

'I'm sorry, but I tried. It was busy every time. Didn't you get my texts?'

He handed her the backpack full of their things.

'Lisa's football practice has changed,' he said acidly. 'It's on Thursdays from now on.'

'You know Thursdays aren't good for me. Isn't there any way we could change it? Maybe she could be in a different group or something?'

'It's not my job to keep track of your working hours, and Lisa wants to stay with her friends, so either you change your schedule or you'll disappoint your daughter.'

Don't fall into the trap, now; don't start arguing.

'Okay, I'll work it out somehow. Are you ready, kids? Shall we go? The car's outside the door.'

'Did you park illegally again, Mum? You got a ticket last time, don't you remember?'

'We won't get one if we hurry.'

'But Mum, if a policeman comes and gives you a ticket, you can just say that you work for the police . . . then they won't do anything.'

'It doesn't work like that, sweetheart.'

'No, because they aren't called that, Arvid . . . they're not real police . . . they're "perking police".'

Farther down the hall, she saw Erika walk by, holding the baby, without even looking in her direction. Ten years younger than she was. She came from the countryside somewhere, Värmland, and was making a career for herself at the same law firm as Ola.

'Mum, it's toy day at nursery tomorrow, and I want to bring my green Bakugan, but Dad can't find it.'

'It's at home, on your bed; you didn't bring it here.'

The relief in her boy's eyes, his serene joy at still having his toy – she realized she had tears in her eyes.

'Was that all, Ola? Is there anything else I should know? Homework?'

'There's a note in Lisa's backpack. They're having a field trip on Tuesday.'

'So, tomorrow. You could have let me know earlier.'

'How about taking some responsibility yourself? Have you heard of the school website? You just have to check there.'

He gave her a look of unadulterated spite before turning to the children with a smile.

'Can I get a hug, kids, before you go with Mum?'

Don't punch him now, don't give him a fist straight to the face, don't split that beautifully shaped lower lip, don't break his revolting fucking nose. The kids are the important thing right now – getting them home to peace and quiet, starting the week off on the best possible foot.

She forced the images away and tried to think of something else as he hugged them for an excessively long time.

Joel Klingberg.

She had received the tip-off about the businessman's disappearance from a young detective who had been at the Economic Crime offices earlier and who knew that she was working on something about Klingberg Aluminium. A few months before, the firm had popped up in connection with a complaint from an employee who had had his contract terminated. It was about an alleged transaction in which one of the firm's subsidiaries had been involved. The claim was that fifty million kronor had secretly been transferred to an account in the Virgin Islands. Moreover, there was no recipient name attached to the account. She had barely started sniffing around before other assignments got in the way. When she had heard that Klingberg's wife had reported him missing she had become curious again.

The investigation into his disappearance had quickly been dropped because all signs indicated that he had left of his own volition. But something had made her dig deeper on her own initiative. And so she had worked overtime when it was Ola's week – she just stayed at the office, going through material from the sacked man's complaint, searching records, wondering at all the tragedies the Klingberg family had experienced throughout the years, going down to the car park where Klingberg had parked his car before he disappeared and asking to see the surveillance tapes.

Not that she had got anywhere. But that didn't matter. What else would she have done during those lonely nights?

Her work phone rang just as Ola waved the children into the stairwell. Lisa made it to the lift first; Arvid yelled that it was his turn to press the button. She dug the phone out of her pocket.

What an odd coincidence, she had time to think: Danielsson, the detective from the violent crimes division who had given her the tip-off about Klingberg. He certainly seemed to be hooked on her, but he would never call if it wasn't important.

'I'm sorry, but I have to get this,' she said, when she noticed Ola's sceptical glance.

She held the phone tight to her ear and listened to the voice on the other end of the line, nodding as she looked over at the kids, who were waiting for her attentively, who wanted to go home, to their room and toys on Torsgatan, to their beds, to the apartment where they didn't have to compete with a baby and a girlfriend for the attention of a father who, at best, ignored their needs.

'Okay,' she said. 'Klingberg's wife. Tell me again . . . so, a nationwide alert has gone out, and there's a suspect. Someone close to her?'

'No. An unrelated person.'

'Do you have a name?'

'Yes . . .'

'Well, tell me!'

'Danny Katz.'

'Can you repeat that?'

'Danny Katz. Translator. Lives in Traneberg.'

The children were already getting into the lift, still arguing about who got to push the down button. The door to the flat was closed. Ola hadn't even looked at her, much less said goodbye. She hung up on Danielsson, walked over and crouched in front of them.

'Something has come up,' she said. 'I'm sorry, but you'll have to stay with Dad tonight, too.'

'Why? I want to go home to my Bakugan!'

'You can't . . . I have to go and do something. I'll pick you up early tomorrow morning. You can stay home from school and nursery if you want to.'

The fried-food smell was gone; instead, she smelled freshly brewed coffee.

Shitty building, she thought. Shady landlord. She would bet a thousand kronor that Ola and Erika had signed an illegal contract for it.

But she would give anything for a cup of coffee right now, something warm to take away the icy cold she felt inside.

The kids walked dejectedly back to the door. It hurt to watch them; she loved them so terribly much. Lisa, her girl – she would never have to live the life she had lived herself, never have to be scared or fear death. It would break her.

Katz. Jorma Hedlund. All of that strange, faraway time when she had been at rock bottom, although she was only a child. She had worked so hard to get away from there; she had never looked over her shoulder, but now it was all coming back.

The T-Centralen metro station was the eye of the storm. People everywhere, on their way home from late shifts at the office and working overtime, gangs of teens using the ticket hall at Sergels Torg as a gathering place, revellers on their way to or from the bars in the town. It calmed him; he could move around relatively unnoticed.

He had left the stolen car in an industrial car park in Alviks Strand. It was too risky to use it right now. Perhaps it would come in handy later.

He had a window of time, he thought, but it was slowly narrowing.

He couldn't remember the last time he had been here. In any case, it had been renovated since then. The public toilets looked like the Gents' in a hotel foyer with their patterned glass doors and oak-panelled walls. The mushroom-shaped columns had been fitted with digital advertising screens.

He stood in the middle of the traffic of passengers, on the alert for suspicious movements. The streams of people subsided like water, flowing off down stairs and escalators, being refilled from endless reservoirs of humans. No plain-clothes cops that he could see.

He went through the turnstiles and scanned the area. A group of tourists was standing by the ticket machines, trying to figure out how they worked. Two junkies, men of about twenty-five, were waiting for Godot outside the Åhléns display window; their movements, their posture, their gazes were universal: withdrawal. Just like him, once upon a time, waiting at that very spot for a chronically late dealer.

Kicks was still there, anyway – the store where the prostitutes from Malmskillnadsgatan would buy cheap lipstick before the night shift started.

Katz saw more junkies: a couple of Kosovo Albanians with gaunt faces, a woman with bad skin taking a mirror from her bag and studying her make-up over by the glass doors.

He took the photo from the inner pocket of his jacket, the picture of the boy from the multi-storey car park. Katz was sure that this was his territory.

The junkies by the display window looked at him expressionlessly as he approached. One turned his head a bit to the left, seemed to realize something, turned back to Katz and gave him a nearly imperceptible signal. He stopped. A gang of teens came down the stairs from Drottninggatan, and behind them were two plain-clothes cops.

Katz backed up a few metres, taking cover in the stream of passengers on their way down to the metro platforms. There were more people now, another bunch being spewed up from the escalators; he felt the mass pressing into him from behind and pushing him in the direction of the exit.

Had the alert already gone out? Was he wanted; was there a picture and everything?

The junkies by the display window were suddenly gone. He couldn't see them anywhere. They had sensed that there was about to be a raid. He looked in the other direction, towards the stairs that led down from Åhléns. More scouts, impossible to miss: two men and a woman in tracksuits.

Katz backed up, heard people swearing at him; someone shoved him and he nearly lost his balance. But when he looked up again, the police were gone. He saw one of their backs vanishing out on to Plattan. He wasn't the one they were searching for, at least not right now.

Five minutes later, in the passageway outside the urinals, he found what he was after. T-Centralen was like an anthill, impossible to flush out. The police could try to destroy it, smoke it out, stomp it and kick it to pieces, but it would only work for a little while. As soon as they were gone, everything went back to the way it was.

The woman with the pocket mirror was back. A prostitute, Katz thought, as he approached her. She walked the streets a few blocks away, but she took care of her hygiene at the public bathrooms in T-Centralen. Once he was standing in front of her, he realized she was younger than he'd first thought.

She recognized the boy in the photograph, but she hadn't seen him in more than a month. The boy had lived at a shelter during the winter, she explained, the same one she stayed at, KarismaCare at Fridhemsplan. But he had been thrown out for hiding drugs in his room. He had a hard time dealing with other people and preferred to keep to himself.

She looked at the picture again.

'Jonas,' she said in her drawling junkie voice. 'That's what he's called, but I don't know if it's his real name. He's mentally ill and more or less deaf. Not even social services can deal with him. He's violent. And he has HIV, I heard.'

'Where does he buy his drugs?'

'I don't know.'

'And where does he usually stay when he's not at the shelter?'

The woman shrugged.

'Here, around Plattan. And in an abandoned building somewhere outside the city. And he sleeps in car tunnels. Like I said, he can't handle people.'

'Which tunnels?'

'Klara tunnel. Like a fucking rat.'

She took out her mirror again, putting more rouge on her deathly pale cheeks. Katz could see her pores as if through a magnifying glass – deep pits, as if she had been hit by a blast of shot; the wrinkles around her mouth and eyes made her look twenty years older than she was.

It was past midnight when Katz entered the tunnel near Vattugatan. The traffic was lighter now. He had taken a short cut across Klara cemetery, past the small church where the diocese handed out food to the homeless during the day, through the iron gates, until he arrived at the artery that led to Central Bridge.

The lights in the tunnel cast a cold glow on the walls. There was a sort of pavement on the right side, running against the traffic; it was used by the streets division when they needed to make repairs.

A car appeared over in the curve, and it dimmed its lights and changed lanes when the driver saw him.

Fifty metres on, he saw the first emergency-phone sign. He hurried on, hearing the fans hum in the ceiling ten metres above his head.

Angela, he thought suddenly. So incomprehensible that she had just been there, just met him, and then she was *gone*. There was no clear boundary, and that was what made it so surreal.

He had come to the recess in the wall. It was about one by two metres. No one was there. The light bulb was still in its ceiling socket. The homeless usually unscrewed them when they wanted to sleep. A bloody tampon and a crumpled beer can lay next to the emergency phone.

The traffic had increased as Katz made his way through the tunnel. Thirty metres on, he came to the next recess, which appeared to be dark.

He turned on the torch he had brought from his flat. An older man lay on the ground in a sleeping bag, on a mattress made of cardboard. A plastic bag of his belongings stood at his feet. Farther up, on some stairs, was a spirit stove. A few canned goods, plastic glasses and some silverware lay in a box, like in a pantry.

The man sat up and looked at him, bewildered.

'What do you want?' he said wearily.

Katz showed him the photo.

'The deaf boy. Why are you looking for him?'

'I just need to get hold of him.'

'Are you a cop?'

'No.'

'Then fuck off.'

The man lay down again, fumbling around on the floor above his head until he found something – a scarf, which he put over his face. Katz pulled it back off.

'Turn off your torch, damn it!'

He sat up again and glared angrily at Katz. There was a moving box with a black garbage bag in it farther up the stairs.

'When was the last time you saw him?'

'A few weeks ago. He usually sleeps in the first part of the tunnel, but the light bulb's been on for several weeks, so I guess he found somewhere else.'

'Where?'

'He stays in the metro sometimes, I know that. Between Hötorget and Rådmansgatan, a friend told me; there are small spots there. God, you should have seen him when he was detoxing. He lay over there whining for two days, wrapped up in some old blankets, and he shit himself so bad I could smell it all the way over here. And there wasn't a single person there to help him. He's just a kid. But now he's clean. I saw him at Centralen a few days ago. He looked really good. Someone must have helped him.'

The man lay down again.

'The kid's nuts,' he said. 'He was abused so much when he was growing up that he lost his hearing. That's what they say, anyway. Now leave me alone.'

Katz suddenly noticed the stench. And all at once he

realized what it was from, what the moving box on the stairs was used for. He turned off his torch and left the tunnel the same way he'd come.

He had to hurry now; he could feel it. The noose was about to be tightened. He crossed the highway by the Sheraton garage and took a left on to Herkulesgatan. The neighbourhood was totally dead; there were only office buildings and a small deli that sold Polish and Hungarian food. He realized he was hungry, but it would have to wait.

He walked across Drottninggatan to Brunkebergstorg, passed the black granite façade of Riksbanken, and walked north along Malmskillnadsgatan. Two whores were patrolling their respective sidewalks. So at least there were no cops nearby.

These blocks were dark, as if they had something to hide. And there were side streets to slip into if one didn't want to be seen, stairs leading down to streets below the ridge.

He passed Oxtorget and the bridge over Kungsgatan. He was tramping around in a sludge of memories that belonged to his old life: buying drugs up here, unscrewing the service panels of streetlights and hiding stamp bags of powder among the cables, getting in a fight outside Nalen, being arrested for possession under the bridge over Kungsgatan, being driven in the ambulance to Karolinska Hospital when someone thought he had overdosed in the bathroom of US Video.

He had robbed people further down Birger Jarlsgatan.

But that had been earlier, when he and Jorma Hedlund had been no more than sixteen. They had taken the train in from the suburbs for the sole purpose of stealing money and watches from drunk upper-class creeps on their way to or from the bar. People like Klingberg. They had loathed them and envied them at the same time. Their terrified faces as Jorma waved his Mora knife around two centimetres from their throats. One guy had, to their great joy, shit himself.

At Restaurant KGB he took a left and walked down the stairs to Olof Palmes Gata. Then he walked along Luntmakargatan, parallel to Sveavägen, until he had come to the metro station at Rådmansgatan.

Katz looked at the clock. Five minutes to one. The last train would soon enter the station. He got his ticket strip stamped by a sleepy turnstile guard and took the stairs down to the platform. Aside from a young couple inter-twined on a bench, he was alone.

Katz called the lift down and waited until it had stopped. Then he held the door open a bit so that no one could call it up again.

Then he waited for the train to come in.

Only one single passenger got off and went towards the exit at the opposite end. The young couple got into the middle compartment. Katz opened the lift door and crouched down as the train driver looked around the empty platform. Then came the sucking sound of the closing doors and the screech of the wheels as the train started moving again and vanished in the direction of Odenplan.

He waited for a few minutes. Up in the ticket hall he heard the turnstile guard close the ticket booth. When the platform lights went dark he stepped out again.

Silence.

Katz stood still until his eyes had adjusted to the darkness. Then he hopped down on to the tracks.

The gravel crunched under his boots as he walked, the beam of the torch dancing before him. At a distance he could see a shaft illuminated by lights on the wall. It was narrow and just over a metre tall. It was some sort of connecting passage which ran between the concrete walls across to the opposite track. He peered in. No sign of life.

He saw movement out of the corner of his eye and reflexively turned his head to see a rat dart off between the tracks. Then it was calm again, that strange silence of an empty metro, of the guts of a city. The ceiling glistened with condensation. Small drops of water fell silently on to the tracks.

He crawled into the shaft. He felt something soft hit the back of his neck and turned around.

A backpack. He hadn't noticed it earlier. It must have fallen down from a partition above him.

Katz rose to his knees and peered in. A passageway for hot-water pipes, just large enough for a person to get in. He turned on his torch and shone it in. The boy's terrified eyes blinked in the sudden light.

The boy had climbed down from the alcove and was squatting in front of him.

He was short for his age. His hair was greasy and it

hung in front of his eyes in chunks. His clothes were dirty, and he smelled like sweat and something else, undeniably sour.

'You're Jonas, aren't you?' said Katz.

The boy's eyes darted back and forth before fixing on Katz's lips.

'Don't be afraid, I'm not going to hurt you. Do you understand what I'm saying? Should I speak more clearly?'

The emptiness in his eyes. But it wasn't from drugs. He was clean.

'Can you hear what I'm saying?'

There was a hearing aid behind one of the boy's ears; it looked as if a flesh-coloured insect had attached itself to his skin. A bandage with dried blood hung loosely around the tip of his index finger. Katz wondered if the woman at T-Centralen was right, if he had HIV.

'I need your help . . . Identifying a man.'

The boy followed his lips as they moved. His gaze sharpened. Then he answered. Tonelessly, like a deaf person who can't hear his own voice.

'How did you find me?'

'That's not important. I just want to identify someone. Then I'll leave you alone.'

Katz took out the photos from the car park. One of the boy. The other of the man in the raincoat, seen from the back.

'Do you remember him? You spoke to him in the stairwell of a multi-storey car park. That was three weeks ago. You were afraid of him.'

The boy mumbled something incomprehensible to himself as he looked at the pictures.

'I'm clean,' he said. 'I quit H.'

'I know.'

'I couldn't do it any more. I want to go home. Home.'

That toneless voice. And yet there was a hint of accent, from the south, maybe Skåne. He stopped talking in the middle of a sentence and looked glassily at Katz.

'Was this the man you spoke to?'

He held out the portrait of Klingberg Julin had printed off from the Internet. The boy gave a start, as if he understood everything, but with a slight delay.

'No.'

'Are you sure?'

'I'm sure.'

'What did he look like, the person you talked to?'

The boy's eyes roamed again.

'Or do you know him?'

'No.'

'So what did you talk about?'

'Don't remember.'

'I think you met someone by the door; you happened to run right into him. And you apologized . . . was that what happened? Because he was annoyed, because he scared you?'

'Maybe.'

'Did you see his face?'

The boy fingered the zip of his backpack. His hands were covered in scars from old track marks. No fresh ones, as far as Katz could see. Then he became more lucid somehow, more focused.

'I have to go now,' he whispered.

'Try to think. Was there anything else about the man?'

'No!'

'I need to know more. About how he looked – was he old, young?'

A metallic noise came from the tunnel; a service train was approaching with its lights on, and there were panicked movements alongside the tracks – rats. There must be a nest somewhere nearby, Katz thought as the train roared by, very close.

When he once more looked at the boy, he realized he was holding a syringe.

'You . . . you . . . you stay here. I have to go.'

Katz didn't move, just looked at the boy's face, noticing how close to his neck he was holding the needle, a centimetre from his artery.

The boy crouched, stood up, the needle still aimed at Katz; he took his rucksack, backed out and disappeared into the darkness.

For two days Katz hid in an allotment cottage in Tantol-
unden. It was secluded and didn't seem to have been used
for a long time. He had no trouble breaking the lock. He
was careful; he didn't let anyone notice that he was there.
He left only at night, after it had got dark. He walked
through the park over to Hornstull, bought provisions at
7-Eleven with his hood pulled up, didn't look anyone in
the eye and bought a SIM card for the phone he'd brought
along.

It was impossible to miss the headlines. They were
about him, but somehow about someone else: a doppel-
gänger who had stolen his identity.

When he linked his laptop to the phone and went
online, he saw himself everywhere. Danny Katz, forty-four
years old, resides in Bromma. Wanted for murder and kidnapping. For abducting Joel Klingberg and killing his wife.

It was incredible how much they'd managed to grub up
on him: his background as a criminal, as a military interpreter, as a homeless junkie.

One of the evening papers had published a photo of
the business card he'd given Angela, with the doodle of a
heart and a flower. 'The killer's declaration of love', the
caption said.

Another paper had dug up the money-begging letter

he'd written to Klingberg fifteen years earlier. Apparently, the family had kept it. Klingberg had been afraid of him even then, the reporter wrote, and had filed a complaint with the police.

This surprised him, because neither Angela nor Pontus Klingberg had mentioned anything about it.

The papers wrote that he had been best friends with Klingberg in the military, but that they had gone their separate ways after a fight. Katz was said to have followed Klingberg's career in the business world from a distance, calling him and writing threatening letters in which he demanded money. Finally – this was the police's theory – he had kidnapped Klingberg and then contacted his wife under the pretence of wishing to help her find her missing husband. And then he had murdered them both.

According to an anonymous source, Angela had told a friend that she suspected Katz had kidnapped her husband.

That couldn't be right. Or was it? Had she suddenly started to suspect him?

There were no pictures of the body, but the murder was described in detail: the kitchen knife that had been driven straight into her heart; the fact that she'd been strangled first, so violently that her hyoid bone had broken. And the bites, the insane bites around her neck, the wounds that she had suffered after she was already dead.

The incident on Grubbholmen twenty-eight years before had been unearthed. They were making him out to be a serial offender.

The fingerprints in the flat and Klingberg's car. His kitchen knife. Strands of his hair in the bedroom, the kitchen, the pools of blood on the floor. Planted by the person who had broken into his apartment.

The raincoat had been found, too, after a tip-off – it was in a construction skip near Central Station. One of the evening papers ran a picture of a detective holding it up to the camera. *His* raincoat, the one the unknown man in the multi-storey car park had been wearing.

He turned off the computer, walked over to the window and peered out through the curtains. Dark cottages and the light from the southern suburbs on the other side of the canal. The falling rain. He felt exhaustion come over him, the weight of everything that had happened; he saw the image of the body on the floor in the flat on Skeppargatan. He blinked when he noticed that tears were welling in his eyes.

What if he *was* the one?

Was it truly impossible? Had things backfired on him? Had the same thing happened that time with Eva Dahlman? The world going black. Not remembering anything afterwards.

Angela had opened the door to someone she knew. And she had been waiting for Katz; she'd arranged to meet him.

But it didn't make sense. He trusted his memory. It wasn't him.

He heard a distant siren; he felt his pulse increase even though he knew it was an ambulance on its way to Söder Hospital.

Cats miaowed in the dark; he heard drunken hooting from a gang of teenagers on their way through the community gardens.

He felt instinctively that he couldn't stay in the cottage much longer. Sooner or later, his hiding place would be exposed.

Jorma, he thought. It had been several years since he had last heard from him. He had to get hold of him.

Katz hadn't seen Jorma Hedlund since the late 2000s. It had been in a café in Gallerian, shortly after Jorma had been released from prison for aiding and abetting in an armed robbery. They had been as happy as little kids to see each other again. Years could go by in between, but each time they got together it felt like it was the day before that they had last seen each other. *Brothers from before*, Katz had thought as he looked at Jorma's jet-black crew cut and the rough fists he could use to renovate buildings, defend his pride or, to everyone's surprise, play piano. A deep friendship had always existed between them, like the love between siblings.

Katz had known Jorma for more than half his life. When Katz was placed in the youth home after his parents' death, Jorma already lived there, forcibly taken into custody according to paragraph three of the Child Welfare Law. In the eyes of the authorities, he was a hopeless case. But the Jewish boy had seen himself in Jorma. Both had black hair and darker skin than the peers they were surrounded by. And then there was the fact that Jorma played the piano; it seemed to run counter to some unknown order – it was like seeing beautiful flowers growing out of a rubbish dump.

At the café, Jorma had told him about his plans to

move to Thailand. An old acquaintance had started his own construction business in Rayong, which was a two-hour drive from Bangkok. Jorma had been offered the chance to be a partner. They were going to build holiday apartments down there, with condos for rich Thais. Jorma would keep an eye on the workforce of locals, play in the piano bar and pitch in when needed. He had saved enough money to invest in it. Money from the robberies, Katz assumed.

So he was surprised when he found Jorma in the local directory, at a new address in Midsommarkransen. No phone number was given. But Katz had no intention of calling anyway.

It was evening when he opened the door to the building on Tellusborgsvägen. He had been waiting outside for half an hour, sizing up the neighbourhood. It was quiet. No one seemed to have made the connection between them.

He heard piano music when he stopped outside the door on the first floor. 'Georgia on My Mind'. Jorma loved old Hoagy Carmichael songs. The music stopped in the middle of a chord when Katz rang the bell.

An instant later Jorma was standing in front of him, big and muscular, with prison tattoos on his arms and a bundle of sheet music in his hand. He let him in without a word.

It took several hours for Katz to explain everything that had happened since the moment he received the phone call from Angela Klingberg. He told Jorma about the boy he had found in the metro, the man in the raincoat who had driven Klingberg's car, the document he had found on Klingberg's computer in which Joel connected his brother's disappearance with the death of his parents. He described his meeting with Pontus Klingberg and the burglary in his flat, the coat that had been stolen from the basement storage area a few months earlier, the embroidered pieces of cloth that Klingberg had received shortly before he vanished into thin air and the strange route he drove before he disappeared. But, as he spoke, he realized the puzzle wasn't even half finished; he had only just started finding the pieces.

'They're pros,' said Jorma, who was sitting before him on the piano stool. 'Whoever is behind this . . . they know what they're doing.'

'What do you mean?'

'That this took resources, but you can see that for yourself.'

Katz looked around the room as he let his thoughts wander freely, trying to find a loose thread somewhere . . . the oil paintings on the walls, painted by Jorma himself during his time in prison, abstract, fantastic colour combinations . . . the piano . . . the furniture . . . but he couldn't think of anything.

'Anyway, someone knows that I was found guilty of a similar crime.'

'And now they're making use of that knowledge. And making it look like you did it.' Jorma looked at him for a long time. 'Someone's trying to frame you. Do we agree on that? And in order for it to work, there must be several people involved.'

'But why?'

'So the perpetrators themselves will go free, of course. And maybe there are other reasons. That's what you have to ask yourself.'

Katz had never asked questions about Jorma's enterprises; this was a silent agreement between them. They had lost contact with one another during Katz's worst years. Jorma had tried to help him, but he hadn't wanted to be helped. Yet they each kept up with the other, as if out of the corners of their eyes. Katz knew what Jorma was up to: he worked for various criminal groups, motorcycle gangs, Finns from his old neighbourhood in western Stockholm. Debt collection, handling stolen money, stealing cash in transit. People in Jorma's world had reason to hurt each other, but in his own world?

'Maybe I shouldn't be here,' he said. 'In case the police start looking. Maybe it would be better to leave the city for a while.'

'Where would you go? And, officially, it's been over twenty-five years since we were listed in the same registry. The cops won't have put us together yet.'

Katz stood up and walked over to the balcony door, which stood ajar; he looked at the cars going by on the street, at the streetlights reflecting in the puddles, like lights from the underworld.

'I have to make a call,' he said. 'I need help if I'm going to manage this.'

As he walked into the kitchen he heard the intro of another Hoagy Carmichael song: 'Stardust'. He closed the door behind him and dialled Julin's number. It rang half a dozen times before he answered: 'Katz, is everything all right?'

'It's under control. Have you checked to see if the police found anything at the place where Kristoffer Klingberg was abducted?'

'Yes. Nothing. That was over forty years ago. All that's left of the official report are the transcripts of the interrogations with the father, and there's no mention of any particular evidence found at the scene. Katz, listen, the police have been here asking about you. I said that I haven't seen you or heard from you in six months, but that I considered it to be out of the question that you'd be behind a murder and a kidnapping.'

'Are you absolutely certain?'

'I know it's not you. But the problem is that you're hiding out, and that's not helping you. They're going to find you. They're putting resources into it. And it doesn't look good. All the newspaper reports, all the new information that's come out . . .'

'So what do you think I should do?'

'Give up. You're a wanted man, and you're running out of room to manoeuvre. Do you even have anywhere to sleep?'

'For a few nights. With an old friend.'

'Where?'

'In Kransen.'

He regretted it the second he'd said it. But why would Julin's phone be bugged?

'Is there anything else I can do for you?'

'Yes. Check out Pontus Klingberg. Where he was the night Angela was murdered.'

He heard Julin sigh heavily on the other end of the line. 'Do you think it was him?'

'No, but I have to start somewhere. Angela opened the door to someone she knew.'

'Okay,' he said. 'I'll see what I can do. Is there a number I can reach you at?'

'I'm going to switch SIM cards after this conversation. I'll call you again within twenty-four hours.'

When he came back to the living room, Jorma had brought his bag in from the hallway.

'You knew I was going to show up?' said Katz.

'The way I see it, you had nowhere else to go. Another day out there and they would have found you.'

'Nothing ever happened with Thailand?'

'No, I had to earn money other ways. Times change. Working alone used to be enough. But now . . . you have to be part of an organization, be loyal to the leaders. I'm thinking of quitting. Starting to work with my hands again. I'm good at construction.'

Katz gave a start as he heard the lift begin to move out in the stairwell, but Jorma shook his head dismissively.

'The neighbours,' he said. 'A retired police commissioner, among others. It's fine, Katz. What do you think of my flat, by the way? I received it as a gift, including the piano. I did time in Norrtälje Prison for three years, and I helped a guy get the other prisoners to leave him alone.

He was very generous afterwards. Come on, I'll show you your room.'

Katz took the bag and followed him to the kitchen and then into a larger room, which was completely devoid of furniture. They stopped in front of a bare wall.

'You're planning on getting to the bottom of this?' said Jorma.

Katz nodded.

'How?'

'I don't know yet.'

'Don't worry. First you have to sleep. I don't know if you've looked in the mirror, but you look like a corpse.'

He pressed the baseboard with his foot. The whole wall slid silently a metre to the side. There was a hidden room on the other side; it was furnished with a reading lamp and a mattress that was already made up.

'This was the first thing I did when I renovated the apartment,' he said. 'Could be good to hide things in, I thought. Stolen goods. Or friends on the run.'

She had always thought of her office as a cloister cell, squeezed between the chamber commissioner's office and the economic auditor on the other side of the wall. The linoleum floor, shades of yellow and orange from the early nineties. The view of Kungsholm Church. She liked to see the cemetery in the different seasons, from the delicate greens of spring to the shadows the large, bare trees cast on the snow in winter. There was a filing cabinet full of folders next to the door. The project cases in one section; the particularly demanding cases in another. A desk with a computer. Hanging on the wall in front of her were portraits of Lisa and Arvid, from when they were babies up to the present. *All the children I'll have*, she thought.

She looked down at the desk as she listened to the voice on the other end of the phone line. Two sheaves of paper lay in folders before her. The verdict against Katz twenty-eight years earlier in one. The investigation of the same matter in the other.

'So what are you planning on doing?' she said to Ola.

'Exactly what I said. In the worst case, I'll contact a lawyer.'

'You're a lawyer yourself.'

'I'm exceptionable in this case. We'll take this to court if you're not prepared to compromise. This is going to be a custody battle, and the way I see it there's a good chance you'll lose. We're going to offer you something along the lines of Thursday to Sunday every other week.'

'You're crazy.'

'Come on, this isn't working any more. It's not good for the kids.'

'That may be, but that's not just my fault.'

'You left them here on Monday and we haven't heard from you since, and that's just the tip of the iceberg. Lisa says she wants to live here for the rest of the spring.'

She heard a clatter from the canteen down the hall. Laughing colleagues. She recognized their voices: Samson, the tax expert from the second economic chamber, and Jelenik, who worked with criminal intelligence in the operational police unit. How long had she worked here? Twelve years, with a short break when she worked the on-call job at the office of the public prosecutor. She had a brain for numbers rather than violent crime. The nose of a truffle pig for financial irregularities, accounting crimes, money laundering.

'You're the one who got her to say that . . . you're the one who made her think that.'

'Erika is in complete agreement with me, especially after what happened at Easter.'

Easter? She didn't want to think about it. That was already history.

'Erika doesn't give a crap about Lisa and Arvid. For God's sake, she looks ill whenever she's in the same room as them.'

'She loves them.'

'Bullshit.'

'Come on, Eva, can you think of a better alternative? The kids are more secure here. They have their own rooms. There are functional adult relationships, routines, definite times for picking them up and dropping them off, two incomes. You don't even show up to get them when you say you will. You break promises, just like always, and it's been like that ever since we got divorced.'

Was that true? Had she let them down, just as her own parents had let her down? She remembered coming home in the middle of the night, thirteen years old, and no one even reacted. Her father in the easy chair in front of the TV, a half-smoked joint in his hand. If he wasn't in the slammer. Her mother, knocked out on pills in the bedroom. Or off in some drunks' hangout somewhere. Pigs, the both of them; she didn't have contact with them any more, didn't even know if they were alive. Was she the same? Not on the surface, but fundamentally? All the times she had shown up late to nursery and to school. That sort of thing had happened too often . . . when a crying Lisa had called Ola from school and he had to pick her up instead, because she herself had got so caught up in her work that she lost all sense of time and place. Not a great track record, she knew.

'Are you listening to me?'

'I'm listening, but please, Ola, I promise things are going to change. I'm working on something right now that I can't drop. All I need is a week. Take care of the kids until then, and tell them I'll be back to our usual schedule soon. Tell them I'll call tonight.'

'Let's do this: the kids can stay with us until the end of the school year. Then we'll see what happens.'

'You're not the boss here. We have joint custody. I want my kids every other week.'

'Just not this week?'

'Exactly.'

Someone was calling on the other line. Oskar Danielsson, according to the screen. He was taking risks by giving her an insight into an investigation that didn't concern her. He wanted to sleep with her, she assumed, although she didn't understand why.

'I'm warning you, Eva: if you fuck this up one more time I'm going to a lawyer. A colleague who never loses a family court case.'

'So you're threatening me?'

'It's not a threat, my dear, it's a promise.'

She ended the call with a swearword and accepted the incoming call. A busy signal: Daniel had already hung up.

The laughter in the canteen had stopped. The door to her office was ajar; she walked over and closed it. The best thing about Ola was his lack of imagination. It made him predictable and gave her an advantage every time they argued. But she hadn't expected this.

She looked at the folders on her desk: the investigation and the sentence where she herself was the victim. Since she no longer went by her maiden name, the investigators hadn't linked her to Katz yet. The investigation was more than a quarter of a century old, and the scars on her neck were no longer visible. For the time being, they had no reason to dig deeper into the old information, but sooner or later they would, and then she would have to answer their questions.

There was another folder at the top of the pile in her left-hand desk drawer. The file from the National Intelligence Service, or NUC, on Katz's military career. The only thing she had managed to get out of the EBM's operational police unit. There was more, she knew, but it was classified. That was damned strange, she thought as she called Danielsson again – this whole military thing bothered her. The answering machine told her that he had gone to lunch and wouldn't be available again until after two o'clock.

It had come as a surprise to her that Katz had done his military service along with Joel Klingberg. She was astonished that he had been selected for special training and then became an interpreter and computer expert for the intelligence service before ending up on the street. But, apparently, they had ignored his background because he was extremely gifted. Just as the office of the public prosecutor had once overlooked her own background, instead choosing to see it as an advantage.

According to the documents she had managed to get hold of, Katz and Klingberg had been recruited at the request of top-ranking military officers within what had once been called the armed forces' Office of Intelligence and Security, or USK, which was the predecessor of MUST, the Military Intelligence and Security Service. As she understood it, they had gone behind the backs of the National Service Administration, which in Katz's case had demanded he be rejected. But USK had got its way. When it came to Klingberg, the interpreter academy hadn't had any objections; his merits as a bookworm at boarding school in Sigtuna were impressive.

And yet . . . both of them were hand-picked. The only ones in their class who were.

And, twenty-five years later, one of them would kidnap the other and then murder his wife.

Lisa and Arvid observed her sceptically from the wall. With good reason, she thought: a workaholic is another sort of addict.

Katz: where was he now?

A nationwide alert had gone out, yet several days had gone by without a single trace of him. This didn't surprise her. He was used to life on the street. According to the excerpts from the registry, he had been homeless and addicted to drugs for most of the nineties. Street smart. He had been even back when she knew him. He knew all sorts of tricks to stay out of sight.

Was he with Jorma? The only west-side thug ever who could, in theory, have got into the Royal College of Music. He'd shocked all her friends at the time by playing piano sonatas at the youth centre. He came from a broken Finnish family where people either became musicians or alcoholics, because that was all society expected of them. Did they still have contact with each other? Once upon a time, they had been like brothers. But, if she understood correctly, no one had put their names together.

They had taken a sample of Katz's DNA during his time in the intelligence service, so it was possible to link him to the scene of the crime by way of hair, left-behind clothes and a puddle of vomit that had been on the floor a few metres from the body. Oddly enough, they hadn't found any traces of saliva in the bites on Angela Klingberg's neck. No DNA at all, aside from the victim's. The forensics team thought this was because the wound had been cleaned with alcohol afterwards; it would have evaporated. It didn't really matter, since everything else pointed to Katz. His fingerprints were in the flat and he had been found guilty of a similar crime before.

She turned on the computer and read through the latest document Danielsson had emailed to her: a short summary of the suspect's relationship to the victim. According to what was known, Angela Klingberg had hired Katz to try to find her missing husband. He had gone to the Royal Library to find information, he had visited Klingberg Aluminium's main office and spoken to Joel Klingberg's uncle and he had visited the same multistorey car park as she had in order to look at the surveillance tapes. He had been at Angela Klingberg's home at least once before the murder occurred.

But the theory Danielsson's team was operating on was that Katz had first kidnapped Klingberg and then murdered his wife. His motive was as yet unknown. As was the question of where Klingberg was, if he was still alive. When it came to the kidnapping, there were a couple of things that pointed to Katz: Klingberg's car had been in the vicinity of his building the day he disappeared, and a raincoat that apparently belonged to Katz had been worn by the man who was seen in the tape from the car park. A person who, in her world, could be anyone at all, since his face wasn't visible.

Or was she wrong? Was it Katz? Had it been him that time in Hässelby, too?

She looked at the crime-scene photos that Danielsson had emailed over: Katz's clothes spread across the floor, hair that belonged to him, the pools of blood, the kitchen knife with his fingerprints, the body with its bite marks and strangulation wounds.

She felt the nausea coming. The memories, as if from a horror film. Would he have done all those things?

For the past few days, since she had starting researching this case, it had felt as if she had taken a time machine back to those days. Pandora's box, she thought, impossible to put things back once it had been opened. The sense memories of how in love she had been, the way you can be only at that age, on the threshold of the adult world, a child's capacity for devotion still intact, how insanely in love she had been with that dark-haired Jewish boy with his inscrutable brown eyes and his strange last name. She remembered the joy she had felt, the butterflies in her stomach every time she saw him; she even remembered the scent of his hair and armpits, the way he kissed her, the taste of his tongue.

What had really happened that night? Jorma and Katz had burgled a yacht. She had been standing in a nearby grove of trees, watching them swim out to the boat. They had been back an hour later with a thousand kronor in cash.

And then?

They had gone to a party in the nearby high-rise development; they'd met people from the same gang but had got bored and moved on to central Hässelby. She recalled that they had felt as if they were being followed, but that had been normal back then; in their circles there was always a certain amount of paranoia. They had bought drugs from a dealer they didn't know but who seemed trustworthy. She didn't remember his face. How could she, almost three decades later?

After that they had gone to the bike storage room.

She had been there several times before; she had got her hands on a key to the room and she slept there when things were particularly bad at home. She had been fourteen years old, a child who had already seen and heard too much. They had shared a needle as a sort of testament to love, to show that they trusted one another in a world where everyone else had let them down. The risk of HIV or hepatitis B – they hadn't given a damn about that back then. She could still picture the crease of Katz's elbow, that slight resistance as the needle punctured the skin. Then it was her turn. *An overdose*, she had time to think before it all went black.

She remembered the period after the incident as if in a fog: the hospital stay, the police interrogations, the trial. Social services had intervened and sent her to a treatment home outside Vilhelmina. Even then she had thought that something didn't add up. It couldn't be Katz; he wasn't a madman. The fact that his whole face was covered in her blood didn't prove anything. Someone had taken advantage of the fact that they had been defenceless after taking

H that was too strong. And then that person carried them to Grubbholmen, assaulted her, bit her and arranged the crime scene so that everything would point to Katz.

But who? And why?

She paged through the investigation report. Thirty measly pages. No DNA test, naturally. Those hadn't been done at the time, and even if it had been possible they wouldn't have considered it necessary: Katz had been doomed from the start.

She had quit heroin that same autumn. She had seen a psychologist. Life had turned around. She finished school in Vilhelmina and realized how bad her life had been up until then. But it took time for her to forget Katz, several years, until she was finished with school and was accepted as a law student.

She gave a start when she heard the phone ring. Ola, she thought automatically. He wanted to keep messing with her, take the kids away from her. But it wasn't her ex-husband; it was Danielsson on his mobile.

'Did you learn anything new?' she asked.

'I don't know. Possibly. Can we meet?'

'When?'

'Preferably in the evening . . . tomorrow.'

He wanted to sleep with her. She could hear it in his voice; she knew he had an erection as he sat there with the phone to his ear.

'Where?'

'Maybe at your place. The walls have ears around here.'

She had to find every loose thread in this investigation, she thought as she hung up: the fact that both Klingberg and Katz had been specially chosen for the interpreter academy, the fact that Klingberg's company had been accused of being involved in transferring fifty million kronor to the Virgin Islands and that the guy had later vanished into thin air – could that just be a coincidence? She didn't believe in coincidences, so she had to get to the bottom of this, find Katz, prove that he was innocent. She owed it to him. And she owed it to herself.

Katz had no idea what time it was when he woke up. It could be the middle of the night or early morning; the room he was in was pitch black. He fumbled for his phone, which was next to the mattress, and looked at the screen: two thirty.

Cop paranoia, he thought. Or general paranoia, his subconscious reminding him that he was being pursued. Or maybe he had woken from a dream he couldn't remember.

He heard the faint sound of cars on Essingeleden two hundred metres away, the lulling rush of the night-time lorry traffic, and he felt his heart pounding in his chest, faster than usual. The sudden tension, as if something electric were running through his limbs. His body was a step ahead of him; it was trying to tell him something.

He resisted the urge to get up. He focused instead.

The rush of traffic . . . and something else, something his senses were still fumbling to grasp.

Then he realized what it was: someone's breathing.

He held his own breath in order to hear more clearly. Yes, there was no doubt, there was someone on the other side of the wall, a few metres away.

Jorma? He had gone out earlier that evening, and Katz

hadn't wanted to ask what he was up to – business, or maybe meeting a woman. Probably business.

Light pressed in under the skirting board. He watched it subside, come back and vanish once more. The light of a torch.

The steps grew more distant, disappearing down the hall.

The cops? he thought, as his pulse increased again. Had Julin's phone been bugged after all?

No. He would have heard them earlier. There would have been half a dozen officers in bulletproof vests breaking down the door and coming in with weapons drawn.

More steps out there, but now they were farther away in the flat. Someone with unfinished business? But Jorma would have said something if people were after him.

The sound of traffic on Essingeleden grew louder. A window was open somewhere, or maybe it was the balcony door.

He lay there, not moving, thinking that he should wait out the situation until whoever it was had gone. At least his hiding spot hadn't been revealed.

Then it struck him that Jorma might be there, too, that he had come home and something had happened to him.

A lorry honked on the highway. Katz acted on reflex, using the sound to mask the low click as he pressed the lock mechanism and allowed the wall to slide open until there was enough room for him to get out.

The blinds were closed.

He carefully sneaked along the wall to the kitchen.

It was empty. Light filtered in from the streetlights

outside. He was naked, he realized, and he suddenly felt vulnerable, almost prudish.

He took shelter behind the refrigerator. He heard steps again, from the room where the piano was. Katz fished a knife out of the dish rack. It would have to do for now.

He crouched down and peered into the hallway. Pitch black.

He held his mouth to his elbow to muffle the sound of his breathing. He weighed the odds. He had the element of surprise on his side. The person didn't know he was there. But it was too risky, he thought. Whoever it was, he would probably be armed.

Someone flushed the toilet in the apartment above. Katz took two quick steps across the hallway and arrived at the smaller hall.

He sank down, his back against the wall, hidden by the clothes that hung from a coat rack.

He sat completely still. No one had noticed him.

A closet-like door led from the recess in the hallway to the living room.

It wasn't completely closed. He opened it a millimetre at a time until the gap was large enough for him to peek through.

A man was standing on the opposite side of the room. He could tell the man was nervous; he kept moving, looking at his watch, peering anxiously towards Jorma's bedroom. Katz couldn't see his face because the man's back was to him.

The varnish on the piano gleamed in the dim light. The

balcony door was wide open. So that was how he had got in.

Katz looked at the man again. Just over average height. No hood or mask. No intention of leaving a witness behind.

Then he realized that there wasn't one person in the flat, but two. He heard another sound, the creak of the parquet from Jorma's bedroom.

Katz drew back into the darkness of the hall again. Was Jorma there? Had they hurt him? He looked around for a better weapon than the knife in his hand. An object he could use to strike, hard, very hard, at a moment when no one expected it.

Then he forced the thought aside, forced away the aggression, because it wouldn't help him.

Were they looking for something Jorma had hidden? Stolen goods? Katz didn't think so.

A car drove by on the street. He cautiously leaned forward. He used the hall mirror to see into Jorma's bedroom. The other person was in there, standing perfectly still by the bed, breathing very calmly. He couldn't tell if Jorma was in there.

The person was dressed in a dark tracksuit. White gym shoes. The hood of the jacket hid his face. A piece of steel wire dangled from his right hand.

It took a few seconds for him to realize what it was: a garrotte.

The same man who had been standing outside his hidden room. Unnaturally calm. He had to be on something.

It's not a person, he thought then, without having any idea where the thought came from. He just felt it instinctively – there was something inhuman about the person by the bed with a loop of wire in his hand.

The man from the multi-storey car park – was it him? And, in that case, he wouldn't be looking for Jorma; he was looking for Katz . . .

The rage again, that cold, hard seed inside him, the inheritance from Benjamin.

The flat was totally silent. He could hear only the very calm breathing from inside the bedroom. The man was standing stock-still in there, as if every joint and muscle in his body was locked in place.

Then he suddenly backed out.

He was two metres from Katz. His face was still shadowed by the hood; there was just a sort of cold flash from his eyes. A faint scent of insect repellant.

The man vanished into the living room, to his accomplice, the person who was keeping watch or who was there as a backup. Neither of them said anything. Katz heard them walk out to the balcony; they were in no hurry. He heard them climb over the railing and jump; heard them land on the gravel behind the building.

He walked into the bedroom and was startled by someone's rapid breathing and gasping, until he realized that it was him.

His eyes had adjusted to the darkness. He didn't have to turn on the lights to see. Jorma was curled up at the head of the bed. The fear was still evident in his lifeless face. He hadn't had time to defend himself. The garrotte had been pulled so tight it had torn the skin on his neck.

Katz felt for a pulse that wasn't there, turned him on his back, crossed his palms over Jorma's chest, pressing and pressing in a frantic tempo. He stopped, bent over, performed artificial respiration. He thought about how strange it was to feel Jorma's lips against his own, to hear his own bestial whimper as he started again, massaging his heart, giving him air, massaging his heart, hoping it wasn't too late.

She didn't know why she had slept with him. The last thing she needed right now was more problems.

He was still lying in her bed, whistling cheerfully as he browsed through a magazine. She was already up and fully dressed.

She looked at the clock. Eight thirty. She needed to get more information out of him and then to get rid of him as quickly as possible.

On the way to the kitchen she passed the children's room. She stopped and looked in. Arvid's green Bakugan was still lying on the bottom bunk. Lisa's football cards were spread out on the floor. All their things in there – the dolls, cars, stuffed animals, loose parts from Barbies and Bratz, a veritable massacre of detached limbs and decapitated heads in little piles on the rug. She closed the door with a vague sense of shame.

Danielsson's briefcase of information about the murder was still in the hallway. Witness statements, lab reports, reports from the scene of the murder, the crime-scene techs' summary. And a copy of Klingberg's hard drive, which he'd promised she could take a look at. She let him think that her interest was because of what had happened in the Virgin Islands.

From across the apartment she heard him get up and

go to the bathroom. Good-natured steps. A jolly mood. The shower started as he sang an idiotic Schlager song.

She could still taste him in her mouth. The head of his penis, like velvet, like the skin on a horse's muzzle.

Had she had sex with him to get back at Ola? That was completely pointless, since she would never tell Ola about it.

Or had she done it because it was about time? Because her body had needed it.

The worst part was that he might become annoying. Clingy. Looking at her with puppy-dog eyes. Confusing love and sex.

She turned into the hall. The postman had been. There was a single envelope on the floor. She picked it up, walked into the kitchen and opened it.

It was a summons to the family support division at social services, on Ola's request. A meeting to discuss the children and the custody arrangements – which place was better, with a single mother, or at home with a stable father with a partner and a new sibling. Ola had decided to raise the stakes.

Nine years earlier, when they'd met at a conference about administrative law, he had idealized her; he'd seen a conscientious girl from the suburbs who had managed to make it in this world, a cheerful careerist who dreamed of a bourgeois life with a husband and children, a dog and a place in the country. But, in the long term, she had never fitted in. Her background, which he thought at first was exotic, suddenly didn't suit his needs. She spoke a little too loudly and badly; she drank a little too much and made small breaches of etiquette that after a while could no longer be notched up under 'charming'. She had tried to adapt, but she was who she was. And then things had gone downhill, until their divorce was a reality.

She felt a twinge of pain at the thought of Lisa and Arvid. Two days had gone by since she had last spoken to them on the phone – or, more precisely, to Lisa, since Arvid had been playing Minecraft on a tablet and didn't want to talk. Lisa had sounded brusque, talking only about the puppy Ola had promised her; she hadn't even asked when they would see each other again.

'I want to live with Dad for the rest of the spring,' she finally said. 'Can I, Mum? It's fun here . . . we might get a dog.'

She placed the letter on the kitchen table, walked back to the bedroom, glanced through the window at the tender green of spring in Vasaparken and kept walking into the living room.

The bottle of Jack Daniel's that she and Danielsson had shared the night before was still on the coffee table. Half empty or half full, depending on how you looked at it. His underwear was on the floor in front of the TV. She had taken him by surprise. She'd put her hand on his cock mid-sentence, outside his jeans, and felt him grow hard. She'd pulled off his jeans and his underwear and taken him into her mouth, rubbing his anus with her index finger at the same time. It had taken fewer than fifteen seconds for him to come. He'd exploded in her mouth like a teenager. He'd looked a bit bewildered when she went back to her glass of JD as if nothing had happened.

And then he had stayed the night.

Why the hell did I let it happen? He doesn't even turn me on. Just like what happened last Easter . . . the last straw for Ola.

Her mobile phone was on the coffee table. Three missed calls from the director general's office, and then there was a criminal-profits case she'd promised to help the legal division with.

She'd have to catch up on work later, just as she'd have to catch up on her relationship with the children. Right now, Katz was the most important thing.

At least things had started looking up in the last twenty-four hours.

She had spoken to the guard at the parking garage again, putting the pressure on when she realized he was hiding something, and she finally worked out what it was. Apparently, a witness had seen the man driving Klingberg's car. The guard had him on a personal tape. Katz, he told her, had also seen it. But the police hadn't.

She hadn't told Danielsson about it. She might do later, once she knew more.

Why would Katz go to all that trouble and pretend to be searching for Klingberg if he was the one who had kidnapped him and even had plans to murder his wife?

She had identified the boy through a contact on the drug squad. He was a seventeen-year-old heroin addict named Jonas Åkesson. The weird thing was that he had been in the morgue for a few days, dead of an overdose. He had been found in the back seat of a car in Märsta, the needle still in his arm.

Odd, she thought. The kid had been clean for almost two months. And then he had suddenly had a fatal relapse.

She looked over towards the bathroom door. Danielsson was taking his time.

She went back to the hall and peeked in his briefcase to see if there was anything else of interest in it. She fished out a copy of materials that had been printed off from Klingberg's GPS. If Danielsson noticed it was missing, she would just say that he had left it here.

Fifty million kronor, she thought as she went back to the kitchen. She had asked the police unit at work to contact Interpol and check on every large transaction between Sweden and the Virgin Islands during the past year. That would take time, she learned, depending on the local banks' secrecy laws.

By the time Danielsson came out of the bathroom – dressed, she was relieved to see – the coffee was already on the table.

'How does it feel?' he said.

'What?'

'Does it feel okay . . . what happened yesterday?'

She poured him a cup of coffee, making an effort to seem friendly.

'Let's just forget it,' she said. 'It never happened. Tell me about the investigation instead. Is there anything else you haven't told me yet?'

He looked wounded, but he nodded.

'I don't think so. I've given you everything we have.'

'You said that the computer was on when Angela Klingberg was found.'

'Yes, there was a slideshow.'

'What kind of pictures were there?'

'Family portraits. Holiday pictures.'

'Randomly chosen?'

'No idea.'

'And you think that the perpetrator started the slideshow?'

'Or the victim. In any case, it was on after the murder was committed. Like I said, I made a copy of the hard drive in case you need to look for information about Klingberg Aluminium on it. You'll find his private photos there, too . . . in case you're curious.'

The sarcastic overtone in his voice told her that she was about to go too far. And yet she couldn't help but ask, 'Are you sure that you're looking for the right man?'

'God, Eva, we found that guy's fingerprints everywhere – on the murder weapon, in the car, on the keys he used to lock the door to the flat from the inside. Plus, he was found guilty of the exact same sort of assault in the eighties. What more do you want?'

They hadn't made the connection between them yet. She was grateful for that.

'Have you found the person who called in the emergency yet?'

'No.'

'And that doesn't bother you?'

'We couldn't do our jobs without anonymous tips. It's not illegal, you know that, and we can't force people to give evidence.'

'You're assuming that the call came from one of the neighbours, who heard her screaming?'

'There are seventeen households in the building. The person called from a prepaid phone that can't be traced. It's probably someone who doesn't want anything to do with the police. All sorts of people live in Östermalm these days. And, like I said, we're still working on getting hold of the informant.'

Danielsson disappeared into the hall and came back with his briefcase; he opened it and took out the hard drive.

'How are things going your end?' he said. 'Have you got any further on the fifty-million-kronor transaction?'

'Just waiting for people to be scared into breaking bank secrecy by a call from Interpol. The Virgin Islands are a tax haven, of course, so they'll try to get out of it and delay giving up the information as long as they can. By the way, you mentioned something about a stolen car yesterday before I . . . how shall I put it? . . . interrupted you.'

A brief smile. At least he had a sense of humour.

'Yes. We found a car that the suspect stole in the vicinity of his home shortly after the murder.'

'Where did he leave it?'

'In Alviks Strand. All traces of him end there.'

'And his old boss, has anyone contacted him?'

'Rickard Julin? We had a chat with him, but he says he hasn't heard from Danny Katz in six months. And he seems trustworthy. Ex-military.'

He should be checked out more thoroughly, she thought; the military part of Katz's history interested her.

'And the bites on Angela Klingberg's neck – have you found a DNA match?'

'We don't need it to link the perpetrator to the scene and the murder.'

They sat in silence for a moment. Not touching their coffee. There was still tension between them. Why the hell had she slept with him?

'Maybe I should get moving,' he said hesitantly. 'Before people start to call, wondering where I am.'

She just nodded.

'Can't we see each other again, Eva?'

'Sure. We'll keep in touch about this.'

'I mean privately.'

'We'll see, Danielsson. I'm not interested in a relationship.'

She turned to him, looked right into his puppy-dog eyes and saw the very clinginess that she couldn't handle. *You get what you deserve*, she thought, *when you mix work and your body*.

As soon as he left, she took out the copy of the printouts from the GPS. The investigators had been interested only in the dates around Joel Klingberg's disappearance and Angela Klingberg's death. But what about in between?

Angela Klingberg had hardly used the car after her husband's disappearance; it seemed she'd only gone on short trips around Östermalm and one slightly longer one to Djursholm.

She checked out the address online. Pontus Klingberg's home address. Angela had driven there ten days before she was murdered, arriving at seven in the evening and leaving again at . . . nine o'clock the next morning.

Surely the divorced CEO of Klingberg Aluminium

would have an explanation for why she had stayed overnight if Danielsson had thought to ask: his nephew's wife had been worried about her missing husband, he had tried to calm her, comfort her, he'd asked her to stay for dinner, and then she'd had some wine and had decided to sleep over in the guest room.

Unless something was going on between them?

She went further back in the GPS log. All the information since the new year had been saved. The car had mostly been driven from the couple's home on Skeppargatan to Klingberg's office at Norrtull. But the trip to Djursholm recurred at regular intervals, and there was an overnight stay each time. She looked for more overnights in other places and found another address, in Sörmland.

She Googled the address.

Pontus Klingberg's country place, a manor house just outside of Katrineholm. Several overnight stays there.

She loaded the copy of the hard drive on to the laptop, searching through the tabs for calendar tools, and she found what she was looking for: Joel Klingberg's digital planner.

The man was organized, that much was clear; his calendar was full of birthdays, to-do memos, appointments for car inspections and doctor's visits, work schedules, meetings, conferences, business trips.

She compared them to the dates in the GPS log. Check. The overnight trips had been made when he was gone.

Kinky, she thought. It seemed Angela had been having an affair with her husband's uncle.

She put this aside for the time being and called up the photo viewer. There were only a few hundred pictures.

She opened the slideshow menu and brought up the most recent series of photos: about fifty of them, set to classical music. Holiday photos. Angela and Joel Klingberg on various trips – celebrating midsummer at a fancy country home; travelling in Italy; lying on a beach in some tropical paradise; sailing pictures from some sort of regatta, maybe in Sandhamn; and standing together on the deck of a luxury yacht.

She stopped the slideshow, clicked back to the yacht, enlarged the picture and zoomed in on the name on the bow: *St Rochus*.

She searched her memory for the time she had stood on the beach in Hässelby, watching Jorma and Katz swim out to a boat. *St Rochus* . . . the name was still there, like an echo from the past.

She stood up, went to the living room, picked up her phone from the sofa where she had seduced Danielsson and dialled the number of the Transport Agency.

'Please transfer me to the Registry of Ships,' she said. 'I need information about the owner of a boat in Stockholm.'

The network posed the question in Russian: '*Kakoi pseu-donim tui vuiberyosh?*' Which alias do you choose? Katz entered the first word that came to him: Baruch. As he entered a password, he wondered why it had been that word. He was starting to feel tired. Eight hours straight on IRC networks in order to find someone who could help him. He'd only found script kiddies so far, kids who used pre-written codes and got scared when they realized what he was looking for.

Baruch? he thought again. Because it was Friday, and that was the first word in the Hebrew Shabbat prayer: *Baruch ata Adonai . . .* Praise be to you, lord our God.

Strange. He hadn't said the Shabbat prayer since he was thirteen, that time with his father in the orthodox syna-gogue on Sankt Paulsgatan where Dad used to take him on the important holidays for some reason. He didn't know much about Benjamin. Just that he'd come to Swe-den as a refugee right before the war and that his parents, Chaim and Sara, had emigrated to Israel in the fifties and lost contact with their son. Or stopped contacting him.

He hit enter. The screen flickered. He was asked to repeat the password. He typed it again.

He thought of Jorma while he waited. He was filled with feelings of hate and revenge. Jorma was on a respirator at

Söder Hospital. Katz had managed to get his heart beating again, and he'd called 112 and propped the door open for the ambulance crew before he left the flat. He had sat in Jorma's car a hundred metres away, watching as he was carried out on a stretcher and driven off. Then he had called the most recently dialled number on Jorma's phone and reached one of his friends, Emir, who helped him find a new hideout in Västberga. That was where he was now. In a one-bedroom flat on the fourth floor.

His looked at the computer screen again. He had come in from the cold; he saw the graphics unfold and the chat room was open. One avatar was of Pikachu. Another was Han Solo from *Star Wars*. People who refused to grow up.

The network was called Oxymoron. The person who had recommended him, a certain Hunky Dory with whom he'd once shared programs online, told him he would find help here.

The temporary operator's name was Trotsky; he had been the first to enter the channel and was denoted by his '@' prefix.

It took several minutes for him to ask who Baruch was and what he wanted: *Kto tui . . . chto tui khotyesh?*

I need help, Katz wrote back: *Mne nuzhna pomosh!*

Dobro pozhalovat, wrote Trotsky. Welcome.

They were alone in the chat room now, him and the operator. Katz explained his errand; he needed help with a 'superuser do' command to take control of a server.

Silence. No reaction at first. There were other

conversations going on simultaneously, in hidden rooms that Trotsky was moderating. Katz couldn't follow them.

It took several minutes for him to answer: *Chto ya polu-tyu vzamen?* What will you give me in return?

This was common in an IRC environment: people would exchange advanced programs or information, often shady things. And it had to be new, something no one had seen before. But Katz had nothing to offer, at least not this time. He explained that he had come empty-handed.

Silence again, and then Trotsky asked him which operating system he was dealing with.

Sun OS Solaris.

Kakuyu versiyu? Which version?

Katz told him what little he knew about the original version and the updates.

Trotsky sent a smiley and asked him to wait.

Then he showed up again and asked if Baruch was Jewish: *Tui yevrey, Baruch?*

Da.

Prove it!

Without thinking, he typed the rest of the Shabbat prayer: . . . *Eloheinu Melech haolam asher kid'shanu b'mitzvotav v'ratzah vanu lehadlik ner shel Shabbat.*

And Trotsky immediately replied: *It wouldn't matter if you were a goy, Baruch. You wouldn't have got access here if Hunky Dory hadn't vouched for you. Who are you going to hurt?*

Evil people, he replied.

Shabbat shalom, Baruch. And good luck.

A link popped up on the screen. A few minutes later,

he had the source code for the program on the hard drive. He would have to add quite a bit of code, he realized, and look for bugs to get it to work just as he wanted it to. A few hours' work. It had been a long time since he'd programmed.

It was one in the morning when he tried to get into Capitol Security's server. He heard a dull hum coming from the networked computers in the closet. His own Linux machine was connected to two hard drives, a router and a modem he had taken from Jorma's apartment.

It had taken him a few hours to get everything in place. A fake IP address registered under a fake name was the closest link in the chain that led to the screen before him. His own server was routed through several other servers with hacked accounts: a university computer in Paris, among others; another one in Boston, finally anonymized in the Tor network's tunnel. In any case, if a system operator were watching the traffic, he would have trouble tracing him.

Everything felt completely unreal. He had considered Julin a friend, almost like an older brother. Everything he had done for Katz throughout the years, helping him get clean, getting him a job, putting him in touch with his contacts, helping him out when he had problems. Their time in St Petersburg when they got to know each other, all the hours they'd sat in cafés in Stockholm, speaking Russian to keep their abilities up. He didn't understand.

But everything was pointing at Julin. He was the only one who had known that Katz was going to meet Angela on the night of the murder. And he was the only one who had known that he was hiding at a friend's house in Midsommarkransen. If it were Julin, Katz swore he would strike back. Mercilessly. At the time of his choosing.

But what he didn't understand was why Julin had first planted evidence that fingered him as the perpetrator, and then sent a person to murder him . . . a person who, accidentally, almost killed Jorma instead.

Because Julin thought he was on his trail? Because he had managed to hide from the police, against all odds?

'Your old army friend,' Julin said, when he'd given him the printout of the photo out in Smedslätten. Katz hadn't managed to capture the thought then, but the crux of the matter was that he'd never told Julin how he knew Klingberg.

The computer-case fans whirred from the open closet. The program was working its way closer and closer to a hole in Capitol's server.

More flows. Another prompt, demanding another command.

The program he'd received was a relative of the legendary 'John the Ripper' program that cracked encrypted passwords, but this one was much, much faster.

Suddenly, Katz stood on the threshold of having full control of the system. The program kept the sudo-command function open and prevented it from sounding an alarm as it worked on decrypting the code. It only took a few minutes and he was in.

He had obtained access to the administrator account. The only question was how much time he had.

He was inside one of the work computers in there; it belonged to someone who hadn't logged out, who was still there, working overtime. The person was surfing the net – an online casino, he saw.

Katz felt his pulse increase.

No one knows I'm here, take it easy.

He closed his eyes and saw Jorma before him, pale as a ghost under an oxygen mask in the ICU. Katz had been in touch with Jorma's sister; she was keeping him informed about his condition. It didn't look good. There were severe wounds to his neck. Suffering, insane amounts of suffering, and he swore he would get revenge.

He looked at the screen.

The user had left the online casino and had started working again, busying himself with an accounting program.

He was right. Julin was involved. There were files about Klingberg Aluminium on the computer.

He worked quickly, copying files and dragging them to a folder, searching through back doors. He found a hidden copy of a payment to a foreign account from one of the Klingberg Group's subsidiaries, personal information about Pontus Klingberg, telephone numbers and a few photographs whose contents he planned to check later. He found files marked with the letters KLINGbergVIP, dragged as much information as he could into the folder and saved it on his hard drive.

Then the security level suddenly increased. A system operator was looking for discrepancies in the data flow and had got nervous. Katz interrupted his hack, deleted the log files, erased his footsteps and shut down the computer.

Fifty million kronor. That was how much had been transferred to a foreign account. The SWIFT code and the IBAN number didn't tell him anything. But the name of the payee was there: Klingberg Aluminium. Extortion, but for what?

Moreover, the company had purchased unspecified security services from Capitol, but, unlike the sum paid to the foreign account, these were recorded in the books.

There were a few scanned newspaper articles about Klingberg Aluminium's previous business interests in the sugar industry, about the low-paid workforce. What did it mean?

There was nothing about Joel.

The files marked 'VIP' were empty and couldn't be restored. He could see that the information in them had been deleted on the same day Joel Klingberg disappeared.

Julin had removed all confidential information from the computer and moved it elsewhere. To his house in Smedslätten, to a personal computer, or to a plain old filing cabinet.

St Rochus. According to the Registry of Ships, it was a thirty-metre luxury yacht that the Klingberg family had owned since the early fifties. It had sometimes sailed under the Dominican flag, but it had always been insured in Sweden. It had been purchased long ago in Santo Domingo by the founder of the empire, Gustav Klingberg, but then his son Pontus had inherited it. It had been moored at various marinas in Lake Mälaren over the years, whenever it wasn't in the West Indies.

In 1984, the year of the incident, it had been in harbour at Ekerö.

At regular intervals it had been kept at the shipyard in Ulvsunda, not far from Katz's home. When Eva checked Klingberg's GPS, she discovered he had been near there on the day he disappeared. She had called the shipyard. The boat hadn't been there for several years, and they couldn't say where it might be. Apparently, it was sailing with a hired crew.

But they did have pictures of it; they faxed them over, and the more she looked at them, the more certain she was. The boat anchored off Hässelby Strand that time had been *St Rochus*.

*

She parked the car outside the office and walked the short distance to the old police station Agnegatan. She showed ID at the reception desk and asked to be let in.

She had searched for more information on the Klingberg family and read more about the tragedies that had befallen them over the years. Like a curse, she thought. Unless there was some connection between them?

The head archivist followed her through the basement hallways to the criminal records, introduced her to the attendant and asked him to help her.

On the other side of the gate were 16,000 shelf-metres of materials about crimes committed before the computer age: crime-scene photos, investigations, records, transcripts of interrogations, all arranged chronologically in folders that were themselves arranged according to the date when they had been entered. There was no physical evidence; that was cleaned out and buried in the archive when an investigation petered out.

She filled out the form the attendant gave her. Fifteen minutes later he showed up with the archive cart and placed the folders on the reading table.

Grey, printed covers: K5253-70. And K2065-79.

She took the first folder, from 1970, and opened it.

A kidnapping investigation. The written materials surrounding Kristoffer Klingberg's abduction forty-two years earlier.

It took her an hour to read through it. The investigation had been put on ice after less than a year. The Klingberg family – aside from the desperate parents, Jan and Joanna – hadn't been particularly cooperative. For example, Gustav, the founding father, had refused to answer the police's questions. They hadn't got any further after the initial police work. Later, when the case had gone cold, it had been handed off to an office of the criminal police, where it gathered dust over the years and eventually fell under the statute of limitations and ended up here.

She moved on to the next folder: the police investigation of Jan and Joanna Klingberg's suicide in 1979, with the attached autopsy report.

They had been found in the garage at the same address in Sörmland she'd seen in Klingberg's GPS log. The manor had belonged to Gustav Klingberg back then. There was no foul play suspected; the deaths had been written off as suicide. And yet it had been stored here. Why?

She took out the autopsy report and read through it. The couple had been sitting in the back seat, holding hands as they slowly went to sleep, lost consciousness, and finally asphyxiated. Respiratory failure and, presumably, severe lactic acidosis. The carbon monoxide had bound to the haemoglobin molecules in the blood at the expense of oxygen and had quickly led to hypoxic heart failure.

They had looked peaceful, the doctor wrote – no signs of regret. The blood tests had shown that they were heavily intoxicated when they died.

She read on, through a more detailed description of the state of the bodies, and gave a start. There had been a suck mark on Joanna Klingberg's neck. And one on Jan Klingberg's. The pathologist had no comment.

She put the paper aside and stared at the wall in front of her. What had the doctor thought? That they had shared some passionate farewell kisses?

Suck marks are not bite marks.

She took out the initial report again. She read the report from the police patrol that had been first on the scene, along with the ambulance.

A short description of what they'd seen. Transcripts of the interrogations of the father, Gustav Klingberg, and the brother, Pontus, as well as two employees, a maid and a chauffeur. And of the twelve-year-old boy who had found the bodies: Joel Klingberg.

It took her some time to work out how it had happened. Jan, Joanna and Joel Klingberg had spent the night at the country manor, along with Gustav and Pontus. The family members had slept in different buildings.

Joel had gone to bed around ten, and his parents had still been awake. When he woke up the following morning he couldn't find them. He had gone outside and called for them; he noticed that the door of the garage was closed but that the faint sound of a car engine was coming from within, walked in, and realized what had happened. He had run the two hundred metres to the main building and woken his grandfather. Gustav Klingberg, in turn, had asked the boy to call for an ambulance, whereupon he himself, along with Pontus, went to the scene of the incident.

No suicide note had been found.

She kept browsing and discovered an addendum in a separate envelope. She pulled out a typewritten page. It was a petition from an investigator in Stockholm from one month after the incident, a certain Ragnar Hirsch, who wrote that he wished to carry on investigating the deaths. There were a number of questions remaining, he wrote, without going into greater detail. An internal memo from higher up was attached at the very bottom, with a rejection of his request.

As far as she could tell, a superior had barred him from continuing. But, nevertheless, this was why it had been saved in the criminal records – because there were lingering questions.

There was probably a natural explanation. Lack of resources, an ambiguous chain of command, someone with greater insight in the matter who thought that Hirsch was making mountains out of molehills. In any case, this had all happened more than thirty years ago.

She put the materials back in the folder. Ragnar Hirsch. Where was he now? Retired, probably, even if he was still alive.

All he could see of Julin's house was the top floor; the wall blocked his view. Katz let his eyes move eastwards. An empty avenue, lined with pruned trees. No cars. No people moving about. The next house was nearly a hundred metres away and was obscured by trees. No one would see him when he climbed over. If there were surveillance cameras, they were on the inside of the wall. He would be safe at least until he reached the top.

In the other direction, to the south-west, was the garage. The door was open. Julin's car wasn't there. According to Emir, who had discreetly staked out the address for him, there hadn't been any traffic to or from the house in nearly twenty-four hours. By all appearances, Julin wasn't home.

Katz fumbled in his coat pocket. He felt the grooved top of the pistol, the slender barrel and the chill of the metal. An Austrian Glock with a silencer, nine-millimetre calibre, fifteen bullets in the magazine. Emir had shown him how it worked. To be safe, in case anything happened. Julin might come back. Maybe someone else was hiding in there . . . the man who had tried to kill Jorma.

It didn't matter. Whatever happened, happened.

He thought of Jorma again. He was a little better now; he'd been taken off the machines but was still in the ICU. According to his sister, he hardly remembered the incident. The police had questioned him, but he hadn't told them anything.

Katz felt the icy chill inside him, the primitive desire to harm Julin. He had to keep it in check.

It was nearly dark now. The floodlights might come on at any moment, and that would make it more difficult for him to approach the house unnoticed.

Just a few more minutes.

He pictured Jorma's and Angela's faces before him as he walked briskly towards the darkest part of the wall. He felt the hard seed in his stomach, the polished stone of rage that had been there as long as he could remember.

It was easier than he had hoped to get over the fence. The mason had been sloppy; there were cracks all the way up. Katz got a grip on the top with his fingers and felt for protruding pieces of glass. To his surprise, the top of the wall was completely smooth.

He lay on his stomach and looked across the yard. He couldn't see any cameras. There was no barking dog.

The house was dark. He wondered if Joel Klingberg was in there somewhere. But he doubted it. If Julin were behind the kidnapping, Joel would be held somewhere more secure.

He landed on the lawn with a dull thud. He heard waves lapping on the shore of the lake a hundred metres away. He took the Glock from his pocket and disengaged the safety. He wriggled out of his backpack straps and opened the pack up. Everything he needed was there: a crowbar, wire cutters, lock picks, equipment for demagnetizing electronic alarms. Emir could have started a wholesale warehouse for burglars.

The house was directly to his left, but the entrance was in the rear. A single window was lit in the daylight basement; the angle it was at meant he hadn't been able to see it from the top of the wall. Someone was moving about inside. A man dressed in a Capitol Security watchman's uniform.

Katz sat perfectly still, watching the man, who walked to a chair in the middle of the room and sat down. A snag in his plan, but he couldn't let it stop him.

He looked around and discovered something else he hadn't counted on: motion sensors in the yard. Faint light came from breakers that stuck up out of the ground every five metres along the entire wall. He had got lucky – he'd landed just within the first sector.

He quickly stood up, took a step forward and triggered the alarm.

Katz circled the house purposefully, under the windows and over to the gravel path by the stairs. Five seconds later, when the guard came out of the door, he was standing in the dark behind him and to one side. He hit the guard in the back of the head with the butt of the pistol.

He turned off the alarm and waited for a few minutes, sniffing for enemies like an animal. Silence. The house was empty. There was no video surveillance indoors.

He took off his mask and stuffed it into his backpack. He turned the lights on and off in each room as he searched them. Nothing of interest. Just furniture and decorations.

Aside from the kitchen, the main floor hardly seemed to be used.

Katz walked through a dining room and into a hallway. To the left was a set of stairs that led down to the basement level.

This level was more lived-in. There was a billiard room and a rec room that seemed to be used by Julin's sons – it was filled with various videogame consoles.

There was no cellar. What had he thought, that he would find Klingberg there, chained to the wall?

A smaller room faced the yard. There was a sewing machine on a table. An easel with a half-finished pastel painting depicting a bathing woman. Must be the wife's domain.

He peeked into the spa area. There was a sunken hot tub and a spacious sauna. A small gym behind a glass wall. Farther on, a bathroom that was undergoing renovation.

He went back up to the main level and continued up to the top floor.

Bedrooms. A two-room suite that seemed to belong to the wife. Two large children's rooms for the boys. A smaller bedroom, which he guessed belonged to Julin.

The balcony doors opened out towards the water. There was an unlocked door to the right, along the short wall.

He found himself in Julin's home office, a small room of perhaps eight square metres. Military certificates on the walls. A regiment flag from the SFOR, from Julin's time in the Balkans. Julin seemed to have left the house in a hurry. A movie was paused on a portable DVD player, a documentary about the invasion of Normandy. There were several electronic alarm systems manuals on a desk. The computer was on, but it was sleeping. Katz touched the keyboard and the screen came to life. The desktop was nearly empty. Aside from the hard disk icon, there was only a program menu.

He clicked on the email program.

There were several emails to Julin's wife in the outbox; she and the kids were still in Skåne. He had deleted everything in the inbox except for an old request for payment from an online bookshop.

In the recycling bin were a dozen emails which hadn't yet been automatically deleted. The top one was from a travel agent. Katz opened it. An electronic receipt for a flight on Air France, Stockholm to Santo Domingo, with a stopover in Paris. The ticket had been booked in Julin's name. Departure in a month.

He clicked on the next email: correspondence with a commercial bank on the island about a transaction from the Virgin Islands. The fifty million kronor, Katz thought.

Julin was on his way down there to get the money – to launder it or forward it on until it was no longer traceable.

He typed the name 'Klingberg' into the search box of the spotlight function, but got no results. Then he searched the hard drive for hidden files, but he found nothing of interest.

He looked around the room. There was a safe under the desk, attached to the wall. The door was open; the safe was empty.

Katz's eyes fell on the wall socket under the desk. It was a newer model than the others in the room. Only the top outlet was in use. The cord led to a transistor radio on a shelf. He hit the power button, heard canned music and noticed that the battery light came on. So it wasn't getting power from the outlet.

He crouched down and took a screwdriver from his backpack. He loosened the screws and pried off the plastic cover. He stuck his hand into the cylindrical space in the wall.

Julin had hidden two objects inside. One was a souvenir bottle wound in black yarn and embroidered with red sequins. The cork was sealed with black wax. Yarn stuck out from the sides like arms, so it looked like a person. The object reminded him of the canvases that Joel Klingberg had received shortly before he disappeared.

The other object was a brown office envelope containing photographs. One of them showed Julin standing on the deck of a sailboat with Pontus Klingberg. Younger versions of them, he noticed. Dressed casually. Both were wearing sunglasses. The photo seemed to have been taken in the early 1980s.

So they had known each other for a long time.

Katz's mind raced. If it wasn't a case of extortion, what was it? Collaboration? Had Pontus Klingberg paid Julin to kidnap Joel and murder his wife?

And, afterwards, Julin had cleaned up his tracks and made it look like Katz had done it.

He realized that Joel Klingberg was probably dead, too. He had been the primary target. The canvases he had received by mail had triggered the chain of events. Information about the disappearance of his brother in the early

1970s. That Pontus had been involved? And then Joel had realized that he was in danger and had planted in Angela the idea of contacting Katz if something should happen to him.

Puzzled, he continued to browse through the photos.

One had been taken outside at a regiment camp. It showed Julin and a uniformed man he vaguely recognized. In the background were recruits with red berets: para-troopers. Karlsborg. The picture had been taken outside the interpreter academy barracks, with someone from the military training staff. Had Julin been in contact with Katz's commanding officers?

Katz put the photographs back in the envelope and stuffed them in his coat pocket, along with the little doll. Then a sound from downstairs startled him. The watch-man was waking up.

In Julin's wife's suite, Katz opened a wardrobe door and took out a pair of black nylons. He pulled one leg over his face, took the Glock from his pocket and went down to the main floor. The watchman was lying where he'd left him, locked to a radiator with his own handcuffs. He was conscious, but he looked groggy.

Katz crouched behind him.

'What do you want?' the man said doggedly.

Katz pressed the barrel of the pistol into his mouth and five centimetres down his windpipe until the man started gagging. He held it there as the man was racked with spasms and nausea. Then he pulled it out and wiped it off on the man's cheek.

'Where's Julin?' he asked calmly.

The man could hardly speak.

'What do you want?' he whispered as sweat broke out on his forehead. 'For God's sake . . . what do you want from me?'

'Did Julin kidnap a man by the name of Klingberg?'

'I don't know what you're talking about.'

Katz put the gun in his mouth again and furtively disengaged the safety.

Then he pulled the trigger. And the man soiled himself when he heard the pistol click.

Katz stood up and walked around him.

'Where is Julin now? I need to get hold of him.'

The man had started to sob.

'He left yesterday. He was going hunting . . . fowl, I think. And I don't know anything about any kidnapping. I guard his house when he's gone; that's all I do. Damn it, you have to believe me.'

'An address . . . where is he?'

'I don't know exactly. In Sörmland somewhere. At some estate down there . . . it belongs to someone he knows.'

'I believe you,' Katz said calmly, as the man cried like a child on the floor in front of him. 'And don't forget to tell Julin, if you should see him before I do, that he was lucky to miss my visit. Tell him I'll come back. Tell him an old friend says hi.'

The Jewish retirement home was housed in a sand-coloured two-storey building in Skarpnäck in southern Stockholm. She should have realized it from his last name, she thought as she parked outside the entrance: Hirsch.

Two security doors led her into a hall, where a nurse received her. There was an aquarium on a table next to a visitors' sofa. Colourful cichlids swam among plastic plants and fake coral. There was a map of Israel on the wall.

To the right was a dining room; according to the menu, it served two kinds of kosher entrées for lunch. Lots of glass. A view of a courtyard with a fountain and flowerbeds.

'I'll show you to Ragnar's room,' said the nurse. 'Just follow me.'

They walked through a long corridor. A door with a sign that read 'OCCUPATIONAL THERAPY' stood ajar. An old woman was sitting on a cot inside, lost to the world. Otherwise, there were no people; it was nearly deserted.

'We have a dementia ward as well,' said the nurse, 'but most of our residents can take care of themselves. Our oldest tenant is one hundred and two. The youngest is seventy-five. Ragnar is closer to the median. He'll be ninety this fall. I don't know what it is, if it's the kosher diet or something else, but old Jewish men and women live for a long time.'

They walked by a common room with a TV and a piano. She glimpsed a small cabinet with Torah scrolls and other liturgical objects behind a curtain.

A weekly programme with information about activities hung on a bulletin board. The actor Basia Frydman would be coming that evening to perform songs in Yiddish.

They entered another corridor, which had regular doors as if to flats on either side. The nurse stopped in front of one and knocked lightly.

'Your visitor is here, Ragnar,' she said. 'Just don't forget our outing this afternoon. The bus leaves at three o'clock.'

She had spoken to him on the phone a few hours earlier, so she was expected. The former police commissioner had made coffee and put out a plate of cookies on the table by the window.

Like a gentleman, he pulled a chair out for her and asked her to sit down.

He looked surprisingly good for his age. He was slender and wiry, with thick, short hair.

'Welcome,' he said. 'This place isn't very big, but it's perfect for an old policeman. The staff are very orderly and proper. There are strict schedules for meals and doctor's visits. And lots of friends. We're a fine old bunch here. We don't even have to go to the synagogue any more. We have our services in the common room instead.'

He poured her coffee from a Thermos.

'It's nice here,' she said. 'Cosy.'

'And best of all . . . it's not going to be sold to venture

capitalists and run privately, as seems to happen every-where nowadays.'

There was an old black-and-white photograph on the wall depicting a teenaged version of Ragnar Hirsch out-side a barracks in the archipelago, along with some other teens; they were all wearing football kit. 'GLÄMSTA SUM-MER CAMP', read a sign in the background. The Jewish camp on Väddö. Katz had spent summers there. When his parents were still alive, he had told her, he had been sent there against his will. He had otherwise hardly spoken about his Jewish identity.

'Jewish policemen must not have been very common in your day,' she said.

'That's absolutely right. There was such a lot of anti-Semitism, and I was taunted all the time. Things like, why the hell I would wear myself out as a detective when I could open a bank instead? You were considered rich and stingy if you were circumcised. And worse things, too, for that matter.'

She thought of Katz again. All the needling he had had to cope with when they were young. Jew bastard. You fucking stingy Jew. And the sick jokes: Katz, do you know how to get six million Jews into a Volkswagen? Two in front, two in back. The rest in the ashtray. A lot of the time he had exploded straight away, which was just what his enemies had hoped for.

'Actually, I think I'm the only Stockholm policeman of my generation who keeps kosher,' Ragnar Hirsch went on. 'And definitely the only police officer here at the home.

My dad wanted me to become a policeman. He was an insurance officer himself, but he thought it was time someone in our family put on a uniform.'

He was interrupted by a scream from another part of the building, a sort of plaintive cry that increased in intensity and then suddenly cut off.

'Miriam Löwenstein,' said the retired police officer in front of her. 'She came to Sweden on the white buses when she was fifteen. She survived Auschwitz-Birkenau against all odds. Saw her mother and younger siblings go into the gas chamber. For some memories, there just isn't any cure.'

He gave her a guilty smile as he brushed a few biscuit crumbs from his lap.

'But that's not why you're here,' he said. 'You wanted to know more about the Klingberg couple's suicide.'

Ragnar Hirsch had known one of the ambulance crew who had come to the manor in Sörmland the morning the Klingbergs had been found dead in their car. The man's name was Holmström, and he had previously worked for the Stockholm fire department. He was the one who had called Hirsch a week or so after the deaths to ask him to take a look at the case.

'The housemaid wanted to tell him something, he told me, but she changed her mind when the police patrol showed up.'

Hirsch told her about how he had tried to research the deaths out of sheer curiosity; partly, he said, because it involved such a well-known business family. He had asked

Holmström to give a statement about what he'd seen at the crime scene, and he'd requested the autopsy report and the reports from the Sörmland police and had gone through those. The pathologist had written that the couple had been intoxicated when they committed suicide, and there was evidence that this was the case. Two empty bottles of cognac and an open but only half-drunk bottle of Château Lafite were found in the car.

Holmström, on the other hand, was an old fox who had seen and heard far too much during his long career in emergency services in Stockholm, and thought it looked more like they had been drugged.

'But it didn't really make a difference,' Hirsch said, as he poured more coffee in her cup. 'Because even that matched the description of the Klingbergs. Both were alcoholics, and they abused sedatives.'

'How do you know that?'

'I asked around a little. Apparently, it started after they lost their elder son to abduction. Their sorrow made them fall deeper and deeper into abuse.'

'But that wasn't what Holmström meant?'

'No . . . he thought the way they were sitting in the car looked unnatural. Arranged, somehow . . . and, according to him, they could have been moved to the car while they were unconscious.'

'But there were no signs to suggest it.'

'Impossible to say, because the police patrol took it for granted that it was a suicide and they tramped around the garage like elephants. If there was any evidence there, it was simply destroyed by accident.'

Hirsch continued his story. He had gone out to the family estate in Djursholm to talk to the next of kin. Everyone had been there. Pontus Klingberg and his wife at the time. The aging patriarch, Gustav. The maid, who had wanted to tell Holmström something but changed her mind. And Joel Klingberg.

'I felt so terribly sorry for that boy,' Hirsch said. 'Twelve years old, and no amount of money in the world could comfort him. Just imagine, finding your own parents gassed to death. He was completely broken. It was impossible to get a rational word out of him. He just started crying as soon as I asked him what he'd seen that morning.'

They sat in silence for a moment. Hirsch looked out the small window towards the other wing of the building. It was as if his ninety years started to show themselves as he searched back through his memories. He suddenly looked tired and very old.

'I was wondering . . . those suck marks on their necks. Why didn't anyone try to find an explanation for them?'

'I never saw the bodies,' said Hirsch. 'Just the photographs, both from the pathologist and the police patrol. But I agree with you – what on earth were they doing there?'

'So you suspected foul play?'

'Well, it was impossible to rule out, let's say that much.'

'But you weren't allowed to move forward?'

He nodded. 'People above me thought that my talents were needed in other areas. There quite simply wasn't enough evidence for me to investigate further. None at all. In addition, Gustav Klingberg's word had great weight in the matter. He knew people high up at police headquarters, and even higher up on a political level. He was completely overcome. First he lost a grandchild, then his younger son and daughter-in-law. He didn't want any more publicity, any more police investigations. He thought there had been enough. And he was also trying to protect his grandson from general curiosity – Joel Klingberg. The boy wasn't far from a mental breakdown, after all, and Gustav . . .'

He stopped talking, hesitating before he went on: 'Gustav . . . had some sort of bizarre fantasy that his family had been struck by a curse. This went for the abduction of his elder grandson nine years earlier . . . and the best way to protect them against further accidents was to stop talking about it, stop giving out any more information about his family.'

'Was that what his maid wanted to tell Holmström?'

'I never found out. *A mayse on a moshl iz vi a moltsayt on a tsimes* . . . a story without a point is like a meal without dessert, as they say in Yiddish. I was bothered for a long time afterwards that I never found out what she wanted.'

'Did you talk to her?'

'Yes.'

'What did she say?'

'Nothing more than that Gustav thought there was a family curse. He even blamed his recurring nosebleeds on it. I suspected that she knew more, but I couldn't force it out of her. Suddenly, she had no comment whatsoever.'

'Do you remember her name?'

'Sandra Dahlström. A young woman, at the time. After the Klingbergs' death she was the one who raised Joel.'

*

She said goodbye to him in the hall, beside the aquarium of cichlids. There were more people around now; lunch was now being served. Old men in *kippahs* were brought into the dining room in wheelchairs, along with elegant ladies with slightly exotic features. She heard people speaking by turns in Polish, Yiddish and Swedish.

Visitors were on their way in – families with children there to visit their grandparents. One of the men reminded her of Katz.

She got into her car and turned the key in the ignition.

No sign of him yet. He was still at large. She couldn't help feeling a certain amount of admiration.

He must have had help hiding somewhere. Maybe from Jorma?

According to the national registry, Jorma lived in Midsommarkransen. He had been released from Norrtälje Prison a few years earlier after a three-year sentence for aiding and abetting in an armed robbery.

She took out her phone and called Marianne Lindblom, a civilian investigator at EBM, asking her to take a closer look at Jorma's file and see if anyone was keeping an eye on him at the moment. She ignored Marianne's questions about when she would be back in the office and hung up.

Klingberg's old maid, Sandra Dahlström. For some reason, she suddenly seemed more important.

Ormnäs Manor was situated in a nature reserve between Katrineholm and Vingåker. The property consisted of eight hundred hectares of forest, water and farmland. The main building was a two-storey stone house from the seventeenth century with one-storey wings of timber, constructed in the Swedish Karoline style.

Surrounding the manor were several farm buildings: stalls, barns, guest houses, coach houses, a mill and an old dairy.

The road that led to the main building was private, a kilometre of chestnut-lined avenue that appeared to end at a fountain in a courtyard.

Katz had checked the place out on Google Earth. In order to approach the main building unnoticed, one would have to come from the south, on foot.

It was past midnight when he parked Jorma's car on a timber road a few kilometres from the property.

He stood still for a moment, letting his eyes adjust to the darkness, listening to the clicking of the warm engine, to the sounds of the forest – the light breeze moving through the trees and a nocturnal bird calling from a marsh.

Then he took his torch from his jacket pocket, turned

it on at the dimmest setting, looked for a path that seemed to lead north and started walking.

It took him half an hour to make his way through the first section of forest. Fault fissures and steep hills forced him to take detours. He crossed another timber road with old tracks left by forestry machines, rounded a small pond and arrived at a fence. He followed it west until he realized that this part of the grounds was enclosed. He swore when he realized that he had left his backpack with the wire cutters in the car.

Since it was too late to go back, he climbed the fence instead. The metal links cut into his fingers as he pulled himself up. He finally reached the top and rested, his arms over the fence. The cloud cover had lessened for the moment; starlight penetrated it. He could see better now. The manor was five hundred metres away, a black monolith where the forest opened up.

He climbed down the other side, jumped the last metre and landed beside the roots of a fallen tree.

He looked in the direction of the buildings and kept moving. The going was easier now. This part of the forest was cultivated and not as thick. The ground was flat.

Then he came to the first field. There were a few hunting stands scattered along the edge, like gloomy wooden sculptures from a vanished hunter culture. He could smell fresh earth.

He closed his eyes, opening them again when the first raindrops fell. At least it would be harder to hear him now.

The rain made a sort of background noise, blocking out all other sounds.

The manor was dark. There were no cars in the drive. The buildings looked like set pieces in the hazy light from the night sky.

He followed the edge of the forest and came to the first barn. He was standing at a gravel road that ran eastwards between the outbuildings, over to a hill.

The avenue to the courtyard was fifty metres away. Katz wondered what he should do. He thought he should just keep going up to the house, to see if anyone was there.

As he approached the courtyard, he discovered that the gravel was perfectly even. No sign of vehicles. The main building brooded in the darkness before him. Six rows of two windows, like rectangular black eyes. Piles of leaves covered the stairs.

Katz didn't know what he'd been thinking. No one was there . . . and no one had been there for a long time. He had just taken for granted that Julin was at the Klingberg family's estate in Sörmland. He'd driven here without thinking, desperately needing to do something, to make something happen, reverse their roles.

The rain was falling more heavily. He looked around to find shelter somewhere and discovered an overhanging roof on a building farther off; he went over to it. He sank down against the wall and blinked when he saw bright lights along the main road. A vehicle turned on to the avenue.

The car rolled past, only forty metres away from him; it was a silver-grey SUV. A lone man was in the driver's seat.

But the car didn't stop near the manor house. It rounded the courtyard and continued eastwards, past the buildings and off towards the wooded ridge. The sound of the engine faded slowly. The headlights flickered through the trees, winding up a hill until they disappeared from sight.

He walked for twenty minutes before he found the car; it was parked outside a log cabin on the gravel road. Faint light came from the windows. He heard the mumbling of male voices.

He retreated into the forest in order to approach unnoticed.

There was a barrier across the road, and another fence started on the other side of it. The entire area seemed to be fenced in.

Katz walked parallel to the fence for twenty metres, into the forest, until he was level with the cabin. He fumbled in his pocket for Jorma's phone to make sure it was turned off.

There was another car in the driveway, a black Volvo station wagon.

Katz sneaked closer and stopped a metre from the fence.

The cabin was made of black-tarred timber, and it was surrounded by forest in three directions. The gravel path widened outside the entrance in order to make room for cars. Farther off, there was a guest cabin with a veranda, and down the road the metal gates for driving in and out.

The adrenalin pumped through Katz's body. He went on through a clearing where the path turned into a slope that led down to a lake. The fence was out of sight of the building here, and it was also a metre shorter. He climbed over it.

He was standing on the path below the crown of the hill, the Glock in his hand. He listened to something he realized was a dog barking. It was faint at first, but then, with no intermediate stage, it was much louder. It was as if it had shown up out of nowhere.

He sank down in a crouch and watched the dog approach from the top of the hill, very slowly, as if it wanted to prolong its task for fun.

The Ovcharka. This was where Julin had brought it. Apparently, it was the only breed in the world that could give a wolf or a bear an honest fight. It weighed eighty kilos, and it stood nearly a metre at the shoulders. Predators couldn't hurt it, he had read somewhere; its pelt was too thick and there were no soft parts to bite.

He was on his knees, in a shooting position, watching the dog approach – it was much larger than he'd expected. Its jaws were wide open; its killing instinct was incredibly keen. It wasn't even barking now, just concentrating on its prey. It was twenty metres away now, ten, five . . . Katz didn't feel a thing, just cold concentration.

It stopped two metres away from him. He could smell the harsh scent of its fur. Its eyes looked like two black buttons. Its growl was like nothing he'd ever heard.

He shot in the same instant it attacked, two shots which, to his surprise, met their mark.

When he stood up a second later, he still had tunnel vision. He didn't notice the person approaching from behind. He didn't notice the violent blow coming to the back of his neck; he was only conscious of the world exploding into a red glow before he fell headlong to the ground.

She sat in the car in a car park in Mörby Centrum, looking over at the high-rises while she smoked. Loreen's 'Euphoria' was coming through the speakers. She was sick of hearing it. Her phone beeped just as she turned off the radio. It was a text message from Ola: Fuck you, you promised to come, the kids and I waited for half an hour, and finally we had to go in on our own, I want you to know that . . .

She exited the message without reading the rest. She looked in her calendar. She had missed the meeting with the family counsellor. Or she had ignored it. Because she couldn't handle such situations. Because she was self-destructive.

Two more messages from Ola, on the same theme. Plus four missed calls from work. They had started to wonder where she was.

She looked over at the high-rises again. Early sixties. The dream of modernity had ended in veritable ghettos. The walls were covered in graffiti. There were cheap satellite dishes on the balconies. Just like in Hässelby Gård, the world she and Katz had come from.

She lit another cigarette. The taste was divine. It had been ten years since she'd given up. She didn't understand how it could still be so good.

*

Her prosecutor's ID seemed to make quite an impression; the woman let her in with no questions asked and led her through a dark hallway to a new-age-inspired living room. A golden Buddha sat on a table. There were pictures of Indian gods on the walls – a blue, dancing figure she guessed was Krishna; another that was probably Shiva. The scent of incense. An unrolled yoga mat on the floor.

To the left, the door to a bedroom stood open. Kitschy Christmas lights were hung on the walls, there were pillows and blankets in a pile at the foot of the bed, and pictures of a woman in colourful clothing on the bedside table. She had a sudden sense of déjà vu, but it went away again before she could hook on to it.

So this was how she lived. Sandra Dahlström. Childless, according to the information in the registry. Born in 1951. On disability for six years now.

She seemed to be freezing. She had slippers on her feet and she was wearing a long-sleeved cardigan. Her gaze was empty. Perhaps she was on medication. Her nose seemed disproportionately tiny compared to her sensual mouth. There were small scars under the wings of her nose, apparently from plastic surgery.

The woman nodded at her to follow her to a glassed-in balcony.

'I've been expecting you,' she said softly.

She took a seat before a game of solitaire that seemed to have been interrupted. There were palms and ferns in pots on the floor. Herbs sprouted from a hotbed. It was horribly warm. Eva couldn't fathom how the woman could be sitting there in a cardigan.

'It's about Joel, isn't it?' she said. 'I read the papers. He's been kidnapped and his wife was murdered. Sooner or later, someone had to come and ask questions.'

Of her own accord – and, chronologically, besides – she began to tell the story, as if it were something she'd waited a long time to do.

'I started working for the Klingberg family in autumn 1969, when I was eighteen. I saw an ad in *Svenska Dagbladet*; they were looking for a new maid. I lived with my mother at the time . . . in this building, in fact, on the first floor. My dad had left us, so it was just the two of us. Mum worked hard as a cleaning woman in the city. I had left school – I didn't even finish compulsory school. We needed the money. Djursholm isn't that far away, of course; it's just a few kilometres in the other direction, towards the water. And yet you can't imagine a greater contrast.'

Sandra Dahlström had moved into servants' quarters that were annexed to the house. She was essentially supposed to be at her employer's disposal twenty-four hours a day. The pay was better than she'd expected.

'What was he like – Gustav?'

'He was pleasant to some and a pig to others. He got pleasure out of being cruel to people he didn't like. It was worst for his older son, Pontus. He treated him as if he didn't exist, and the more Pontus tried to please him the worse it got.'

'Was it the same with the younger brother?'

'No, Jan was the exception. The favourite . . . the lost son. He lived a bohemian life when he was young. He distanced himself from his capitalist father. Which just made Gustav love him even more. Gustav did everything for him . . . tried to buy his love, wanted to give him important positions in the group, but Jan refused. I think it had to do with his mother. The brothers had different mothers, you know. Jan's mother was a black woman from the Dominican Republic, Marie Bennoit. The love of Gustav Klingberg's life, the rumours went, but he ran out on her when the family moved back to Sweden.'

This surprised Eva, but she just took it in; she'd have to work through it later if she were to concentrate on the woman's story.

'What was it that Russian author wrote, that all happy families are alike but those that are unhappy are unhappy in their own ways? I used to think of that during the twelve years I was employed there. About all the tragedies that happened to them, and how their fortune didn't help a bit.'

'What sort of relationship did the brothers have?'

'Not much of one. And it didn't help that Gustav played favourites with his younger son. I think he went so far as to change his will and make Jan the primary heir in order to humiliate his other son. Pontus hated his brother after that.'

Maybe to the point that he wanted to destroy his life? Eva thought, as she let her eyes wander back to the living room, the bookshelf, the knick-knacks and a portrait of a young boy she hadn't noticed earlier.

'You worked for the family when Kristoffer Klingberg was kidnapped?' she said.

'That's right. I had been there for about eight months

when it happened. I'd never seen such wealth in my entire life. Servants, chauffeurs, a thirty-room mansion; parties, often organized by Pontus, where people scarfed down Iranian caviar and drank vintage champagne like it was juice. I'm from a working-class home . . . it was like finding yourself in a strange waking dream that suddenly transformed into a nightmare. He was so lovely, that little boy, Kristoffer. Biracial. The black heritage showed up in him, strangely enough, not in his father or his little brother. And plus, he was Gustav's favourite grandchild; maybe he reminded him of his lost love. Gustav would play with him for hours when he visited. And then it happened . . .'

She stopped talking and looked out of the window at the car park below. She was sweating in her cardigan; dark spots as large as the palms of her hands had formed under her arms. 'Gustav thought it was all because of a curse. Because he had left Marie and taken Jan with him. He was a superstitious one. He'd grown up in the Caribbean . . . believed in the evil eye and all that. That people could harm you and get revenge from a distance. He blamed his migraines on it. And the nosebleeds that the whole family suffered from, even though that was probably something hereditary. He considered losing blood to be the worst thing of all. And it added fuel to the fire when someone sent him strange objects in connection with the abduction.'

'What were they?'

'Some things that came by post a few days before Kristoffer disappeared. A doll, among other things; I remember it upset Gustav terribly. Marie Bennoit came from a family where people were involved with things like that. I never found out any details; these are just things I picked up in passing. But Gustav was terrified; I could see that for myself. He was absolutely stricken. He feared for his life. It wasn't rational, but that's how it was. When Kristoffer disappeared, he gave up all hope of getting him back. He considered him lost . . . and thought that this was their fate, a punishment they just had to submit to.'

'Did he ever show those objects to the police?'

'No. He thought that would just give the curse even more power. I know it sounds strange, but it didn't seem that way when you were in the middle of it. It was like I just got used to all these peculiar things, for better or for worse.'

'So you stayed with the family?'

'Yes. I just had to avoid Pontus. He clashed with the servants, too. I lived in the house year round, and never even got time off. I didn't think I needed it, because I got to go along on the family's holidays.'

'Sailing trips?'

'Luxury cruises. Spa vacations. Once, they rented out an entire ski resort in Switzerland. And we spent a lot of time in the Caribbean, in the Bahamas, Jamaica, the Dominican Republic. Gustav still had business interests there. Sugarcane plantations. Bauxite mines. Hundreds of employees who slaved away like animals. Only black men. There was that contrast again; it defined the family . . . the contrasts in their lives. Their wealth, and the poverty of their workers. Jan refused to come along. But Pontus was usually there, with various girlfriends or new wives. And Joel, whom his grandfather always wanted to bring along; he had taken

Kristoffer's place. They would sail around down there in a luxury yacht with a hired crew that brought her over from Sweden.'

'*St Rochus*?'

Sandra Dahlström looked at her in surprise.

'Yes.'

'I know this sounds like a strange question, but the summer of 1984 – do you know if the boat was in Lake Mälaren then, and if it was ever moored at Hässelby?'

By now the sweat was running down Sandra's face as well. Eva didn't understand why she was wearing long sleeves.

'I wouldn't venture to answer that. I no longer worked for them then, but it's definitely possible. It would have been on Pontus's orders. He was the only one who used the boat when it was in Sweden.'

She stood up and wiped the sweat from her brow with the sleeve of her cardigan.

'Do you have anything against going outside for a bit?' she said. 'I think I need some fresh air.'

They walked to a nearby park. There were immigrant families on picnics, with blankets and disposable grills. Women in veils and ankle-length dresses. They followed a path towards a wooded area.

'You were there at the time of the second tragedy, too, when Jan and Joanna were found.'

She noticed that Sandra stiffened and slowed down.

'Yes, that was dreadful. All the pain it caused. And for Joel to be the one to find them. I hadn't got to know

Kristoffer very well before he disappeared, but it was different with Joel. I had watched him grow up. I'd seen the torture he went through, being the one who was left. Kristoffer lived on in the family like a ghost . . . invisible, but terribly present. I think Joel suffered from survivor's guilt.'

She picked up a small rock from the ground; she let it slide between her fingers to calm herself down.

'When it happened, at Ormnäs Manor . . . it was like the ground was pulled out from under him; the last bit of security was taken from him.'

'How did he react?'

'With apathy, at first. Then with rage. I was the one who took care of him in the year after his parents' death. He moved in with us in Djursholm. Gustav didn't have the strength to raise him; he was too broken. So I did instead . . . maybe not like another mum, but like an older sister.'

'How did it go?'

'Good, sometimes . . . worse, on other occasions. He didn't know how to work through the catastrophe. He hurt himself . . . attacked objects, too. He destroyed things. But I could handle it. I was the only one who could get him to calm down, and then his attacks of rage would turn into unfathomable despair. It was unbearable to see so much pain in such a little boy.'

Eva noticed that she was starting to have trouble steering the conversation. So she told the story of her meeting with Ragnar Hirsch, about how he suspected that things hadn't been handled correctly.

'The morning when Joel found his parents,' she said. 'You were there, of course . . . did you notice anything that might have been of interest to the police?'

She stared into Sandra's face, which was turned towards her as they stood on the path; it was relaxed, and there was no sign that she was trying to conceal anything.

'You wanted to tell something to a man in the ambulance crew that was first on the scene. That's how he understood it, anyway.'

'Yes . . . but it seemed so stupid at the time, so silly, the fantasy of a little boy. A few nights before they killed themselves, I was with Joel out in the country. Jan and Joanna were off somewhere, maybe in the hunting cabin; they would sit out there and drink . . . both of them had drinking problems. Joel suddenly started telling me about how his older brother had disappeared nine years earlier, and how he remembered a number of details from that day.'

'He was just a little boy when it happened.'

'I know, and that's why I had trouble believing him.'

'So what did he say?'

'That they had been followed that day. That a man had got on the same bus and got off at the same stop. That he'd had a companion who'd acted like a drunk, and that the driver of a car, a Volvo, had acted strangely as they crossed the street to the metro station where Kristoffer would later disappear. And there had been strange objects at the place where Kristoffer was taken. Chicken feathers in the shape of a cross, among other things.'

'Did he tell anyone else about it?'

'No. He had kept quiet about it all those years, but he told his dad about it the same week they killed themselves. And when he found them in the garage, he came to the conclusion that it was his fault, that they had died because he gave them a dangerous clue.'

'So Joel didn't believe that they had killed themselves?'

'He thought they were murdered. But then he got over it. I convinced him otherwise.'

They had walked around the wooded area in a circle and were back at the grassy area outside the high-rises.

'And that was what you wanted to tell the ambulance driver?'

'Yes . . . but then I decided not to. It was only a child's fantasies. A few years later, I met a certain person and put in my notice. We lived together until very recently, when she got breast cancer and died.'

The woman in the photographs, she thought; a childless lesbian couple.

'And Joel. Have you seen him since then?'

'No. And I haven't seen anyone else in the family either. I've just read about them. I feel sorry for them. Money is certainly no guarantee of happiness.'

In the car back to the city, she felt strangely absent. She scanned through the radio stations until she found the most boring one, Easy Favourites. She listened to cheesy hard-rock ballads as she watched downtown Stockholm grow closer.

The traffic became heavier and nearly stopped at the bottleneck by Norrtull. She picked up her phone from the passenger seat. She had one new message. She called her voicemail as the traffic crept slowly into the city.

Marianne Lindblom's voice. She had news about Jorma. He was in the ICU at Söder Hospital.

Darkness, slowly filling with sounds. Voices speaking in another room, someone swearing. Visions detaching from a wall of ashes, stepping out like 3D figures on an internal movie screen. Julin, pale and sweaty, with Emir's Glock in his hand. The other man, the one in the white tennis shoes, the one who had wanted to murder him but attacked Jorma by mistake . . . he didn't have a face; he kept it hidden inside his hood. He didn't speak. He was mute, as if someone had cut out his vocal cords. So there had to be a third person in the background, the one Julin had been talking to.

He heard sentences in Russian, but he realized that they weren't coming from the real world; instead, they were somehow part of the drug haze they'd put him in, the narcotic state he didn't recognize. Katz had tried most things, but this was like nothing else. The apathy . . . a sense of no longer wanting to be alive.

Kak delya, Danya, said a voice. How are you, Danny?

He answered with a colloquial Russian word: *Normalno!*

The person vanished through a door in his consciousness as suddenly as he had appeared, mumbling a lofty verse.

Then came the darkness again . . . his brain being chloroformed, his body lying dormant. He saw Julin through a narrow gap in his consciousness. Julin was bending over him as he lay there, bound to a cot; he was breathing so close that he could feel the warmth of his skin.

'Who else knows that you're here, Katz?'

Don't answer, don't give him anything. That was what had been drummed into him in the military. *If you give them information, you are no longer of use, they'll have what they want and you are spent and soon dead.*

'We found the car. Did you come here with someone?'

He pretended to whisper something.

'What did you say? Speak louder!'

He whispered even more quietly. Julin bent down to hear.

He couldn't miss, no matter how much they had drugged him.

He spat in Julin's face. 'Fuck you, asshole.'

The fist came up; Julin was about to hit him when someone whistled from a part of the room he couldn't see.

Julin disappeared and, instead, the man in the hood was standing before him. From his skin came the scent of insect repellant. And the scent of burning birchwood; there was a fire in a stove somewhere.

Katz tried to spit again but didn't have the strength; his head rolled back, into unconsciousness.

He was in a server now; he was a sort of electrical impulse travelling at the speed of light through semiconductors, deeper into the operating system; he saw a gap in the source code and he installed a back door, disguised as a system file. In case I need to come back, he thought triumphantly: in case I need to run away from here!

Glämsta. Suddenly he was there . . . at the Jewish summer camp. He walked past the Falu-red cabins, the kiosk, the Secret Cave, Lake Klappis, the football field where they held their Junior Maccabiad every year. He had only gone there for two summers, and he had hated it. He'd always felt like an outsider . . . he didn't even fit in as a Jew.

The man in the hood bent over him, as if he didn't know what to do. His breathing was abnormally slow; he only took a breath every thirty seconds.

The bottle wound with fabric was protecting him; the figure with the outstretched arms. Katz knew it, but he didn't know how. He didn't even know where this idea came from, but it was very strong. They hadn't found it when they searched his clothes; the figure had fallen into the lining of his jacket through a hole in the inner pocket. He felt it against his hip, and he felt the power that radiated from it. The man in the hood felt it, too. Only him. Not Julin. He felt it and was afraid of it.

The third man's voice: *What the hell are we going to do with him?*

Who was it . . . Pontus Klingberg?

He slipped away from the room again, deeper into unconsciousness. All of a sudden he was standing in a kitchen in his pyjamas. Benjamin was at the table with a passport in his hand. There was a large 'J' stamped on the front endpaper. Anne tried to calm him, tried to take the passport from him, but he wouldn't let her. He raised his arm instead, striking her face with the back of his hand. The anguish he felt as he watched his mother fall to the floor was not of this world. Two rivulets of pinkish blood ran from her nose.

'*Ferdamte shikse*,' his father said in Yiddish, in a strange voice, and he meant it as an insult – that she wasn't a Jewish woman, that she was Swedish, from a village just south of Krokom in Jämtland.

His mother got up without answering, walked over to Benjamin and tried once again to take the passport from him. And this time she succeeded.

Benjamin, in only his underwear, his circumcised cock peeking out of the gap. You are reminded of your identity every time you piss, he liked to say.

His father cried, his face buried in his hands, as Anne stood at the sink and washed the blood away from her nose. No one noticed Katz; it was as if he had become invisible.

His mother put the passport – an Austrian passport, he realized, with the Jewish stamp on the first page – back in the top drawer of the kitchen cupboard. His father said something about his parents, whom Katz had never met, Chaim and Sara, buried in a kibbutz between Jaffa and Tel Aviv; said something about the man he had to kill for the sake of the passport and his parents. Katz didn't understand. Who had his father been forced to kill?

He had asked the question as he stood in the doorway: 'Who did you kill, Dad?'

He remembered the silence and realized that they hadn't noticed he was there until that moment.

'A swine,' his mother said, without looking at him. 'It was a long time ago. The man deserved it.'

*

Darkness again, but it was weaker this time, as if it were washed out. He climbed up through thin layers of consciousness. He opened his eyes. It was day; stripes of sunshine trickled in at the edges of the lowered blinds.

The man with the hood was standing next to him. He caught a glimpse of his face. Dark. Squinting eyes.

He couldn't explain it. *He's dead*, he thought. The man wasn't alive. Pseudo-life.

His body ached. He tried to move, but nothing happened. He was still bound – but not to a cot, he realized, to a wide board that stood on sawhorses.

He wasn't afraid. He had no feelings at all. He was paralysed somehow. He couldn't even move his fingers, couldn't move his feet; only his breathing worked. And his eyelids. He could blink. He could see.

He still had his clothes on. They had taken off his shoes and socks. As if from a great distance, he felt the power from the bottle in the lining of his jacket. He didn't understand how it worked, but it was protecting him. The man in the hood couldn't hurt him as long as the power was emanating from it.

The dead man. He did only what others ordered him to, because he lacked his own will, because he lacked true life.

All imagination, he thought; they had drugged him, and he was suffering from hallucinations.

He saw something moving across the room. The third man stood with his back to him, dressed in a thin, dark coat, speaking softly with Julin. He couldn't make out what they were saying; there was just a dull mumbling when his name popped up. The man with the hood stroked his hand

lightly. His hand was ice-cold . . . he had never felt anything like it; it was not only cool, but chilled from the inside,
as if the blood that ran under his skin were freezing.

He felt the draw of heroin; it suddenly came out of
nowhere.

*It's been a long time since I went to NA, but when I get out of
here I'll go to a meeting, that's a promise.*

Then Julin was standing before him. 'Can you hear me,
Katz?'

He wanted to spit at him again, but again he didn't have
the strength. He just blinked.

'You should be able to talk soon. The stuff we gave you
doesn't affect your speech organs. I want you to use your
voice. Say something, anything at all.'

'No . . .'

It was true. He could speak, but his voice was weak.

'Good, so we know you can communicate. I want you
to tell me what you learned about Angela's murder and
Klingberg's abduction. And what you told to others . . .
who you've been in contact with.'

He didn't understand.

'Does anyone else know you're here?'

He didn't answer; why should he give him anything?

'Okay. We're in no rush. But I'm going to make you tell
me, do you understand?'

Julin held up the photos that Katz had found in the
hiding place behind the power socket.

'I know you took these from my house. Look at me
when I'm speaking to you!'

'You fucking asshole . . . you made it look like I did it.'

He couldn't believe he was talking to him, but it must have been the hate, because he added, 'And I swear, Julin, I'm going to get revenge.'

Julin didn't bat an eye.

'You're right. I'll be honest with you – you ended up the scapegoat. And now I want you to be honest with me. Who else have you told?'

'Go to hell . . .'

Julin just nodded, and he left the room with the others; Katz saw a door open and daylight pouring in and being sucked back out as they closed the door behind them. He was left alone in the room. His eyes searched for something that could help him get the rope loose, but he couldn't find anything. What did it matter? He was paralysed. The drug they had given him had disabled his muscles.

He dozed off again. He saw an old black woman he understood to be Marie Bennoit. She was holding a bone rattle in one hand and a brush made of chicken feathers in the other . . . she shuffled through the room, humming a song, until she transformed into Eva Dahlman, with bite marks around her neck.

Sorry, Eva, he thought as he fell once more through a blood-red shaft, deep into himself.

She was on the highway, halfway to Katrineholm. Her visit to Söder Hospital had changed everything. Jorma had left the ICU that afternoon and been moved to an aftercare ward. A single police officer had been sitting on a stool in the hallway outside his room. She had shown him her EBM ID and, to her surprise, he had let her in.

They hadn't seen each other since she was fourteen, and yet he looked the same. Handsome in his own way, not unlike Katz. Black hair, dark brown eyes. But he was larger and calmer. He had a faint Finnish accent even though he'd lived in Sweden all his life. He was nice, one of the few truly kind-hearted people she had ever met. As long as you weren't his enemy.

She must look the same, too, she guessed, because he recognized her and chose to trust her. So far he hadn't said a word to the police who had tried to question him.

What are they going to do? I don't want to get the cops involved in this. Are you a cop, Eva? I can smell it on you.

'A prosecutor,' she said. 'I have to get hold of him . . . and no one has made the connection between you and Katz yet.'

His vocal cords were damaged. He had to whisper when he told her what had happened.

Katz had found him and told him about everything

that had happened leading up to Angela Klingberg's murder. He was convinced that there was a conspiracy against him. Jorma had helped him stay hidden. Katz was on the trail of something; it had to do with his old boss Rickard Julin from Capitol Security. *But some fucking Judas had betrayed him!*

He gave her a pained smile as he told her how he had woken up in the middle of the night to find a person standing beside his bed. Then it had all gone black. He had been knocked unconscious and, after that, someone had tried to strangle him. He'd been lucky to survive. Apparently, Katz had saved him.

But they weren't after me. It was him. They got the wrong person.

Since he'd woken from the anaesthetic, he had only had indirect contact with Katz, through his sister and a third person named Emir.

What had happened after that? She tried to put the puzzle together as she drove south on the highway.

Katz had broken into Julin's house and not found what he was looking for. Evidence, she supposed, to show that Julin was involved. Emir had said as much to Jorma's sister. Katz had borrowed a weapon from him, a Glock. He'd called afterwards to ask if he could keep the pistol for a little while longer. He hadn't been able to find Julin, but he thought he knew where he was. That was over twenty-four hours ago, and there had been so sign of him since.

She was coming up on Strängnäs now, and she saw the darkness of the evening rub at the car windows; contours of the landscape flying by at 140 kilometres per hour.

Had Katz fallen in love with Angela Klingberg? Jorma had hinted at it, and that bothered her.

Jealous . . . it's not possible.

The memories had come over her as she sat beside Jorma's hospital bed. The three of them together, that summer. What a terribly destructive life they'd lived, but it was just what they'd wanted – to feel something, because pain meant you were alive. She had truly loved Katz, and had gone a little bit crazy with desire just from being in the same room as him. She'd had three or four lovers before him, older men who took advantage of her, but Katz had felt like the first.

Her thoughts were fluttering about of their own accord. Rickard Julin – what did she actually know about him? Almost nothing. He was former military, according to Danielsson. He'd had a high-ranking position in counterespionage before he changed professions and entered the security industry. And it was the military angle that bothered her.

She turned off the motorway at Katrineholm, and the road became smaller and the forest thicker; she had to slow down.

She had the feeling that something serious had happened to him. Katz had taken Jorma's car and phone when he left the apartment in Midsommarkransen.

If you promise not to tattle to the cops, Eva, there's a tracking function on the phone in case it gets stolen or forgotten somewhere. You just need a code.

The phone had been at the Klingberg family's property in Sörmland for more than a day; according to the satellite

219

signal it was in a forested area a few kilometres from the house.

She had called Klingberg Aluminium and asked for Pontus. All she was told was that he was away on business.

She increased her speed as she tested the thought that Pontus Klingberg was the one behind everything. In order to destroy the life of the man he hated most of all, his own brother, he had started by having his brother's elder son kidnapped and murdered.

He had managed to scare Gustav by sending Caribbean objects to him, and that had delayed the investigation. Gustav had refused to answer questions when he was interrogated, and he had asked his contacts in the police not to prioritize the case.

Nine years later, so that the incident wouldn't seem *too* suspicious, Pontus had murdered Jan and Joanna Klingberg and made it look like suicide.

Gustav had changed his will and made his lost son, Jan, the principal heir, but money wasn't the most important thing – Pontus wanted to avenge his humiliation.

Finally, it had been Joel's turn, and his wife's. The last drop of black blood would be eliminated from the family tree. But first he had seduced her, degrading his nephew by cuckolding him.

The only question was, why had he chosen Katz as the scapegoat?

When he woke up, he was lying at a different angle, leaning back at a fifteen-degree angle. They had taken away one sawhorse and bound his arms under the board. He could touch the floor with his fingers.

An empty beer bottle stood at the end by his feet. If he could get to it, break it somehow . . . but that would require his body to obey him.

He felt the blood rushing to his head, a slight pain at his temples; it was harder to breathe. He felt the electrical tape across his forehead and skull, wound several times around the board. He might as well have been in a vice.

Julin was standing at a sink, filling a plastic bucket with water. He could hear faint sounds from outside: a laughing magpie. The buzz of a generator.

He closed his eyes, and when he opened them again Julin was standing in front of him with a black piece of fabric in his hand. He knew the face, but it had suddenly become so foreign – it belonged to someone he had never really known, despite what he had thought.

It was as if someone had turned out the lights. Sudden darkness. The smell of fabric. The cloth covered his whole face, stretched across his mouth and nose, pulled tight.

Go inside yourself if you can't escape.

He started to gag as soon as the water started to run across the cloth. His whole stomach turned. The muscles of his chest and throat hurt. It felt as if there were water everywhere, water that he was inhaling, as if he were drowning.

He tried to remain calm; he told himself it was an illusion, that his senses were being tricked. *It's just water. It won't kill you.*

He coughed, breathed in and felt his lungs filling with fluid again. More convulsions; he vomited bile.

'I know you were in Capitol's database, Katz; you left footprints behind. And you broke into my home. I want you to tell me what you learned.'

It wasn't true; Julin was just guessing about the hacking – it was impossible to trace.

'And I want to know if you told anything to anyone else. You told your friend Jorma, of course, but he's not a problem any more.'

He was wrong about that, too.

'We assumed he would be there, but not that you would be gone. You were somewhere else. Thus there might be more people who know what you know. I want names.'

More water flowed over the cloth. He tried to breathe as calmly as possible, trying to step inside himself, sink to the bottom of his consciousness . . . but the water was everywhere and his heaves came more and more often; he started to panic, to hyperventilate, and it felt as if his lungs were about to explode.

'Of course, none of this would have needed to happen

if the police had done their job. But now you're here, and I want to know who you've been in contact with.'

I'm going to kill you. I'm going to get out of this for only one reason: to get revenge, to kill you, you fucking bastard.

'Who does the car belong to?'

Have to buy time, he thought, as he roared with pain. He gurgled, felt mucus and blood loosening in his throat and tried to swallow but couldn't.

Then it stopped. He sank down again, into sleep. Soon he would be dead; they wouldn't let him live.

When he woke up again, the room was quiet. Outside the window, it was dusk. He heard a blackbird singing. Julin was sitting in an easy chair on the other side of the room.

'What are we going to do with you, Katz?' he said.

He moved his head a bit; they had removed the tape. The water on the floor had been mopped up.

'You're a dead man, Julin.'

'I'm trembling with fear.'

Julin leaned back in the chair, crossing one leg over the other.

'Where's Joel?' Katz said, as he tried to look around. The beer bottle was still on the floor, a bit closer to his feet now. 'Is he dead?'

'Why?'

'Tell me what all this is about.'

The effects of the drug had faded, he noticed; his thoughts were clearer and the sensation in his body was coming back. The ropes sat more slackly around his feet.

223

Someone had loosened them a bit, or perhaps he had stretched them out as he resisted the waterboarding.

'Money and secrets, Katz. It's nothing personal.'

'Who paid you . . . Pontus Klingberg?'

Julin stood up, walked over to the window, carefully lifted the curtain and peered out.

'What does it matter?'

The cabin was totally silent. Katz wondered where the others were. Had they left, with Julin staying behind to finish the job? He couldn't picture his own death. That was what made up a life – the inability to comprehend its opposite.

'Why did you help me in the first place? You got information for me, about Joel, and later about Angela.'

'I expected you to be caught.'

Julin let the curtain fall again, and then he nodded curtly at Katz and left the room.

Ten minutes went by in which nothing happened. Katz pulled at the rope with his legs and felt it loosen further; he strained his ankle and managed to reach the bottle with his foot. Careful now . . . he needed to tip it in the right direction if it were going to roll towards him. He felt his calf start to cramp as he clenched his toes, stretched them a little farther, made contact and tipped the bottle over. He heard the clatter as it started rolling, lost momentum and stopped on the floor just beside him.

He lay still for a while, listening. Still no sounds. Just the blackbird outside. He got a finger into the neck of the bottle, lifted it, felt the rope straining against his wrists and bashed the bottle against the floor. Just as the neck of the bottle broke off, he coughed very loudly and the body of the bottle rolled into the corner.

The neck of the bottle sat on his right index finger like a thimble. When he turned his head he could see jagged edges sticking up.

Then he heard a sound outside, a shot being fired, and then another that was more muffled. Then silence again.

Two shots. Like an execution, he thought. But who had shot at whom? He listened intently, trying to find some explanation, waiting for someone to yell or for another shot to be fired, but nothing happened.

He started hacking at the rope with the edge of the bottle; he could feel it chewing at the fibres and knew that he had to hurry. He pressed more firmly, swallowing hard when he realized he'd hurt himself. Blood ran from his wrist and made his fingers sticky; he couldn't feel the pain.

Someone had been shooting out there. But who . . . and at whom?

The door opened and the man in the hood came in. He approached Katz with his head turned away. The scent of insect repellant emanated from his skin and clothes. He started to look for something in Katz's jacket.

Blood was still flowing from Katz's wrist; the wound was deeper than he'd thought.

The man didn't notice when the rope came loose. Katz aimed at the shadow within the hood and smiled briefly before he drove the neck of the bottle into the man's face with as much force as he could. There was a soft, rubbery resistance before it penetrated the flesh and stuck there, in the man's cheek, he thought.

The man didn't even react. He just kept searching his jacket until he found the fabric-covered miniature bottle in the lining. His blood dripped on to Katz's chest. A dead man, he thought, a being without life.

Katz couldn't explain it, but the man seemed to be afraid of the object. He put it back in Katz's pocket and got up.

The neck of the bottle was still stuck in his face, but he didn't seem conscious of what had happened. Apparently, he couldn't feel pain. He had to be on some drug; there was no other explanation.

Then someone shouted outside, and the man left the room.

When Katz came to again, the blood on his wrist had congealed. It was night-time. He lay on the floor in front of the easy chair. His legs hardly held him as he stood up.

Out on the road, where the cars had been, was a large pool of blood. The Glock had been tossed on to the gravel next to it. Katz fished it up and put it in his jacket pocket. The tyre tracks on the road . . . they didn't lead to the manor house but in the other direction, through the forest to Vingåker.

He went back to the cabin and searched it, one room at a time. There was no sign of life. No indication that anyone had even been there. It had been cleaned. The furniture was covered with sheets. There was nothing to suggest that Joel Klingberg had been held prisoner there.

It was inconceivable, he thought, as he followed the

gravel path down towards Ormnäs Manor. Why had they tried to murder him at first and then just let him go? And who had been shot? It was as if the person behind it all was a child, playing by his own rules . . . and they might change at any time.

She was standing in a hall with a blackened stone floor and walnut-panelled walls. A ten-armed crystal chandelier hung from the ceiling. On the right was a vaulted staircase that led up to the second floor. At the other end of the room was a ceramic stove with hand-painted tiles depicting nature scenes and sprays of flowers, with a beautiful crown moulding above it.

An oak door stood ajar. Light came from within. The crackling of a fire. She opened the door and stepped into a parlour. Windows faced a terraced garden, which was faintly lit by the moon. An oriental rug covered the floor. Empire-style furniture. Wooden-armed chairs with cushions. Mirror sconces with lit candles in their arms. Like a church, she thought, a temple.

Two stuffed moose heads stared down at her from one of the short walls. Ten metres away, a fire burned in an enormous fireplace. The ornamentation on the mantel was a noble coat of arms.

Pontus Klingberg was sitting in an easy chair before the fire, his feet up on a footstool. He noticed her presence but didn't look in her direction.

'The shield of the Bielke family,' he said, nodding at the ornamentation. 'Dad bought the manor from one of the barons. The man couldn't pay his debts. Gustav built his whole business concept on that very principle: buy cheap, preferably from desperate people. Take advantage of your superior position in the market.'

The light from the flames danced back and forth across the floor. There were paper napkins on the rug. Spotted with blood, she saw.

'Who are you?' he suddenly asked.

'I know Danny Katz.'

'Do you know where he is?'

'I – I thought you knew.'

She felt the stutter coming, noticed it in her head before she had even formulated the words. It hadn't happened for a long time, since before the children were born. Maybe she was afraid. She ought to be, anyway. No one besides Jorma knew she was here. Danielsson could have helped her out with a service weapon, or she could have taken one from the weapons cabinet at EBM. She had the code, and the pistols were used so seldom that no one would have noticed. But she had driven here without thinking.

'If I knew where he was I would kill him. With my bare hands, if I had to.'

He started to cry very quietly.

'He murdered her, that fucking Jew bastard.'

His voice was faint, almost a whisper. His stubble glistened with moisture.

'We would meet here sometimes, when Joel was away. We took risks, but I was so in love I didn't even have a guilty conscience. Their relationship was coming to an end. She wanted kids . . . I could have given them to her.'

He nodded to himself as if to lend weight to the words. He picked up a glass of water from the floor, drank from it and put it back down.

'We were going to tell him; we'd picked a day and everything. Even though we knew the chaos it would unleash. Poor Joel, I can picture his despair. His wife, leaving him for his uncle. But we didn't have time. He disappeared before we could tell him. That psychopath Jew kidnapped him. And murdered him, I suppose. Just like he murdered Angela.'

Pontus Klingberg was deep inside his own mind. He didn't care that she was there, didn't care who she was or what she wanted; he was just talking to himself, trying to put his pain into words.

'She changed her mind when Joel vanished. As if he weren't important until then, when she was worried about him. She didn't want to see me any more . . . she came out to Djursholm one night just to tell me that nothing more would happen between us, and then she contacted Katz, who pretended to want to help her.'

Blood suddenly streamed out of both of his nostrils, dripping on to the front of his shirt. He picked up a tissue and held it over his face as he pinched the bridge of his nose until it stopped bleeding.

'A family curse,' he said. 'The attacks pass as quickly as they begin.'

When he stirred, she took a step backwards on reflex. But he remained seated, staring emptily into the fire.

'1970,' she said. 'You had Kristoffer taken.'

'Are you out of your mind?'

'Joel said something about a man dressed as a drunk who was posted near the site of the abduction. And he said they'd been followed that day.'

'Joel has always had an active imagination.'

He looked at her in confusion, shaking his head quietly.

'Some objects were sent to Gustav in connection with Kristoffer's abduction.'

'That happened all the time. Jan's mother had put a curse on the family . . . part of that is sending that sort of message, to keep the fear alive. You've never been over there; you don't know anything about it, how strong the beliefs in fukú and Vodou can be . . . the things a person can imagine, how self-fulfilling they can be.'

The blood was flowing again; he swore under his breath as he leaned back with the tissue over his face.

'Those dolls that came by mail . . . Marassa, Erzulie Freda and all of those . . . they had nothing to do with Kristoffer's kidnapping, even if Dad was convinced they did. A woman took him. On her own initiative, because she could. Maybe she was a paedophile. We received indications to suggest she was. Jan and I had never been great friends, but that changed after Kristoffer vanished. We hired people to look for him privately. Security experts . . . private investigators . . . military people who wanted to earn some extra money on the side. The police got nowhere, of course – or, more accurately, Dad made sure they didn't get anywhere because he was terrified of Caribbean superstitions. Shortly before my brother died we got news from Holland. That the woman supposedly sold Kristoffer to a ring of paedophiles shortly after his abduction. They abused him . . . and after about a year they had him killed. We received that information in June 1979, nine years after he'd disappeared, and that was the death blow for my brother and his wife. If it was true, there was no hope. A few weeks later, they killed themselves.'

Pontus Klingberg stopped speaking, stared into the fire and pinched himself hard on the arm.

She was wrong, she thought. She had misunderstood everything. And Sandra Dahlström hadn't understood what had happened, either.

'Fifty million kronor was recently transferred from one of Klingberg Aluminium's subsidiaries to an account in the Virgin Islands. Can you tell me what that was about?'

Pontus Klingberg gave her an icy look.

'I don't believe you've identified yourself yet. You're a police officer, I presume?'

There was a sound from the front door. She turned around and saw a person walking across the hallway by the staircase. It was Katz, with a pistol in his hand. A man she hadn't seen since she was a teenager.

What if nothing was as she believed it to be, she thought, as a thousand contradictory thoughts washed through her. What if it *was* him, both times?

She turned to Klingberg. His nose was bleeding again, violently this time.

'Who are you?' he asked again. 'I want to know what this is about.'

But she didn't answer. She had made her choice. She backed out of the room with one thought in her head. Get Katz out of there before he did something they would both regret.

PART 3

She sat down on a bench fifty metres from the playground and watched them through the trees, watched them playing by the trampolines. She found him immediately by the way he moved, as if she were equipped with a particular sort of radar. He was wearing his Blixten McQueen cap. And expensive brand-name trainers Ola had bought. And the denim jacket he'd inherited from Lisa. He was standing apart from the others, holding a teacher by the hand. The small, huddled figure seemed so fragile in the sunlight.

Then he said something and looked up at his teacher. She wondered how it felt to stand with your neck bent so far back, talking to someone who was twice your height.

It was incredible that they'd been a family once upon a time, that she'd loved Ola and couldn't have imagined a life with the children without him.

She looked down at the letter in her lap. It was a militarily short message to say that he had contacted a family lawyer and applied for sole custody of the children.

Full-out war, she thought.

It was the first real week of summer, and the whole city was bursting with green. The parks smelled of lilacs. An atmosphere of excitement.

She thought about calling home to see how Katz was

doing, to listen to his voice and try to say something hopeful.

He was hiding at her house now. It was insane, but what could they do?

The police were still looking for him, but at least the media had started writing about other things. The upcoming European Championship, for example.

Jorma was the only one who knew where Katz was hiding. He had come home from the hospital now, completely recovered.

She herself had called her family doctor and said that she felt burnt out. Generously enough, he had written her a certificate for a week's sick leave.

She wondered if that would be enough to make any progress. After all, they didn't even know where to start.

She would never forget the sight of Katz at the manor. Exhausted and confused by what he'd been through: drugged, bound and tortured. She hadn't seen him in nearly three decades, and yet she would have been able to pick him out of a crowd from a hundred metres away. He was a different person, and yet he was also the same. Without a doubt, he would have tried to hurt Pontus Klingberg if she hadn't managed to get him out of there; Pontus Klingberg, who was innocent . . .

A truck carrying students celebrating their graduation drove by on its way to the city. A bare-chested jogger passed the bench she was sitting on. There were more people in the park now; another nursery group was on its way to the playground.

Two women stood at the ice-cream stand, speaking to

one another in sign language. She had always admired that spatial syntax, the beauty and the drama of the movements, hands as tools for language. But not right now; it only bothered her.

She looked at her phone. Four missed calls from Danielsson – or, rather, they had been rejected with a push of a button. She wondered if her former identity had been revealed at last. But she didn't think so.

The deaf women had each bought an ice cream, and they sat down on a park bench.

She looked over at the playground again, at Arvid, who had started playing with the other children. Her little boy.

She gave a start as a man approached the playground from the opposite direction. He was wearing a jacket with the hood pulled up. He walked purposefully towards the kids, holding something in his hand.

Another man came from the other direction, by the sandpits. He was wearing a brown leather jacket, with a cap and black gloves. He turned so he was walking diagonally up to the bouncy house.

Her heart beat violently. Yet she remained seated, as if she were frozen.

The sunlight seemed to curdle in the air. A few pigeons picked at the ground two metres from her feet.

The man in the hooded jacket was walking faster now; he was only thirty metres from the children. Arvid was talking to his teacher again, laughing at what she said, taking something from his trouser pocket to show her.

She looked in the other direction. The other man was no longer visible; he had vanished behind a storage building. The pigeons took off and flew away as she moved her head suddenly.

The man was ten metres from Arvid.

She felt like she was going to die. She watched him lift his hand and bellow something that made the children jump. Then she realized what he was holding – a dog's leash. And then she saw the runaway Border collie running off between the trees. He started jogging after it, past the nursery children, off through the park, where the man in the leather coat had shown up again, on his way to a café.

She stood up and walked back to the car, aware of how her hand shook as she put the key in the ignition. She fished her phone out of her purse. She dialled her home number and let it ring four times before she hung up and called again – the code they'd agreed on. But Katz didn't answer.

For some reason she pictured Sandra Dahlström's face before her. The photograph of the boy on the bookshelf. The portrait of the woman on the bedside table. The strange sense of déjà vu she'd had when she visited the woman.

The lawyer's office was on Narvavägen, not far from Karlaplan. A receptionist was sitting behind a marble desk, talking on the phone via a headset, when she came through the door.

'Do you have an appointment with someone?' the receptionist asked.

'Ola Westin.'

'And your name is?'

'Eva Westin.'

Tinted picture windows looked out on to the street. Behind the reception desk was a glass wall that looked into the office landscape. Ola was inside, leaning over a pushchair. Erika was visiting. He looked at the clock, said something to her and disappeared towards a door.

A few minutes later she was shown into his office.

'What are you doing here?' he asked.

'We have to talk.'

'About what? You don't care about anything. Lisa has tried to call every night and you won't even answer your mobile.'

'I'm sorry about that.'

She looked at his hand, which was resting on the desk. The Breitling watch with its thick steel links, the pale hairs on the back of his hand; she had the absurd thought that this very hand had cupped her breasts and slid along her thighs late at night when the kids had gone to bed. Or had stroked her cheek when she was tired or sad.

'It's not the first time,' he said. 'And nothing happens to fix it. You just act like an addict . . . and don't blame your upbringing and your parents. Everyone has to take responsibility for their own life.'

'Once a junkie, always a junkie, is that what you think?'

'No. I just want our kids to be happy.'

She turned her head and discovered that Erika was on the other side of the glass wall. She had taken the baby out of the pushchair and was rocking it in her arms. She glanced nervously in their direction.

'And the kids have started talking about that one time again, about what happened at Easter. Lisa is a big girl now. I've started dropping her off at the bus stop outside the school, and she's allowed to walk the last hundred metres by herself. She understands everything that goes on around her.'

She didn't like the idea that he let her little girl walk by herself. But she didn't say so.

'I thought they were sleeping,' she said instead.

'But they weren't.'

That casual hook-up. She didn't even remember his name – he was just a man she'd met out one evening when the kids were at Ola's, and she'd brought him home with her in her drunkenness. Then he'd shown up again spontaneously one night during Easter week. She couldn't think of a good reason to explain why she'd let him come in. Because she felt like she owed him something?

The children had been sleeping in their room. That was what she had thought, anyway. It had been after 11 p.m.; incredibly enough, he had remembered the entrance code to her building, although he'd only been there once – a one-night stand, she'd thought.

'You got sloshed and fucked some guy until the kids woke up. That's not okay, damn it.'

No, it wasn't. She had offered him some JD, and she'd had some herself . . . too much. Ola was right, she'd lost her good judgement and, God knows how, ended up in bed with him. The image of the kids at the bedroom door. They must have been standing there for a long time before she realized they were there. Her moans had woken them. They had been scared, so they got up.

'And now you're going to punish me for it?' she said.

'No. You need help. With this whole self-destructive thing, which you've had as long as I can remember.'

He had taken a pencil from the desk and was nervously twirling it between his fingers. His nails were neat, manicured. She looked at her own: blunt, short, unfeminine.

'Is the lawyer planning to take it to court?'

'Maybe, I don't know. Listen, all I want is for the kids to be happy. Not least with you. But it's not working. They aren't doing well; Lisa's teacher says she's been having trouble concentrating all spring. No matter how much you love them, because I know you do, you don't seem capable of taking care of them. Maybe you will be eventually . . . I really hope so. But until then, they're going to live with me.'

Erika had put the baby back in the pushchair. She seemed to be contemplating whether she should come into Ola's office and ask if he needed help throwing her out.

'Okay,' she said. 'I'll back off. You can call your family lawyer and say we'll work it out on our own. I'll let the kids go if I can see them twice a week. You can be there if you want; that's okay with me. Then we'll see. I'll try to shape up. I'll go to a psychologist or something. You're right on every count.'

He looked at her searchingly.

'But that's not all, is it?'

She shook her head.

'It's about a woman,' she said. 'Sandra Dahlström. I think you had her as a client once.'

The room's twenty square metres were filled with books and decorations, strangely painted toys, wooden masks, statuettes, children's dolls and figurines made of cloth. An open bottle of rum stood on a serving table. The strong scent of perfume hung in the air.

The man before them noticed their curious glances.

'It's not all from the Caribbean,' he said. 'I started out as an expert on West Africa, but my studies of the slave trade led me to Haiti. Vodou is an incredibly interesting area of research, because it's as much a philosophy of life and a cultural heritage as it is a religion . . . and it's the history of the slave trade expressed in symbols.'

He went over to one of the dolls which was sitting on a small throne on the other side of the room; it was made of rigid plastic and looked like the average child's doll, but it wore the make-up of a grown woman and was dressed in gaudy clothes.

'Erzulie Freda,' he said. 'One of the four hundred deities in the Vodou nation. The prima donna of the spirits. The Caribbean's answer to Venus. She's the goddess of love and a gay icon in the same being. Vodou practitioners who become possessed by her become incredibly flirty, even with members of their own sex. Erzulie Freda loves jewels, French perfumes and expensive champagne. If she doesn't get a shower of perfume at night before I go to bed, she makes a big mess in here. Unless it's pure coincidence that a whole section of folders happened to fall off the shelf during the night, or that the toilet suddenly won't flush. So you'll have to excuse the excessive scent of Calvin Klein perfume.'

Champagne, Katz thought, looking over at the serving table. Joel Klingberg had painted a champagne cork in the commemorative painting of what he'd seen when his brother was abducted. And a perfume bottle.

Jan Hammarberg, lecturer in cultural anthropology and the country's leading expert in the field, had agreed to meet them in his home just outside Uppsala, without asking any questions. Perhaps he had been frightened by the sight of Jorma, his prison tattoos, the bandage around his neck, the look that wouldn't take no for an answer. They were taking a risk by coming here, but they had to find a clue somewhere.

'Is that a voodoo doll?' he asked, nodding at Erzulie Freda.

'That depends on how you define the word. "Vodou" just means to serve the *loa*, or the 401 spirits that are part of the belief system. The dolls represent the spirits. Here's another one of my favourites: Marassa!' Hammarberg had picked up two more dolls from the shelf; they had African features and were identically dressed in pink baby clothes. They were tied together at the waist with a string.

'Marassa is a pair of twins, but they're one and the same *loa*. The problem is that she has to have two of every offering. And because Marassa is a child, she prefers sweet things:

sweets, fruit, pastries and ice cream. If you happen to become possessed by her, you yourself start acting like a child – begging for presents and complaining that you don't get enough sweets or that you don't get to be the boss of everyone and everything. She can be a bit trying, this little cutie.'

He smiled a stiff, academic smile and looked at them searchingly. Katz wondered if he recognized him. He didn't think so; the photographs that had been published in the papers were old and he didn't look the same these days. He'd also allowed his beard and his hair to grow out.

'Oh, goodness, I'm standing here giving a lecture as if you were two of my students. I understand you had some specific questions?'

Katz handed the first embroidered cloth to Hammarberg.

'A ceremonial flag,' he said, after studying it closely. '*Drapo sèvis.* Most Vodou societies own a few. They're used during certain rituals, and when one is invoking the gods. The swordmaster is in charge of them. They're arranged in pairs, or triads, just like in military parades.'

'What do the letters mean . . . MK? And the kneeling man?'

'This is the flag of Maître Carrefour. Or Met Kalfou, as he's called in Creole. The master of the crossroads. He belongs to the *petro* spirits, the hot spirits. You might know him from American blues. The devil at the crossroads. One can invoke him to cause injury or to kill an enemy. Every *loa* has its own flag. And Met Kalfou's flag depicts a man kneeling before two crossed arrows, or a fork in the road.'

Katz handed him the other piece of cloth.

'Legba!' said Hammarberg. 'The first spirit invoked in any ceremony. He opens the passage for all the other spirits. He's usually depicted like this, as St Rochus, tortured by boils that are being licked by dogs . . . not unlike the condition the slaves found themselves in when they reached the coast of Hispaniola. And the colours . . . red and black . . . it's a Bizango flag.'

The man carefully folded the pieces of cloth and handed them back to Katz.

'Bizango?' he said.

'Vodou of the night. The Bizango society's secret Vodou goes hand in hand with Haiti's violent history. Pride in being the first black nation to win its independence from a colonial power. The society was formed in the eighteenth century during the great slave uprisings. Runaway slaves – maroons – waged guerilla warfare against the French along with the few Taino Indians who had survived the ravages and diseases of the Europeans. But they had a severe shortage of weapons, so the spiritual battle was at least as important. They got power from the Vodou, from the Indians' cool healing spirits, and from the dangerous *petro* spirits from Africa, and they used the magic in their warfare.'

Hammarberg grew silent and walked over to his gigantic bookcase, where he retrieved a thick volume from the shelves and showed them a page of it. Pictures of people-sized dolls. All of them made of red-and-black cloth. They looked grotesque, with open wounds and fabric intestines hanging out. Some were in chains; others had crutches. Some had amputated limbs.

'Textile sculptures from a temple in the Artibonite district. They bear witness to the military history of the movement. They're mutilated because they were once slaves.'

He turned the pages to another part of the book.

'A Bizango captain with rank insignia and a bottle of rum in his hand. A Bizango grandmother with enormous, sagging breasts. The general of the three swamps. And here's a Bizango executioner.'

A cloth figure with a black hood was holding a sharp machete out towards the photographer.

'When the usual social institutions didn't come through, the Bizango functioned as a court. They could even sentence people to death, but most of the time it ended in a symbolic execution.'

Hammarberg looked at his watch, gave a quick smile and then opened a bottle of rum.

'Time for offerings,' he said self-consciously. 'I have a Petit Papa Bossou Trois Cornes who's angry because I didn't manage to acquire his wife during my last trip to Port-au-Prince. And to be appeased, he needs double servings of rum.'

He went over to a small, horned wooden sculpture that stood on the windowsill, poured a splash of rum on its head and then placed the glass with the rest of its contents on a plate at its feet.

'Do you have any idea what this means?'

Katz had taken the fabric-wrapped souvenir bottle from his jacket pocket. Hammarberg inspected the object with interest.

'A *paké*,' he said at last. 'A sort of talisman. We call this particular kind a Congo *paké*, because they have their origins in Congo. They're carried under the shirt, directly against the skin as protection against *ounga-mort*, or bewitchment. I like to compare them to batteries, magical batteries with concentrated power. Where did you get it?'

'A friend.'

'Are you interested in selling it? I'll pay handsomely. No? I understand, a strong *paké* is better than life insurance.'

Hammarberg handed the object back with a smile. Then he sat down in an easy chair with his hands behind his head.

'You said something about the administration of justice earlier,' said Katz. 'Something about symbolically sentencing people to death.'

'Yes. N'zambi. To turn the convicted person into a zombie. I don't usually talk about that side of Vodou, because it results in a lot of misunderstandings.'

Hammarberg looked at them seriously.

'In popular belief, a zombie is a body without a soul, a dead body endowed with mechanical life by way of bewitching. The conjurer steals a recently buried body before it has had time to rot, gives the dead person new life, shows it how to move and work, enslaves it and forces it into hard labour. It's said that the night shift on the sugarcane plantations used to be made up of zombies. They could work twelve hours at a time, seven days a week, without eating or drinking. In Haiti, people often guard graves until it's absolutely certain that the corpse has begun to rot. But if you're unlucky, the conjurer will get there first.'

'Bewitched by some sort of autosuggestion, you mean?'

'It's a complex issue. It might be a state of mental illness that is interpreted as a display of magic, or be about social shunning of someone who has violated the collective or the community. A sort of ritual punishment or – how should I put it? – vicarious suicide. There are rumours about medicinal herbs that can chemically lobotomize a person. And it does take a certain amount of suggestion or autosuggestion . . . or witchcraft, if you choose to believe in it.'

Hammarberg bent down and pulled on a pair of jogging shoes.

'Please excuse me, gentlemen,' he said, 'but I think I've given you as much information as I can. I have to go out and get some exercise before my lectures begin.'

They took the scenic route back to Stockholm; Jorma drove and Katz sat in the back seat, to be safe. He thought of Hammarberg's bizarre claims about people in suspended animation, but he put these thoughts aside for the time being because he didn't know what he should think.

He felt a chill inside; he'd become so closed off.

Someone was toying with him, and that was why there was no logic to what had happened. Julin had wanted to kill him in the hunting cabin, but something had prevented him. Shots had been fired and, shortly afterwards, the building had been emptied. Someone had set him free so that his nightmare could continue. The pistol had been left on the gravel outside the house. They wanted him to feel hunted. Or had they hoped that he would shoot Pontus Klingberg in the manor house, so that he would be accused of yet another murder? But Eva had got him out of there in time.

Eva. He wondered if she had got back to the flat by now, and if she had been anxious when he wasn't there. The strange feeling of seeing her again after all these years. It had unleashed an avalanche of memories inside him, the sensation of falling backwards in time to places and events he didn't know if he wanted to revisit. It was the sensation of having met a total stranger who was also a close friend.

Near Vallentuna, Jorma slowed down as they encountered squad cars: two of them, heading north.

Katz sank down, but Jorma smiled at him in the rearview mirror. 'The amulet will protect you,' he said. 'The Congo packet, or whatever it was called.'

'Hammarberg seemed to believe in it.'

'Or else he's playing it safe.'

'Do you think he recognized me?'

'From the papers? No. But he must have wondered who we were.'

They drove through the northern suburbs. Katz wished things could feel the way they used to. He and Jorma, together again. And Eva, waiting for him. As if no time had passed at all. But it wasn't real. They were no longer the same people.

She decided to take the stairs up to the eighth floor. She needed to think, to buy time.

According to Ola, Sandra Dahlström and Linnie Holm had been living together for nearly twenty years when they decided to apply for adoption. The child in question was a seven-year-old boy they'd got to know during a holiday in the Philippines. They had completed all the paperwork at the adoption centre, followed all the rules, arranged things with the authorities in Manila and the institution where the orphaned boy lived, but they were rejected by the social services in Stockholm.

The decision had come as a shock. They were desperate and decided to bring in a lawyer. This was in the mid-2000s. Ola had taken the case:

I did what I could, but they were rejected again because they were considered too old. Sandra Dahlström was over fifty and, in addition, her partner, Linnie Holm, had been diagnosed with an aggressive form of breast cancer that the doctors said would kill her within a few years.

So there was yet another reason for the authorities to throw a spanner in the works for the childless lesbian couple. More bitterness. Both had been convinced they were being discriminated against on the basis of their sexual orientation. People in the Philippines had already said yes, and the boy was just waiting to travel to Sweden. They had begged Ola to appeal the case in a higher court. He had advised against it. They were outraged; they threatened to sue him for breach of faith and sent threatening letters to the solicitors' office.

Eva remembered the case because Ola had been so troubled by it, because there was nothing to their claims that they were discriminated against and because, in the midst of it all, he felt sorry for them.

At the same time, the couple had been there for vulnerable children, and they wanted Ola to use this as an argument when he appealed. She had a faint memory of him telling her about this, saying that, among others, they had taken in a deaf boy because Linnie Holm was fluent in sign language.

The boy's name was Jonas Åkesson; he lived with them on and off for a few years.

Jonas . . . the boy in the photograph on Sandra's bookshelf. The guy from the security tapes in the multi-storey car park who had been found dead of an overdose.

The fourth floor. The scent of Middle Eastern food in the stairwell, clattering and shouting from the flats.

Sandra had got her to suspect Pontus Klingberg, and maybe she'd done that on purpose. Her thoughts whirled as she moved on, almost running now. The person who had killed Angela Klingberg wasn't trying to imitate Katz, or what he thought Katz had done. It was no copycat case. Because it was the same person: the same perpetrator as on Grubbholmen.

She wanted to tell Katz, but he didn't answer when she called the number to Torsgatan.

The same person both times. The biting madman.

*

253

The door was unlocked. Eva saw Sandra Dahlström through the hall. She was sitting on the glassed-in balcony in front of the same game of solitaire as last time. She raised her eyes as she discovered Eva there, and pulled on her cardigan, which was hanging over the back of her chair. There was a lit candle in front of the picture of the boy.

Eva walked up to her, took her left arm and rolled up the sleeve. Old scars, from bites, several dozen of them. Ugly edges. Others looked better – scars from actual operations.

The woman looked down at her arm as if she didn't really understand that it was her own.

'There are more,' she said quietly, 'on my stomach and my breasts, worse than the ones on my arms. Once, he almost bit off my nose. He bit so hard that the cartilage snapped and the tip of my nose came off. They were barely able to save it. Gustav paid for the plastic surgery.'

The tiny neat scars under the wings of her nose were hardly visible in the bright sunlight.

'Who knew about it?'

'Only Gustav, and he did everything he could to keep it quiet.'

'Not Pontus?'

'No.'

'What about the police . . . didn't you ever report him?'

'Gustav gave me plenty to make up for it. Like an allowance, almost, up until he died. After all, I was the only one who could manage him when he had his rages; no one else could handle it. I know it sounds sick, but I really loved him . . . he was just a little boy.'

She was in mourning, Eva thought; she was taking anti-anxiety medication, but she didn't know that the deaf boy's death had any connection to this.

Joel had had the boy killed because he saw the person who parked Joel's car in the garage – whether it was Joel himself, or someone else.

Shortly before this, he had murdered Angela out of jealousy. He must have learned about the affair she was having with his uncle, and that had set him off. He was a person driven by getting sick revenge. He had hired Julin, transferred money to an account in the Virgin Islands so that Julin would take part in a conspiracy to frame Katz. That is, the person who was convicted for Joel's first attack, on Grubbholmen. But, first, he had faked his own disappearance.

She didn't know exactly how, but it made sense. Joel Klingberg must have been on board the boat that night. He'd managed to hide when Jorma and Katz broke in, but then he followed them, decided to get revenge, to hurt one of them, and had struck when he found her and Katz in the bike room, knocked out on heroin.

'You've continued to see Joel, haven't you? And he's met Jonas, too?'

'Yes . . . he couldn't seem to let me go. I left my job, but he kept visiting me. I know it's difficult to understand, but I watched Joel grow up, and he had become like family to me.'

She grew quiet, as if something had come into her head.

'When was the last time you saw him?'

'A few years ago. When Jonas lived here. Linnie was still alive. But I asked him to leave. Jonas was afraid of him.'

She stood up and gathered her playing cards.

'And Rickard Julin? What did he have to do with it all?'

Sandra looked at her in surprise. 'Why?'

'Just tell me!'

Warning bells were ringing inside her, but she ignored them. She looked up at the milky eye of the camera lens, waiting for someone to let her in.

She had called the office and asked for Pontus Kling-berg. A younger man had said he was working from home this week. Unfortunately, he couldn't give out the phone number.

She rang the bell again. Felt the button vibrate against her fingertip. Looked up at the camera, which was at the very top of the wall outside the house in Djursholm. She felt exposed to the gaze of an invisible person.

Pontus Klingberg didn't know that his nephew had murdered Angela, and that Julin had helped him. He didn't even know what had happened in the hunting cabin at Ormnäs Manor. If it was a case of revenge, he might reasonably be next in line. She had to warn him.

She had tried to call Katz again, but with no luck. She'd left a message on the answering machine to say that she was coming here. Why hadn't he answered? If the police had found him, she ought to have known by now; Dan-ielsson would have called.

She heard the dull buzz of an electric lock and a click as a bolt lifted in the metal gates and they folded back like the wings of a mechanical butterfly.

She walked up the gravel apron to the house. She'd never seen anything like it. At least thirty rooms. Views of the water from two verandas. A 25-metre pool on the lawn behind the house. Two tennis courts beyond that. A private beach with a pavilion on a dock. A boathouse as big as an average home.

The gate slid shut behind her. She went up the stairs to the door, which had been left open.

Once inside the house, she called out, but didn't receive an answer. The curtains in the foyer were drawn closed. She opened a pair of French doors and found herself in the largest private dining room she'd ever seen. A table with room for thirty guests. A marble floor. Expensive art. One Carl Larsson painting covered almost an entire wall.

She called out again, but no one revealed himself.

She went on through various lounges until she got to a smaller parlour. She thought of what Sandra Dahlström had said about Julin, but she didn't know how it was connected. In the mid-seventies, as a young officer in counter-intelligence, he had been contracted to try to find out what had happened to Kristoffer. Pontus Klingberg had mentioned that he and his brother Jan had contacted people in the military to try to get help. So Julin was one of them, maybe even the one who had brought the terrible news from Holland.

She was back in the foyer again, having gone through the entire first floor without seeing anyone. She smelled a strange odour; it was sweet and sickly at the same time, but she couldn't work out where it was coming from. She

THE BOY IN THE SHADOWS

thought Pontus must be in the house somewhere; after all, the gate had opened.

She went up the stairs to the second floor, starting to sweat even though the house was air-conditioned. The odour was stronger now; it smelled like something was rotting, something old and putrid. More art on the walls; she was in the modern section. She recognized the grotesque style of one of the paintings – an Englishman, what was his name? . . . Francis Bacon?

She called out again, but there was no answer. Could he be in one of the other buildings on the property?

She had to warn him. And work things out. Pontus Klingberg was the one who could give her answers. So, Julin had become friends with him. Started spending time with the family. And, according to Sandra Dahlström, he had started to take an interest in Joel. This was before Joel had been sent to Sigtuna. He had gone to a private school in Danдеryd back then and was extremely gifted. Julin was fascinated by his intelligence . . . and, according to Sandra, by his attacks of rage.

Was Julin the one who had seen to it that he eventually ended up at the interpreter academy along with Katz?

Had he run some sort of programme, with what he thought were psychopaths who were gifted at languages?

It was speculation, but maybe Pontus Klingberg knew.

She gave a start when she heard steps nearby. She stood still, but couldn't hear anything more.

Again according to Sandra Dahlström, Julin had also become interested in everything to do with Vodou. In the curse Marie Bennoit was alleged to have placed on the family. He had come along on several of the family's trips to the Dominican Republic; he'd visited Gustav's sugar-cane plantation.

She entered a room containing Caribbean antiques. Wooden masks and statues. Two machetes in a cross on the wall. Paintings depicting black people working in a field of sugar cane. It was racist, but it was hard to put your finger on just why. A slave-trade feeling. Gustav's old office, she realized.

She went on through a corridor which had a suite of rooms that faced the water. She felt her heart beating as if it wanted to pound its way out of her chest. The sickly smell was stronger. She opened one of the doors to a bedroom and peered in. She absorbed what she didn't want to see . . . a scene that looked staged. Pontus Klingberg's body, sitting with its back against the wall. The swollen male body that lay with its head in Pontus's lap had gunshot wounds on the forehead. Pontus Klingberg's fingers had been laced with Julin's, as if they were praying together. She saw Klingberg's eyes bulging out like someone with a goitre, and his tongue, which had been pulled out of his mouth, was grotesquely long because the bone had been broken as he was strangled. The bites around his neck, like jewellery made of wounds.

There was an entrance into Eva's flat from the rear court-yard. They used it to be on the safe side. Katz called out for her, but there was no answer.

The flat looked as he had left it that morning. Messy, and somehow makeshift. Furniture that didn't really match, a home she didn't really care about, as if she were only a temporary guest in her own life.

He opened the refrigerator and took out two light beers, handed one to Jorma and sat down with the other on the living-room sofa. There was an empty bottle of Jack Daniel's on the table. She drank too much. Other than that, he didn't know very much about her, except that she had been married, had two kids and was fighting with her ex about custody. And she had lived alone for the past few years. She had told him things, starting to stutter at one point – just like when they were young – about casual love affairs, men who came and went, how she kept them at a distance, uninterested in more serious relationships.

What would their lives have been like if the incident on Grubbholmen had never happened? Maybe better, but probably worse. At least the incident had got her on a different track; she'd stopped taking drugs and taken control of her life. If they had stayed together, the downward slope would have become steeper; they would have gone downhill faster and faster, until they crashed at the bottom.

'Where is she?' said Jorma.

'I don't know. She had plans to visit her son at the nursery.'

Jorma had emptied the beer; he looked around as if for a piano to play, and was disappointed when he didn't see one.

It struck Katz that he was longing to see Eva step through the door with her sad smile, and he was surprised at how strong the feeling was.

'I think I'll go out to Kransen,' said Jorma. 'The doctor wants me to take it easy.'

'And the police . . . don't they want more information?'

'I've been called in for questioning by the criminal police next week. The county police's expert on gang-related crime wants to have a chat with me. I'll have to see which story I tell.'

Katz nodded and took a drink of his beer.

'We have to find the people who are behind all this.'

'I know. But not tonight.'

The answering machine was blinking amidst the mess on the table. Her children might have called and left a message. He shouldn't be there, in her life. There was no reason for her to be dragged deeper into what was going on.

'Do you think Emir's apartment is still safe?' he asked.

'It'd be better for you to stay here . . . in the eye of the storm. Don't you trust her?'

'Yeah, I do.'

Jorma nodded at the answering machine.

'I think you should listen to that,' he said. 'She must have been worried if she called here and you didn't answer.'

She had backed out of the room and was standing in the hall again. She listened for steps, but didn't hear any. There was opera music coming from the first floor. He was somewhere in the house: Joel Klingberg.

Her hand was shaking so hard she could hardly use it to get her phone out of her purse. Dead. How could that be? She never forgot to charge it. She looked around for some sort of weapon, but didn't see anything. The opera music was louder now, and it was coming from the second floor, too, from remote-controlled speakers.

She kept going down the hall, turned a corner and stood before a glass door. There was a sun porch on the other side. But it was eight metres down to the ground from it, and she would break her legs if she jumped.

Her heart was beating more calmly now. Gustav's office, she thought: there had been knives hanging there, machetes from the Dominican Republic.

The corridor felt endlessly long as she retraced her steps. All the doors were closed, except for the one to the room the bodies were in.

She didn't want to look in, but her eyes had a will of their own. Pontus Klingberg's head had fallen forward, as if he were about to kiss the man who lay in his lap.

The opera music stopped, but only for a few seconds, until the next movement began – an aria sung by a tenor.

How the hell could she have been so fucking stupid as to come out here alone?

She had come to Gustav's office. The room lay half in shadow and it took a few seconds for her eyes to adjust. She took the heavy knife from the wall, weighed it in her hand – it was as much an axe as it was a weapon for stabbing. Then she froze, an icy feeling in her body. One knife. There had been two the first time she walked past the room . . .

She slowly turned 180 degrees and looked into a strange mirror with a baroque frame, adorned with a skull at the very top. Voodoo crap . . . the old man had really believed in such things.

She noticed a movement in the mirror, behind her, but when she turned around there was no one there.

Fear – this was how it manifested itself.

There was a telephone on the desk. Her fingers felt like clay as she lifted it. Silence. He had cut the line dead.

She went over to the window. This one was just as high up; she had to get out some other way.

She kept going, to the top of the stairs. The elegant turn of the marble, the sleek cast-iron banister, the imitation-rococo form. The opera music suddenly sounded louder; it was coming from the first floor now, but she couldn't see anyone there. Her legs started to shake, and the tremors spread up her whole body until she lost all her strength and sank down on to the top step.

The music stopped. She realized she was crying. She didn't know how long she had been sitting there, before the image of Lisa and Arvid forced her to get up again and walk cautiously to the first floor.

She stopped in the hall past the stairs. She jumped when she heard the sound of the electric motor that opened the curtains in the dining room. Cascades of sunshine were flung in. The terrace doors were closed and locked. She could see the water down there, and the islands of the inner archipelago. Somehow, she knew that the first floor was burglar-proof, that the glass in the windows was unbreakable.

The curtains closed again, like a theatre curtain.

The door that led to the foyer was wide open. She saw the front door she had entered through, the one that led out to the courtyard and the drive, but there were dark recesses on either side of it.

She held the machete up over her right shoulder as she approached. Her lower body was shaking; it felt as if she weren't getting enough air.

The recesses were empty. She placed her hand on the heavy bronze handle of the door, pulled it down and let go again. The upper security lock was engaged.

She knew she was going to die, that he was standing right behind her, weapon in hand. She slowly turned around so that she would at least see his face. But it was her imagination again. There was no one there. She went back towards the inner parts of the house. There must be an exit somewhere, she thought; he was playing with her.

They drove through Solna, past Järva Krog and Berg-shamra.

They went over the bridge to Stocksund, and took a right on Vendevägen. The wealthy neighbourhood came up suddenly, as if they had travelled into another dimension at the speed of light. Gigantic mansions with gardens as large as parks. Luxury cars in the drives. They kept going until they arrived in Djursholm.

The Palme family's old neighbourhood, built in competition with the Wallenbergs' Saltsjöbaden. The streets ended in culs-de-sac. The waterfront properties were at a comfortable distance from one another. An archipelago feel. You could see the yachts on Stora Värtan.

They parked the car in a public car park and started walking purposefully so as not to arouse any suspicions. The area was guarded by private security companies.

They walked by the wall outside Klingberg's home, ignored the cameras and walked down towards the water. Katz had tried to call Eva, but she hadn't answered. It went straight to voicemail. He couldn't explain it, but he knew something was wrong.

The street ended at the water. An inlet curved into the property.

Katz didn't think as he climbed down from the dock

and waded over to a stony beach. He heard Jorma swearing just behind him.

Thick bushes grew along the closest part of the shoreline. Twenty metres away, a cement block with barbed wire on top stuck out of the water. Katz took the Glock out of his pocket and held it above water as he swam around. Jorma followed him.

By now they were on the property. The house was a hundred metres up the hillside. When they reached the front lawn, they split up.

Katz walked towards the nearest terrace; Jorma went in the other direction.

The feeling that Eva was in danger was so strong that it settled in Katz's body, like aching muscles. Katz turned towards a more wooded part of the property, continuing on past the tennis courts and a six-car garage and turning up in the direction of the house again.

Remote-controlled curtains were closing and opening behind a pane of glass. He heard music, opera, someone turning the volume up and down.

He took a short cut across the garden. Out of the corner of his eye, he saw Jorma approaching from the other direction, as if he'd read his mind.

He ran the last few metres over to the entrance. He felt the door handle. Locked. A camera moved back and forth three metres up on the façade. Apparently, it was motion-activated. The camera's aperture adjusted, and it zoomed in on him.

'It's locked on the other side, too,' said Jorma.

The opera music vacillated between loud and soft

inside, like a parody of Morse code – a tenor singing at an insane volume and then fading away again, rising and falling, rising and falling. Pontus Klingberg, Katz thought – was he behind everything, after all?

He looked up at the façade. A downpipe ran from the roof straight down to where he was standing. There was a trellis of climbing roses attached to the wall next to the second-floor terrace, seven metres up.

Katz started climbing, but his hands slipped and he slid back to the ground. He took off his shoes and socks and tried again. It was easier this time; his feet had a better grip.

Thirty seconds later he had made it. He felt dizzy when he looked down. He tugged at the trellis to see if it would bear his weight. It seemed to hold.

He hung straight up and down, his legs dangling, and carefully made his way to the left, one hand at a time, climbing like a monkey.

He didn't know how but, suddenly, he was up on the terrace. There were large tears in his jacket, he discovered, and his fingers had thorns stuck in them. Jorma climbed up after him.

The music in the house had stopped. Waves lapped the beach and the dock a hundred metres away.

He put out a hand and helped Jorma over the railing; he could hear him panting with exertion. Katz took the Glock from his pocket. The door was ajar.

They came into a second-floor foyer and followed a hall towards the interior parts of the house. The smell of decay, a nauseating odour of rotten meat. Katz shouted Eva's name, but there was no answer. He looked to the right, where a door stood open. There were two bodies on the floor. Julin's and Pontus Klingberg's.

He pushed aside his disgust and started running. He shouted her name again and heard it fall to the floor like a brittle object.

The hall ended in a staircase. As he walked down, his pistol aimed ahead of him, he realized that Pontus Klingberg and Julin had been murdered by a person who was still in the house.

The opera music had begun again, but this time it was at normal volume.

They passed a dining room and came to a servants' passage, following the sound of the music to an alcove in a lounge. A CD player was built into the wall; Katz turned it off. The silence sounded somehow like an explosion in reverse.

'I'll check the other way,' said Jorma. 'There has to be another exit.'

Katz nodded and went on, into the next room. He gave a start when he saw her. She was crouched next to a radiator, with a large knife in her hands.

'Are you okay?'

She didn't answer; her head was buried in her knees. She tried to say something when he touched her, but all she could do was stutter; all that came out was a pile of consonants.

He heard Jorma call to him from the other side of the house.

He tried to say something comforting to her, to tell her that she was out of danger, that they had got there in time; he felt a sharp stab of pain, as if she were his child and he hadn't been able to protect her when she needed it most. Then he helped her to her feet, took her by the arm, supporting her as they walked towards Jorma's voice.

Jorma was waiting for them at a door just inside the back entrance to the house. A spiral staircase led down to what appeared to be a cellar.

'He went this way . . . I heard sounds.'

Lamps shaped like torches were set into recesses in the walls. They walked down cautiously, with Katz in the lead.

The stairs ended ten metres below ground. The remote control to the CD player lay on the last step. Right next to it was a machete.

This was no cellar. Instead, it was some sort of underground passage. It probably led to the garage – a warm, dry short cut when it was snowing or pouring rain. They heard the sound of footsteps at a distance; the sound of someone jogging or walking very quickly.

They kept going, keeping close to the wall. Eva walked on her own, no longer needing support. There were dim spotlights on the ceiling. Katz suddenly remembered that he was barefoot.

The tunnel bent away in a curve and, after thirty metres, it split in two. They could no longer hear the footsteps. They stood there for a few seconds, at a loss, discussing what to do.

'I think this way leads to the garage,' said Jorma, 'but he didn't go there. He kept going straight ahead.'

There was another sound from the other direction, a sucking, electrical noise as something was set in motion.

They moved on, towards the source of the noise, until the tunnel ended.

They were in the boathouse, or rather in some sort of anteroom one storey below ground. A lift went straight up to the quay berth. Through a thick pane of glass they could see the water, as if they were looking at an aquarium.

Katz ran up the stairs beside the lift. He heard the roar of an accelerating motor. Through a sheet of Plexiglas, he watched a covered boat glide past the stone pier and disappear into the bay.

There was a bloody jacket on a bench on the edge of the quay: Julin's. This was where his corpse had been unloaded and then carried through the underground passage up to the house.

Her phone was ringing somewhere in the living room. Katz woke up just as the last ring died away. He looked at her, lying there next to him, naked, one hand entangled in her hair. It took a microsecond for him to remember why she was there. They had slept together. Because it was unavoidable, and even though both of them knew that it would get complicated. There was always the risk that one would push the wrong buttons.

He let her stay in bed, sleeping; he went into the hall and picked up the morning paper from the letter box. He went to the kitchen and browsed through the headlines in the news section.

There was nothing about a double murder in Djursholm. So the bodies were still there, thirty-six hours after they'd left. It didn't matter that they'd deleted the files from the security cameras. It was only a matter of time before the bodies would be found and suspicion would be hurled at him once again.

He opened the refrigerator and peered into the empty space. A jar of Dijon mustard. Cheese that had seen better days. The only thing that differentiated this fridge from his own was the nail polish in the top rack on the door.

He went back to the bedroom and stood in the doorway. From the twitching of her face he could tell that she

273

was dreaming. About her kids, maybe. She missed them, and the intensity of her yearning was something he would never be able to understand.

The blanket was about to slide down to the floor; he picked it up, tucked her back in and went out to the living room.

He sat down in front of the computer on her desk and checked his emails. Trotsky's new program had arrived. Apparently, he'd worked on it during the night, writing code and debugging. Now it was ready, an exploit kit designed to make its way into encrypted servers. Trotsky was a genius. He didn't even want to be paid; he did it for the challenge.

Angela had been murdered by Joel Klingberg, Katz thought as he linked the computer to the hacked server chain that went via Montreal, Tel Aviv and Warsaw. Out of jealousy, because she had had an affair with his uncle. After that he had shot Julin outside the hunting cabin in Sörmland and brought the corpse to the house in Djursholm, where he murdered his uncle to get revenge.

But why Julin? Had they ended up in a dispute over something, or had Klingberg wanted him out of the way to be on the safe side? Or was there a completely different reason?

At least he knew where he would start looking.

It took him less than an hour to find a way in through Project Prio, the armed forces' new IT system. The program was built on solutions from the German systems supplier SAP, and it had authorization issues. The operating system was from Sun Microsystems. Viraltech, a large British anti-virus company, had created the shield against malicious code. From what Katz had heard, there were security holes that hadn't been patched.

He'd got authorization via a logged-in computer at the Material Administration. Trotsky's program had no problem hijacking the computer. He clicked his way on, typing in commands, moving quickly through the flow.

He found an internal search engine and typed in Julin's name. He was allowed through, to the Defence Recruiting Authority. He typed the name into another search box and found Julin's wartime posting in the register. On Lovön, he saw, with FRA, the National Defence Radio Establishment. No details about the post, not even his rank. But there was a strange addendum: Legba. Like that Vodou spirit Hammarberg had mentioned.

Katz went back to the database and found another search path. Like a digital ghost, he thought, a phantom that could go through walls, thanks to Trotsky. He typed in 'Legba' and got a hit at a department within MUST, the Military Intelligence and Security Service. Project Legba. Classified information. His search ended in a dead end.

He descended deeper and deeper into the flow of information, interpreting what he saw, executing more commands, letting the exploit program do his work for him. It was like a sort of dance, or acrobatics, and he made decisions based on intuition.

He found another hole, a computer that had just logged in from FRA. With full permission, he realized, but still he hesitated.

It's a honeytrap . . . someone's trying to make it easy for me . . . putting it out there in the system to see if it will be attacked.

He was still hesitant, but he didn't want to abort the hack. He was being paranoid. He ought to take the chance.

Her phone rang again; it was on the desk next to the computer. He looked at the screen: it was Ola, her ex. He didn't want to wake her, didn't want to know any more about her problems with her former husband. He grunted in irritation and set the phone to silent.

There was no activity on the logged-in computer; it was just there, free for the taking. *Too easy*, he thought, moving his search to another part of the system.

All at once, things became more interesting. There was a large cluster of password-protected files. It was MUST's database at Gärdet. He didn't know how he'd suddenly ended up there.

He could see traces of old botnets, hackers, or maybe another defence establishment that had tried to infect the database with malicious code. Unless it was a simulation the techs had done. The shadow of a zombie network. He shuddered at the thought of the word and let Trotsky's new program look for a hole.

Then he found it and was in. The files were encrypted, but there was an open register. He typed in both 'Legba' and 'Julin' and got hits in about ten files that were linked to SSI, the Section for Special Collection, which was the predecessor of KSI, the Office for Special Collection, a secret intelligence bureau within the armed forces.

Project Legba. He copied them to the computer.

There were strange traffic flows in the server; he knew

it was a sign of anxiety. He was more or less certain that the open FRA computer had been a honeytrap. One or more sysops were on his trail; they'd found the logs in the firewall and were trying to trace where he'd come from and how he'd got in. There were more techs out there; he'd set off major alarms.

He felt a cold sweat running down his spine, as if the ghosts in the server were real, as if they might climb out of the computer screen at any moment. He transferred the last few files, heard the whir of the CPU fan, the sound of Eva mumbling something in her sleep and the buzzing of the mobile phone he'd put on silent, someone calling again and again. A person walking in the stairwell; Katz felt panicked, imagining things: that they'd already found him, that they were faster than he was, with resources he hadn't counted on.

He dragged the last encrypted file to the hard drive and shut down the computer. He listened for sounds from the stairwell. *Just my imagination*, he thought.

Project Legba had been initiated by Julin in the late seventies, as part of the armed forces' effort to modernize the intelligence agency. But Julin hadn't worked alone. Superiors had helped and supported him.

Katz didn't understand it all yet, how all the threads were connected, because he had only been able to restore parts of the files. He would need help with them later; maybe Trotsky could create a better decryption program for him.

The documents mentioned a certain 'L' or 'Lynx' at

SSI, a separate entity that was loosely connected to MUST. Was Lynx Julin's boss? Katz had learned what little he knew about SSI from his time at the Ministry for Foreign Affairs. The employees, all of whom worked under aliases, dealt with human intelligence, infiltrating foreign spy organizations and doing security analyses on behalf of the defence staff. Project Legba had been partially financed with funds from SSI.

G was another initial that popped up in several places. A person from the business world, who, as far as Katz could tell, had supported Julin with money and contacts. Gustav Klingberg? Was it that simple?

What had the project dealt with? An experiment in which they tried to develop better methods of forcing information out of POWs in a war zone? The documents were sketchy, as if they had been hesitant to include too much information out of security concerns. Some of the text consisted only of code words that he would need an encryption key to interpret.

They had carried out clinical trials with psychoactive and hallucinogenic drugs. The interpreter academy had somehow been involved in the programme.

He saw his own name in one of the documents. He had belonged to 'Unit B'. A small group of recruits who had, without their knowledge, been selected as 'special interrogators'. Joel Klingberg was another member, and there were two more from the class ahead of theirs. All of them had been diagnosed as psychopaths by a military psychologist, and they had been classified as extremely gifted with languages. Unit B had never been activated.

What had they been planning to do with them? Seeing what they were capable of under the influence of specially prepared drugs? Creating totally callous torturers and murderers?

Julin and Lynx had been in contact with the interpreter academy for several years. Katz was starting to see how it was all connected: Julin had made sure that he was selected to serve in the Ministry for Foreign Affairs and that he eventually ended up in St Petersburg so he could be placed in any conflict situation that might come up. But there had never been such a situation. Instead, the Soviet empire had collapsed like a house of cards. Julin had made sure to keep him within the armed forces like some sort of sleeper cell, without Katz knowing it.

Experiments had been done on coastal commandos. The recruits had been required to sign documents stating that they would never leak the details of what they'd experienced to outsiders. Fragments of a document were attached. The experiment had taken place under the supervision of a small team of military psychologists. A few doctors had also been present: experts in toxicology from the Institute of Tropical Medicine in Berlin, experts on natural drugs, antivenom and antitoxins.

One soldier said that the intoxication made him lose all his will. He became apathetic and only did what others told him to, 'no matter how absurd or dangerous it seemed'.

What had they done? Subjected one another to torture? To interrogations while drugged?

So they had done experiments with a drug, but which drug was it?

He searched on, looking for more pieces of the puzzle. One document mentioned something about 'the amount of tetrodotoxin that was to be modified'. It was a very potent neurotoxin, one of the German toxicologists had added in a report, and there was no known antidote. The name was derived from *Tetraodontiformes*, the order of fish that includes pufferfish, porcupine fish, sunfish and triggerfish. 'May produce a state of apparent death. Cardiac activity cannot be appreciated with a stethoscope, but can of course be measured by EKG.'

Katz remembered a television programme he'd seen about the Pacific fish called fugu that was a delicacy in Japan. Only specially licensed chefs were allowed to clean and prepare it, otherwise there was a risk that the restaurant patrons would die.

More illegible text, until he got to a part about *Datura*, nightshade, and a hallucinogenic substance called bufotenin. 'The test subject hallucinates and becomes very violent,' the doctors had written.

Next came some chemical notations that didn't mean anything to him, and then a list of ingredients for a kind of tincture that was called 'Legba' and contained Caribbean porcupine fish, nightshade, animal fats from a particular kind of toad and 'bone powder from a child's cranium'.

This information had come from sources close to 'G'. Gustav Klingberg, he thought again. He had been familiar with that sort of thing; he believed in Vodou.

More tests and evaluations had been done on select

people. But the results had not been satisfactory. The project had been put on ice.

What had they been looking for? The ingredients for the drug that Vodou sorcerers had used to make people appear dead? The very drug he had been subjected to in the Klingberg family's hunting cabin?

Katz sat in the kitchen and read, vaguely aware of the mobile that kept buzzing out in the living room. The experiments involved trying to change personalities, to make people ignore all the rules, give up all personal morals. He and Klingberg and a few other military interpreters had been part of this project in some way, although he didn't understand how.

And the other man in the hunting cabin, the zombie-like one – the person who didn't seem to feel pain, the person who had tried to kill Jorma . . . was he another result of these experiments?

He went back to the living room and picked up Eva's phone. Eight missed calls from her ex-husband. Plus messages on voicemail and several texts. He brought up the most recent one and felt an icy chill flow through his body.

The seconds it took for him to walk over to the bedroom felt like an eternity.

She was still lying in bed, just about to wake up.

'What is it?' she said sleepily.

'You have to call your ex. Something happened with your daughter.'

She had never felt anything like this before. Animal terror – it ached within her. She couldn't combine her thoughts into a functioning whole; there were only fragments, sketches of thoughts. She felt like she was going to throw up.

She was sitting on the designer sofa in Ola's apartment, listening, but not understanding.

'Start from the beginning,' she said. 'You dropped her off near the school . . .'

He explained again, for which time in a row she didn't know, that he had dropped her off at the bus stop, from the car, at twenty minutes past eight that morning, a hundred metres from the schoolyard gate. She had walked towards the schoolyard, throwing him a kiss before he made a U-turn and drove into the city. Waved until he was out of sight.

Why hadn't she said it the last time she saw him, she thought, that she didn't like it, that Lisa was too little to walk by herself? But she had no say in situations like that; Ola was the organized one, the one who knew what to do and could set limits.

'No one has seen her since – none of her classmates, none of the staff. Ida – you know, her friend – usually waits for her at the door, and she was waiting yesterday, too, up until the bell rang.'

He had aged ten years in only a few hours. He looked ugly, ravaged and vicious.

Erika came into the room, cautiously wondering if they wanted coffee. Ola snapped at her to go away and looked at his hands, which were shaking like an old man's.

'And after that what happened?'

'Anne-Marie, the form teacher, tried to get hold of me during the morning break, but I was in a planning meeting. I got the message just before ten. I called her right away. She sounded normal; she asked if Lisa was sick and if so how long she would be out of school. Because they're going on a field trip tomorrow. To the Tom Tits museum in Södertälje.'

He started to cry, and she was shocked. She'd never seen him cry before, not even during their divorce, not even when his mother had died the fall after they got married.

She had taken the car to Söder as soon as she got the news, driving through the city with tunnel vision, hyperventilating at every red light until she had arrived and sank down on to Ola's sofa because her legs wouldn't hold her any more. Now she looked around as if that could alleviate her panic. Furniture from Room. Decorations from NK Interior. Tasteful, planned by people with style. A sort of negative of her own flat. She didn't know what she'd seen in him once upon a time. They were each other's opposites, like water and fire.

'What did you do after that?'

'I panicked.'

'Didn't you call the police?'

'That was the first thing I did. They sent a patrol car. I gave them Lisa's description.'

'There are usually natural explanations for these kinds of things. In normal cases, people show up again, children too. Maybe she ran off with a friend? Decided to do something other than go to school – just bunking off.'

She heard her own voice as if from a distance. Professionally calm, so as not to break down entirely. She was talking about the incident as if it were a fraud investigation. And she could hear how absurd she sounded – it would be completely unlike her dutiful little girl.

'So you started looking for her?'

'Yes, but at the same time I tried to get hold of you. But you didn't answer. I thought she had gone to your place, that she missed her mum. Or that you picked her up outside the school . . . anything that resembled a simple explanation.'

He was no longer crying. He seemed calmer and more collected.

'And then I called the police again, three or four times, but got the same answer. Wait and see.'

'Did you talk to her teacher again?'

'Yes, and her classmates. They're all worried. No one has any good idea about why she didn't show up.'

'Does she hang out with anyone else outside the class? Does she have friends here in the neighbourhood?'

'There's a girl in the building she plays with sometimes. Lottie. One year younger. But they're gone this week. Her dad is a pilot for SAS; he takes the family along on trips sometimes. They fly for free.'

There must be someone else, she thought, another

child she knew, some friend who convinced her to leave school. But to do what?

Erika came back into the room. She'd put the baby down in the nursery; it wasn't screaming any more. She was walking towards her with her arms out in a grotesque gesture, and it wasn't until Erika had her in her arms that Eva realized Erika wanted to hug her. She pulled away and walked over to the window.

'You have to use your contacts,' said Ola. 'You know people at the police station. You have to tell them to do more.'

'I already called, before I came here.'

'And what did they say?'

'They're doing everything they can. The patrol cars have been given the description. And I talked to the emergency centre. At least no traffic accidents have been reported downtown this morning.'

The quiet was unbearable – the faint hum of traffic on Ringvägen, the sounds of conversation from the pavement . . . unbearable. She needed a cigarette, but she didn't have any. She wondered why she was pretending for Ola. So that she would appear to be strong and collected for once. But, in reality, she had made over a dozen calls to the police station, screamed at people in a complete panic, begged people she knew to try to do something to find her daughter.

'Can you show me Lisa's room?' she said.

'Sure.'

She followed him down the hall to where the bedrooms

were. She'd never seen the way the children lived at Ola's. She'd never been invited to.

The room was the exact opposite of the one they shared on Torsgatan. It was a girl's dream. A pink bed with a matching child-size easy chair. A lace bed canopy. Dress-up clothes in their own wardrobe. String system shelves on the wall. Children's books in neat rows. Her own computer. Toys arranged on shelves. A CD player on a bench. A Loreen CD was out – she noticed it was autographed.

In the bed was her favourite doll, Engla.

At the thought of what could have happened to Lisa, she nearly threw up.

'Do you know if she keeps a diary? Maybe there's something there.'

Ola shook his head.

'She's seven, she just learned to write.'

She was grasping at straws, she realized. Searching for clues to what had happened in her room. Absurd. As if there would be anything in here. As if she had written something that could help them. Engla stared at her beseechingly. The scent of her little girl lingered in the room; she could feel the warmth of her body, hear her voice.

They spent the entire day looking for her, driving around in Ola's car, using the school as a sort of hub around which they made ever-wider circles.

They asked about her at playgrounds, at leisure centres, outside schools; they called around to her classmates and asked them if they knew anything about other children or adults: had she ever mentioned another person she often saw, had she said or done anything strange or unusual recently, had she mentioned anything about strangers? And, during all this, Eva was in contact with the police station, pulling at threads, screaming at people, getting them to start working.

At eight that night she went home. Every patrol car in the county was now keeping an eye out for Lisa. An investigator had called the hospitals to see if she was there, but with no result. She didn't know if she ought to feel relieved. Because, at the same time, of course, she knew how it worked – the more time that passed without finding Lisa, the more likely it was that they would not find her alive.

And then came the call. It was as if she had been waiting for it, she thought. As if she'd known beforehand what was going to happen. She knew that she would remember every detail for the rest of her life. That certain things were etched forever into a person's mind.

She had hardly been able to look at Katz since she came back to the apartment; she just gave him a summary of what had happened and what she knew. It was impossible to look any other person in the eye, not least a person she had slept with less than twenty-four hours earlier – except for Ola, who, for a change, was the only one who understood her, the only one who was feeling the same boundless fear.

She didn't want Katz there. She just wanted to be alone. To take a sleeping pill and fade away, to wake up and hope that it had all been a dream.

But it wasn't. This was just the beginning, she realized the same instant she picked up the phone.

'Is this Eva Westin?'

She knew it was him even though she hadn't heard his voice before.

He explained very calmly that he had Lisa, and that she was unharmed. He explained that he knew who she was, that he knew most things about her: where she worked, where she lived, her family situation.

'We did meet once before,' he said, 'a long time ago. But I don't think you remember much of the actual event. And then again recently, in the house where I grew up, but you didn't see me.'

Grubbholmen, that was what he meant, and the house in Djursholm. He sounded completely normal, as if this were just any old conversation; he sounded like one of those telemarketers who called sometimes, wanting to sell mobile-phone contracts or some strange insurance – professionally friendly.

'What do you want from me?' she said.

'I'll explain in a little bit.'

'I want to talk to Lisa.'

Her voice disappeared as she ran out of air. Katz was standing next to her now, as she sat on the bed with the phone pressed hard to her ear. She knew he understood everything: who she was talking to, and that it was the worst news possible.

'Lisa is fine. You don't need to worry about her. She's sleeping right now.'

'What do you want from me?' she said again.

'For one thing, I don't want you to tell anyone that I called. Not Lisa's dad, and definitely not the police. That's a prerequisite for us to be able to work together.'

'I want to talk to her now; wake her up . . .'

'For another thing, I don't want to be interrupted. From now on, you speak when I ask you to; otherwise, you keep quiet and listen. Is that understood?'

'Yes.'

'Good, then I want something from you in return.'

She was quiet, waiting.

'I want Katz. Do you understand? My guess is that he's nearby. May I speak to him?'

She handed the phone to Katz. For one instant, she hated him. She didn't want him there; she didn't understand why he was part of her life and how she could have let herself be dragged into this mess.

Katz took the phone with the sensation of being outside his own body.

'Yes,' he said. 'It's me.'

289

Silence at first, just Klingberg's breathing. Then the voice he hadn't heard in a quarter of a century:

'Danny, it's been a long time.'

He didn't answer, because what could he say?

'Is it possible for you to sit down? And perhaps take out a pen and paper – I was planning on giving you some instructions.'

Katz went over to the computer desk and took a sheet of A4 from the printer and a pen from his pocket.

'I'm ready,' he said.

'Don't stress, Katz. I'm trusting in you. Remember . . . *the only person I've ever really trusted.*'

Those words again, another variation of them that brought something nameless to life. He just couldn't think what.

'I'm sorry,' he said. 'But I don't remember.'

'No? Listen carefully. I've got Eva's little girl here. And I want to trade her for you.'

Silence on the line again, just the breathing, and in the background a sleepy girl's voice that suddenly shouted something. But Klingberg must have immediately gone into another room, because everything was quiet again, and more compact, as if he were in a very small area, close to a wall.

'Tell me what to do.'

'I want you to go to the Dominican Republic. To Santo Domingo. I want you to be there by three days from now.'

'I'm wanted by the police.'

'That's not my problem. Right now it's . . .' Silence again.

The girl had to be there, somewhere in the background – the terror she must be feeling. 'Ten-oh-five p.m. The time difference is minus six hours. So you have to be there by four-oh-five p.m. in three calendar days.'

'That won't be possible.'

'Everything is possible. You'll have to improvise. You'll be given further instructions once you get there.'

The girl's voice again; Klingberg had returned to the room she was in. She was calling for her dad.

'Lisa is awake now,' Klingberg said matter-of-factly. 'Do you want to talk to your mum, Lisa? Hold on, here she comes . . .'

It was her turn again. She hoped that her stutter wouldn't show itself, that she could keep it together for Lisa's sake. The phone slid through her fingers; she had to use both hands to press it to her ear.

'Hi darling, it's Mum. Listen to me. Everything will be okay, no matter what you think right now. I promise you. Everything will work itself out.'

She could hear Lisa's panicked breathing on the other end.

'Calm down, Lisa; it's important. You have to try to breathe normally. Nothing dangerous is going to happen. I promise you. I'm your mum and you can trust me.'

Lisa settled down a little bit, seemingly calmed by her voice.

'Where are you, Mum?'

'I'm at my house.'

'Are my things there? Did you find Arvid's Bakugan?'

'I found it. Everything is perfectly normal here, but I cleaned your room so it will be nice for when you come back.'

Lisa gave a small whimper, as if she were in pain.

'I don't want to be here, Mum.'

'I know.'

'What's going to happen?'

'Nothing's going to happen. We'll be together again soon, and you'll get to go home. It might take a little while, but eventually it will happen. I promise. I don't know if we're going to get to talk on the phone very much until then, but in the meantime I want you to try to think of things that make you happy. Things you can look forward to.'

Was this her own voice? She couldn't fathom it. Memories of Lisa fluttered by on an inner screen, a sort of résumé of her seven years on earth, from when she had been a newborn at BB Stockholm on that beautiful snow-sparkling February day to the last time she'd seen her in the stairwell at Ola's.

'I love you, Lisa.'

'I love you too, Mum.'

Then she started crying again, and her sobs faded into the background like a murmur. She thought that Klingberg would take the phone again to say something. But the call had been ended.

Katz was driving south on the E4 alongside Lake Vättern. He could see Visingsö like a floating graphic object out in the water. The traffic was light, mostly lorries and commuters. Tender greenery on the slopes that led down to the lake.

Near Gränna, he turned off at a rest stop and remained in the car to eat the lunch he'd brought along. He felt safe behind the tinted windows.

He would drive the rental car to Malmö, park it near Central Station and drop the keys off in the slot at Hertz. That way he would avoid anyone seeing him. That was the most important thing right now, not to be recognized.

In the inner pocket of his jacket was the passport that one of Jorma's friends had managed to arrange for him. It was issued by the embassy of the Russian Federation in Stockholm. He was travelling under the name Igor Liebermann. A Jewish-Russian journalist born in Rostov the same year as he was. The airline tickets had been purchased under the same name. If anyone started asking questions, he would answer in Russian.

The suitcase in the trunk was packed as if for a normal holiday. Clothes, toiletries, a guidebook about the Dominican Republic. And a miniature satellite phone, no larger than a matchbook. It could be used to call from anywhere, even from the South Pole, according to Eva. She had managed to obtain it from the operational police unit at EBM.

On the seat next to him was the little fabric doll, the *paké*. He didn't know why he'd brought it along. Like an amulet, maybe, even though he didn't believe in superstitions.

Katz continued southwards, past Huskvarna and Jönköping. He was careful to stick to the speed limit, and he kept the radio on in case there were any traffic updates.

He looked at the fuel gauge. The car was efficient; he still had over two thirds of a tank. He wouldn't need to get gas before he got to Malmö.

The forest closed in around him as he drove on through Småland, kilometre after kilometre of planted firs.

Just north of Värnamo he passed a speed trap: a patrol car and two motorcycles; he took his foot off the accelerator on reflex and watched the rear-view mirror for a long time until he was sure they weren't following him.

He was going to make it. He would get to the airport in Santo Domingo, Aeropuerto Las Américas, go up to a particular car-rental agency and receive further instructions. Meanwhile, Eva and Jorma would look for the girl. But after that . . . what was the point?

At one thirty in the afternoon, he parked the car at Malmö Central, left the key in the box outside Hertz and walked into the arrivals hall. He cautiously looked around for police in plain clothes; things seemed to be okay.

According to the information board, an Öresund train

was on the platform. Soon he could relax a bit, he thought, if only he could make it to the Danish side.

He took a window seat and read a paper someone had left behind as the conductor went by, clipping his ticket without looking at him. No customs officials; they worked the opposite direction.

He was up on Öresund Bridge now. It was a beautiful day; the sky was deep blue with hazy clouds along the horizon. The sea below was greenish black.

When the train stopped at Kastrup, he avoided looking at the people who got on; he sank into himself, keeping his face turned away, looking out of the window.

He suddenly remembered a trip he'd taken to Copenhagen in the early 2000s when he'd been at rock bottom. He'd been there with a younger man from Uppsala who was going to pick up a shipment of heroin from a distributor in Vesterbro. Katz's job was to be a decoy. He would sit a few seats away in the same compartment on the way back. If customs were to do a random inspection, they would pick out Katz, the obvious junkie, and not the well-dressed young guy with the briefcase who was paging through a business magazine.

What had he been paid – fifteen grams of H? That was the price he thought he was worth back then.

It was quarter past two when he arrived at Hovedbanegården, took the escalator up to the ticketing hall and purchased a one-way ticket to Hamburg. Good timing again. The train would be leaving in ten minutes. He had seven hours before the plane would take off from Fuhlsbüttel.

She hadn't been to the office in ages. People stared at her as she walked past them on the way to her desk. She heard voices from the conference room. 'An implementation time of ninety days is super fucking rough . . . it's unreasonable . . . can someone tell me what the Financial Crimes Unit is thinking?'

She closed the door behind her and turned on the computer. She checked her emails from the legal division, but didn't see anything that couldn't wait. She had received a reply from the London office of Interpol, as well. The Virgin Islands were still trying to delay the bank-transaction matter; it might take up to six months before they learned who the account belonged to.

She scrolled down through her inbox. Four messages from Danielsson. He wanted to see her, but apparently he didn't dare call. She glanced through the most recent one, which had been sent the night before. He wondered if she was feeling better and suggested that they have dinner at a Chinese restaurant once she was back; he wanted to give her some info on how far they'd come in the investigation surrounding Angela Klingberg.

Nothing about Julin or Pontus Klingberg. So, the bodies were still in Djursholm.

She changed into her indoor shoes, went to the canteen

and got a cup of coffee from the machine. She had gone into the police station on her way to the office. She'd met the female inspector who was in charge of investigating Lisa's disappearance. Publishing the description hadn't brought any results; no witnesses had seen her since she disappeared. The woman had asked the standard questions in her office. Had Lisa been acting strangely in the past few weeks? What sort of friends did she have; had she ever run away? The woman had patted Eva's shoulder before she left and lied, saying that they would find her soon.

She'd been on the verge of confessing everything, the way things really were, but she realized it was so complicated that they would have a hard time believing her. And yet that's not what decided it for her. It was Joel Klingberg. She knew he was in a position where he might do anything. He would kill Lisa at the least suspicion that she had cooperated with the police.

How had he managed to abduct her? In a car, she thought as she returned to her office, probably a stolen one that he dumped somewhere afterwards. He or his accomplice had been lucky; no one seemed to have seen it happen. The papers had just begun to write about it. Perhaps that would bring out some witnesses.

Her mobile rang. Ola. She accepted the call.

'Have you heard anything new?' he said.

His voice was hoarse with exhaustion.

'No, nothing new. I met with the investigator in charge again an hour ago. They haven't made a single step of progress.'

The lies continued, the withholding of information,

and she hated herself for it. But if only Lisa were rescued she would tell him everything. And the police. Even the part about Katz. That was a promise.

'And the hospitals?'

'Nothing there either.'

'This just can't be happening!'

He took a deep breath before he went on.

'Could she have drowned?' he said. 'This whole city is full of water . . . did she go somewhere and fall in?'

'I don't think so.'

'So what the hell is it? Paedophiles?'

'I don't know, Ola. Go and get some sleep if you can. You seem absolutely exhausted. I'll call you as soon as I hear anything more.'

They hung up. The National Intelligence Centre's report on Katz's time in the military was still on her desk. She hadn't heard anything from him yet, and she didn't know if she should take that as a good sign or not. On his way to the Dominican Republic with a fake passport. From Fuhlsbüttel in Hamburg to Madrid, and then on to Santo Domingo. What the hell were they thinking?

Lisa . . . she didn't want to think about how she was, because as soon as she did she was paralysed with fear. She hadn't been able to talk to her since the first time Klingberg contacted her. The second time he called, he had just asked to speak to Katz and had told him what to do when he arrived in Santo Domingo.

She had to keep thoughts of Lisa at bay in order to think clearly. Imagine that she was someone else's daughter.

Where was she? In Stockholm, she thought, at a place Klingberg considered secure.

Her only inroad was Sandra Dahlström. She had to have told Klingberg about Eva's visit, thus putting him on her trail. It was the only reasonable explanation. But she had disappeared. Jorma had gone out to Mörby to look for her. He had peered in through the letter box; there had been a big pile of post on the hall rug.

She spent the rest of the morning doing more searches on Sandra Dahlström. The results were meagre. There was nothing on her in the criminal registry or the general registry. Nothing at the Enforcement Authority. She didn't own any property or any vehicles. She didn't even have a dog. She surfed around the Net for a while and found that name in a number of contexts, but they seemed to involve different people. To be on the safe side, she did an image search to see if there was a picture of her anywhere, but she found no results.

She had just shut down the computer when her phone rang again. The number was blocked; her voice hardly held up as she answered.

'Eva Westin.'

'Mum, it's me.'

'Sweetie . . . are you okay?'

Someone coughed in the background. It was important, it was all important, every detail, no matter how irrelevant it might seem, if she was going to find her.

'I miss you and Dad. Why can't I talk to Dad, too?'

'I don't get to decide that . . . Lisa . . . everything is going to be okay; you'll get to come home again soon.'

'I know, Mum.'

She listened intently for background noises. But she couldn't hear anything.

'I'm allowed to talk to you for a little while, Mum, isn't that good?'

'Yes, it's very good. Listen, Lisa . . . tell me something, anything you think sounds fun.'

'About what?'

'What you want to do this summer, for example; just do it. Now!'

She must have understood somehow, because she started telling a long, complicated story about what she was going to do on her summer holiday.

'Good, Lisa, just keep going, and at the same time I'm going to ask questions that you just have to answer yes or no to, as if it were part of the story.'

She seemed to understand what Eva meant, because she continued to describe the puppy Ola was going to give her and what she would do when she took it out to the country.

'Are there any windows where you are, that you can see out of? Only answer yes or no; that's important.'

'*No* . . . the puppy won't have its own kennel, it's going to sleep in a basket next to my bed.'

'So there are no windows in the room. Is it a basement, do you think, yes or no?'

'*No* . . . its name is going to be Charlie, because that was Dad's dog's name, the one he had when he was little.'

'Good. Did it take a long time to get to where you are?'

'*No* . . . not long, except Dad thinks the puppy should be named Gruffen, but I don't think so.'

'I understand . . . could you see anything on the way there, where you were going or anything?'

'*No* . . . just a little *water* that the dog could drink . . . and then there were *thorns* that got stuck in its fur . . . Mum, I'm tired of telling.'

She was playing with fire. If there was a speakerphone function, he had heard everything she'd said. But it wasn't on; if it had been, Lisa's voice would have sounded different: brighter, more high-frequency.

Water, she had seen or heard water when they took her out of the car. And thorns . . . something with thorns.

'I want to go home now, Mum . . . I don't want to stay here.'

'I know, darling. And you will get to come home soon, I promise.'

She heard a sudden rumbling in the background. She recognized the sound and tried desperately to define it. Blasting; they were blasting nearby!

'Tell me how many toys you want to get when you come home. And it should be the same as the number of people you've seen since all this happened.'

'Three toys. But now there's only one toy. The other toys are gone. I don't know where they went. Mum, I have to stop now, but I think . . .'

Lisa's voice disappeared mid-sentence. It took several seconds for her to realize that they'd hung up.

The Lufthansa flight to Madrid went according to plan; he slept for a while and woke up shortly before they landed at Barajas. He looked for the terminal for transatlantic flights – his bags were checked all the way to Santo Domingo – and he waited for a few hours in a bar next to the gate and was among the first to board the Iberia plane to Santo Domingo.

He had a nine-hour flight ahead of him; he would land well before the time was up.

An air steward was walking around with blankets and inflatable neck cushions. Katz's closest neighbour was an older Spanish woman with blue hair and a cat in a carrier between her feet. To his relief, she seemed uninterested in conversing with him.

As the plane taxied to the runway, he had the sensation of being observed. Paranoia, he thought, as he looked around. Mostly white Spaniards, most of them old. People who had been visiting relatives in Spain and were on their way home now. A black flight attendant with incredibly beautiful facial features smiled at him from the door of the nearest galley.

After the light meal that was served when they reached cruising altitude, he started to think about Joel Klingberg again.

What had sparked the chain of events? Klingberg had learned that his wife had had an affair with his uncle, so he had gone underground to get revenge.

But where had he hidden for the first few weeks? In the hunting cabin in Sörmland? That didn't seem likely; it was too close to the manor, and Pontus or Angela could have shown up at any time.

Katz ate some of the dessert that was still on the tray in front of him – a chilli-spiced Caribbean fruit salad. It was too hot, he noticed; he pushed it away.

Joel had returned to his home several weeks after he disappeared; Angela hadn't opened the door to the perpetrator as Katz had first thought, because Joel had his own set of keys.

What had she thought when she saw him? Had she been relieved that he was back, unharmed, that he hadn't been the victim of an accident or a crime as she had suspected? After all, she had broken it off with Pontus when her husband had vanished; she regretted her actions and wanted her husband back.

Had he said anything to her? That he knew that she had cheated on him? Or had he attacked her straight away?

Julin had been involved from the start. Julin was the one who had broken into Katz's place and stolen things that were later planted in the apartment. And he had been paid an absurd amount of money. Fifty million kronor had been put in a secret account in the Virgin Islands.

Julin and Klingberg had known each other for a long time. They had met for the first time in the seventies, when Joel was still a child and Julin had been hired to find out what had happened to his brother. Julin had started to spend time with the family, going on trips to the Caribbean with them, becoming interested in Joel – in his gift for studies, his ear for languages and his bursts of rage. And he had become interested in Vodou.

Through the Klingberg family, he had come into contact with Caribbean folk beliefs – that one could drug people with certain medicinal herbs, influence their free will and get them to do the most bizarre things. At the same time, he had managed a secret programme within the armed forces. Katz was still uncertain about exactly what it had entailed, but it involved personality-changing drugs.

Katz stopped a flight attendant who was walking by and asked her for a refill of coffee. Then he leaned back again and continued his train of thought.

Julin had made sure that both Katz and Joel Klingberg were accepted into the interpreter academy. Katz because he had been convicted of an extremely brutal violent crime. But what Julin hadn't known was that it was actually Klingberg who was behind the attack on Grubbholmen. What made Julin become interested in Katz was his belief that Katz was capable of such bestial violence. As for Joel, he must have suspected or known about his attacks on the maid, Sandra Dahlström.

Or did he suspect that Joel had murdered his own parents?

It was impossible to know what had happened in the years that followed, but the two men must have kept in contact. And a few months ago, Klingberg had shown up with his offer.

Julin had become involved in conspiracy to murder. It was part of the plan for Angela to contact Katz to ask for help in finding her missing husband; they had purposely set her in motion against him, made sure that she hired him, all to create a personal connection between him and the murder victim. But why had they chosen Katz in particular? So that Klingberg could live out his violent fantasies again? Or had he wanted to get revenge . . . but for what?

Katz stopped his thoughts the same way one might press pause on a music player.

Two rows behind him, an argument had broken out between a father and his son, a five-year-old boy who apparently refused to finish his food. The man was in his thirties and was incredibly drunk. Katz watched as he grabbed the boy by the back of the neck and forced his face into the tray. The boy was crying. Those around them looked troubled, but no one intervened. Katz could understand why not. The man was a bodybuilder and had gang tattoos on his neck and arms. His eyes looked spaced-out.

'*Pide disculpas!*' he said. 'Say you're sorry!'

'*Perdoneme, papá*' . . . 'I'm sorry, Dad.'

'*No te oigo,*' said the man as he cuffed the boy's ear. 'I can't hear you!'

A woman in the next seat, probably the boy's mother, looked down at her lap, clearly terrified of her husband.

'Stay out of it,' the man said, when he noticed Katz looking. Then he tousled his son's hair before opening a miniature bottle of brandy and pouring it into a glass.

Katz pressed play again.

Klingberg and Julin had ended up on a collision course after Angela's murder. Julin had tried to murder Katz on his own. Julin had been the one to send an assassin to Jorma's apartment in Kransen. Because he had got cold feet. Not only had Katz managed to evade the police against all odds, Julin thought Katz was on his trail. The military secrets. That was what he'd wanted to keep hidden, and it had been more important than the murder plot he was involved in.

But Klingberg had opposed the idea of silencing Katz and had instead had Julin killed outside the hunting cabin in Sörmland. And let Katz go so the game could continue?

The only reason they had been there at all was because they were going to murder Pontus Klingberg, who'd been on his way to the manor. But then Katz showed up and created confusion.

He closed his eyes and pictured a kidnapped seven-year-old girl before him. Nothing must happen to her; he would never forgive himself.

The man behind him had started arguing again, but not with his son – with the black flight attendant. He tried to grab her as she walked by. When she didn't seem amused, he became furious. *'Puta negra!'* he yelled. 'Black whore!'

Katz got out of his seat, stretched his legs and sat down on the armrest, looking towards the man. The flight attendant walked by again, and the man stuck his foot into the aisle. When she stepped over it, he put his hand up under her skirt. She gave a shout, backed up, tripped and ended up on the floor. An air steward purser showed up to help her to her feet.

Katz looked at the man and received a scornful smile in return. An experienced fighter, he thought. His eyes suggested as much – their hardness, the disdain, the way he sought out confrontation. A swastika was tattooed on his lower arm.

Half an hour later, Katz saw the man get up and walk to the lavatory in the rear of the Airbus. The cabin lights had been dimmed. The passengers were sleeping. The flight attendant who had been molested had switched areas and was now behind the curtains of business class. The crew hadn't known how to deal with the man; he was too unpredictable and they didn't want to risk him becoming violent. The steward had been serving him since the flight attendant had vanished: three large rums. Katz had kept count.

His wife and son were sleeping, each under a blanket. The boy's face was still red from crying.

Katz waited until the 'occupied' light lit up outside the lavatory, and then he stood up, used the parallel aisle, to be on the safe side, crossed at the connecting aisle and stood beside the lavatory door.

There was no queue. The people in the seats nearby were sleeping. He discovered a curtain that the crew used when they were preparing trays of food in the rear galley and carefully pulled it closed.

No one from the cabin could see in now; he was standing in the dark, and the only light was from the red lamp above the lavatory.

When the man opened the door, Katz pressed his left thumb into the man's right eye and saw him double in pain. He met the movement with full power, kneeing him in the face. The man fell backwards and struck the back of his head on the toilet. A bloody front tooth was sticking out between his lips. Katz kicked him in the crotch. Then he grabbed hold – one hand in the hair at the back of his neck and the other around his throat – and turned him around, shoving his head into the toilet as he used his foot to close the accordion door behind him. The man's throat was pressing hard against the edge of the seat; he fought to breathe.

'*Señor, quiero que me escuche con mucho cuidado. Si le veo a Usted golpear a un niño o hostigar a una mujer, le mato. Me entiende?*'

Katz hadn't spoken Spanish for twenty-five years, since he had been a student at the interpreter academy, where he took an intensive course in the language because he had some extra time, and he was surprised at how easy it was to formulate the words, as if they were born in his mouth just as he spoke them.

When the man didn't answer, he lifted his head by the hair. He was about to pound the man's face against the steel edge of the toilet, but he managed to stop himself at the last second. He looked at his bloody hands with disgust. He looked at the man, who was lying on the floor in shock.

'*No me mate!*' he whispered. 'Don't kill me!'

Katz rinsed himself off in the sink, avoiding his reflection in the mirror – the empty eyes that stared hatefully out into nothingness. He heard the man whimper on the floor at his feet.

That is the language you have mastered best of all, he thought as he went back to his seat, *the language of violence. What kind of person are you . . . what is wrong with you?*

Two out of three toys are gone; which one is left and which is it?

Like a riddle, she thought, and if she could find it, she would find Lisa.

So she was alone somewhere, with one person, but she couldn't imagine where and with whom.

In Stockholm, because the car trip hadn't taken long. Near the water. And there were thorns that got stuck in her clothes.

The light went out with a faint click, and the stairwell grew dark. She was in Mörby Centrum with Jorma, half a floor below Sandra Dahlström's apartment. It was 2 a.m.

Jorma . . . she hadn't spent time with him since they were teenagers. And yet she trusted him. Because they were made of the same frayed material, because they were from the same time and place, from the same circumstances, where no one cared.

He signalled for her to follow him. They could hear the sound of a TV somewhere. It sounded like an action film.

They were standing in front of her door now. No light from the neighbours' peepholes. Jorma felt for something along the top hinge – a match. And she remembered it from the days when she had been involved in break-ins, the old trick to check if someone had come back home after you'd been there scouting it out. The match would have broken if someone had opened the door.

He took a feeler gauge out of his pocket – *from Biltema, best in the business* – selected one of the blades, bent the top with his thumb and stuck it in at the edge of the door, just below the lock.

It was an ASSA cylinder lock. She'd had a hard time believing him when he said it would take thirty seconds max to get it open. But it didn't even take ten. Two or three turns, some plain old flat-nosed pliers to help push it up, and she heard the bolt roll back into the lock.

They stood still for a moment, listening for sounds in the building. All they could hear was the TV from the neighbour who was awake two floors down.

Jorma quickly walked through the room, lowering the blinds and pulling the curtains across all the windows before he turned on his torch.

As he looked through the wardrobes in the bedroom, she thought again of what Lisa had said: *A small, windowless room near the water. Thorns that got stuck in her clothes.*

And it was near a place where they were blasting.

She had called the Transport Administration to try to find out about large blasting projects that were currently underway in the Stockholm area. An administrator had reluctantly given her the information. Excavation at Norra Länken near Roslagstull. Blasting in Vasastan for the new City Line. *The rats are running amok; the explosions scare them up out of the sewers, monsters bigger than one kilo are running around in Vasaparken* . . . Blasting for the new commuter rail station under Odenplan. Farther away – at Arlanda – new underground garages were being built, old buildings were being torn down to build new ones by Söder Hospital, and there was blasting for a new electricity connection through the rock from the Danderyd transformer station over to Järva, where planning was underway for a new part of the city. The administrator had continued to rattle off municipal projects until Eva realized she would never find Lisa that way. Furthermore, there were a number of private contractors who did blasting for pools, single-family homes and excavation, and for the stone industry.

Was there a protocol for blasting times? she had asked.

Possibly, but she'd have to ask the contractors about that.

She'd called the Stockholm Blasting Centre and a few other, larger firms to find out. After all, she knew the time of the explosions she'd heard on the phone. A friendly man at the centre promised to try to check with the blasters themselves. But it might take some time; she'd have to be patient.

There were four wardrobes in the bedroom, and she went through them one by one. Nothing valuable, just clothing.

She kept searching – in the bedside table, in a chest of drawers, in the drawers of a dressing table.

The scent of another person's life: Sandra Dahlström's. She might not have anything to do with this; she might be travelling, on holiday, visiting a relative or another part of the country. But that didn't make sense. How else would Klingberg have known who she was? Sandra was the one who had told him about her, that she had been there asking questions.

Had she been murdered? Had Klingberg got her out of

the way, just as he had done with Julin? It was a distinct possibility.

Eva peered over towards the living room. The beam of light from Jorma's torch danced across the floor as he walked between the bookcases. She heard him humming a tune and was amazed at how calm he was.

She checked under the bed; there was a box on wheels which she rolled out and inspected. More clothes, but in larger sizes. They had belonged to Linnie Holm, she thought. Sandra had saved them.

The lift stopped in the stairwell. There were footsteps on the stone floor, the lift doors closed, someone's keys jingled.

She saw Jorma in the hall, cautiously working a pistol out of his jacket pocket. An Israeli Desert Eagle. She remembered what it was called because it was so absurd. Because Jorma had shown it to her, explaining how to use it in case it became necessary. As if this were the most natural information in the world.

Jorma crouched down, aiming his pistol at the door to the flat. He carefully blew a stray lock of hair out of his eyes, not nervous at all.

Two more steps out there, more jingling of keys; the person was drunk. Then she heard the lock of the flat next door being turned. The door was opened, closed and locked.

They waited for five minutes before they started searching again. Faint music came from the neighbouring flat.

When she was finished in the bedroom, she went out to join Jorma. He was sitting in an easy chair under the Shiva poster, smoking. He had an address book and a small photo album in his lap.

'It was in the laundry basket,' he said, picking up the photo album. 'Lots of people hide their valuables there. And in the freezer.' He held up the address book, and she could see that there was frost on it. 'For some reason, people think that burglars won't look there, but of course it's the first thing they do. Otherwise, there are no valuables in this apartment, unless you found something in the bedroom. No computer or tablet, no jewellery or cash. I'm disappointed.'

He gave a crooked smile and put out his cigarette in a flowerpot.

'But for some reason she thinks a photo album and an address book are valuable.'

She started leafing through them. The address book first. The phone numbers to her doctor and dentist, an administrator at the social insurance office, a few more numbers to a nurse hotline, an insurance company and an electric company. *A lonely person*, she thought, as she flipped to the last page.

Åkesson, Jonas. No address, just a crossed-out mobile number. The homeless boy she had taken care of. Next to the phone number she had written down six numbers, organized in pairs: 05 16 12. The day he had been found dead in a car in Märsta.

She leafed backwards, and the names of a few acquaintances fluttered by – a certain Anki Rågklint, another woman by the name of Myriam Pettersson, who lived a few streets away.

She stopped at the letter K. There were several numbers there, to mobile phones, but there weren't any names. The numbers had been written with different pens, in chronological order. Old numbers had been crossed out as new ones appeared. To Joel Klingberg, she guessed.

The last one had been written there recently; the pencil lead was fresh. It was a long number – a foreign number.

She put down the address book and opened the photo album to the first page. Photos of Jonas Åkesson as a child; the pictures had been taken in this apartment. He was sitting on the floor, playing with Lego, maybe ten years old.

More photos of the boy as she browsed on; he was a bit older here. In one of them he was standing on a Djurgården ferry with Linnie Holm, and in another he was in front of the entrance to Gröna Lund, the amusement park. After that he was photographed in front of a car, with a well-dressed couple – maybe his biological parents; there was a certain similarity to their features.

She leafed through a bit further. Jonas on vacation with Sandra Dahlström and Linnie Holm. In the Greek archipelago, it looked like. Someone else was holding the camera. He was older now; maybe thirteen. He looked worn out – had he started taking drugs already?

Then there were a few pages of empty plastic sleeves, but he showed up again on the last page. With Rickard Julin.

It took a minute for her surprise to subside.

She guessed that the picture had been taken a few years earlier. Who was the photographer? Sandra Dahlström, one could assume. The two men were standing next to

each other in front of something that looked like an abandoned house. Neither of them was looking at the camera;
the picture seemed to have been taken by mistake, as if
someone had slipped and hit the button. Julin was mid-
step, moving away from the camera.

She was bewildered. How were these two connected?

She looked at the photo again. It had been taken in the
autumn; the leaves in the yard in front of the house had
turned yellow. The windows were broken, and part of the
roof had caved in. It had been a beautiful house once
upon a time, designed by an architect. From the fifties, she
would guess. Behind the house was a glimpse of an overgrown garden.

The sky above them was lofty and deep blue. Her intuition told her that they were near the water.

The approach over the Caribbean Sea was bumpy. For a moment, Katz thought they were about to have an emergency landing in the turquoise water before the runway showed up on the coast at the last second. The sky was cloudy, almost black at the horizon; hurricane season was only a few weeks away.

He caught a glimpse of the man he had assaulted as they got off the plane. He was leaning on his wife and limping down the ramp. The man pretended not to recognize him, but Katz saw the fear of death in his eyes and he knew it would remain there for a long time.

It was 7 a.m. local time and the heat was already oppressive. A faint scent of decay hung in the air. The humidity was nearly one hundred per cent.

After he'd retrieved his luggage from the conveyor belt he went through customs and walked into the arrivals hall. Merengue music streamed out of the taxis outside the building. A mixed bag of European tourists, Dominicans with Spanish and African roots, and every shade in between went in and out of the automatic doors.

At the other end of the arrivals hall he saw the sign for car rentals.

*

He introduced himself as Señor Katz to a woman in her twenties and received a professional smile in response before she found an envelope with a car key in a cupboard behind the desk.

'Your car is in parking slot 91A,' she said, pointing at an outlined map of the airport. 'Welcome to the Dominican Republic, Señor Katz, I hope you have a pleasant stay here.'

He found the car in its assigned spot: a white Land Rover with a detachable top. When he'd closed the door behind him, a mobile phone started ringing in the glove compartment.

It was under the car manual. He pressed the answer button and heard Klingberg's voice.

'I'll make this quick: there's a hotel room reserved under your name in Zona Colonial, the old part of Santo Domingo. You'll like it. It's first class. Pool on the roof. Parking in the basement; you can leave the car there until I contact you again. It's all paid for, so don't worry. The address of the hotel is in an envelope in the glove compartment. Understood?'

He answered in the affirmative.

'Good. You just have to do as I tell you. And have this phone available twenty-four hours a day so you can receive further instructions. Outgoing calls are blocked. It's important for you to follow my instructions to the letter. Otherwise, the girl will not survive.'

'I realize that.'

'Good, Katz. Did you sleep with her, by the way?'

'Who?'

'Angela.'

He didn't answer, because he didn't know what to say. He just looked across the car park, where steam was rising from the heated asphalt, over to the northern horizon, where the coastal landscape turned into soft hills.

'More your type than mine, right? But you didn't get a chance before everything got out of hand. Oh God, I knew it . . . from the very start I knew it would be like this. Now drive to the hotel. You need to rest after your trip.'

He peered in the rear-view mirror as he turned out of the car park and aimed for the highway. Buses and taxis came and went from the terminals; there were people everywhere, and tropical greenery, air shimmering with heat. Apparently, Klingberg had hired people to keep him under surveillance. He looked around for cars that might be tailing him, but he didn't see any that seemed suspicious.

The hotel was on the other side of the Ozama River in the southern part of Santo Domingo's old city centre. Katz checked in and took the lift up to his room, a suite with a view of the harbour and the old Spanish fort at the mouth of the river. He put the phone on the bedside table and connected it to a charger he'd found in the car. He went through the call log and realized that it had been used only once, when Klingberg called him at the airport from a blocked number.

The phone couldn't make outgoing calls. The SIM card inside it was from the Dominican state telecom company.

He left the phone there as he unpacked his bags, putting his clothes in the wardrobe, his razor and toothbrush in the bathroom; he put the amulet on the desk without really knowing why, and he started up his laptop and connected to the hotel Wi-Fi. He thought about calling Eva from the satellite phone to tell her he had arrived, but he changed his mind and sent an email instead.

A miniature bottle of three-star rum and a good cigar stood on the coffee table like a welcome present from the hotel. Katz took ice and cola from the refrigerator, mixed a weak Cuba Libre and went out to the balcony. He sat down in a rattan chair under the awning and left the balcony door open.

The hotel faced a small street that was beyond the tourist district. A fruit seller was standing in a corner, cooling himself with a fan. A one-armed man in a straw hat rode by on a mule. Two children were begging outside the hotel entrance. Katz sat there for an hour, waiting for a call. In the end, he gave up and left the hotel.

He devoted the rest of the morning to walking around the city with the phone in his breast pocket. He visited Santa Maria, the oldest cathedral in the New World, built by the Spanish colonists. He walked past Alcázar de Colón, the viceroy's palace, and through Parque Colón, the city park, where dusty palms and hibiscus shrubs drooped in the heat.

He navigated through the old grid of streets that had once set the standard for Spanish cities in the New World. The throngs of people were incredible: American tourists, destitute beggars – extreme poverty alongside equally extreme luxury.

At regular intervals he looked at the phone, worried that he had missed Klingberg. But it was quiet, and there was nothing he could do but wait.

After he'd eaten lunch on the oceanfront promenade, Malecón, he took out the guidebook and read about the island's history as he drank two cups of coffee.

Hispaniola had been discovered by Christopher Columbus during his first expedition to the New World in 1492. The island sat under the Spanish crown for two hundred years, until the western part was ceded to France and given the name Haiti. In practice, both of the countries were controlled by rich plantation owners, and they built their fortunes on exporting sugar.

Slave uprisings broke out on the French part of the island in conjunction with the Napoleonic Wars. The black rebel leader Toussaint Louverture succeeded in throwing out the Frenchmen and then proclaimed himself emperor. A bloody civil war ensued, but slavery came to an end and there was land reform at the plantation owners' expense.

On the Spanish side of Hispaniola, however, slavery continued – a bone of contention that led to fifty years of border conflicts and war with Haiti, conflicts that revolved around race and language, around hatred between blacks and whites, around freedom versus slavery.

In the thirties, the United States-friendly General Trujillo seized power in the Dominican Republic. 'The Benefactor', as the people called him, renamed the capital city after himself – Ciudad Trujillo – and pursued racist policies against ethnic Haitians in the country. This led to more tension between the governments in Santo Domingo and Port-au-Prince. The so-called Parsley Massacre that Angela Klingberg had told him about took place in 1937. Using machetes, the army slaughtered thirty thousand Haitians in the border regions between the two countries.

Trujillo was murdered in the early sixties in a conspiracy led by younger officers. Eventually, a fragile democracy was established, the tourist industry grew, agriculture was modernized and, today, the country was one of the richest in the Caribbean. Haiti, on the other hand, remained impoverished.

Katz put down the book and looked out at the palm-edged promenade. Two white women at the table next to him were complaining about the service. They preferred not to be served by *africanos*. On the other side of the quay was a marina with luxury boats. The sky grew darker and darker, and he saw flashes of lightning above the mountains to the north. He decided to go back to the hotel.

A tropical storm broke out minutes after he was back in his room. The electricity was out when he sat down in front of his laptop. The Internet connection didn't work, and the computer's batteries had run out.

He took out the satellite phone Eva had given him before he left. Same thing there: the batteries were almost dead. He had the sense that she needed to get hold of him, that something important had happened since he'd been gone.

The social worker at the Maria Youth Agency was a short woman of about thirty with a birthmark just under her left eye. She had put the folder in front of Eva so she could look at its contents while she spoke.

'The confidentiality rules no longer apply to Jonas,' she said sadly, 'not now that he's dead. I just don't understand it. I saw him less than three months ago and he had given up drugs. For good, I thought.'

'What made you think that?'

'Experience. He truly wanted to give up, it was an existential decision, and that is better than all the compulsory care and treatment programmes in the world. And then there was the fact that he had managed to get clean all on his own. That is a delicate mission indeed. One's will must be greater than the addiction. Do you know how the body reacts when a person gives up heroin cold turkey?'

'Yes, I do, actually.'

'Pain. It creeps through your whole body, as if there were insects under your skin. Agony, of course, sleeplessness . . . more pain, stomach cramps, vomiting, diarrhoea . . . your bones feel like plaster, and the slightest touch feels like a punch.'

'How did he manage to get clean?'

'He got hold of some tramadol and codeine to use as he detoxed, and that would have relieved the pain, of course, but it doesn't explain how he did it. He really wanted to give up and start a new life.'

'How did you communicate with him? I understand he was deaf.'

'My parents are deaf; I grew up in sign-language culture, and I'm actually the only person in the county who is dedicated to helping deaf junkies – there are more than you'd think. And also, Jonas could hear a little bit when he used his hearing aid.'

Eva leafed through the folder the social worker had put out for her. There was information about the boy's mental health and previous treatment programmes, and about caregivers – Sandra Dahlström and Linnie Holm seemed to be the most important ones. Old reports, decisions about foster-home placements, but nothing about his biological parents. They were probably protected by the confidentiality law. There were some documents that she would be allowed to see only if she applied for permission through the police authority.

'You said earlier that he wanted to see you shortly before he died?'

'Yes. He wanted to tell me something.'

'What was it?'

'I don't know; it all seemed so muddled. He said he wanted to get out of something, a medical experiment he'd been involved in, which funded his drug abuse for several years. He wanted to give it up, he said, and the first step he had to take was to become drug-free. We had scheduled a meeting here two days before he was found dead. He was supposed to fill me in more then.'

'It sounds mysterious.'

'You have to take into consideration that Jonas wasn't totally reliable. He mixed up fantasy and reality, because it made it easier to tolerate his existence. He'd had several emergency admits to Sankt Göran's Hospital for toxic psychosis in recent years. He heard voices that told him what to do, and he claimed they controlled his desires. And he also became extremely violent, more violent than usual.'

'Was he as a child, too? Violent?'

'He nearly beat his younger sister to death when he was ten. That was the last straw for his biological parents. They handed him over to social services.'

'Would you classify him as a psychopath? That's what it says in the documents here.'

'That's a doctor's opinion, from several years ago. But I don't actually think he was. He didn't completely lack empathy; he could feel compassion for others.'

'And you never heard anything more about that medical experiment?'

'No. But I take it for granted that it was something he made up.'

Eva looked out the window, at the rain that had started to fall on the car park. She pictured Lisa before her, but she forced the image away.

'Have you had any contact with a certain Sandra Dahlström or Linnie Holm – they're mentioned in your documents?'

'I know who you're talking about, but they were his caregivers long before my time, before I took over, so to speak, because no one else could handle Jonas. In the end there were essentially no authorities who were willing to help him, except for the staff at the emergency mental hospital, because they had to.'

'Do you know where he stayed those last few months, after he got clean?'

'He was homeless because he had burned all his bridges with the shelters. He lived in tunnels, among other places. Seventeen years old. It's appalling.'

'Did he ever mention staying at an abandoned house?'

'Yes, actually, he did. I didn't think there were any in Stockholm, given the property values.'

'Did he say where it was?'

'No. Just that he could be alone there. There was an entrance to the house that no one else knew about. And he was glad for it. Junkies tend to steal from one another, after all . . .'

On the way back to EBM she tried to call Katz, but no one answered the satellite phone. Actually, it didn't ring at all. A vague sense of unease crept over her. She ought to have heard something more from him; there should have been a reaction to the photo she'd scanned and emailed, in which Julin and Jonas Åkesson were standing together in front of a ramshackle house. But the only sign of life she'd received was an email in which he briefly stated that he'd landed.

She dialled the number of the Stockholm Blasting

Centre and reached the same man she'd spoken to the day before.

'I've received some information from the blasters,' he said, 'but none of it matches the time you're looking for, 12.05 the day before yesterday.'

'How many are you still waiting on?'

'About ten.'

'Can you call me as soon as you get anything that matches the time?'

'You bet. What is this about? Is it something important?'

'It has to do with locating a girl who's been kidnapped.'

There was silence for a moment.

'I think I can get some of the guys to hurry up,' he said. 'I'll call you this afternoon.'

An abandoned house, she thought, as she hung up, with a hiding place that only a few people knew about . . . blasting . . . she knew they were connected.

Fifteen minutes later she was back at EBM on Hant-verkargatan. To her surprise, Danielsson was waiting for her in her office. Four printed-out photos were on her desk. The top one showed Eva herself outside the gates of Klingberg's estate in Djursholm.

'Can you explain to me what this is all about, Eva?'

This was the end; she couldn't keep lying any more.

'How did you get those?'

'We were alerted by the elder daughter, who became worried about her father and went there to see what had happened. I was first on the scene. There are surveillance cameras around the property. Someone had deleted the video, but we found a back-up function.'

'What are you going to do . . . detain me?'

'Maybe.'

He stood up from the visitor's chair, took the photographs from the desk and looked at them sceptically.

'There were two bodies inside. Pontus Klingberg and Katz's former boss, Rickard Julin. Do you know what this means? It's going to be a fucking mess!'

'Who else knows I was there?'

'I'm the only one, so far. The surveillance videos landed on my desk, and I haven't released the contents yet. But, naturally, it's only a matter of time until I have to.'

'How long?'

'Time's already up. Now tell me what the hell is going on!'

'I can't.'

'You have no choice.'

'There's always a choice. My daughter's safety is at stake.'

He looked at her for a long time, realized she wasn't going to tell him anything, that nothing would help – not threats, not pleading.

'I can't believe I'm going to say this,' he said. 'But I'll give you three hours to finish whatever the hell it is you're up to. Then I'm going to bring you in for questioning and demand an explanation for why there is a picture of you outside a house that contains two bodies, and not only that – you were with one person who is wanted for murder and another who is a known criminal.'

She went up to the desk and looked at the other

photographs. Katz and Jorma were also in the picture. 'Are you the one who's hiding him?' said Danielsson. 'You don't have to answer now. But you're going to have to, and soon, damn it. I'm putting my career on the line for you. And I don't really know why. Because we slept together? Don't think so. Whatever we started, it's over. You're not my type, Eva, I'm coming to realize that.'

He gave her a pained smile and went to the door.

'Eva Dahlman,' he said. 'Your maiden name . . . victim of an attack much like the one on Angela Klingberg, in 1984. Danny Katz was convicted of the crime. But you refused to testify against him.'

She looked beseechingly at him.

'Can you help me with one more thing? One last favour, I promise.'

He just sighed, and she took that as a yes.

'A phone number. I think it's to the Dominican Republic, to a mobile phone. It must be possible to trace the phone, see where the user is.'

'Why don't you just call and ask?'

'I can't. It's very important that this person doesn't suspect anything. I'll explain everything later.'

The phone call came early in the morning. Klingberg's voice sounded distant, as if reception was bad wherever he was. Katz had to leave immediately, had to drive west, towards San Juan de la Maguana. The route had been programmed into the car's GPS. He would receive further instructions on the way. It was important that he not take anything with him, just the clothes he was wearing and the mobile phone.

Tell the hotel staff that you're going on a trip and you'll be back in a few days. Leave your bags and luggage in the room. And, believe me, I have the ability to make sure you do as I say.

It was dark in the garage. The electricity hadn't been restored yet. A valet brought up the car for him.

He weaved his way through the old city centre and followed Avenida George Washington until he was out of the area. Slums lined the motorway; shacks of sheet metal and plastic that would blow away during the hurricane season. Children in rags played among the rubbish.

One hour later, as he turned north-west, he found himself in the Middle Ages. Farm workers with hoes and machetes in the fields. Carts pulled by oxen. No more white faces, except in the passing cars.

The traffic became lighter and lighter the farther into the countryside he drove. The scenery changed, becoming greener; the ridges were forested. The valleys he drove through were like savannas. The cloud-encircled top of Pico Duarte towered three thousand metres above sea level, directly to the north.

He stopped at a rest stop. A man in broken sandals tried to sell him petrol from a plastic can. The man had a faint Creole accent. When Katz declined, he took the can and vanished into the fields.

He opened the hood of the car and pretended to inspect the engine. He stood there for five minutes, during which time no cars passed. He stepped around to the other side, opened the door and took out the miniature satellite phone and the charger he'd placed under the mat on the passenger side. He tore off a piece of the electrical tape he'd brought along, walked back to the open hood and taped the objects under the radiator.

He had to find an outlet soon so he could call Eva.

Then he got back into the car and drove on. One hour later, he had arrived in San Juan de la Maguana.

The city was a sleepy provincial hole. Men in straw hats sat in the shade of tattered umbrellas, waiting for nothing. Beggar children ran after the car. Katz stopped outside a chemist's in what appeared to be the centre. He sat there with the air conditioning on for ten minutes before Klingberg called.

'I'm guessing you've arrived.'

'Yes, I'm here.'

'I understand you made a stop along the way?'

The car itself was bugged, Katz thought; Klingberg

had either linked into the GPS or stuck a transmitter somewhere on the Land Rover.

'The engine sounded strange; I was afraid it was going to overheat. But it was a false alarm.'

'I'm glad to hear it. I hope you were able to enjoy the scenery. The sierra. The sea as you drove out of Santo Domingo. My old neighbourhood in the summer when I was young. I spent a few months each year on the island with my father. Only happy memories, on my part.'

He stopped talking and breathed very close to the receiver.

'You're getting close,' he said. 'From now on, you have to listen carefully to my instructions. Do you understand what I'm saying?'

He answered in the affirmative.

'Keep driving west towards Las Matas de Farfán. A few kilometres after the village you'll see a small church. You'll turn off there, on to a smaller country road. I'll call you again once you're there.'

He hung up without waiting for an answer. Katz started the car and drove on.

She had to get hold of Katz, to inform him of what had come up. If she managed to find Lisa, her muddled thoughts said, he had to know. So he could come home again.

But no one answered the fucking satellite phone.

Danielsson had managed to locate the number she'd found in Sandra Dahlström's address book. It went to a subscription in the Dominican Republic. Two days earlier, someone had called it from an unknown number. The call lasted for three minutes. Before that, there had been no activity on the number at all.

She looked over at the house that stood brooding behind the overgrown garden. Lisa . . . she dared to think about her a little more now that there was a ray of hope.

She'd got lucky at the Blasting Centre. The man she had spoken to called in the afternoon with what he hoped was good news. Two days earlier, at 12.05, four explosive charges of two kilos each had been detonated under the rock at Margretelundsvägen in Traneberg. It was a delayed excavation for the new Tvärbana light-rail line between Alvik and Solna.

'The explosions would have been clearly audible within a radius of five hundred metres,' he had explained to her, 'and the vibrations might have been felt in an area double that size.'

So this was where she was locked up – along the route Klingberg had driven the same day he had staged his own disappearance.

The reason Klingberg had been in Traneberg had nothing to do with his brother's kidnapping, as Katz had first thought when he followed Joel's route. Nor did it have anything to do with the fact that Katz lived there, with trying to make it look like Katz was behind the disappearance, or with the fact that the family's luxury yacht had once been in the shipyard nearby. Julin had been with Klingberg, she thought. Julin dropped him off there and then drove the car to the multi-storey car park in the centre, where he ran into Jonas Åkesson.

She'd come here as fast as she could as soon after she had talked to the man at the Blasting Centre, and there it was – the abandoned house, two hundred metres from where they were blasting, hardly visible behind the overgrown garden.

The house had been purchased by Capitol Security ten years earlier. Marianne Lindblom, her faithful helper at EBM, had checked it out for her. There was a building permit for a new office building on the property, but the company had never had the old house torn down; it had been allowed to remain and decay. She sat in the car, watching the property through binoculars as she waited for Jorma to show up. No movement so far; no car traffic. The shipyard and the other small industries in the area were closed for the day. The phone rang and she took the call without thinking, in the hope that it was Jorma. It was Ola.

'Any news?' he asked.

'No.'

'I feel like I'm about to go crazy. I can't work, can't eat, can't sleep. My thoughts just keep going around and around.'

'We're going to find her.'

'How do you know that? We have to face it – she might be dead.'

She didn't want to think about that. And she couldn't tell him anything she knew. She couldn't even involve the police, because if there was one thing she understood, it was that Klingberg was a man who kept his word.

'Where are you? I have to see you . . . just to talk a little. Erika can't stand me.'

She looked at the house. The painted yellow façade, the missing balcony floor, the roof that had partially caved in. It had been beautiful once upon a time, a luxurious, architect-designed villa, three storeys, a view of Ulvsundasjön. She guessed that there must be about ten rooms inside. And a basement. It was impossible to see what was behind it. Outbuildings. A garage?

'Are you listening to me, Eva, are you still there?'

Near the water and a place where they're blasting . . . And what if she was wrong? It couldn't be. This was her only chance.

'I'm here.'

'So what are the police actually doing? I haven't heard anything from them in a day. Are they ignoring us? They can't do that, damn it! You have to use your contacts. I'm going crazy, because I can't do anything. And Arvid, what the hell am I supposed to tell Arvid? He doesn't have any idea what's going on . . .'

A broken man, she thought. If the worst were to happen, he would never recover. Nor would she.

Then she saw movement farther down the road, at the curve. She hoped it was Jorma's car approaching at high speed. But it wasn't. She saw a small car, which stopped fifty metres from the house. A woman stepped out, looking around suspiciously. She was wearing a grey cardigan.

'I have to go now,' she said. 'I'll call later. There's something I have to do. Try to take it easy for now. We'll work this out.'

He was approaching the border with Haiti. Thick jungle along the road. Here and there he saw a clearing, tobacco fields in the forest. He didn't see any people; there was no traffic. Colourful butterflies were flushed out of the ditches as he drove by.

Klingberg had called him again and guided him on to smaller roads, which brought him farther and farther into the wilderness.

He turned on the car radio and listened to the staticky broadcast from Port-au-Prince. He flipped between music stations that alternated between playing salsa and Jamaican reggae. He found a talk show with a female host, but the French they were speaking was so full of Creole expressions that he hardly understood half of it. On the other end of the FM dial, a Dominican station was broadcasting the news in Spanish. A minor hurricane was expected to reach the east coast within twenty-four hours. People in Punta Cana and La Romana were advised to stay indoors and continue to follow the news on the radio; it might become necessary to evacuate parts of the coast.

He was at a higher altitude now. A flock of chattering parrots flew down the mountainside. The ground was cut through with streams. Mud spattered on to the windshield. As the road bent sharply to the left, the Land Rover started to skid and Katz couldn't stop it until he'd come out of the curve.

At the edge of the road, just where he'd stopped, was an altar. The severed head of a snake lay in a pool of blood on a piece of white cloth. Next to it stood a bottle of rum, a crucifix and a candelabra holding red candles. Shoes had been nailed to the tree trunks in the clearing.

He continued through the forest for another hour as the road got worse and worse, a sea of mud that created a narrow path through the trees. Then it suddenly broadened again; the landscape opened up.

There were half-overgrown sugar-cane fields on either side of the road.

Ramshackle metal shacks with signs in French and Spanish.

There were more buildings here: sugar-cane mills, a concrete structure that he guessed was a sugar refinery. Small homes made of corrugated iron and bamboo with verandas. And a larger building in colonial style, surrounded by palms. A few feral dogs ran across the yard, barking.

The phone rang just as he stopped. The reception was poor; he could hardly hear Klingberg's voice.

'You've arrived. There's a room ready for you in the big house.'

The house didn't seem to have been inhabited for several years. The shutters were closed. The furniture was covered in damp sheets. A thick layer of undisturbed dust blanketed the floor in the parlour.

No electricity. Empty water calabashes in the kitchen. Rat droppings on the floor.

He walked into a library with a wall of shelves that were full of leather-bound books. The titles were in Spanish and French. On the opposite wall was a gallery of paintings. Oil portraits of the former owners of the house, he guessed, in chronological order. The oldest one depicted a man with a plumed hat and a clay pipe in his hand; it appeared to be from the seventeenth century. The most recent was a portrait of Gustav Klingberg in his forties, dressed in a chalk-stripe suit with a bloodhound lying at his feet.

Katz went up to the second floor and found the room Klingberg had mentioned. A bottle of mineral water stood on a table. A canopied bed draped in mosquito netting towered in the middle of the room. There was heavy mahogany furniture along the walls. Behind a balcony door was a terrace with a view of a pool full of sludge.

The entire afternoon went by without a trace of any other people. He walked around aimlessly in what he guessed had once been a plantation belonging to the Klingberg family. The sugar mills didn't seem to have been used for several years. The buildings had been emptied of machines and inventory.

One of the sheds contained slaughtering masks and bolt pistols as well as a slaughtering pen ingrained with blackened blood. Pig skulls and other animal bones were piled behind the door.

He took one of the bolt pistols from the wall and

weighed it in his hand. The construction was simple; a spring drove the bolt itself out of the cylinder. The iron had rusted, but the spring mechanism seemed to work. Katz stuck it in his pocket. At least it was a weapon.

He kept walking along a half-overgrown mud path, peering into old workers' dwellings: huts with trampled earthen floors and roofs of corrugated metal. The windows and doors had been removed, but rusty bunk beds remained. Yellowed advertisements for Haitian rum hung on the wall. There were rotted clothes and shoes in the wardrobes.

More rainclouds were gathering on the horizon. The sky was grey as a corpse.

Someone had painted a bleeding black man being licked by dogs on the door of one cement building. Legba, or St Rochus, the patron saint of the Haitian slaves. The building had no windows, and the door was locked with a thick padlock. A wooden barrel that was half full of salt stood outside the door.

He kept walking along the road he'd driven in the car, then turned on to a path that led to the edge of the forest and a smaller building.

He saw a chapel as he approached and, next to it, a small cemetery. There were only two graves there, marked with iron crosses. There were glass-encased photographs attached to the crosses. One was of an old black woman. She was lying in a casket, wrapped in a white shift. He read the name and the years: Marie Bennoit, born 27 September 1921; died 11 November 1978.

He looked at the other cross. The blurry picture showed

a young boy with biracial features; he, too, was lying in a casket. There was no name, just the years of birth and death: 1963–79. The boy looked like Kristoffer Klingberg.

Swarms of mosquitoes followed him as he walked back towards the house. Night was falling quickly. There was no moon, no stars; the layer of cloud was growing thicker. He saw the pack of feral dogs again; they were on the road, growling, showing their teeth, but when he picked up a rock from the ground they ran off.

A storm broke; big lightning bolts split the sky and made the mountains light up as if from fluorescent bulbs. It started to rain, big, warm drops of water that fell thicker and thicker and whipped at his face. Strong gusts of wind ploughed through the sugar-cane fields like invisible giants.

Katz went up to the room that had been prepared for him, lit the candles in the candelabra next to the bed and closed the windows and shutters. The rain was like an endless drum roll on the room. He looked at the phone. Hardly any battery power left, and he wouldn't be able to charge it. If Klingberg wanted to call him again, he'd have to do it soon. But maybe that wasn't his intention.

He lay down on the mattress and looked up at the tattered canopy.

He suddenly remembered everything.

Klingberg's girlfriend in Uppsala. What was her name, Ingrid?

That was what the drugs had done to him – perforated his memory, poked holes in it, picking out important bits of information and destroying them.

They had been together during their last term in Uppsala. Klingberg's old girlfriend from Sigtuna, teenage love that had lasted for a few months before she went to France to attend a language school and, as far as Katz knew, they broke up.

She had visited them in their shared dorm. Klingberg had discreetly asked Katz to stay away for a few hours. He'd gone to Ofvandahls Hovkonditori to study Russian over half a dozen cups of black coffee before he returned to the dorm, where Klingberg and Ingrid met him with a mix of shame and satisfaction in their eyes.

She was from the upper class, just like him. She'd driven a red Porsche 911, which she'd received as a graduation present from her parents.

At one point, in May, he remembered, she had come to a party in the dorm; Katz had ended up alone with her on the balcony. He'd offered her a Gauloise, joked with her in French – he'd studied the language at *gymnasiet*, done six terms' worth in less than a year – and lent her his leather jacket when she said she was cold. They had drunk alcohol, he remembered, vintage whiskey she'd brought from home. These were drinking habits he'd never come across before meeting Klingberg. Their whole lives were so foreign to his own, with their language courses abroad, their family fortunes, their sports cars, private chauffeurs and a never-ending supply of money.

He'd put his hand under her skirt, run his finger along the edge of her panties; she was already wet. Then he'd groped further, under the fabric, touching her slippery labia as he continued to make jokes in French. He stood with his back to the balcony door so that none of the others could see what was going on.

Had he been high? He didn't remember. It was definitely possible that he had taken something. He still had relapses sometimes. But he had no memory of regret. In any case, he hadn't been hampered by moral imperatives. Not back then. He had thought of it as a form of tax refund: taking from the rich and giving to the poor.

The contempt he felt for Klingberg, deep down . . . that weakling, that nerd . . . wasn't it the case that he very well might have done it to ruin things between them?

She'd come back two days later, on a Saturday, when Klingberg was at his grandfather's home in Djursholm. They'd slept together in Klingberg's bed. Katz recalled that his feelings of guilt made him cry afterwards.

Klingberg came back on Sunday night. Katz hadn't even bothered to get rid of the evidence. The condom wrapper was still in Klingberg's unmade bed. The shawl she'd left behind was on the floor. Klingberg asked if it was true, if he'd slept with her, and Katz had only laughed in reply. *I don't understand*, Klingberg mumbled before he left the room. *The only person I ever trusted.*

They were discharged not long after that. Katz had been sure they'd never meet again.

He woke up in the middle of the night to the sound of drums. The photo in the cemetery – was it really Kristoffer in that grave, and if it was, how had he come to be there? He remembered Ingrid again. It hadn't been important back then, just something he'd done without a guilty conscience, because that was who he was at the time – and that was why, with the help of the drugs he'd stuffed himself with in the decade that followed, he had forgotten everything.

The storm seemed to have let up, or perhaps it was only temporary. Katz lay in bed, listening to the drums, a quick, pattering rhythm far away. He looked at the phone on the bedside table; there was still a little bit of battery left. But Klingberg wouldn't call.

He got up and put on his clothes. He heard the rustle of cockroaches running across the floor. He didn't think anything in particular; he was just drawn farther into the surreal feeling. How had he ended up here . . . how had it all started?

The landscape looked like it had been plated with chrome when he stepped into the yard. He could see scattered clusters of stars through the high, thin clouds. The sound of the drums had taken on a different character.

He walked past the barracks and down to the cane fields. Bats were performing acrobatic acts in the air in front of him; the full moon hung from an invisible thread at the horizon. He kept walking towards the sound of the drums, or towards where he thought they were coming from. He passed the sugar mills and arrived in an open field. On the other side of it was the jungle, a black wall. Faint lights flickered between the tree trunks.

He followed an irrigation ditch towards the glow of the lights. The smell of mud and rotting plants rose from the stagnant water. Frogs hopped out of the way of his feet, croaking. Then he had come to the edge of the forest. He found a sort of portal, cut by machetes, in the wall of vegetation, and he entered the jungle along a cleared path.

He walked for five minutes before a clearing opened before him. A fire was burning in a pit that had been dug in the middle. Katz took twenty steps into the forest so that he was hidden among the trees.

A party, ecstatically dancing people. He saw a drunk man swig from a bottle of rum, wipe off the neck and hand it to a young boy. There were more people farther off; some were crouching and playing drums, and an older woman was shaking some sort of rattle. They were all poor, dressed in rags.

On a chair next to the drummers was a man covered in a white sheet. There was a human skull in his lap. A cigar had been stuck between its teeth, and a pair of aviator sunglasses covered its empty eye sockets. The person under the sheet was sitting perfectly still.

A man took a glowing coal from the fire and started eating it as a woman brushed his back with a live chicken and chanted in Creole. Some of the people were white . . . but he was mistaken, he realized then; they were naked and covered in pale mud.

The dancing and singing continued. He watched people falling into trances and writhing on the ground like snakes. He heard people screaming in ecstasy and bestial sorrow. He saw a piglet carried to an altar, squealing furiously, and he saw a woman cut its throat with a dagger in one slice. She released it on the ground and let it run into the forest with its neck spouting blood. A pig, sacrificed and sent to the spirit world.

His eyes kept returning to the man under the sheet: the white trainers sticking out from under the fabric, the skull in his lap, with its sunglasses and the cigar in its jaws.

There could be no doubt that it was Sandra Dahlström. Eva could see her clearly through the binoculars. She had parked her car fifty metres from the abandoned house.

Her greying hair was in a ponytail. She looked around suspiciously, walked away from the house, took a right on to a path that led up to the hill behind the property and disappeared from sight.

Eva felt it instinctively – she couldn't wait any longer, she had to act immediately.

She stepped out of the car and started running. She saw her own shadow darting in front of her as her mind spooled out memories of Lisa, and she promised to herself that she would be a better mother, a better role model, a less self-destructive person, if only her daughter were unharmed.

She slowed down as she approached the path. She looked up warily and saw movement – a person vanishing around a bend. She cautiously followed. Her yearning for Lisa brought tears to her eyes.

She went another hundred metres before she found herself on a rise above the property.

There was no movement down there. She could see the garden and the house more clearly from the hill where she stood. The windows and doors were covered with boards and sheet metal. Even the second-floor windows had been boarded up. Like a fort, she thought.

There was a hidden entrance somewhere, but she couldn't see it. Sandra Dahlström could have led her to it. She had missed her by a few seconds.

There was a dilapidated shed to the right of the building. To the left was a garage without a door, full of old building materials.

She let her eyes wander on. Overgrown apple trees, a lawn that had been transformed into a meadow; the poppies glowed bright red against the yellow grass.

She moved on, stooping, shuffling down the slope towards the short side of the garage.

She was twenty metres from the house now, but she still couldn't hear anything. The grass was trampled where Sandra Dahlström had just walked; it led to a gravel path that went around the house in both directions.

Somewhere inside, Lisa was alone with her. There was one person left, she had said on the phone; the others were gone. The room she was in wasn't soundproofed, otherwise she wouldn't have been able to hear the blasting.

But where was the entrance?

Time was running out. She was having trouble thinking clearly; she just wanted to follow her instincts, which told her that she had to find Lisa right away. But wouldn't it be better to go back to the car and wait for Jorma? She didn't even have a weapon. Wouldn't it be better to wait until Sandra Dahlström showed up again, and then force her to lead them to Lisa? It would be crazy to try to catch her by surprise if she was in the same room as her daughter; Lisa might end up injured.

She slowly retreated to the garage, but she stumbled on a broken rain barrel, fell down and found herself on the ground.

To her left was a tall rosebush. She never would have discovered what was behind it if she had been standing; only down by the trunks where the bush was thinner was it possible to see that the rosebush had grown around a well like a protective wall. A ladder was sticking out of the opening.

And then there were thorns that got stuck . . .

She stood up, bent the branches out of the way and stepped into the clearing. Her shawl got stuck in the bush but she didn't have time to pull it loose. The well cover lay alongside the brick edge. She grabbed the ladder and climbed down.

The well was dry. When she came to the bottom she discovered a small passage that led in the direction of the house. She had to stoop as she walked, using her hand to feel the way ahead in the pitch black. After ten steps the passage bent sharply to the left. She could glimpse light up ahead.

A door was ajar. She opened it cautiously. The ceiling lights were on. She was standing in a laboratory. *Julin's*, she thought, as she looked around. She just knew it – this was where he had experimented with psychoactive drugs. There were separators for examining plant toxins on a long counter. On the shelves were test tubes, jars and

349

containers of chemical compounds. An open cupboard contained syringes in plastic packaging.

She opened another door and stepped into a small bedroom. There was an unmade bed along the wall and an open wardrobe in a recess opposite it. There were jeans and T-shirts on the shelves. A suit hung from a hanger. A container of food with silverware stood on a folding table. On the rolled-up bedspread was a leather strap and an insulin syringe. Jonas Åkesson had stayed there. He had been murdered in his bed, given an overdose when Julin realized that Katz was on his trail.

And Klingberg had stayed there after faking his disappearance. The suit was his.

She heard sounds now, coming from somewhere deeper in the house. Faint, sobbing cries. Lisa. So she was alive, at least.

She opened a sliding door and stepped into a hallway that led up to a staircase. Daylight shone down from above. She cautiously walked towards the stairs and was suddenly aware of how defenceless she was, that she had nothing to protect herself with.

Then she noticed movement out of the corner of her eye and turned around. She saw an electric arc just as the pain came and her muscles seemed to loosen from their attachments to her body. Sandra Dahlström was standing two metres away, aiming a taser at her; she discharged it again and the world went black.

Katz couldn't tell what time it was when he woke up. Early morning, he guessed. The light outside was grey.

The wind sounded like creaking metal. He heard the tiles on the roof moving. The thuds of trees falling, far away. Klingberg was sitting on a chair by the wall, watching him.

'A hurricane,' he said. 'A twelve on the Beaufort scale. That's how they sound, creaking as they increase in strength. Soon you won't be able to hear anything but a roar.'

He was taller than Katz remembered, or perhaps it was a trick of his thin body. He resembled his grandfather in the portrait on the floor below. His hair was still brown, with no hint of any grey strands. His eyes were inscrutable. He was wearing khaki pants, a thin jacket and a pale shirt.

'Gustav told me a story once,' he said. 'It was about a doctor who was going to help a Dominican man get rid of the black colour of his skin. The only problem was that the man couldn't decide which colour he wanted instead. Whether he wanted to be *moreno*, dark; *canelo*, cinnamon-coloured; *blanco-oscuro*, dark white . . . it's actually called that . . . or wheat-coloured, *trigueño*. But none of those colours are white, they're just variations and euphemisms for black skin. I don't remember how the story

351

ended, but I know what it was about: African heritage is a curse.'

He looked at the legs of his trousers, finding a speck of dirt which he rubbed at with the nail of his thumb.

'You saw a ceremony tonight,' he said. 'In the forest. After you'd been to the cemetery. Desperate people, looking for comfort in the only thing they have left: their faith. My grandmother was involved in that sort of thing. Marie Bennoit. She was a priest in a *perestil*, a Vodou church on the other side of the border. She was from a family that used black magic. Or superstition, if you prefer.'

On the table in front of him was the cloth doll from the hotel room, and the satellite phone Katz had hidden in the car engine.

'I brought a few things with me,' he said, when he noticed where Katz was looking. 'You won't be returning.'

'Where's the girl?' said Katz. 'You were going to let her go.'

Klingberg didn't answer. He went over to a window and opened the shutters. The palms were bending in the wind. From far away came a rumble Katz had never before experienced, a sort of howl that slowly increased in strength.

'I think this was where he told me the story . . . Gustav's heaven on earth. A classic batey, a sugar workers' town, the first one he had built and the only one he kept until his death. Two hundred Haitians worked here during the heyday, in the late forties. Gustav would organize parties in the house. He invited Ramfis Trujillo and his entourage, people like Porfirio Rubirosa. Have you heard of him? He was one of the international jet-setters at the time, a play-boy and ladies' man. Gustav hired whores for his guests. They were sent here on mules from the bordellos in Port-au-Prince. Rich white men and penniless black women had poolside orgies. The whores were paid in as much food as they could carry home with them afterwards. Blacks were just a sort of human livestock to do with as one pleased. That went for Marie Bennoit, too . . . and, eventually, Kristoffer.'

The butt of a revolver was sticking out of his jacket pocket. Klingberg nodded when he realized Katz had seen it.

'Grandfather became nostalgic as soon as we got here. Once . . . I was twelve at the time . . . I saw him set the dogs on one of the employees. It was the summer before Mum and Dad died. Gustav and I were here on our own. A Haitian foreman had stolen money from the office. Gustav thought it would be good for me to watch, educational. He was bitten in the throat, like a bloody necklace . . . I'll never forget it.'

He stopped talking and looked sadly at Katz. Far away, the feral dogs started howling.

'It was the summer of 1978. Kristoffer must have been here then, although he was kept hidden from me. Julin found him in the end, here at the plantation, but with only faint memories of who he was. Julin realized that Grand-father was the one behind it all. Gustav had organized the abduction, sent him back to Marie Bennoit, who had placed a curse on the family. Gustav hoped it would appease her. He was terrified of her – business deals that failed just before they went through; his wife, Lisbet, who was suddenly struck by inexplicable fainting spells – and his fear of sorcery was greater than his love for his own grandchild. Julin found proof of everything. He had a hold on Gustav after that, for the rest of his life.'

He grew quiet, looking at Katz glassily.

'Is there anything else you're wondering about?' he said. 'What happened on the boat that time in Hässelby?'

Katz nodded as he touched his trouser pocket carefully. He had fallen asleep with his clothes on. The bolt pistol was still there.

'I woke up to someone breaking in. I was terrified and hid under a berth. The adults had gone into town. Pontus and his friends were going to the pub. I could see out through the crack under the top of the cot. I witnessed two guys my age vandalizing the furnishings. And I decided that I wouldn't let it go unpunished.'

'So you followed us?'

'You and the other guy went separate ways; you went off with a girl. Eva, Lisa's mum. You went to a bike room, took too many drugs . . . you were completely knocked out.'

'But you weren't alone.'

Klingberg looked at him sadly, as if he wanted to ask forgiveness.

'No. I called my old nursemaid. Sandra Dahlström. She came and helped me, gave you more drugs while you were unconscious. We took you to a nearby islet. Then I was able to do as I wished. I think I inherited my desire for revenge from my grandfather.'

Klingberg stopped talking and looked at the clock.

'Get up,' he said. 'We have to finish this before the storm comes.'

The roar of the approaching hurricane had increased by the time they came out into the yard. The feral dogs had stopped barking. Klingberg pressed the barrel of the revolver to Katz's back and pushed him ahead. They walked slowly along the gravel path through the village as Joel continued to tell him everything that had happened, filling in the holes, tightening up the story as if he wanted to make sure that Katz understood every detail.

He talked about the hatred he'd felt for his parents and missing older brother, the hatred for being the one left alone, because, despite his absence, Kristoffer had been the centre of their world, the loss his parents had always come back to, since they had no idea that he was alive and on a sugar-cane plantation in the borderlands between Haiti and the Dominican Republic; the hatred from having lived in the shadow of a missing older brother.

He talked about the murder of his parents at the manor house in Sörmland, how he'd found them falling-down drunk one evening, each sleeping on a sofa in the big parlour, and realized that it was the opportunity he'd been waiting for. How he'd managed to drag them out to the garage, then got them into the car, placed bottles of alcohol in their laps, laced their fingers together, attached the garden hose to the exhaust pipe and the interior of the car . . . bent in and gave them each a farewell kiss, a suck mark on the neck, without really understanding why . . .

before starting the engine, almost in shock – not about what he'd done but because he'd dared to do it. How Gustav had suspected it had been him but chose to keep quiet anyway.

He talked about how Julin had become interested in him when he was a teenager, in his outbursts of rage and his gift for languages. He told Katz what he knew about Julin's secret military programme, about how he had become inspired by what he'd seen during his trips to the Dominican Republic, about the money that had come from Gustav thanks to the hold Julin had on the old man. He explained that Julin had helped him with the murder of Angela Klingberg and everything that happened after that, and he was saying all of this in the certainty that Katz would not survive.

By the time he had finished, they were a kilometre down the road. They were standing outside the cement building with St Rochus painted on the door. The lid was missing from the salt barrel outside. The door was open.

'Go in! You can't scare him any more. Not when you don't have this.'

In one hand Klingberg held the cloth doll, the *paké*, and with the other he pointed the revolver at Katz. Katz did as he was told.

A person was sitting motionlessly on a chair by the far wall, covered by a dirty sheet. A pair of white trainers stuck out under the hem. The roar of the hurricane was still growing stronger. Klingberg had to raise his voice to make himself heard.

'Take some salt from the barrel and throw it at him.'

Katz did as he asked. The person gave a start as the salt hit the sheet.

'Once more! That's how you wake them, the seemingly dead.'

He threw another fistful. Convulsions went through the body. Its feet scraped nervously at the floor. Then the sheet fell off him.

It was a man in his fifties, a half-black man. He was dressed in ragged jeans and a dirty T-shirt. His eyes were empty, lifeless, like those of a junkie. He could see the Nordic features in the face. The green eyes, the blond hair that was interrupted by the brown skin.

'He thinks he's dead,' said Klingberg. 'Because he *wants* to be dead . . . because he has nothing to live for.'

Katz saw the wound on the man's cheek where he'd stabbed him with the neck of the broken bottle in the hunting cabin. The man's face drew into a grimace as he showed his teeth and gave a low growl.

'My brother died of a tropical illness shortly after Julin found him, and just a few months after Marie Bennoit's death. She had taken care of him like a mother, doing her best, given the limited circumstances.'

Klingberg stopped talking and looked contemptuously at him.

'This man claims that he's Kristoffer, that he was taken out of the earth shortly after he was buried. Our grandmother could no longer protect him from all the hate that Gustav had created here.'

Klingberg was still aiming the revolver at him; he, too,

took a handful of salt from the barrel and threw it at the man, who convulsed again.

'What do you think, Katz, is this Kristoffer?'

He didn't answer; he just waited for something to happen.

'He was one of the ones Julin studied . . . along with a number of others with similar symptoms. There's a hospital on the other side of the border, a psychiatric clinic where they try to treat people like him. Julin went there, too. And to Port-au-Prince. Look at him. He has no will of his own. You can make him do anything at all; he thinks he has to obey.'

That was the last thing Katz knew; he just heard the crack of the gunshot and noticed a burning sensation in his right thigh. He fell down head first. His cheek struck the floor and he passed out.

She woke up on the floor in a space that stank of mould. Her hands were bound to a warm-water pipe with plastic ties. Her body still ached from the electric shocks.

'Mum . . . are you there?'

Lisa's voice came from another part of the house. She wanted to shout back, that she was there, that everything would be fine, but she didn't have the strength.

'Mum . . . answer me!'

She started crying. She couldn't believe she had risked everything by going in alone.

'Mum, please . . .'

The voice was suddenly cut off as someone closed the door to the room Lisa was in. She made every effort not to panic.

A few minutes went by. Her body seemed to be recovering; her brain was starting to work again. She heard steps approaching, a door opened, and Sandra Dahlström stood before her.

'Does anyone know you were coming here?' she asked.

'No.'

'You're lying, you cunt.'

'I came alone.'

She aimed the taser at her again and fired it. The pain

was indescribable, as if someone were igniting her from the inside.

'Tell the truth!'

It took nearly a minute for her to be able to answer:

'I swear . . . I came by myself.'

'How did you find it?'

'There was blasting nearby . . . I recognized the sound on the phone. I managed to get the times from the firm that did the job.'

She wanted to say something more, but her stutter showed up and blocked her whole body.

Sandra Dahlström just nodded, bent forward and checked to make sure that the plastic ties were still where they should be. Then she straightened up again, walked over to a metal cabinet and took out a roll of electrical tape.

Eva realized that she had to buy time, at any price. Time was the only thing that could give her the possibility of finding a way to escape. But pain from the electric shock was still running through her body; her muscles were numb.

Talk to her, she thought, *stall her . . . without stuttering*.

'I don't understand,' she said quietly. 'You knew that Julin was doing experiments on Jonas and you didn't do anything to help him.'

Sandra ignored her, searching for something else in the cabinet: a kitchen towel that she rolled into a ball.

'You knew that Klingberg and Julin had him killed because Katz was on their trail. In this house, with an overdose of heroin.'

Her voice hardly carried. She watched as Sandra peeled off a piece of electrical tape, held it between her teeth and ripped it from the roll. The scars from the bite marks on her arm were shiny in the light from the doorway.

'Why does he have such power over you . . . Joel?'

'Love,' she said. 'It's as simple as that.'

They'd had a relationship since Klingberg was a teenager, thought Eva, as she cautiously tugged at the ties to test how firmly she was bound. They both had needs, and they found an outlet for them. Sandra had hoped that she would be able to transfer her love for him to Linnie, but it had never succeeded; she'd continued to see him even though he abused her.

'You still haven't told me the truth. Does anyone else know that you're here?'

'No.'

Sandra turned a knob on the taser and checked the settings.

'Now it's on the highest voltage. I think I'll go and visit your daughter and see how it works.'

The hate that rose in her was even stronger than her fear and pain.

'I'll kill you if you touch her.'

Sandra Dahlström looked at her expressionlessly, bent down and pressed the kitchen towel into her mouth, and wound the electrical tape around her head several times to keep it in place. Then she nodded and left the room.

Ten seconds went by, a period of time completely taken up with the thought that her little girl was going to die, and that she herself was going to die – that only Arvid would be left when it was all over. She heard Lisa calling for her again, faintly, far away. The kitchen towel made her feel like she was suffocating; she breathed wildly through her nose.

Then she heard two quick shots from a handgun in the next room; someone screamed and ran off.

She must have passed out, because when she came to again Jorma was bending over her and loosening the ties from the warm-water pipe.

'Lisa?' she said. 'Where is she?'

'In another room. She's okay.'

'And Sandra?'

'I don't know. She disappeared.'

She saw the pistol he was holding in his hand.

'You shot her?'

'I don't know if I hit her. I didn't even know if I was in the right place. I saw your scarf; it was caught on a rose-bush . . . that's how I found the entrance. I went in, saw a woman with a taser and shot at her without asking any questions.'

He led her along a hall, over to a windowless room on the other side of the house. All the pain and despair flowed through her as she saw her little girl bound to a hospital bed. But she was alive; that was all that mattered right now.

She didn't remember what order things happened in after that. She only knew that she sat with Lisa in her arms for a long time as Jorma searched the house, both of them crying with fear and relief. At some point he had called for her to come, and she found him in the laboratory in the cellar along with the lifeless body of Sandra Dahlström. She had swallowed some poison, she guessed, because her face was blackish blue and she was already dead. She wasn't sure if Lisa was there with her or if she'd left her in the room, or if she had perhaps already got her out, had called Ola to tell him, crying, that the nightmare was over.

He was in the slaughterhouse, on his knees in the pen. He was groggy, drugged. It was the same sort of intoxication as in the hunting cabin, but stronger. Klingberg didn't need to tie him up; his muscles didn't work.

Something was fastened around his head, some sort of metal band that chafed his forehead. A slaughtering mask.

Klingberg was standing before him with a plastic bottle in hand. He sniffed the contents.

'Tetrodotoxin,' he said. 'And a hallucinogenic ingredient, bufotenin. In olden times, the poison was placed in the victim's shoes or poured on to his back. When the person showed all the symptoms of death and had been buried, the witch doctor who had performed the poisoning went to the grave and dug up the body.'

Blood was streaming from a wound on the front of Katz's thigh. The bullet seemed to have gone through the muscle tissue without harming the bone or artery.

Klingberg bent forward, pouring another couple of drops from the bottle into the wound. Then he turned around and said a few words in Spanish to the man in the trainers.

The door was open. Katz saw the feral dogs on the road. They could smell the blood. They would come once his body had been left; the door would be open, his body would be covered in blood from the entry wound in his forehead where the bolt would strike him. The ravenous dogs would lick the blood off him first, and then they would try to find the soft bits . . . perhaps his throat . . . which Klingberg would have already bitten to shreds, just as he had seen a bloodhound do to a farm worker long ago on his grandfather's plantation.

He was flooded with a powerful feeling of peace, not unlike the one from a heroin rush. His muscles were useless, but the endorphins were there. Was this how he would die, high on a Caribbean drug?

He was still on his knees in the slaughtering pen, unable to move. The wind roared outside. The door was open. Roof tiles flew by in the air, light as leaves. And every other conceivable sort of rubbish: wood, branches, bushes that had been torn up by their roots. Large roofing sheets came loose from some building, rising and floating off twenty metres up in the air before they landed out of sight with a crash.

It was remarkably calm in the room he was in. The man in front of him was striking a hammer lightly against his leg. He seemed totally absent, higher than Katz was. A penniless man in a shithole at the edge of the world. Who was he? Kristoffer Klingberg? His body was covered in the scars of abuse. There were welts on his back where he'd been whipped like an animal. Like a child? Like a slave on a white man's sugar-cane plantation. Dead – a person who hadn't lived for years. What sort of trauma was behind such incomprehensible autosuggestion, that a person could consider himself dead? And yet he knew, because hadn't he himself lived that way for more than ten years, like a zombie?

Klingberg was standing next to him. Perhaps he wanted to witness his execution. He heard him speak as if from the other end of a kilometre-long corridor. Shouting to drown out the roar of the storm: 'It's logical, Katz, when you die I'll let the girl go. Are you prepared to sacrifice yourself?'

He said yes with his eyes, because he couldn't speak. He couldn't even swallow. He still didn't believe it. Why would Klingberg spare someone when everything had gone this far?

'I would have been able to come back . . . or maybe I still can. Everything points at you, after all. Nothing has changed on that front. Even the murder of Julin, the only one who, theoretically, could have testified against me. Do you know why I killed him?'

He looked intently at Katz.

'Because he wanted to kill you. You were on the trail of the deaf boy, and Julin didn't want to take any chances. But I was opposed to it. I saved your life. Because I liked the thought that you would be pursued for something I had done . . .'

Joel yelled something more that he didn't catch. His hearing was starting to give way; there were long pauses during which the background noise was transformed into a tinnitus-like buzz. As if someone was turning a relay on and off in his head.

'It was so easy to use you, Katz. You were doomed from the start, just like that time in Hässelby.'

He said something about how he hadn't realized that Katz was the same person before the night he came back from Djursholm and realized that Katz had slept with Ingrid. He suddenly seemed to recognize the hard, cold facial expression from the time a few years earlier when Katz had broken into the *St Rochus*. It was easy to confirm his suspicions. Katz, the person he had admired because he'd defended him against a paratrooper in Karlsborg. He said something about how much he hated Ingrid and Katz for what they'd done. How much he hated betrayal . . . ever since his brother had disappeared, since his parents had betrayed him with their sorrow. Ingrid had gone on a language trip to France the summer after they were discharged and had never returned. She disappeared during a mountain climb in the Pyrenees. Her body had never been found. But, naturally, he knew where it was, what was left of it.

The rage, Katz thought, that terrible rage they both carried. And he had to muster it in himself if he were going to survive this. Only with the help of his rage could he get free. He laughed internally at himself, at his foolishness.

'The pieces of cloth,' he managed to say. 'Someone sent embroidered Vodou cloths to you shortly before you vanished.'

'Yes. Strange, isn't it?'

Klingberg laughed.

'A black killing a Jew. Isn't it ironic? Soon he's going to drive that bolt into your head, nine centimetres straight into your brain. As soon as I leave.'

Klingberg was an anti-Semite, always had been, a racist and an anti-Semite, just like his uncle and grandfather. He'd known this back when they were acquaintances at the interpreter academy, but had ignored it, just as he'd ignored everything else to do with Klingberg, because he felt contempt for him.

'You wouldn't want to see yourself right now, Katz. With a slaughtering mask on your head . . . on your knees . . . covered in your own shit.'

It was true; he could smell the odour of his total degradation, but he didn't care. He was high on the drug Joel had given him, which had transformed him into a lifeless person. Klingberg's nose was bleeding, he noticed; it was running down his chin and neck, but he didn't seem to be aware of it.

'I have to go now,' he said. 'While the roads are still passable.'

Then he nodded at the man with the hammer and backed out of the room. He stood in the doorway for a moment as the wind tore at his clothes; then he turned around and disappeared down the path, hunched up.

Katz felt dizzy as the realization came to him that he had perhaps ten or twenty breaths left to live.

The man with the hammer took two steps towards him. He would have to bend down and sit across from Katz in order to drive the bolt into his brain. Unless he lifted him up first and propped him against something. Or laid him on his back.

The rage, he thought, *it has to come out now, the hate, it has to come*, because that was the only thing that had helped him survive all his years on the street.

His hands were clenched tight. He was still holding salt in one of them. He concentrated on Angela and Eva, on Lisa, whom Klingberg was holding captive somewhere and wouldn't spare; he felt his high give way and the darkness and the hate came out.

The man had got to his knees in front of him. He slowly lifted the hammer, but he seemed to realize that he wouldn't be able to strike the bolt at that angle, that it would go crooked.

He got up again, shoving Katz backwards with his foot so that Katz's back was leaning against the board wall. The storm just kept going outside; a tree trunk rolled past on the path, more roof tiles, more metal sheeting. Katz felt the hatred growing, all the collected hate he had carried within him since his childhood. He had got a hand up to his face now; the man watched as he licked the salt out of his open palm, but didn't seem to understand what he was doing and used his foot to push Katz's hand down until it was resting against his hip. Katz felt the bolt pistol in his pocket, groaned with pain as his muscles started to obey him, concentrated on his rage and let it wake him from the dead.

The man bent forward, raising his hand with the hammer. *The salt*, Katz thought: his body was reacting to it, the muscle cramps subsided, his body began to convulse and he fell over on to his side. He kept the bolt pistol hidden in his hand as the man bent over to lift him up. A little closer now. He had to grab Katz's arms to lay him on his back. Katz saw his head moving closer; he could smell his breath and the scent of insect repellant on his skin.

Twenty centimetres away now. He was surprised by the precision of his actions, as if he had always known what he would do in this very situation. The man looked at him in surprise as he suddenly lifted his hand and placed a cold object against the man's temple. Katz pulled the trigger and felt the recoil go through his arm. The man tumbled on to him with the left portion of his frontal bone indented into his brain.

He had no idea how long he lay there in the slaughter-house with the body on top of him. An hour . . . a day? He had auditory hallucinations; he thought that the dead man was talking, and the language he spoke was Swedish. Kristoffer – was it him, after all?

Finally, the high drew back, like the tide. He could move; the strength returned to his muscles.

It was evening when he stood on the path outside the slaughterhouse. The storm had passed. The sugar-cane village looked like an abandoned battlefield. The windows in the manor house were broken; the roof had blown off. There was rubbish and wreckage everywhere, heavy objects that had been carried a long distance. The feral dogs watched him from the edge of the forest as he stag-gered along the path towards the house. The Land Rover was gone. Klingberg had vanished in it, without making sure he was dead.

The mobile phone and wallet were still on the bed in the room on the second floor. His phone rang at the same instant he found it. *Klingberg*, he thought. But instead he heard Jorma's voice from far away:

'Katz, are you there? We found Lisa . . . she's okay . . .'

The line was broken as the last per cent of power left the battery.

He rented a small room in Barrio Las Malvinas in northern Santo Domingo. The furnishings were meagre: a bed, a lamp, a metal sink. The toilet and shower were in the hall.

On the first night he bought a few grams of Jamaican grass from a street dealer. He rolled joints and smoked them while sitting at the open window as he absently watched the sunset. The darkness came quickly, like when a lamp is rapidly dimmed. The sea was dead calm. The storm had passed by the coast without causing any great damage.

He'd hitched a ride on a lorry that was carrying pottery from Port-au-Prince to Santo Domingo. He didn't know where he got the strength. First, he'd limped along a jungle road for an hour, before he came to a village on the Haitian side of the border. Helpful people had taken care of him: a doctor from Doctors without Borders looked at his bullet wound, the people in the village let him sleep in a hammock in a mission hall overnight, gave him food and water and stopped the lorry as it came through the village streets early the next morning.

'Erzulie Freda?' he'd asked, when he saw the child's doll in a sequinned dress hanging from the rear-view mirror of the truck. The driver had given him the biggest smile he'd seen in several years.

He didn't know how long he would stay. Until the

view had cleared. And he'd done what he demanded of himself.

He was slowly recovering. The poison was still in his body, affecting his muscles, but the wound in his leg was healing surprisingly quickly. He tried not to think of the man he'd killed.

He called Eva the day he arrived.

'I miss you,' she said. 'When are you coming back?'

'I don't know.'

'Do you regret us sleeping together?'

'I don't think so.'

He'd listened to her calm breathing. Felt her relief that her little girl was unharmed. She'd tried to explain everything that had happened, but he hadn't had the strength to absorb it or tell her what had happened to him. He'd just said that it was all under control.

'Give me a call as soon as you're back, Katz. There's a lot we need to work out.'

He did what he had to; he scouted, thought, bought a map of the port district. One morning, he went to Avenida Sarasota some distance from the city centre. The pink building was from the late fifties. The relief above the entrance depicted a menorah, the seven-armed candelabra.

It was Saturday and the morning services were already underway. Katz took a *kippah* and a prayer book from a shelf and opened it to the right spot in the Amidah. The right-hand page was in Spanish, the left-hand in Hebrew. The cantor was standing on the *bema*, reciting.

About thirty men and women were on either side of

the centre aisle. Most of them had Sephardic roots – they were dark-skinned and short. There was a curtain as a *mechitza*, but it wasn't being used. People didn't seem to notice him; perhaps they were used to American tourists.

The cantor's voice was lulling and beautiful. He read the week's *parashah* from the Torah in a deep bass tone. The verse was about revenge, about the revenge of God, which was righteous but almost always incomprehensible. The vengefulness of man, which was conceivable but futile.

The cantor came up and introduced himself after the service; he was surprised when Katz said he was from Sweden, and he told Katz about the congregation, which was the oldest in the New World. The first Sephardim had come with the Spanish colonists and had kept their faith a secret. Later, more Jews had arrived from the Dutch Antilles, and Jewish refugees came from Europe during the war. Trujillo had allowed their immigration, generously enough; they'd received their own territory on the northern part of the island, in the enclave of Sosúa. The Jewish World Congress had bought land and livestock for them.

The cantor laughed as he talked about German-speaking academics who became farmers and stockbreeders.

'Do you need help with anything?' he asked, as Katz was about to leave.

'Yes . . .'

'Just name it.'

'I don't mean to alarm you, but I need to buy a pistol.'

The cantor looked at him earnestly.

'Are you in trouble?'

'I need it for self-defence. Hopefully, I won't have to use it.'

Hesitation. The cantor didn't know him, after all, and his request must have sounded absurd. And yet he must have seen something in Katz's eyes, the honesty of his seriousness.

'All I can give you is a phone number,' he said. 'You'll have to take care of the rest yourself. It's Shabbat for another eight hours. Come back after Havdalah.'

The boat was in the marina, at the farthest pier, among the luxury yachts. He could see it through the binoculars: *St Rochus*. It was sailing under the Panamanian flag these days.

'I'll give you a thousand pesos if you take me out there.'

The man who ran sightseeing boats up the Ozama River gave him a sceptical look.

'Now? It's going to be dark soon.'

'Yes, now.'

'What are you going to do? I don't want to get dragged into anything.'

'I just want to look around.'

Katz took a wad of bills from his pocket, added a fifty-dollar bill and handed the money to the man. He felt the rage inside him again as he climbed down into the motorboat; he had to find an outlet for it so as not to suffocate.

He took off his waterproof backpack and placed it on the floor of the boat. It didn't weigh much. All it contained was a torch, a can of pepper spray and a tiny Colt revolver.

The darkness fell quickly as they left the mouth of the river. Lanterns were being lit on the boats in the marina.

St Rochus was at the farthest dock – the boat he had broken into in another life.

They rounded the outer pier and continued towards the docks. Katz looked at his watch. Six thirty. The warmth still hung in the air like a warm, wet wrapper.

'I'm not going any closer,' said the man driving the motorboat. 'The docks are patrolled by guards. Do you want to turn around, or should I take you over to the seafront?'

But when he turned around, his passenger was gone.

The dock was illuminated by lanterns. A guard was standing at the gate that blocked the area off from the land side. Katz aimed for the stern of the nearest boat, swimming silently. There was a party underway farther off, on something that looked like a floating three-storey house.

He was out of sight, in the shadows behind the stern of the nearest boat. A man in a tuxedo was pissing from the railing ten metres away. Katz held still in the water, no pain in his injured leg, holding on to an anchor chain, inhaling the scents of waste oil and grilled food. When the man vanished, he kept going.

The *St Rochus* was dark. Klingberg was elsewhere, but sooner or later he would come back. Katz wasn't in any rush. He could wait for him. Revenge was a dish best served cold.

He swam around the craft, close to the hull. He listened for sounds, but didn't hear any. The cabins were dark. The deck was empty.

There was a ladder next to the water trampoline. Katz climbed up and dropped down behind the nearest cabin wall. Sighing sounds came as waves surged against the hull. He had a flashback to the slaughterhouse at the sugar-cane plantation. He hadn't had any choice, and yet he would have to live the rest of his life with the knowledge that he'd killed a man. He felt the hatred again, aimed at Klingberg. He felt the blackness coming behind his eyes.

He took off his backpack and his soaking-wet shirt. He waited until the guard was at the other end of the dock and crawled across the deck up to the door that led down to the cabins and the lounge. Unlocked.

He went down the stairs just as he had that time with Jorma in Hässelby. He held the revolver in one hand and the torch in the other. One cabin door was open. He shone the light into the room. A dirty bunk bed, scraps of food in a cellophane package, a strong scent of insect repellant – the same kind he'd smelled on the man he'd killed.

He entered the lounge. The room looked just as he remembered it, with furniture bolted to the floor: a dining table and a teak bar counter.

'Have a seat, Katz!'

The voice came from the dark corner astern. A Swedish voice, but it didn't belong to Klingberg. Two men were sitting on a sofa, reclining comfortably. A third was crouching by a safe that was set into the wall. The one who was speaking aimed a pistol with a silencer at him.

'Put the revolver on the table. I don't want there to be an accident.'

Katz did as he said.

'Empty your pockets, please.'

The pepper spray, his last lifeline . . . he put it on the table.

'Great, now have a seat. Don't worry, nothing's going to happen to you. We're just going to have a little chat.'

The man followed his movements with the barrel of the pistol. A professional – his hand was unbelievably steady; it didn't tremble in the least.

'Where's Klingberg?' Katz asked, as he sat down.

'You don't need to worry about him any more. In a few years he'll be declared dead. His body won't be found. He quite simply doesn't exist any longer.'

He had no idea what was going on; he just looked in amazement at the man who was speaking to him. It was difficult to make out his features in the darkness. He had a large build, and he was bearded, but his head was shaved.

'Unfortunately, I can't introduce myself. And the same goes for my colleagues.'

Lynx. Julin's superior.

The man who was crouching by the wall took something from the safe – it looked like a hard drive – put it in his bag and stood up.

'I want you to forget everything about this meeting when we're done. It simply never happened.'

Katz nodded, waiting for some sort of explanation.

'I think you've guessed who I am, or rather my alias. That's going to disappear, too, and you will never mention it in the future. Not under any circumstances. You created a number of problems for us. There is no safe way to store information, except for here!' He tapped a finger lightly against his head. 'And if, against all odds, you should trespass in our computers again, you won't find anything. What you saw . . . let's call it fragments of a larger whole . . . is no longer there. It's all been erased.'

The man crossed one leg over the other and looked intently at Katz from the corner, still pointing the pistol at him.

'It wasn't even supposed to be in the system any more. That was carelessness on our part.'

He leaned back so that his face almost disappeared in the darkness.

'You must have lots of questions,' he said. 'And I might consider answering some of them . . . because we owe you that.'

'Who do you work for?' said Katz. 'SSI?'

'It's more complicated than that. Project Legba was an international matter. And there are many of us who had to clean up traces of it years after it was discontinued. My two friends here, for example, speak only English. And Hebrew.'

The man who had put the hard drive into a bag gave Katz a quick smile. A *chai* symbol was hanging around his neck on a gold chain. *Mossad*, he thought, *or maybe Shin Bet*.

'It started a long time ago, at the end of the Cold War. We were faced with a worst-case scenario, that the Russians would do something rash out of pure desperation, urged on by an arms race they couldn't afford . . . a strategic attack on a neutral country to show their strength. Certain information we received supported those suspicions. My task was rapidly to develop better methods of information gathering. Better interrogators, quite simply, who were prepared to go against the Geneva Convention in order to get information in an urgent situation, and preferably even before one came up.'

'You wanted to train people in torture?'

'If you ask my friends here, they see it from a completely different perspective. It's a classic problem in practical philosophy: when is it okay to take one life to save others?'

He was silent for a moment, before going on.

'Julin was directly under me back then. I gave him free rein to create a training programme for a new generation of military interpreters. The problem was that the recruits couldn't be aware of it themselves. We had laws to think of, but we wanted it to be there if an urgent situation should come up. It was no mistake that you ended up in the programme.'

'I was falsely convicted of assaulting a woman.'

'I know. And Julin knew it, too. But, still, your list of strengths was quite solid. You were a known fighter, a criminal, with several cases of armed robbery and assault that no one could put you away for because you were a juvenile. And, beyond that, you had enormous talent for languages and computers. You were sent on through the system, like a weapon ready to be fired when the time was right.'

'And what if it didn't work – what if I had refused?'

'I don't think you would have, Katz.'

He tried to see himself from the outside, the person he had been and the person he had become. But it didn't match up; he was no torpedo, no psychopath.

'And the drugs that Julin experimented with?'

'Our joint project from the start. But when the funding was cut, he continued it on his own, with help from Gustav Klingberg. And, eventually, from Joel Klingberg.'

'And the military looked the other way?'

'Soldiers who don't feel fear. Soldiers who kill without thinking. That's very unusual. What army doesn't dream about men like that? And, at the same time, we could wash our hands of it. One or two people on the defence staff were informed. Neither the Supreme Commander nor the department knew anything.'

'But you were involved?'

'Julin kept us informed. And also several other organizations, foreign ones, related to my own.' He threw a glance at the man sitting next to him on the sofa. 'We never operate in a vacuum. We are on the right side, the winning side, and no matter how much we brag about our neutrality we do have certain allies. Many people were interested in Julin's experiments. The Americans were working on something similar at the same time. So were the Russians. Siberian peoples have a lot of phytotoxins that can change a person's personality. The problem was that Julin went too far in the end. There was a risk that heads would start to roll, that he would harm my organization. He used people in a manner that was incompatible with our principles of voluntary service. Junkies, for example, seldom have a choice, but, above all, they're not trustworthy; sooner or later, they start to leak. But Klingberg solved that problem for us . . . Julin no longer exists.'

'And the fifty million kronor?' said Katz. 'Where did that come from?'

'Some came from Joel Klingberg, and another portion came from international security firms that have started to take an interest in the project. The money was transferred through Klingberg Aluminium instead of Capitol Security in order to avoid a direct link to Julin. The money was meant to be laundered in the Virgin Islands before it was sent on to one of Julin's foreign accounts. But then there was the thing with Klingberg's wife – she cheated on him with his uncle, and the whole revenge machination was set into motion.'

'How did he convince Julin to help murder his wife?'

'He had a hold on him. They had been mixed up together for decades, Julin and the Klingberg family. Threats of cutting off the flow of money. We don't know exactly, and now it's too late to ask.'

Lynx stood up. He had put away the pistol and was standing at such an angle that Katz could get a glimpse of his face in the light from the lanterns that came in through the cabin window. He was in his seventies. In good condition. Fit. With old stabbing scars on his throat. A man who had recently killed another: Klingberg. To save his own skin. And he had done it with no hesitation.

He took a passport from his inner pocket and placed it on the table in front of Katz. A Russian passport.

'The question is, what are we going to do with you? As I see it, you have two options. One, you can stay here. We can help you. You've already got the beginnings of a new identity . . . as the Russian journalist Igor Liebermann. No family at home, no one waiting for you. There's fifty million in an anonymous account in Banco Popular

Dominicano; it would be easy for us to change the information so that part of that sum suddenly belongs to you. Let's say, fifteen million. And if you don't like living in the Caribbean, my friends here can work things out so you can go with them. You'd be following in your grandparents' footsteps, so to speak.'

He knows all about me, Katz thought; he's followed me at a distance all these years, he's watched me like a scientist through a magnifying glass.

'And what's my other option?'

'We'll fix the mess that Klingberg left behind. You'll be exonerated and you can go on with your regular life in Stockholm, but on one condition: you will be at our disposal. I must admit that I'm impressed by you.'

'What if I say no?'

'It would be rough. Pretty soon you might need to help a friend who is about to get into trouble.'

He stopped talking, looked intently at Katz, letting the enigmatic message take hold.

'In any case . . . we have one basic demand, no matter what you choose . . . and that's that this meeting never happened.'

Stockholm, June 2012

They were sitting in the living room of Jorma's apartment in Midsommarkransen. It was the last week of June. The night was painfully bright. Cool air streamed in through the open balcony door.

'What are you thinking about?'

Eva's voice, right next to him. He filled her glass from the bottle of rum he'd brought with him – Haitian Barbancourt.

'Nothing.'

'Are you sure? It looked like you were.'

'Absolutely sure.'

They knew almost everything by now. He'd told them what had happened, except for the meeting with Lynx. He'd explained that Klingberg was dead, that the information came from a reliable source, but that he didn't know how it had happened. He'd told them about Ingrid, Joel Klingberg's girlfriend, about what had happened to him at the sugar-cane plantation, about Julin's role in the story and about Gustav Klingberg's involvement in Kristoffer Klingberg's abduction. They'd asked questions that he'd answered as best he could. Then the conversation died out. They were exhausted, he thought, after all they'd been through.

'A Star of David, just like when you were sixteen.'

She touched the trinket that was hanging at his throat.

'I got it from my dad when I did my bar mitzvah. I put it on today. For the first time in years.'

He had thought a lot about Benjamin recently. Katz had been only fourteen when he died. His memories had faded. He supposed he hadn't wanted to remember him, that it was too painful.

He closed his eyes and, before him, he saw the synagogue on Sankt Paulsgatan as he was called forth to bless the Torah and read a passage in Hebrew. His father's pride as he saw that he had learned to place the *tefillin*, the small prayer boxes, in the right places: the *shel rosh* behind his hairline above his forehead, the *shel yad* on his right bicep, because he was left-handed. He had worn a *tallit*, too, a prayer shawl, for the first and only time in his life, and his father had beamed like the sun from his place in the front row with the *kippah* on his bald pate. Six months later, he was gone.

His parents had visited him like ghosts in Santo Domingo. They'd forced their way to him with their mysteriousness, causing him to wonder about things he'd never thought about before. Why had they left him in the lurch; why had they always moved around? Benjamin's rage, where had it come from? And had he really killed a person for the sake of a passport? Anne, his mother, had been fifteen years younger. Katz had never got to know her either; they'd kept him at a distance. It had been the two of them against the world.

He realized he was cold. Eva got up, walked over to the balcony door and closed it.

'I'm curious about something,' she said. 'The file you

found in Klingberg's computer, with the notes. Why was it there? He linked his brother's kidnapping to his parents' death.'

'Because he wanted to appear innocent. After all, he didn't know exactly what would happen once everything was set into motion. And if anyone were to start digging deeper, in his computer, for example, there would be small, subtle things that pointed to his innocence.'

Jorma nodded at them from the piano stool:

'He wanted to be able to come back and say, "Look, I have nothing to do with this."'

Jorma's voice – it wasn't quite *there*. Katz wondered if he was starting to get drunk.

'And Jonas Åkesson . . . there must be more people like him out there, drug addicts Julin experimented on?'

Maybe, he thought; they didn't know. And they would probably never find out. Lynx would clean up this mess.

Jorma had started playing again. Katz followed his fingers – the left hand, leading its own life among the low notes, striking colourful chords as the right hand delicately groped for the melody. Something by Carmichael; it was incredibly beautiful.

He felt Eva's arm around his waist. He pretended not to notice it.

Had it been a mistake not to stay in Santo Domingo? He had lingered for two weeks, living under the name Igor Liebermann at a beachfront hotel, seeing how it felt. Lynx was right; he had no family, no relatives – no one would miss him, except for the two people in the room right now. Jorma and Eva.

A new identity, the chance just to disappear. Wasn't that what he'd dreamed of for all these years? With fifteen million in starting capital. Why hadn't he taken the chance? Because he couldn't fool himself.

He poured more rum into the glass and took Eva's hand, which was searching its way around his waist again. She was a bit too drunk; that's the sort of person she was. A leopard can't change its spots, he thought, the time and the place it comes from.

Jorma was playing a classical piece now, a piano sonata. A long time ago, when they were living in the youth home in Hässelby Gård, a music teacher had said that Jorma was the most talented person he'd ever had, and that the world would fall at his feet if he got the right education. But it had never happened. No one had had the strength to guide them into the right sort of future.

He looked at Jorma, his oldest friend: his closed face, his eyes in another world. The little gleam of pain in the corner of his eye.

His thoughts slid on. The money-begging letter he'd sent Klingberg fifteen years earlier . . . in the end, it had come back to bite him: Klingberg had anonymously sent it to the papers after Angela was murdered, so that Katz would appear guilty. His drug abuse had made him grovel; he would never allow it to happen again.

Jorma seemed distant as he played. Something wasn't right. A friend who found himself in trouble? Was Jorma the one Lynx had been referring to? Or was he just imagining things?

Katz hadn't replied to the offer yet. How could he? A

person like Lynx wasn't in the phone book. He guessed that he would be contacted at some point . . . unless it all came to nothing.

In any case, Danielsson had received the information he needed for Katz to be exonerated. Eva had taken care of that part. And people higher up had become involved. The investigation had been marked classified. Perhaps Lynx was pulling strings in the background.

It slowly grew dark outside the windows; the light became weaker, but it wouldn't vanish entirely. White nights in Stockholm. His city. He reached for the bottle of rum and poured a little bit into his glass. That would be enough. He wanted to wake up sober.

Ten Questions for Carl-Johan Vallgren

Where did you grow up?
In a small village on the Swedish west coast; Falkenberg. Two younger sisters, hard working parents. Middle-class. Boring neighbourhood, but secure. The perfect childhood for an author.

Is there a person who has significantly influenced your life?
My wife Rebecka, the wisest person on the planet.

What place fascinates you most?
Gotland, the island in the Baltic – it's simply magical.

What are you afraid of?
Death – everything else is peanuts.

What makes you happy?
Writing.

Can you imagine a day without music?
Of course, when I'm writing I can't listen to music at all.

Which role in a film would you have loved to play?
I prefer cameo appearances, but if I had talent: Walter White in *Breaking Bad*.

**If you only had ten Euros left, what
would you spend them on?**
Swedish chewing tobacco – 'snus' – I'm totally addicted.

Do heaven and hell exist?
No.

What's important in life?
Love.

Carl-Johan Vallgren on
The Boy in the Shadows

How did it come to pass that as a 'literary' author you decided to write a crime series? What was your biggest challenge?

I felt a little weary at the thought of writing another 'literary' novel. I needed something new, to surprise myself with, to develop myself as an author, and to find new pleasure in writing. And because I love the crime genre – in movies and books – it seemed the most obvious thing to move in that direction. The biggest challenge was to write in a less 'literary' style, and with more pace, but without losing the depth. To think more of the plot, but without forgetting the scene-setting.

Are there suspense writers you especially love reading or you see as an inspiration?

New and old noir authors, of course, from Chandler to Ellroy, but I wanted to write in a more modern style, for readers of our time.

The Scandinavian crime thriller boom has had major international impact in the last few years. What do you think of this development?

I don't measure myself against other Scandinavian writers; I am trying to do my own thing. And don't forget: there are also some very bad Scandinavian crime novels and the fact is that most stuff from there is rubbish. That said, the competition is very tough, which is something good – you have to offer something new in order to widen your audience.

Your two main protagonists Danny Katz and Eva Westin both have lived through dark times in their pasts. What do you think is the appeal of these 'broken' characters?

Firstly: they are facets of me. One can't write literature without using oneself as 'material'. But this kind of protagonist is also part of the genre. It all has to be dark and bitter. Violent people. The dark side of life. Night. Darkness. Drugs. Suffering. Life right at the bottom of society. That's how one creates atmosphere. I'm very interested in Danny and Eva, both of them are very lonely and don't fit into society. But they are also very talented people, and with their criminal background and street-smarts there's a lot of room to develop their characters in the novel.

You're also active as a singer/songwriter – where is the biggest difference between writing a song and writing a novel?

Music is my hobby, just like others paint or play chess – and coincidentally I've had a bit of success with it. But writing novels is my profession and my life. I'd never compare them that way.